"Do it."

The cilia thickening, growing, branching, eating through the wood, curling round bluevein threads, taking the energy, raw, strange, dark.

Powerful.

Sick.

Flowing into him. He felt himself call out. Felt a thrill at the strength. Fell backwards, his body alive. A single moment of pleasure swiftly followed by revulsion. Tasted rot in his mouth. Wanted to run, to fly, to escape himself. Could almost sense the forest trying to move away from him. A faint sense of... satisfaction? But not his, nor the cowls.

"Well," said Nahac, "it worked."

"How do you know?" he said, lying on his back, breathing hard, fighting the urge to commit.

"I know," she said.

"How?"

"Your eyes have turned black."

Praise for RJ Barker

Praise for the Forsaken Trilogy

"This is a splendid fantasy work, full of RJ's trademark invention. Highly recommended."

—Adrian Tchaikovsky, Arthur C. Clarke Award–winning author of *Children of Time*

"A triple-threat of world-building, character and plot, *Gods of the Wyrdwood* represents the work of an experienced novelist at the top of his game. This is *Avatar* meets *Dune*—on shrooms."

—*SFX*

"A sweeping story of destiny and redemption. Weighty, deliberate, tender and brutal, this is a big, wonderful book and an utterly involving read."

—*Daily Mail*

"At times lyrical and others stark in its depiction of battle, *Gods of the Wyrdwood* has all the delicious worldbuilding of a '90s fantasy you'd want to cut your teeth on but with characters and situations that resonate with modernity."

—Linden A. Lewis, author of *The First Sister*

Praise for the Tide Child Trilogy

"A vividly realized high-seas epic that pulls you deep into its world and keeps you tangled there until the very last word."

—Evan Winter, author of *The Rage of Dragons*

"I absolutely loved it. A whole lot of swashbuckling awesomeness by RJ Barker. He has crafted a fascinating world and a twisty plot, both rooted in characters I came to care about. A definite winner for me."

—John Gwynne, author of *The Shadow of the Gods*

"An epic tale of duty and obligation and honor, and what bravery really means. I can't recommend it enough."

—Peter McLean, author of *Priest of Bones*

"A unique and memorable world—harsh and brutal and full of sharply realized, powerful female characters. Barker has managed to craft a story inspired by *Moby Dick*, *Game of Thrones*, and pirate lore, and readers will be drawn in and fascinated."

—*Booklist* (starred review)

Praise for the Wounded Kingdom

"Often poignant and always intriguing, *Age of Assassins* reveals its mysteries with the style of a magic show and the artful grace of a gifted storyteller."

—Nicholas Eames, author of *Kings of the Wyld*

"Outstanding. Beautifully written, perfectly paced, and assured. Kept me reading well into the early hours of the morning. A wonderful first book—a wonderful book, period—that should be at the very top of your to-read list."

—James Islington, author of *The Shadow of What Was Lost*

By RJ Barker

THE WOUNDED KINGDOM

Age of Assassins

Blood of Assassins

King of Assassins

THE TIDE CHILD TRILOGY

The Bone Ships

Call of the Bone Ships

The Bone Ship's Wake

THE FORSAKEN TRILOGY

Gods of the Wyrdwood

Warlords of Wyrdwood

WAR LORDS OF WYRD WOOD

The Forsaken Trilogy:
Book Two

R J BARKER

orbitbooks.net

Cover design by Duncan Spilling—LBBG
Cover images by Shutterstock
Map by Tom Parker Illustration

Orbit
Hachette Book Group
1290 Avenue of the Americas
New York, NY 10104
orbitbooks.net

First Edition: September 2024
Simultaneously published in Great Britain by Orbit

Orbit is an imprint of Hachette Book Group.
The Orbit name and logo are registered trademarks of Little, Brown Book Group Limited.

Library of Congress Control Number: 2024938042

ISBNs: 9780316401883 (trade paperback), 9780316401982 (ebook)

Printed in the United States of America

LSC-C

Printing 1, 2024

For my Mum, without her I'd never
have loved language the way I do.

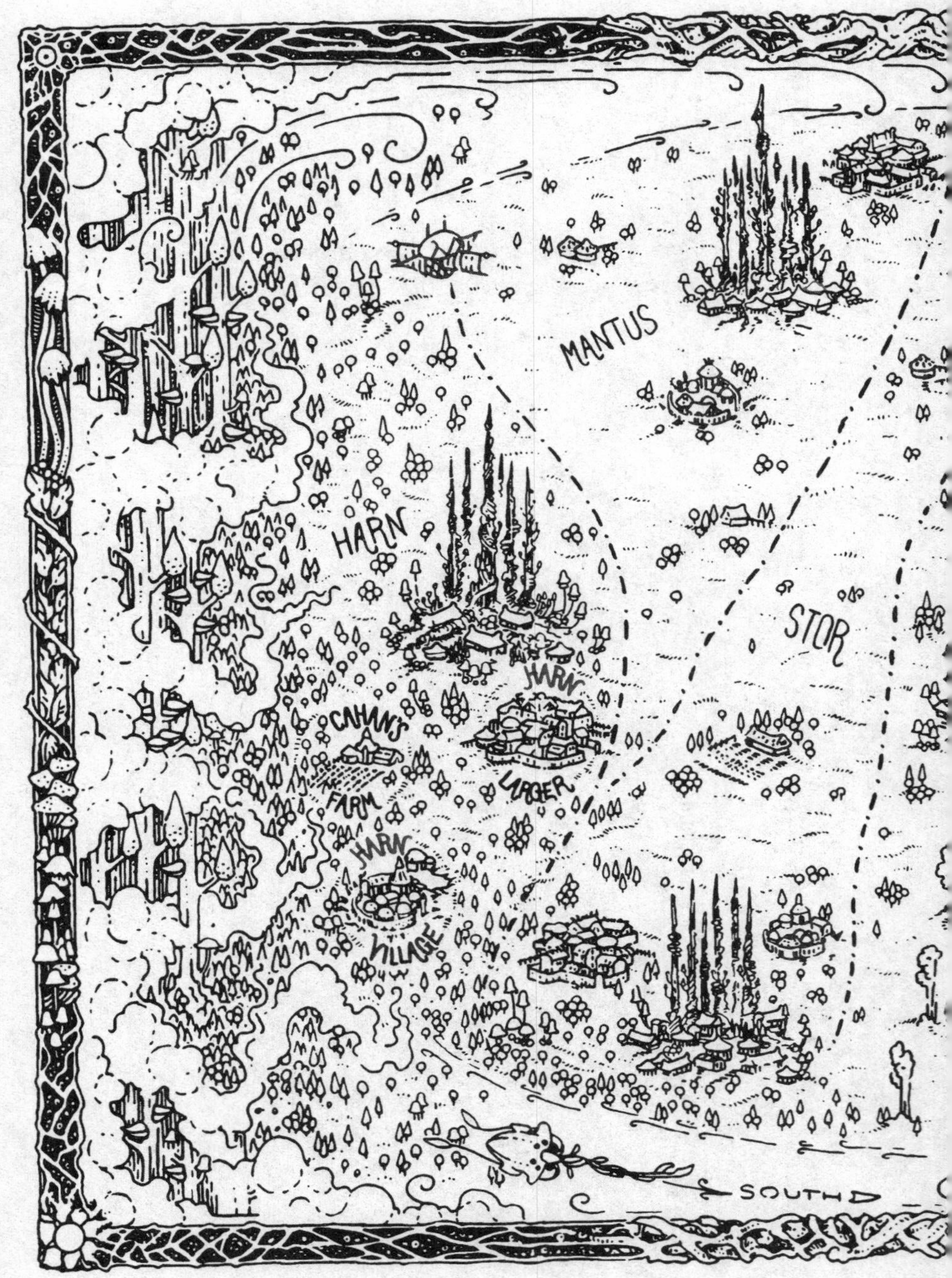
MANTUS
HARN
STOR
HARN
LARGER
CAHAN'S
FARM
HARN
VILLAGE
SOUTH

NORTH
JINNENG
SEERSTEM
MYDAL
ILT

What Has Gone Before

The Rai are the ruling warrior caste of Crua, bonded with cowls which live beneath their skin and allow them to steal the lives of others to fuel their own power. The strongest of all cowl users is the Cowl-Rai, who comes into existence only once in a generation and brings a new god, to whom all others must bow.

Or so it is believed.

Cahan Du-Nahere was the Cowl-Rai, the chosen one destined to remake his world in the image of a god named Zorir, but he was a gentle child and unsuited to the cruelty of the Rai. He only managed to wake his cowl through killing when his sister was murdered, and the murderer was brought before him.

Before Cahan could fully embrace his power, however, another Cowl-Rai rose and took his place. Cahan was abandoned by the monks who raised him, left alone and unwanted, an inconvenience to be wiped out by this new, unnamed ruler. In his confusion and rage, his new power overwhelmed him, destroying his pursuers and anyone caught between them.

Since then he swore never to use his power, and he

became a hermit, living in anonymity on the edge of Crua's huge and alien forests near a small village named Harn.

Named "the forester" by the villagers, he spends his life farming; fighting against a hard land and the bluevein which sickens crops. The forester is the only one who can navigate Wyrdwood, a dark and deep forest filled with volatile plants, dangerous wildlife, monsters from the land's darkest folklore . . . and worse.

The new Cowl-Rai has taken most of Crua for Tarl-an-Gig, beating back the forces of the old god, Chyi, they seem set on wiping out servants of all the old gods. And another Cowl-Rai cannot be allowed to exist. The county's capital city of Harnspire sends assassins to kill the forester. Cahan escapes death by a stroke of luck, and though others died in his place he believes himself safe.

The world has other ideas. Strange undying warriors, the Reborn, seek him out convinced he can free them from the curse of eternal life. Cahan wants nothing to do with them. Believing his only option is to escape he leaves Harn but is arrested as a vagrant and offered as sacrifice to wake the cowl of a trion, one of Crua's third sex, named Venn. Unknown to Cahan, Venn is the child of the ruler of Harnspire, and the only trion with a cowl. Venn's tormentors had reckoned without Cahan. Unable to give in to death, his cowl wakes, killing two of the Rai accompanying Venn and stripping the third, Sorha, of her cowl and her power. Doing this almost kills Cahan but Venn saves him, by giving themselves back to the warriors sent to find them, allowing Cahan to escape even though it may cost Venn dearly.

Unknown to Cahan, the Rai Sorha survives having her cowl burned from her, usually this is a death sentence for the Rai, but she has become a null spot that negates the cowls of those near her. This makes her a pariah among her own people and she becomes obsessed with Cahan, vowing vengeance.

With the Rai once more believing he is dead, Cahan returns to his farm with the idea of again becoming anonymous. But even Cahan cannot be completely alone, and must trade with his nearest village for necessities. Little by little he is pulled into the lives of Harn's villagers. His knowledge of Wyrdwood means he is called upon when Issofur, the child of the village's Leoric, Furin, has strayed into the dark and strange forest where most fear to go. Accompanied by Udinny, monk of a forgotten god called Ranya, Cahan journeys through Wyrdwood searching for the lost child.

There he comes into contact with the Forestals, outlaws of Wyrdwood who rebel against the cruel Rai, and he finds the boy Issofur in the company of the Boughry, strange and vicious gods of the deep forest. The Boughry allow Cahan and Udinny to reclaim the boy, but only after Udinny promises to serve them. They also find out that one of the great cloudtrees, the unfathomably huge trees of Wyrdwood, has fallen. Such a thing is rare and can make people rich beyond imagining, though it also brings dangers.

As does Cahan's existence.

The Rai Sorha comes for Cahan, taking over Harn and demanding his life in exchange for the villagers. With her she brings the trion, Venn. Cahan is forced to choose whether he flees, leaving the villagers in Sorha's cruel hands, or finally makes a stand and accepts that his power allows him to help others, not to simply destroy. He chooses to help the village, and together with Venn and the Reborn he frees the village, but Sorha escapes.

The people of Harn rejoice in their victory but Cahan does not. He knows the Rai will return; they cannot leave an insult to their power unanswered and it is not long before Sorha returns, as part of a large army intent on the destruction of the village.

Faced with overwhelming odds, the village of Harn, assisted by a small group of Forestals led by a woman called

Ania, stand against the might of Harnspire's army. It is a battle they cannot win even though Venn has discovered an ability to heal, and the Forestals reveal they have cowls and can work together to create shields. Little by little the defenders are whittled down. Cahan refuses to kill to feed his cowl, even though it would give him more power.

In the end, Cahan's decision is taken out of his hands. The wounded and dying of the village sacrifice themselves, forcing their lifeforce onto Cahan. The fact that it is given freely and not forced magnifies this power into something Cahan can barely hold. It is then that the Boughry of Wyrdwood make their claim on Udinny. Cahan, Venn and Udinny join, Venn channelling Cahan's power to Udinny, and the monk, with the guidance of the Boughry, assists Cahan in growing a forest, a vicious and hungry one that slays the attacking army, saving Cahan, Venn and the people of Harn – though it costs Udinny her life and the village is destroyed.

Once more, Sorha escapes. Her vengeance thwarted and her life forfeit for failure she knows she cannot return to the Rai without something on this new enemy or her quest for vengeance will be over.

In Tilt, the central county of Crua, an old secret awaits. The real ruler of Crua is Saradis, the high priest of Zorir, the same woman who raised Cahan, to make him Cowl-Rai. Now she is Skua-Rai, high priest of Tarl-an-Gig, and she keeps the Cowl-Rai of her god in a cage, imprisoned to protect everyone from the twisted power of the bluevein sickness. And this Cowl-Rai, this new chosen one?

It is Cahan's sister. She did not die as Cahan was told, but she is *changed*.

1

Udinny

It is entirely true and real and to the point to say that I lived a life which involved many mistakes. Sometimes those mistakes hurt others, which I regret enormously, but mostly those mistakes only hurt me; and though I wish I could have avoided them, to some degree I deserved the pain that followed. It was earned. Nonetheless, each and every mistake I made was a step along a path in which I learnt: about myself, the world and the people within it. So I cannot truly say I would undo anything I have done. At least not without undoing myself in the process.

Life is complicated like that.

In fact, it is far, far more complicated than I ever imagined.

There is, however, one mistake that I do regret, and that is becoming dead. Given the chance and knowing what I know now, I would undo that entirely. Though, I would not have been able to, as I would not have known what I know. This must sound like a riddle. Well, I understand little enough of it myself. Suffice to say, before I died, I had thought death to be a very definite full stop. A movement from the land of Crua, cold and hard and unpleasant and full of people who were gruff and often unfair to me, to the land of the dead where my Lady Ranya would take my hand and guide me along the star path to a better place. There I would find a kinder land populated by those I had met in life and missed the most. We would eat and drink too much in the god's city of Great Anjiin, once more rebuilt after the breaking of Iftal, and we would not even suffer the pain of the morning after.

And yet.

Here we are.

Me, talking to you, whoever you may be. I suspect that you may be me, a me I am yet to meet or one of me who I have left behind. Yes, I talk like a mad person, but I exist as one. I have woken in a room of a million mirrors, each one containing a reflection of a person I was and yet I have never known.

Of course, they are not actually mirrors.

It is too dark here for mirrors.

Which one should expect from being dead, I suppose.

Forgive me, I know this makes little sense. I am using our dialogue to make sense of it myself. We are involved in a process. You, who may be me, and I who is definitely me.

I gave my life to Ranya, our lady of the lost, whose web stretches throughout Crua and touches all things. But I died on the word of the Boughry, the cruel lords of the forest, who are the strength, the spirit and the bridge. I thought them separate, and they are, but I should also not be surprised to find out that, in some way I have yet to fathom, they are also the same creature. I felt it, though now I do not feel anything.

Riddles upon riddles upon riddles.

I live within a vast space (if I can still use the word live; I am not sure it is truly applicable) but it is also a small space. Like I sit in a box made of glass looking out at a plain that runs into an eternity before me. Though I do not actually see it, as I have no eyes. Or ears. Or mouth. Or sense of touch.

How strange, I did not know any of these things until I thought about them. How can I be aware of anything when I have no senses to be aware of them with? Really, it seems death is a mystery that is not even solved by dying; it only becomes more complex and more mysterious. If I were you, which I may or may not be as we have previously discussed, I would avoid dying. If that is at all possible.

I imagine that were I the type to go mad, this is exactly the sort of thing that would send me so. It may be that I am already mad, or that this is some strange and powerful new torture dreamed up by the Rai of Crua and I did not die in a little village where a forest grew from nothing to vanquish our enemies. Though that is unlikely as I feel no pain, and the Rai – the rulers of Crua – enjoy inflicting pain and are too lacking in imagination to believe being stuck within a darkness that poses nothing but questions and offers no answers could be a torture all of its own.

I imagine if my friend Cahan found himself in this place he would not enjoy it at all. He would rage and scream and fight, and of course that would all be useless. You cannot fight a prison without bars, especially when you have no hands. Or feet. Or body.

I did not know I had no hands or feet or body until I thought about it.

Being dead really is a constant journey of both discovery and frustration.

Oh, and wonder, though if I were Cahan I would feel only frustration; he is man who is very good at being frustrated, and surly. He truly has a talent for being surly that is beyond that of any other human I have ever met, and I have met a lot. And a fair few of them were quite surly. Maybe it is an effect I have on people?

I cannot see or hear or speak or touch, and yet I am aware. I have no hands or legs and yet I move. I cannot see anything but darkness and yet I know there is a beyond that I am currently denied. It is strange, and new, and that is a wonder.

I am in a prison.

I am lost.

But I serve Ranya, the lady of the lost, and she has been the one to guide my steps throughout my life, and never has she led me wrong. Even though she led me to my death. Now I consider it, she has also led me to prison, more than once. Many times in fact.

But I have always escaped.

There are stars here. But not the single star of Crua. There are many.

How strange.

How fascinating.

2

Cahan

Thirty-seven of the villagers of Harn died in the fight with the Rai, including four children. The village burned, orange light painting the trees in flickering shadows, distorting the faces of those around him. They were all changed, no longer the same people who had woken in a Woodedge village in the days before the forces of Rai Galderin turned up.

Had he changed? Or had he reverted to what he had once been? He did not know.

Cahan could barely walk after the release of power. Furin and Venn supported him as they passed through the new forest around Harn, the one he had grown, his power passing through the conduit of Venn, targeted by Udinny at the life in the ground. At the thought of the little monk, a pain in his heart. He stumbled. Heard Furin and Venn gasp as they took his weight, kept him upright. Grief as vicious as any blade cut him, a gasp escaped. Worse than the gnawing pain of his cowl, hungering for life and making it a fight to stop it taking from Furin.

"Cahan," said Furin, her face hidden in shadow, her hair a halo, orange with firelight. "Are you hurt?"

"Just weak, is all," he said. "Weak."

He had been weak all his life, running from the truth of what he was: something dark, monstrous. If he doubted it the truth hung from the trees that had grown up around them on his command. An eightday ago, eight hours ago, this had been a village surrounded by fields. Now it was dense forest studded with burning houses, and from the trees hung the army that had come to kill everyone who had lived in Harn. These new trees were twisted, strange, and some more than others; the most misshapen had streaks of blue running up them, infected with bluevein which had made them grow into tortuous shapes.

In the time it had taken the people of Harn to make ready to leave the corpses on the trees had become skeletons; what little flesh remained was dry and tight as old leather. On the blueveined trees the skeletons had strange accretions, like glowing rocks. Sightless skulls stared out from branches, each one finding him. Accusing him.

"Cahan," said Venn, "if you are weak can you take from the trees?" The trion and Furin steered him towards a trunk, two corpses hanging from it. He lifted his hand to place against the bark, ready to make the entreaty to the forest, to ask for its kindness.

Stop.

The hiss of the cowl in his mind. At the same time he felt its gnawing hunger, its huge desire for life, vanish. Not quickly enough to stop him, and neither did he trust it enough to obey its desperate whisper. Maybe he was simply not strong enough to react quickly, maybe he still resented the thing for what it made him into: Cahan Du-Nahere, Cowl-Rai, ruler of rulers, unwilling saviour.

Cahan touched the tree.

Hunger.

Pure and powerful and red. An unbearable need, stronger than the cowl within him.

He had felt the power of trees before, the slow aggregation of life that gave them their might and their strength. The tenacity of forests was built up over generations, and in the case of the Cloudtrees of Wyrdwood, over time beyond knowing.

These trees, *his* trees, they were not made that way. They were forced. Forced by him. The many lifetimes of power, taken gently and naturally, were denied to them. The connection to Crua through the invisible net that Udinny had called Ranya's web, it was not there for them.

They hungered.

Lances of red reaching into him. Pain, immediate and excruciating. Life drawn from him. His hand held against the bark by an alien will. He must have screamed. Must have given some sign as the Reborn were there. The undying sisters sworn to his service. Pulling him from the tree, laying him on the ground.

"What is wrong?" said Venn. They tried to step nearer but one of the Reborn, the silent one, stood in their way, spear raised.

"The trees," Cahan said, forcing words out through a mouth that did not want to move, "don't touch the trees."

"Let me help," said Venn.

"We will protect him," said Nahac, the speaker for the two Reborn, who he had named for his murdered sister. Never really understanding why.

"Venn can heal, you know that." Furin speaking.

"They did not heal us," the Reborn's words dull, dead.

"You are not part of life, not any more," said Venn. The two Reborn froze. Cahan wondered for a moment if they would kill the trion; something of their attitude was of the mortally insulted. The silent one raised her spear but Venn showed no fear of her. "You will kill me, because I tell the truth?"

"Stop." The word was all Cahan could manage. The Reborn looked to him. Then Nahac, the one who spoke, who carried the name of his long dead sister, nodded. The silent one moved aside and Venn stepped closer to him.

"Venn." It was all he could manage, he wanted to tell them it was not safe. That his cowl hungered after what he had expended here, even more so now the tree had also taken from him.

"I know, Cahan, why you are frightened," said the trion. "But I can control it." From the look on their face he knew they were not sure, but they were going to try and he, weak as a new-born raniri, could do little to stop them. The trion reached out for him. His cowl howled within, its hunger was every bit as empty and desperate as the trees'. Too strong for him to fight.

Too weak to stop anything.

He had lost Udinny, he did not want to lose Venn as well.

Trying to scream out, "No!"

Venn touched his forehead with the flat of one hand.

A cool, green, wave washing over him.

Connection.

The pain within, not gone, but dulled, like a roaring fire being banked, the flames covered, smothered. Still there, still burning, but now it would burn longer and slower. Venn controlled it, passed him some of what they were, sharing themselves with him and they gave selflessly. As they did, Cahan's world grew, his vision cleared. A change of perspective. He saw the trion bent over him. He saw the Reborn behind them; he saw Furin, and Ont and the rest of the villagers watching. Behind them the Forestals, those thieves and outlaws whose bows had been so useful in the battle, were watching thoughtfully.

"Enough," he said, words coming more easily. He managed to stand unaided, a moment of dizziness and then the Reborn were there, holding him up. He held a hand to his forehead. Fought for clarity.

"What do we do, Cowl-Rai?" The butcher, Ont, spoke from behind him, the man who had stood against him and resented him once. A man who now looked at him entirely differently. It made Cahan uncomfortable.

"My name is Cahan, call me that." Cahan turned and Ont nodded, kept his head bowed. All the villagers did. "Look at me." Some did as he asked, some did not. "I am just a man, just a clanless man."

The villagers were frightened.

Of what this place had become.

Of him.

Who could blame them?

"The plan has not changed," said Furin, their Leoric, their leader. With her stood Ania and one of her Forestals; had only they survived the fight? "Has it, Cahan?" He shook his head.

"No, it has not. We leave here, make for the forest and safety." Cahan looked around. No one argued with him, he wished they would. He would feel more like one of the people then. "It is not safe here." But where was? Sooner expect to stumble across Anjiin, the fabled ruined city of the ancients, than safety in Crua.

"They will come back?" This from the crowd.

"Yes," he said, "and these trees they are . . ." He let his voice tail off. Took a breath. "They are not safe, do not touch them."

"They are just trees," came another voice. "What can trees do?" How could he explain it so they understood?

"These trees were raised to kill." He looked around. "And trees think slowly, they have not realised yet they have done what is needed. So take no chances."

Silence. Utter silence, like none they had ever heard before. No animals called, no gasmaws hissed and chirped, no foliage moved as histi pushed through it. The forest was quiet as the dead that decorated it. It hungered, and nothing which walked carelessly here would live. Nothing had. "We must go, take nothing. Head for Wyrdwood. Safety is there if it is anywhere."

"What makes you think Wyrdwood will take you?" said Ania.

"It will," he said.

"Not for free," said the Forestal, "the forest always wants its price." Cahan looked around, at the bedraggled, tired, bloodied and grief-stricken, and wondered what these people had left to give.

"If it is where the Cowl-R—" Ont broke off. "If it is where Cahan says we go, then it is where we will go." Cahan looked at him, gave him a nod.

The people of Harn left most of their possessions, their houses, their professions and all that they had been behind them. They were no longer villagers. All they carried away were the clothes they wore, what few things they could drag on a travois and the weapons they had trained to use; and maybe Cahan lied to himself, but he felt they carried their bowstaffs with a sense of pride he had not noticed before. These people were villagers no longer, but neither were they warriors. They were something else, a people changed by the truth of their land. Like him, they were in the process of becoming, and they were yet to find out what it was they would become.

He thought that, of them all, Ania the Forestal was the only one not frightened by the future. They moved into her world now.

Furin and Venn helped him walk, he was still weak.

"We shall take him, we are strong," said Nahac of the Reborn, her sister standing by her. Furin and the trion looked at the two warriors. "We do not tire," said Nahac. "You do." Furin nodded and pulled Venn back. Cahan noticed his garaur, Segur, flee as the Reborn approached, the lithe furred body of the herding animal vanishing into the trees. The Reborn put his arms around their shoulders, and he hoped the garaur had the sense to keep away from this hungry forest.

"Where do we go?" asked Ont.

"North," said Ania. "It is always North for you now." Ont looked to Cahan who nodded.

Their journey began.

The first death was before the Light Above had passed out of the early eight. A woman, Jader, stumbled and put her hand out to catch herself on the trunk of a tree. Such a normal and natural reaction. Her body stiffened, she screamed once. A short echo through the hungry trees. It contained so much pain. She fell against the trunk that had taken her life and if they had stayed they would see her body reduced to bones, like the warriors who had attacked Harn. Cahan thought no good could come of such a sight.

Thankfully, he was not the only one who saw the danger.

"Keep going," said Furin, "and be careful, Cahan has warned us of the danger in these trees. They saved us, but they do not love us." There was no argument, no outcry; the villagers of Harn walked on. Too tired to do anything else, too worn by battle and death and the horror that had been brought into their lives.

"You told me this was coming," He said it softly, and the Reborn Nahac turned to him, an eyebrow raised in question. "'I can sense death, Cahan Du-Nahere and it is drawn to you.' That is what you told me. You warned me and I did not listen."

"You cannot run from the dead, Cowl-Rai," she said.

"Do not call me that."

"It is what you are." She nodded at the villagers. "In yourself and in their eyes."

"You are not to call me it." She shrugged, as if it made little difference to her what he was called. "So many dead because of me."

"Put your self-pity aside," she said, "they would all have died without you. There has been Treefall. With the death of the great cloudtree, so would come death to this village; the Rai would never let some Woodedge villagers enjoy such riches." What she said was true, but it did not make him feel any better. "Think on how you will pay your debt to us. You promised us death, we expect it."

The journey through the silent, hungering wood was one

of misery, and it followed them into Woodedge, where once more the forest sprang into life and noise.

Tiny flying creatures gathered in clouds, biting at any exposed skin. The bites were painful, the itching afterwards worse and Cahan's instruction not to slap at the creatures was poorly received. He felt his anger and frustration rise, even as his strength began to return. How could these people have lived so near Harnwood and Wyrdwood and not know the most basic rules of the forest? *Harm not and remain unharmed*. Their lives depended on the forest accepting them. Even away from the hungry wood it felt as though the forest still thirsted for their lives. Every vine and bush they passed thorned, and the littercrawlers, always an annoyance, were more aggressive than he had ever known them. Only the Reborn remained untouched, even the simplest of creatures knew to stay away from them.

Every step they took increased the misery of the villagers. When they stopped at a clearing, infested with the small biting creatures, he took Furin to one side.

"Are they all as miserable as I am?" he said. Furin nodded, put her hand on the top of his arm, the warmth of her contact a shock.

"They are, and frightened. It is turning to anger in some of them; they blame Ont for convincing them to stay in the village and not leaving when you told them they should." She looked over his shoulder, at the villagers. "They are not wrong to."

"He only told them what they all wanted to hear."

"It could lead to violence, Cahan." He closed his eyes at her words, tried to find clarity in his tired mind.

"We should kill those who will not serve the Cowl-Rai," said Nahac. Cahan pretended not to hear.

"Is there anything else?" he asked. The Leoric pushed hair from her face, the white make-up on her skin beginning to flake away.

"Some talk of going back."

"Fools," said Nahac.

"All are not as you," said the Leoric, words sharp, and she turned back to Cahan. "You would do well to have your warriors remember that. And they are not like you either, Cahan. These people do not know the forest, they are not used to this sort of hardship." She spoke more gently. "Leading is not simply about fighting. It is about bringing people together, helping them find strength."

"I am not their leader, you are," he told her.

"I was Leoric of Harn but Harn is gone. Give me a village to run and I will run it. But here," she grimaced as one of the flying things bit her cheek, managed not to slap at it, "well, here I am as miserable as anyone else. This is your domain." And my doing, he thought, though she was kind enough not to say it.

"I do not know people." He looked around. "I know wood, and forests, and crownheads."

"Then you will need to get to know people," said the Leoric, she squeezed his arm. Their eyes met and he looked away, then Furin left to go to where the hunter, Sark, was sharing out dried meats.

"Make them part of this." Cahan turned to find it was Ont speaking to him, the big man somehow shrunken by his experience of war even though the butcher loomed over him, gesturing towards the trees and thick underbrush. "I saw you when you came to Harn, you always looked lost." Cahan studied Ont. Taking in how violence, and learning the truth about the Rai, had changed him, though Cahan still did not feel like he could trust the butcher. "That is how these people feel now, lost."

"I wish Udinny were here." He did not know why he said that, least of all to Ont. Udinny would no doubt have told him it was Ranya showing him the path. Udinny said that about everything. Then she would say something that both amused him and made him feel foolish, but that was gone now. She was gone.

"Udinny gave her life, to save us, Cahan." The forester nodded at the butcher's words; pain stole his voice. "Her god, your god," Ont spoke hesitantly, "they asked that of her and she obeyed." He looked as though this was a puzzle he was struggling to make sense of. "I heard her say, more than once, that Ranya was a kind god but taking her life does not seem . . ." Cahan tried not to be frustrated with the man, to think about how pleased Udinny would be to hear the butcher's interest in her god, him of all people. And how impish the monk would have been about it.

"Ranya is kind," said Cahan but he could not look at Ont as he spoke. "Udinny would tell you that she puts the pieces she needs in the right place, she guides them along the path. What they do when they arrive is up to them."

"She did not command her to die?" said Ont. Cahan shook his head, almost spoke, almost mentioned the Boughry, the darker, older gods of the wood, but knew it would not help anyone. Not him, Udinny or Ont. But why lie? Would Udinny want that?

"Another made that request of her." Cahan looked Ont in the face. "Udinny offered herself to the Boughry, the Woodhewn Nobles of the forest."

"Why?" he said.

"For the Leoric's boy, Issofur."

"Her god made her do it?" The look of horror on his face, that someone would walk willingly to creatures that were the nightmares of every villager. The monstrous old gods of Wyrdwood.

"No," said Cahan. "Ranya asks nothing of anyone. Udinny did it purely to save the boy. And me, I think." Ont stared at Cahan. "She believed it was right." The butcher took a breath, nodded and scratched his nose.

"Asks nothing," he said, "but puts you in a place to do something?"

"Aye, that's it." Cahan stood, sighing. It was still an effort, "Sounds exactly like the sort of thing Udinny would have said." The butcher was about to say more but Venn interrupted.

"Cahan," said the young trion softly. He turned; they were clothed in the shadows of the trees. "Rai are coming."

He went to the trion, his steps careful, slow, and took their arm, leading them away from the villagers. "They are all dead, Venn," he said. The trion shook their head.

"There are more, further out." Venn knelt, put their hand in the leaf litter. "I could not feel them until they entered the forest you raised." They looked up. "I can feel nothing else there, it frightens me."

"How many?" The trion shrugged.

"Not a lot, no more than ten." They looked away, holding something back.

"And?"

"They have Hetton with them." Fear in the trion's voice, and rightly so. Only the Reborn were in a state to face the shock troops of Tarl-an-Gig, devolved into something obscene and almost unstoppable.

"Hetton?" Venn nodded and Cahan looked around, caught Furin's eye. As she approached he found Nahac of the Reborn and beckoned her over to join them.

"What is it?" said Furin.

"We must move, and we must make all speed."

"The people are tired, Cahan," said Furin. "To push them now is to—"

"We did not kill all the Rai, Furin," he said quietly. "A small force remains. Scouts, probably." She stared at him.

"My people are in no state to fight."

"I know."

You need me.

Cahan took a deep breath. Looked around the clearing, the villagers had gathered in small groups, huddling together for warmth because he had forbidden them fire, the forest hated fire. Breath hung in clouds around them.

"Where are the Forestals?"

"Gone," said Venn.

"Where?" They shrugged.

"Just gone. They walked away and then they were gone."

Cahan hissed through his teeth. He thought that maybe fighting alongside Ania had given them some bond, but it was clearly not so. She had been forced back to Harn, fought because she had to and now she had left them, was that his fault. Cahan had asked about how her people made shields that saved Harn from rai fire, but she had quickly changed the subject. He could not blame her for keeping secrets, but it annoyed him nonetheless. He reached into his pocket and took out the walknut, the direction finder given to him by Tall Sera, the leader of the Forestals. He took Venn's hand and put the walknut in it.

"You know how this works. You and Furin, take the people North. If I have not caught up with you by the time you reach the edge of Wyrdwood, then wait. The Forestals will find you I am sure. Ask them for help." Venn looked at the shiny nut. Furin nodded.

"What will you do?" said Venn.

"Take the Reborn, stop the Rai following us."

"Why?" they said.

"Because they will tell others where we go." He looked up. "And then they will come after us."

"Even to Wyrdwood?"

"Even there."

"But Cahan," said Venn. "You are still weak."

"I will ask the trees to lend me power," he said.

He knew it was a lie, but he also had an idea though it was not one he wished to share.

You need me.

3

Saradis

There was a creature native to Tilt called a nettile, a type of very small gasmaw that hung in the air, and from within its body it spun a single string of the very finest silk. The nettile used it to catch the small flying creatures that buzzed around rooms, looking for food or sweat to feed upon. Such creatures brought disease, and nuisance, and sometimes bit, leaving great welts upon the skin that lasted for days. So nettiles were encouraged throughout Tilt, from the smallest hovel in the reaches of the spires to the grandest halls in the low levels. And if sometimes a person was to walk into a nettile thread, and feel a shiver as if a hand reached out for them from beyond death, well, that was a small price to pay to keep away the flyers.

For over a week, a flyer had buzzed around the rooms of Saradis, Skua-Rai of Tarl-an-Gig. Despite there being numerous nettiles floating around near the ceiling the creature remained annoyingly uncaught. It zipped and flew and twisted through the air. And though it annoyed her, and bit her on the cheek leaving a welt she had to cover with an even thicker layer of make-up than was usual, in some ways she found herself feeling admiration for it, a certain sense of kinship. The flyer was only kept alive through its own senses and speed, while all around it waited traps and certain death.

Very like her position. A woman without a cowl surrounded by those with them. Each and every interaction with those in power here was fraught with danger; they could burn her with a thought, drown her for their own amusement or, more likely, out of spite.

Like the flyer, she twisted and turned and span and survived.

And just like the flyer, she also bit.

Saradis. Skua-Rai, high priest of all Crua, or most of it, fought her wars with documents and in meeting rooms, armed with knowledge that made the Rai fear her despite her lack of a cowl. The Cowl-Rai listened when she advised who to send to war, and through her Saradis controlled the shrines of Tarl-an-Gig where the people came to give of themselves to the god, and through that, to give power to the Rai. Each citizen sacrificing a little of their lives to power the cowls of the rai.

So if you did not respect the power of Saradis, high priest of the god Tarl-an-Gig, you did not feed the thing within you.

Or maybe some other fate would befall you.

The kind of fate that can only befall the Rai, those things known by them but never spoken about. Saradis was not the sort of woman who was slow to use her weapons; fear was a tool and she believed it was good to use your tools, to keep in practice. The dullers, that blocked the power of the Rai, and the Hetton, who killed with a single-minded obsession, answered only to her.

Then there was her god, the true god, Zorir, the coming fire. Worshipped in secret and always growing in power, and with their growth came her own. She would burn this world with cleansing flame for Zorir. Once she had thought it might not happen in her lifetime, that she would need to recruit others, but now she was more confident. Something had changed, her communions with her god had been stronger and all this had happened since they had lost Harn. Something had happened there when the weakling Cahan Du-Nahere had surprised them all by *becoming*. It infuriated her, but maybe it had been meant to be? Maybe this was planned all along.

She did not know. All she knew was that she was closer, closer than ever.

The flyer in her room had begun to tax her patience. She caught it. One hand darting out to imprison it. She closed her hand, killing it.

That was how she dealt with problems. How she was dealing with a problem right now. A Rai named Feryn Dar-Hansal, from a small house somewhere far to the north. She had watched him for many days, seen him following her around. Watching as they waited around the entrance to the Cowl-Rai's room. They had even asked for an audience, he said to honour the Cowl-Rai, to give their allegiance. But Saradis could not have anyone getting too close to the Cowl-Rai, and neither could the Cowl-Rai.

Not simply because she was unstable. But because of other, more dangerous things about her that Saradis had no wish for anyone to know. Not yet.

Outside a room, above the main level of Tiltspire's central point, waited her right hand. Laha, who had been with her since the start. The only one who could be trusted entirely. Nothing she could say or do would turn him from the path they walked. Laha was tall, and painfully thin, and many mistook that for him being weak, but he had trained in the arts of killing; there was no weapon that Laha could not use, and even without one the man was lethal.

Especially to the Rai.

"He is in there?" said Saradis as she approached her second, and Laha nodded. He very rarely spoke. Only nodded that bald head, every patch of skin painted in white, the characters spelling out his long, long lineage expertly applied around his left eye which was a startling green, the right a washed out blue. "Well, let us get to it then. Be ready for my call." She walked into the room. The walls of dressed stone were bare; Rai aside, the only thing they contained was a taffistone, like the ones used to take sacrifice, at the back of the room. If the lights were out then it would have an odd blue glow to it. The type of glow that you were not sure was there or not, that you could only see when you looked at it askance, from the corner of your eye.

Feryn Dal-Hansal stared at it, the stone was almost as tall as him. Turning as she entered. Handsome, she supposed, in that foolish youthful way. It was risky for the un-cowled to make love to one with a cowl, if they lost control in the throes of passion the Rai would kill their partners. Saradis had found such risks a thrill once, but it had waned with familiarity and whether he was handsome or not held little sway with her now.

"You asked me here, Skua-Rai," he said, managing to sound like she had insulted him by requesting his presence.

"I did." She gave him a cold smile. "You were looking at that," she said, and nodded at the stone.

"Yes, it has writing on it, I cannot read it though." He stood straighter, the hiss of his clothing beneath the burnished wood of his armour the only sound in the room. "But I did not come here to talk about stones." He stared at her, all the arrogance of youth, all the low cunning of someone given a cowl young and allowed to use that power however they wished. "Your Cowl-Rai is a lie, Saradis," he said. "I want to know what you will offer me to keep that secret."

She let his statement hang in the air, see if he would quail at what he said. If he would realise the enormity of it.

But he was Rai, so he did not.

"Have you ever made a terrible mistake, Rai?" The Rai opened his mouth, about to speak but she did not let him. "I have. I was once Skua-Rai of another god. Like many small monasteries, we raised one who we hoped would be Cowl-Rai. Then one day an army was at my door. It had swept through the north in the name of a new god, Tarl-an-Gig. Their own Cowl-Rai at their head, and I thought I had made a mistake. And in that moment, when I realised the armies of the new Cowl-Rai would come, destroy anyone they saw as a threat, I betrayed my god. I ran, with all my people. We hid, then we found monasteries and committed to this new Cowl-Rai, and just like you, I found out they were not what I thought. Not who I thought." He was smiling at her. Sure in his power over her as she confirmed what he believed. She stepped a little closer. "My god was called Zorir, and they showed me the world. Opened my eyes to its cruelty, its waste. They saw an end to it. They would make the whole world burn, send everyone along the Star Path to true paradise. For many years I thought I had betrayed them, especially when I realised the truth of the Cowl-Rai. I struggled, Rai, truly. Until I had a revelation. I had simply altered my path; the destination was still the same, only the route had changed."

"Why are you telling me this?" he said. "I am not interested in your past. I am only interested in what power you will offer for my silence."

"I am telling you," she said, "because I want you to know that I understand how you feel."

"Why would I care?" He looked genuinely puzzled.

She smiled at him, then shouted, "Laha!" The door opened and her second came in. The Rai gathered fire to his hand, ready to burn her to a cinder where she stood.

The fire went out. Confusion fought nausea on the Rai's face.

"Laha," she said, "is one of a very rare breed. Your cowl

will not work around him." The Rai went for his blade. Laha moved, liquid quick across the room. The Rai drew his sword and thrust but Laha went around the blade, his robe swinging gently, barely even disturbed so smooth was his movement. He grabbed the Rai's arm, twisted his hand so he dropped the blade and then he was behind him, one arm around his neck, the other holding his hand out and the Rai, though he struggled, could not move. Saradis smiled at him.

"The language on the rock, Rai," she said, "is that of darkness, of the enemies of life. It is the words of the Osere below. It took me many, many years to translate it, to understand how to use them for my own ends. Because you cannot have a Cowl-Rai without power, without magic, can you?" She nodded at the stone and Laha manoeuvred the man towards it. "But this stone, is special, one of very few dotted around Crua. Kept in secret places, for secret people and secret purposes." She stood close enough to see the fear and confusion in the Rai's eyes. "It is awful, to be helpless, is it not?" He said nothing. "You do not need to read the words to know how the stone works. A practical demonstration is best. Laha will show you." With that her second forced the Rai's hand onto the stone. The man's body stiffened, he made a noise, part sigh, part scream, part denial as the cowl was changed within him. Then he fell. Became simply an inert thing on the floor.

"He breathes," said Laha, and looked up at her, waiting for direction.

"If he lives, put him in a duller pod or the Hetton pens, otherwise get rid of the body. I will write to the family, tell them he died in the north fighting the outlaw, Cahan Du-Nahere."

With that she left; she had more important tasks to be about.

4

Cahan

"You must talk to them before you leave." Furin held on to his arm, not softly as she had before. Hard, insistent.

"No, I must stop those following us." He tried to pull his arm away but though his strength slowly returned he remained weak, unable to fight off even the Leoric, and she was as tired and weak as any of them.

"Anjiin's ruins, Cahan, they need to hear from you." The pressure of her fingers on his arm, her brown eyes alight with a strength her body lacked. "Remember what I said about leadership? It is more than being gruff and standing tall." Still he did not speak. He did not know what to say.

"This place, Cahan," she looked around, "most of them have never been past Woodedge. You have given some solemn warnings about not starting fires. Told them that speech you are so fond of – 'Harm not and you shall not be harmed'," she said, briefly slipping into a parody of his voice. Then she spoke more softly. "They do not know what it means, Cahan. You need to help them understand." It was as if his voice dried in his throat. As if what she asked sucked life from him as surely as his cowl or the trees of the hungry forest they had left behind. She softened a little. "Tell them what they can do, Cahan. Not what they can't." He held her gaze for a moment longer, then nodded.

"Gather the people, but needs must this is quick." She let go of him, shouting out to the gathered villagers. Her voice filled the clearing, but it went no further as the forest held their sound close, keeping them to itself; cocooning them in the bare branches of Harsh, catching the sound in the closely knit and deep, dark green needles of the evergreens. The people came slowly, the bright colours of their crownhead wool clothes dulled by mud, spattered with the deep brown of dried blood. For some it would be the blood of their invaders, for others it would be the blood of their friends and for many it would be both. The stains of battle would wash out, but he knew it left deeper stains that could not be washed away.

He found a fallen log to stand on, being careful of his footing as the wood was already splitting, falling away where the plants and fungi of the forest had begun to break it down. Sprays of colourful moss grew on the bark, and his feet smeared them across the wood as he mounted it.

Silence.

The background noise of the forest existing as it had done for time past time, with little care for the people within. The drip of snow melting from the branches. The chirp of gasmaws. The whirr of wings, the bark of raniri.

He looked at them. Gathering his words and thoughts the way he once would have herded crownheads.

"You fear the forest." They did not answer, only watched. "It is not foolish." His words rang like bells in the clearing, each face reacting to their clangour. "But the forest does not hate you, it does not hunt you. It does not care about you." They drank his words like they slaked a great thirst. "Think of yourself as tiny creatures moving around a great sleeping animal. It cares nothing for you, as long as you do not disturb it."

"Must we starve?" said a voice from the crowd. "We

have children to feed." Before he could speak, Issofur, the Leoric's child walked out of the wood. In his hands he held nuts and berries.

"No, you will not starve. It will feed you as it has fed Issofur." Cahan pointed at the boy. "Berries and nuts and leaves. Take small amounts without killing the plant and the forest will not mind. As for these buzzing things that bite? Venn can show you how to make a necklace of mint-wort to keep them away and a balm for the bites." The crowd stared. "There is more; garaur can hunt for us. Larger animals, if wounded or weak, can be taken. I will show you more when I return."

"You are leaving us?" This from Ont.

"A group of Rai follows us." His words settled, like brackish black water thick with rot. "They must be stopped." The group became silent and still, coalescing around Ont as if he had become their spokesperson. From the back of the group a voice, soft, resigned.

"You need sacrifice," said Ont. "Who must die to make you strong?"

"Or maybe you can take a little from all of us," said another.

"No!" His voice, and that of Venn who stood to one side of the villagers with Furin, Segur wrapped around their neck.

"But you need strength," said another voice. "To fight them." He clasped his hands behind his back to stop them shaking. Part of him wanted it, so much.

He hungered.

"I am not Rai," he said softly. They did not understand, he could see it. Their world had been in service to others, even the battle of Harn, to them he had been their saviour. They could not see past what the world had impressed upon them. "You do not exist to serve. Dyon, and all those who gave their lives in Harn, saved you. I was simply a vessel." Venn watched, their eyes wide – surprise? Were they surprised? "I go to fight the Rai, I do it to give you a chance to find your own way."

Silence. Confusion.

"We could bring our bows," said a voice and he was sure he saw Furin stand a little taller. He shook his head.

"I will find a way. And if I do not return, find yours. What comes to us is change. But change is life."

"And if we cannot change?" said another voice.

"Then you will die," he said, "but at least not under the weight of the Rai. Look around you, the forest is vast and you are small. It will not bend for you." His words floating in the clearing. Furin looked at him and he knew these were not the words she expected. "But you," he raised his voice, pushing it out beyond the trees around them, "you are the people of Harn. You are strong. You are versatile, you paint the marks of your families across your faces, because you are proud." He let out a breath, a cloud hanging in the biting air. "You will change, and you will live. You have fought the Rai, and like very few others, you won! I was only one among you."

They looked shocked. As if this had not truly occurred to them until this moment.

"He is right," said Ont, looking around. "We can change, we threw the priest of Tarl-an-Gig from our village. We stood against the power of the Rai." He stood straighter. "You know me," he said, "I stood against the forester and his ideas. Blame me for your losses, not him." The crowd were confused, made uncomfortable by Ont's words. "But I have seen the truth now, that the forester was right. The monk, Udinny, and all those who gave their lives, were right. Ranya has touched our village, a gentler god has come to us."

"This gentle god destroyed our village," shouted another voice.

"The Rai did that," said Ont.

"And Treefall was bringing them no matter what, Cahan just meant we were prepared," said Furin.

"Ranya," said Ont, turning to the people of Harn, hesitant, unsure, confused. Almost like the words were using him, rather than him using the words. "She shows us a path, and we must choose to walk it. We can stay and die, or go into the forest, and build our own Anjiin, a place for our god, a different way of being." Silence met this. A long silence and he wondered if talking of the fabled lost city of the gods had been too much, until someone, one of the people in the front, the tanner, Tirra, spoke.

"We better get walking then," she said, "all we are getting here is cold." It was not agreement, not acceptance, only true. The crowd turned, getting ready to travel. Only Ont, Furin, Venn and the two Reborn stayed by Cahan.

"Thank you," he said to the Leoric and the butcher. "For your help, though I am not sure I convinced them." Furin smiled and put a hand on his arm.

"We will wait for you before we enter Wyrdwood," said Furin. "Make sure you come back to us."

"I will find a way."

She nodded, let go of him and put a hand on Ont's arm. Cahan was surprised that he felt a stab of jealousy. "Come, monk of Ranya." Ont looked at her as if he did not understand the words she had spoken.

"Do you think that is my path?" asked the butcher.

"I can only show you it; you must choose where to walk." They left; Venn, Segur and the Reborn stayed.

"We should go," he said to the Reborn. "Venn, help Furin look after them." The trion nodded. "There is much that is dangerous in the forest, you may be able to—"

"It hungers," said Venn, "like the trees you raised but less so."

"Make them go slow, Venn," he said. "Tell Furin that weapons must always be a last resort."

"Cahan," said Venn, "they are right, you are not strong enough to fight. You—"

"I will be strong enough when it is needed."

"The trees may not give, Cahan," they said, and he wondered why they looked so pained, so worried.

"They gave to you, Venn. The land gave to you."

"I think I am different. You need more than the trees will give." They knew what he intended. "You mean to take from the Rai, so you can fight their Hetton."

"It is what Cowl-Rai do," said Nahac.

"You said you would not take from people, Cahan, said it hardened you. Made you cruel." Cahan did not know how to answer.

"I will only do what is needed, Venn," he said quietly, nodded towards the villagers organising themselves to leave, "for them." Venn did not look away; the trion had grown a lot in only a few days. There was power in them and he could feel it. It was power of a different kind, a sort he had never known.

You need me.

"I will protect those people, Venn, it is all I have left." For a moment the trion held his gaze then nodded, more to themselves than the forester. They looked terribly sad. How could he explain what he knew; that the fire that burned dark and cruel within him was not of the cowl, it was him. The cowl only made him more of what he was.

"If you can delay the fight," said Venn, voice on the edge of desperation, "maybe we could find other ways, the Forestals may—"

"The Rai are coming."

"It is not what Udinny would want for you."

"Udinny is gone."

Silence.

"Very well," said Venn. "I only hope it is still you that returns." For a moment, an infinitesimal movement of the Light Above, he could not do anything. Could not speak. Felt frozen in time and place.

"I will come back, Venn," he said. They nodded, moved away to help the villagers. Cahan joined the Reborn.

"You will take from the Rai?" said Nahac, the Reborn's face hidden behind their visor, the mask of a beautiful woman, forever frozen in painted wood.

"I will do what I must," he said.

"It is the easiest way and the trion is right, you need more strength."

"I have this," he said, and lifted his forestbow.

"And if they get near to you?"

"I have you."

"And if we are stopped?"

"Then as I said, I will do what I must, Nahac." She nodded and began to turn. He grabbed her arm, stopped her. "We need to talk of your tactics."

"We kill," she said.

"You kill foolishly. You risk your bodies. In Harn you sacrificed yourself so one Rai could be taken down."

"It worked," she said. "The Rai died, we broke their shield wall."

"It took you both out of the fight."

"We killed the Rai," she sounded puzzled. "You would rather they had lived?"

"You told me that you would fight for me." She nodded, an almost imperceptible movement of her head. "Then that means you obey me."

"We have worshipped at the Blade of Our Lady of Violent Blooms for more years than you can even imagine," the voice behind the mask brittle.

"Maybe you have become too used to chasing the death you say you crave." Her posture changed, or maybe it was something he felt through the cowl, he did not know. He only knew his words hit home. "Without the magics cast in Harn by Venn, you would still be gravely wounded, and your sister would still be a smoking corpse. I need your spears, I cannot afford to have you out of action for a year or more to heal or regrow or whatever it is you do." She remained still, in that unnerving way the Reborn had of becoming statues no matter how awkward the position they stood in.

"Then what do you suggest, Cowl-Rai?" No mistaking the sneer in her voice when she called him that.

"Firstly, that you do not call me that. It is a title that we both hate, and I have done nothing to earn your hate."

"Not yet," she said, "and do not." Cold. Implacable.

"Secondly," he said, "I want you to fight as if you can die. As if you fear it." Again, the stillness.

"We can do that," she said. "But what if sacrifice is the only way for us to win?"

"Then that will be the way."

She nodded. Looked at the bow in his hand.

"Even with that," she said, "you are too weak to fight. You can barely stand." It was true, and she had been too long a warrior for him to lie to her.

"First thing we do, when we come across the Rai," he took a deep breath, "is you bring me one of their soldiers, alive." That beautiful mask, staring at him. Behind her the other Reborn, just as fixed. "I will take the strength I need." The saying of those words, it had the same rancid flavour as when the Hetton were near.

"And yet," she said, "you do not want to be called Cowl-Rai." Then she turned and walked away, and he, weak as he was, had to struggle after her.

5

Dassit

Two hundred soldiers of Chyi, tired and demoralised from multiple retreats in the face of Tarl-an-Gig's armies, sweating in the heat while Dassit waited for her Rai to give an order. She had been waiting for a long time. The Rai did not feel the heat, they did not sweat or suffer, their armour did not rub their skin raw, their muscles did not ache. She could not hurry them, not only because if she tried they would take longer out of spite, but it would also be a poor example to her soldiers and her branch commander, Vir, would rib her for it later. All she could do was stand and wait and listen to the chink of porcelain chains, the flap of flags and the creak of armour as soldiers moved to ease aching feet.

"Why do you think they do it, Trunk Commander?" said the Rai standing by her.

"Do what, Rai?" She was quite sure she knew, but had learnt early in her military career it was best not to presume. Even with a Rai as low down the ranks as this one.

"Betray us, Trunk Commander." She heard Vir cough from behind her and knew he was disguising a laugh. "We are the chosen of the Cowl-Rai, the betrayer from the north presses us and yet these people . . ." The Rai waved towards the walls of Surin-Larger, raised tall and built of thick wood, though the gates now hung off their hinges, smouldering where the Rai's fire had brought them down. "All we ask is they send us soldiers, or sacrifice the weak for us," the Rai sounded genuinely confused, "and yet they refuse."

"I think they are frightened that their children will die." Dassit did not add, "for a lost cause." It was not something the Rai wanted to hear, maybe not something they even could hear. The Rai turned to her, pale eyes locking onto her face.

"But surely they know that to defy the will of Chyi and the Cowl-Rai is to die and deny themselves the Star Path?"

"Maybe they thought you would be too busy fighting the war to bother with them?"

"Well," said the Rai, "they were wrong, weren't they?"

"Will you be leading the final assault, Rai?" she asked. Again, it was a question she felt sure she knew the answer to. The Rai, having already spent her power on the gates, had been eyeing the few prisoners they had caught in front of the walls hungrily.

"I will let you have that honour, Trunk Commander."

"Thank you, Rai."

"Why do you think they still fight?" The Rai touched her lip, rubbing at the skin. "They are beaten."

Because they are brave, thought Dassit, though she could never say that to one of the Rai. Not unless she wanted to join the prisoners.

"Because they are fools and traitors," she said. The Rai nodded.

"How many are left in there?"

"Not many, mostly the very elderly, a few that think themselves soldiers. My scouts say they have taken to the guardhouse in the centre, it is stone on the ground floor."

"And they think it will protect them." The Rai shook her

head. "Well, we do not need the old. Burn the place down with them in it."

"But Rai . . ."

"Are you questioning me?"

"No Rai." Dassit bowed her head and the Rai walked away. Dassit watched her make her way towards where the prisoners were kept, then caught the eye of her second, Vir. He had been with her for years, her lover on occasion, though not for a long time now.

"Are we storming it?" said Vir. Dassit shook her head.

"Burning it. Bring your branch in case they have any surprises in the town."

"They barely put up a fight when we first hit them, can't imagine that—"

"Better to have the numbers and not need them, branch leader, than to . . ."

". . . need 'em and not have 'em." He finished off the sentence for her with a grin and began to call to his troops.

They walked in through the broken gates. Surin-Larger was barely worth of being called a larger. No more than fifty houses, and many of them in poor repair. They'd made a show of standing against her troops but broken within seconds of the gate going down. Had it not been for her strict order to take prisoners it would have been a massacre. The forces of Chyi had known only defeat recently and her troops were angry. She could feel it in them and she hated it. Angry troops couldn't be trusted, they were always looking for someone to blame.

"Fan out!" she shouted. "Check the streets. I don't want any surprises." From the corner of her eyes she saw troops with spear and shield breaking off in groups of four. Angry maybe, but still well disciplined.

"Anjiin's ruins, Dass, they're wasting you here, you're better than kicking over some badly behaved larger." As if to ram home his point Vir kicked a rock, sending it bouncing down the path between two houses. "You held the Osere-cursed traitors at Seerspire, sent 'em packing. They should have us on the frontlines."

She nodded but didn't reply. Vir would neither like nor understand her reply. His world was a simple one of right and wrong. The people on his side were right and everyone else was wrong. She had held the enemy but not in the spire city of Seerstem. She had made her stand in a well-fortified town called Hallick-Larger, just south of the spire city. Her Rai had been killed and with no one but her left she had organised a defence. Stopped the soldiers of Tarl-an-Gig dead and was ready to mount a counter-offensive when the order came to fall back. Even that she was proud of. Lost no one in her retreat.

She did well.

Too well, though she hadn't thought about it at the time. That was why she was here, doing jobs any first day spear-carrier could do. That's what happened when you showed up the Rai. If she'd known her Rai had sent a skipper, saying that the position couldn't be held, she would have fallen back, not fought to hold Hallick-Larger, not wasted her people on the walls.

But she hadn't known and she was no more able to rebuild Anjiin and fix Broken Iftal than she was to change that.

It hadn't been the last time she'd shown up the Rai either. Usually she gave them her ideas, and that was fine, but sometimes she just acted because you had to. War didn't wait for you.

Now here she was.

"Welcoming committee," said Vir, pointing towards the town square. An old man waited for them, long hair, face white with clay. His lineage and the markings of a Leoric on his face. "That the same one you spoke to when you brought the message from the Rai?"

"Yes."

"Shall I kill him?" Vir's hand went to his blade.

"No, I want to talk to him."

"What for?" An air of annoyance in his words. "It's not like they deserve any mercy is it? They've already raised arms against Chyi, let's send 'em to the Osere and be done."

"Wait here, Vir." He gave her a look, as if he thought her mad. Whether he did or not, she did not care, instead she walked across the stony ground and met the Leoric. Maybe twenty paces behind him was the guardhouse. Stone with two floors of wood above it. A good defence in a place like that could kill a lot of people, but she didn't think she had much to worry about here. When she was within two paces of the man she stopped.

"Leoric," she said, a small bow as his position deserved.

"Blessings of Broken Iftal on you, Trunk Commander," he replied softly. It was not lost on her that he did not bless her in Chyi's name; she could not really blame him.

"Why didn't you leave?" she said. "I sent a message, told you we were coming, you should have left." He nodded.

"You were kind to warn us, but this is our home."

"It will be your grave." He smiled at her.

"Better here than ground that we are strangers to." He nodded to himself. "You have seen what is on the borders where Tarl-an-Gig now rules – bodies and heads on spikes, a warning of what waits any who once worshipped the wrong god."

"And your children think that too?" Again, the smile of a man resigned to his fate.

"No, thanks to you the few babes we had here are gone. They at least will find a new life."

"You should have sent people to join the fight when they asked," she said quietly, "then there would have been no need for this." He laughed, not loud but real. Scratched at the side of his beard.

"Trunk Commander, you faced our best at the gate here and barely even noticed them. So you must know there was no one left we could send to fight." He was right of course. Old men and women make poor soldiers and they had proved it here. But the Rai only cared that they were disobeyed, for that a price must be paid.

"I have been ordered to fire the guardhouse," she said. The man nodded. "But I have been in the business of death for a long time, Leoric. I can finish you here and now. Make it quick. Fire is no way to go." He stared at her, then shook his head.

"No," he told her. "I have lived here with my people for my whole life. I will die here with them too. Whatever our fate, we shall share it."

"Very well," she told him.

"For what it is worth, Trunk Commander, and even considering what you are about to do, I think you are a good person." With that he turned, never seeing her expression, never knowing that his words felt like a knife in her guts. When the Leoric was back in the guardhouse she returned to Vir.

"Give the order, Vir," she spoke softly, "torch it." Her branch leader grinned.

"About Osere-cursed time too," he walked forward, "I like a good fire, Dassit. When they start screaming, you know you're doing Chyi's work." Dassit said nothing, only watched as oil was thrown over the building, then the torches lofted up and the fire began to take hold.

When the screaming started she cursed all the gods, but not loud enough to be heard.

6

Cahan

He felt the Hetton as a sickness in the forest. Raised a hand to stop the Reborn and went down on one knee, touching the floor and letting his consciousness drift into the wood along the vast and unseen tangle of Ranya's web. As he did it he felt a pang within: he missed Udinny. He had learned so much from the monk and never thanked her. Udinny had led him along a gentler path, one that had made him care about others and in turn realise he had never cared for himself.

"That way," said Cahan, raising a hand and pointing. Only partly there, his consciousness hovering between the cold skeletons of the trees and the bright net of Ranya's web. The Reborn began to move, battle and death a magnet to them. "Wait." They froze, as if his words had the power to bind them. "Just wait a moment." He fell deeper into the web, the ever-moving and changing crystalline threads against a background of darkness. Searching. Seeing the spots of darkness that were Hetton, the way the life of the forest avoided them. Feeling similar spots growing all over the web where the bluevein sickness touched it

Four.

That voice within, not as unwelcome as it once was. Not welcome though. He tried to see it the way he saw his axes, not as something he wished to use, but as something he may have to. Ranya had placed him into the lives of the villagers of Harn, Udinny had made him realise they were in his care. He would sacrifice himself for them if needs be, as they had for him. Memories that had come back to him, events of his past life, had left him confused about who and what he was, about the fire that burned within him and what fuelled it.

Who fuelled it.

The web was slipping away and he renewed his concentration. Pulled it back, fell into it once more. The throb of life a comfort, behind the hollows where the Hetton were he found the Rai – wrong too, not as wrong as the Hetton, but still something the forest was uncomfortable with. Around them more dots of life, soldiers.

Three Rai.

Six soldiers.

All that had escaped the hungry forest from almost three hundred. His doing, though he felt no guilt. They had come to kill everyone in Harn because they knew about him, because they wanted Venn, because a cloudtree had fallen in the forest, because the Rai considered those people worthless.

He did not consider them worthless.

Cahan knelt a moment longer until he was sure of the direction the Rai headed. Then he stood, a tremor in his legs and arms reminding him of his weakness. He pulled a string from his pocket, leant on his bow but lacked the strength to bend it enough to put the string on.

"Let me," said Nahac. Cahan shook his head.

"You are strong – bend too hard you may break it, and if I lack the strength to string it, I lack the strength to draw it."

"We will take a soldier for you," she said. Her sister stood behind her, silent as always. When he had touched

Ranya's web he had not felt the Reborn at all. It was as if they did not exist. "Or two."

He longed for it. The strength, the power.

"No," he said. The wounded and dying of Harn had given him their lives as a gift; and now he was so close to the act to steal the life of even an enemy felt wrong. Dangerous. There must be other ways. A thought rose within him, blue and unbidden: he had felt, more than once, another power behind Ranya's web. A different power. Maybe there was a way there? Venn did not kill for power, and he did not believe the Forestals did either, or the forest would shun them the way it did the Rai. "They are few," he looked at Nahac, "they are in the forest which they fear, and Rai fear for their own lives more than anything. If we kill one of the Rai, I am sure the rest will run."

"Even if they do, their beasts, these Hetton, will pursue us. You are in no state to run, never mind fight." True again, he should not have come, though he did not trust the Reborn to go alone as they were reckless with their safety and he needed them walking, not slowly healing on a travois.

He had put himself into an impossible position.

"The trees." He walked towards one. Put his hand on the rough bark. "Lend me your strength," he said. He could feel it, the ancient strength of the tree flowing up through it from deep below in an exchange with the Light Above, transmuting its power and the fertility within the ground. Far below a power beyond his understanding, but that was where the Osere held sway, a place he hoped he was not bound for. And behind it . . .

Gone.

There was no strength for him here. The tree denied him. Its strength, so cool and wonderful and pure, slipped around his wishes and denied him.

"Are you strong now?" said Nahac.

"No," he said.

"If the trees do not obey you, then kill one. Make an example," she said. It was all he could do not to laugh. The idea you could somehow fight something as huge and eternal as the trees of Crua. "Why do you smile?" she said. "Everything can die." She was right of course. The fertility of Crua was fed by death, by the rotting of bodies and wood and wasn't that a kind of life? A kind of power.

He had never thought about it before. Was that what he felt behind Ranya's web? Behind the interconnectedness of all things? Could he feel death, soaking away as it fed the world? Death was everywhere – did Venn and the Forestals somehow take from it? Was that the huge well below? He had never truly considered it, the slow seep of life from the ground, where it went. It made sense.

No.

The cowl would think that. It desired life above all things.

Something of the idea worried at him though. The thoughts felt almost alien, not his. Like they seeped into him and unlike the power of the land these thoughts were cold, blue like ice.

"Find me a fallen log. An old one." The Reborn stared at him, no expression. A sudden ache that shot through him, his bones and his muscles, as if his cowl was trying to stop him.

No.

He let out a grunt, pushed the pain away.

Nahac spoke to her sister, words in a language Cahan did not know, something ancient and forgotten. The sister vanished into the wood and Nahac turned back to him.

"You seek power through death."

"I want to try something."

"Sometimes it is better to walk away than fight."

"I am surprised to hear that from you," he said. She pulled down her visor, the grey skin of her finely chiselled face vanishing behind the carved visage of a beautiful woman, only her eyes visible through it.

"We know death, Cahan Du-Nahere, my sister and I." She stepped a little closer. "It is not life, and it can never be. Our creation brought a sickness to the land."

"You do not approve." The silent sister came back, pointed into the wood. "I need strength to fight."

"Reach out for me with your cowl," she said. He tried, but he may as well have tried to catch air.

"I cannot." He felt his brows knit in puzzlement. "You are not there."

"Take it from the living, it is better. We will bring you one of their soldiers. They will die anyway."

He expected something from his cowl, some feeling of desire but there was only the ache in his bones.

"I do not want to become Rai," he said. For a moment he felt a ghost of the power he had used to bring into being the hungry wood. All those lives given to him freely, intoxicating, wonderful. Deadly to Udinny. Nahac moved in front of him.

"There are worse things to be than Rai. Sometimes, it is not about what we want."

"Are you stopping me?" She stared at him, pale eyes behind the visor. Then turned towards her sister who shrugged.

"No." Nahac stepped aside. "Maybe you are a man who only learns through action." Did he detect humour there? He was not sure, he had not thought the Reborn understood humour.

He walked in the direction indicated, every step a fight not only with tiredness but with himself. Twice he fell, as if the cowl was attempting to trip him. Are you afraid, cowl? he wondered. Why? Power is power. He found the log, the remains of some great forest giant, now blackened where moisture had soaked into it, the wood splintered and speckled with bright lichens and fungus. Home to its own ecosystem which slowly broke it down and released the energy within. All around it plants and ferns were springing up, a sapling growing out from underneath and reaching up for the light, maybe even the child of the tree that lay rotting in the mulch. He could not sense the ebb and flow of energy within the log the way he did within the trees, though he could feel the life of what lived within it. When he concentrated he could see the way even those tiny specks of life connected to Ranya's web. He could also feel bluevein, deep in the earth, a different energy, unpleasant. But some things in nature were.

Corruption.

He knelt before the log, felt the coldness of the earth through his armour just as he would if he knelt without it. Damp and cold and fertile. He reached out a hand.

"Are you sure of this, Cahan Du-Nahere?" Nahac behind him, not stopping him, but near enough that he felt her disapproval.

"We have already spoken on this, Nahac, my mind is made up." She remained there, for just long enough to make him uncomfortable and then stood back. He took a breath, the forest air fresh, clear and green. Full of the scent of growing things.

He placed a hand on the log. Damp, slippery with its own fluids as it was slowly broken down.

No.

He paused again. He had never known the voice within turn down power, not since that first time so long ago in the monastery of Zorir when his sister's murderer knelt before him. Another breath, the air alive and strong.

No.

Yes.

He pushed his consciousness down, like a dagger into rotting wood full of spaces where life was absent. He passed by all that was alive – all that was taking sustenance from the rotting log, each point, no matter how infinitesimal it may be on Ranya's web, he put aside. He would not take life; even the briefest touch from him would extinguish these tiny points and he did not want that. Did not want them. He moved further in, seeking the slow discorporation of life within the rot. It denied him. He felt like it spoke a different language, one he knew was communication, but had no way of understanding. He could feel where things had rotted down entirely, feel creatures and roots and cilia changing it to energy but at that point it was part of something living again.

He needed translation.

Corruption.

Our creation brought a sickness to the land.

Did the Reborn mean the bluevein?

It glowed in his mind in a way it never had before

No.

Was that the link?

He had never really studied the bluevein. *No.* Only dragged it from the ground and burned it, thought of it as disease but it always grew where there was death. *No.* Dead trees, corpses, crops that had rotted on the ground. *No.* He pushed his mind towards it, it was not alive but not dead. It was in between, unlike anything else he had come across. Almost – it was like Ranya's web, a medium of something else but at the same time it was not.

Do not.

Could he use it?

Do not.

He reached out for it.

Corrupti—

At its touch the voice of his cowl silenced.

The air no longer as fresh.

The Light Above not so bright.

A tantalising hint of power. Strength. He waited for the cowl to try and stop him but felt only the oddest sensation. Like falling but without moving. Like speaking without words. He gagged, as if on something foul, panicked that the Hetton were near. No. Nahac would have told him.

This feeling is a warning. His thought not the cowl's. But he needed strength. He could always withdraw. Going forward slowly, as if stuck in mud, and that mud becoming thicker and darker. Enclosing him, entombing him. A hunger. A deep blue that was almost black. A maw, a howling darkness. A sense of something else, something beyond what was there but it was gone so quickly he wondered if he imagined it. A faint memory of height and strength and great power and something within the bluevein desired all of that again. He wanted to leave, to reverse. He had made a mistake. Too late. The bluevein pulled at him like a thousand hands. It was a trap sprung around him. A faint blue glow filled his vision, becoming brighter with every moment. He had made a terrible mistake. Pain, in his hands where he touched the log, as if the skin was being flayed from him. Dimly aware the Reborn were trying to pull him away but he had reached too far, death was a howling gale dragging him towards something that pulsated and reached for him. Something he did not understand, an unending hunger that would swallow him up. Take all that was "him" and destroy it.

You need me.

The cowl's voice, but heard as if from very far away. He was being sublimated, eaten away, stretched out flat and thin, replaced.

Let me.

He could not. This was the opposite of what he had been taught, what he had thought all of his life – that he must control the cowl. Him. That without stamping down on it, making it obey him, he would lose all control.

Let me save you.

No. What if . . . what if . . .

Death.

The howling around him, the black wind, the deep hunger. Was his cowl going to end him?

He had been fighting his whole life. Fighting the cowl,

fighting to be alone, fighting others, fighting himself. He did not know how to let go.

Death.

He could not give in, could not die yet.

Agonies like none he had known. It felt like his flesh was afire and at the same time it was freezing. It felt like every muscle worked against another, like his bones were splitting into shards. These agonies, growing and growing as he fought what desired his essence, his being, and at the same time he fought his cowl.

Let me.

The agony growing, heightening, he felt every hair on his body as point of pain. Every piece of him wracked as pain spiralled up and up into new heights. Past was what was bearable and each time he thought it was as painful as could be, it grew. The gnawing, howling darkness hungered for him. Within it another voice. One he did not know.

"Cahan."

Until.

He could not bear it.

Death, even the complete oblivion the hunger offered him, that was better than the pain he felt. Being in such torment that every heartbeat felt like an eternity stretched out across hot coals.

Better death than this.

Better death.

He felt himself give up. Felt his heart stop. Felt the howling hunger rush forth to engulf him and just before it did he heard the third voice again, not his, not the cowl's. "Mine," it said, the word as insidious and slow as the pain was fast and sure.

No.

Something burning through his body. A light that was not light. A being that was not a being. With it came an understanding of the cowl, alive but not aware, not like he was. Part of him, it borrowed his consciousness just as he borrowed its strength. It was him and he was it.

And it did not feel pain.

It could not be persuaded.

It was life.

Part of Ranya's web just as he was. He let go.

The cowl stood as a wall between him and the hunger. The pain stopped but Cahan still could not move and the Reborn pulled at him in vain. No, that was not true, he was aware he could move if he wanted. That it was possible. Or he could stay and do what he had intended. Take the power through the bluevein. He could see it now. Between him, the bluevein, and whatever else was out there. He could feel that the cowl did not want that, but that it would do what he requested. As if in this moment, it chose to show him it could be trusted, should be trusted. The cowl was the wind that blew the skyraft, but he was the hand on the tiller.

Do not take it.

But he needed it.

He felt the cilia burst from his palms, through the gloves of his armour.

Connection.

The hidden web within the wood; within it a second web, the bluevein. A slowly strengthening network growing there, touching Ranya's web. The web was part of Crua. It did not live off the slow work of dissolution but was part of it. The bluevein was different, plugged directly into the rot and the decay, gathering its heat as well as stealing power from what lived. A momentary hesitation, as if to give him time to change his mind. He did not. He would not suffer all that pain for nothing.

"Do it."

The cilia thickening, growing, branching, eating through the wood, curling round bluevein threads, taking the energy, raw, strange, dark.

Powerful.

Sick.

Flowing into him. He felt himself call out. Felt a thrill at the strength. Fell backwards, his body alive. A single moment of pleasure swiftly followed by revulsion. Tasted rot in his mouth. Wanted to run, to fly, to escape himself. Could almost sense the forest trying to move away from him. A faint sense of . . . satisfaction? But not his, nor the cowls.

"Well," said Nahac, "it worked."

"How do you know?" he said, lying on his back, breathing hard, fighting the urge to commit.

"I know," she said.

"How?"

"Your eyes have turned black."

7
Cahan

Revolted by himself. Mind screaming. Nausea. Almost overwhelming. Flowing over and through him in waves as he stepped through the wood. He felt as though a hundred thousand tiny orits crawled between his skin and his armour. As if a million tiny legs marched over his skin.

This was wrong.

He was no longer connected to the armour, it was not part of him. He was not complete. With the waves of nausea came waves of disconnection. Stabs of pain that made him grit his teeth which felt brittle, like chalk, as if they would break under the pressure of his jaw muscles.

A constant high ringing in his ears, barely audible, almost painful.

. . . ou . . . ee . . . m . . .

He was a pariah to the forest. He felt that as keenly as the nausea and the pain. The life, animals and tiny flyers, moving away from him. Even the plants were affected, beginning to change as if his passing brought the falling of the Light Above, flowers shutting, leaves drooping.

He could feel the Hetton clearly. He did not need to reach into Ranya's web for them, and was not going to. He was sure he would not be able to. He was apart from nature now, no longer within the web. What he had done with the rotten log and the bluevein had put him outside of it. Made him outcast.

He coughed and tasted rot, but it did not revolt him as it once would have.

"We told you not to," said Nahac. "Death is not for the living." The Reborn looked different, not grey, they were striped with pulsing energy.

"I am like you," he said, felt a sibilance in his words, a fur upon his tongue. The creeping of his flesh. The lines running along Nahac's armour twisted and shifted.

"No," she said, "for you it is temporary, a lesson in what is forbidden. And why." Her sister joined her, they seemed brighter and more real than the trees and plants around them, more alive. He reached out a hand to touch her. "No," she said. Not a request. A command. "Do not." He let his hand fall, a wave of nausea and self-revulsion passed across him.

"You feel this way."

"It is our eternity." He could not speak. Could not imagine it. "The Cowl-Rai of Cahrasi-Who-Enslaves, they sought the power of the Osere, raised one hundred Reborn from the dead of the battlefield. On the day we were born so was the bluevein. We are born of what you feel."

"A hundred." The words felt like they oozed from his mouth. "Where are the others? Are they the Hetton?" Nahac stared at him, unnaturally still. Then she shook her head, a slow deliberate movement.

"No. They are weak compared to us. My sisters were strong. They lasted hundreds of years before the silence fell upon them."

"The silence? Then your sister?" He looked at the other Reborn. "That is why she does not speak?"

"She is a sister of violent blooms, my lover in a life ended long ago," said Nahac. "And yes, that is one reason why she does not speak. The horror has become too much. If she opens her mouth she will scream, and the screaming will never stop."

Even in his mire of self-loathing he felt the awful truth of what she said, and now he understood the Reborn's wish for death.

"I will find you a way to die," he said. He wanted to wash his hands. "I promise."

"But not today," and if she felt some resentment or emotion she did not show it. "Today others must die." He nodded. Pointed.

"That way." He picked up the bow, it felt strange in his hand, the wood slimy and hard to grip.

"It rejects you," she said.

"I will make it work for me." He felt anger at the bow.

"It will never be the same again if you do."

"But . . ."

She took a sword from her hip. "This is inert, it does not care if you are alive, dead, or somewhere in between." He took the sword, felt a difference.

"I had hoped to use arrows."

"We have throwing spears if you can use them." He nodded and she turned to her sister who took spears from a pack on her back, smaller, lighter and fletched like large arrows. The ends were barbed. "Four each," she said. He picked them up, smooth and dry in his hands. The silent Reborn stepped forward and took his bow, put it into her weapons pack. The sword he held in his hand; he did not reach for his axes. "How many, Cahan?" said Nahac.

"Four Hetton, three Rai." The Hetton pulsed in his mind like lights, the Rai similar but different.

"How many soldiers?"

He put a hand in the dirt, felt the worms, the rot, the slow breakdown of vegetable matter. Dead flesh liquifying, one creature digesting another. It was a song, a strange and discordant song and through it ran the high notes of bluevein which both disgusted and attracted him. There was a scream in his veins that interfered with any chance he had of touching Ranya's web. For a moment he felt himself comfortable among the death. He pulled his hand away as if the ground burned him.

"I do not know," he said. "I cannot find the soldiers." The Reborn nodded, as if this was expected.

"We do not need to fear the soldiers," she said then stood, waiting. "You said we must obey your orders, so give them."

He concentrated, trying to push away the crawling of his skin, the miasma in his mind.

"The Rai will push the Hetton out before them, any soldiers will follow. We head that way," he pointed, "come in behind them."

"And then?"

"We kill the Rai with thrown spears, close with the soldiers and the Hetton." He looked from one Reborn to the other. "We kill them all; any who walk away may report back on the survivors of Harn."

"No prisoners," said Nahac.

"None," he said. He was aware, in the back of his mind, that giving such an order, even if necessary, would have filled him with a sense of guilt once. Not now. Instead he felt a dark elation, pleasure at feeding the land with blood and death.

You . . . ne . . . me.

The voice of the cowl, but as if from very far away. He did not think he needed it. The revulsion he had felt at first was ebbing, the itching of his skin leaving. Now he felt there were other ways to strength and power and they did not involve killing. The urge to vomit flooded through him, doubling him over. His mouth filling with foul-tasting saliva, bringing back the sense of revulsion. He felt the flickering of fire somewhere far away.

"Cahan Du-Nahere?"

"I am all right."

"It is life fighting death and sickness," she said. "You must use this power quickly, remove it from you. Both cannot exist in a living body for long. Something must give." He nodded, spat a foul black liquid into the ferns.

"Let us go," his voice sounded different, deeper, hoarser. He saw the world through a haze. He felt the bluevein in the ground reaching for him.

They pushed through the undergrowth. Leaves dripped a liquid that felt like some foul ichor burning his skin. When he checked it was only water, the gentle normal drip of the forest.

What had happened to him? How could the Reborn bear this? He took a breath and the air was black in his lungs. Nahac was right, he had to get it out of him. Kill. Kill with it. Kill and kill and kill.

He felt himself smiling.

A hand on his arm.

"We must keep moving." He blinked; he had stopped walking, was standing there. "Concentrate," she said. He nodded, they moved on and rather than think about himself he locked on to the feeling of the Hetton, made them lodestones in his mind, shining stars in the darkness.

They closed and he ducked down, hiding in the undergrowth at the side of a forest path and waiting for the enemy to pass. The Reborn positioned themselves further down on either side of the path. He did not feel the same loathing when the Hetton approached. He did not hear their voices as barely understandable sibilance. He heard their speech as song, high and sweet. It spoke to him.

"Follow, follow them. Find them. Follow them find them. Kill them." The words bouncing backwards and forward between the four creatures. Then the soldiers came, he could feel their fear of the Hetton and how much they disliked being around them. Six soldiers. Next came the Rai, three of them. Not speaking, arrogant despite their recent defeat. Not checking the wood around them. Foolish. They did not learn.

They deserved to die.

He looked across, found Nahac among the trees. Exchanged a nod.

Felt a thrill run through him. A pleasure purer and bluer than any other.

He stood, drew his arm back and let strength flow through him. The Reborn stood, launched their own spears.

Two spears.

Two deaths.

Each Reborn spear hitting a Rai in the head, piercing through wood, bone and flesh. The last of the three Rai had time to turn. Hands coming up, fire blossoming, and Cahan threw his spear. The hardened wood smashing through the Rai's visor, through their head. He wanted to howl, to caper and gibber with glee, he felt the floor of the forest – no not the floor, something else, something deeper and darker – fill with joy at being fed. A mirror of his own feelings. There was more power there, power for him and—

"Cahan!"

The voice shook him. He had been lost again, lost in the reverie of death. Soldiers running towards him. Angry and frightened. So weak. They ran and he moved. Faster, stronger, more powerful. The Reborn spinning around him like ghosts, the sword in his hand an extension of his body. Cutting off a limb here, opening a throat there. Reborn spears punctured flesh in explosions of glorious red. Then the soldiers were dead and he felt the power in their corpses. He was unstoppable. This was him. This was what it was to be Cowl-Rai, to wield the power of Zorir.

You . . . ed . . . me.

The voice of the cowl, so quiet and distant. So easy to ignore.

"Cahan, the Hetton!"

They came, glorious glowing powerful creatures. In their fury they were almost too bright for him to look at. Blue lines over their bodies, like the Reborn but brighter, the lines thicker. He could not move.

"Cahan!" Shaken loose by his name. Images flowed away. The Hetton no longer bright but monsters once more. Four of them, armour splintered and dry. Faces stretched and wasted, eyes white and dead. Two with swords, two with spears. The Reborn threw their remaining spears. Concentrating on the first Hetton. The creature pierced multiple times. Falling to its knees and the light of it, the blue haze and lines, winked out. The other three came on. Nahac engaged first. She was swift, fighting in that beautiful spinning style of the devotees of the Lady of Violent Blooms. The Hetton matched her blow for blow but its fighting was ugly, jerky. Her sister engaged, not quite as fast or balletic. Then he was fighting. No time to watch. The Hetton were fast, fluid, vicious. He met each blow with the borrowed sword. Felt the power within him. He did not have to fight.

He brought fire. It leapt from his hand, dark and hungry, splashing against the armour of the Hetton. The creature screamed. This fire did not act like fire, the flames deep blue and purple, flickering over the creature's armour as if alive, searching for a way in. Then the Hetton was trying to rip off its own armour, screeching in a high, painful voice as smoke rose from it. Cahan turned. Saw the silent sister being forced back and reached out with the fire again. His strength ebbing, knowing the silent sister was struggling, not as strong or fast as Nahac. His fire, squirming, stretching, covered the Hetton. Oozed along its armour, looking for a way in, sending it running and screaming. At the same time Nahac ran the last Hetton through with her spear. It screeched and she drove a knife into its eye, cutting off its noise with one hard thrust and stepping back. Watching it fall to the forest floor. Cahan felt the death, felt a small rejoicing at it. The shimmer of bluevein in the ground.

He fell to his knees, weak once more.

"Come, Cowl-Rai," said Nahac and she helped him stand. Looked him in the face. "Your eyes are clear, let us return to your people." He did not move, not at first. He was empty. The power was there, below him. In the corpses. The patches of bluevein were ways to reach out and take the energy of death. He wanted it. "Cahan!" said Nahac. He grunted. Nodded, and the two Reborn helped him limp back into the forest, towards Wyrdwood where the people of Harn waited.

Behind them, unseen, a woman they could not sense, could not feel, and who did not exist within Ranya's web watched. When they had vanished into the undergrowth, she stood and made to follow them, carrying thoughts of vengeance on the man who had destroyed her cowl with her.

8
Cahan

He felt more himself by the time he arrived where the villagers camped. They had not made it as far as he hoped through Harnwood, their going slow and careful. He found the villagers huddled together against the cold air.

"They need fire," said Nahac. He was surprised the Reborn gave an opinion. She turned her visor to him. "The morale of an army is important."

"The forest dislikes fire, and smoke would allow us to be found."

"By who?" she said. "None are following now." He felt a little ashamed at the memory of how much he had enjoyed killing in the forest. The thought made his mouth water and he had to push it away. The Reborn had been right – he should not have taken power from death, it was a mistake. Yet, somewhere, deep within, he had felt a connection. It had felt right, more right than taking life for his cowl, and he hated himself for it. There had been no guilt at the time, the freedom had been a wonderful thing.

Maybe, if he reached out again, then . . .

He cleared his throat, nodded to Nahac.

"I will think on it."

As he approached the camp Segur came racing out, but as it came closer the garaur slowed, stopped. Then it whined, growled at him, turned and raced back into the camp.

It felt like a punch to his gut.

Venn and Furin came out to meet him. They had become closer since the battle at Harn, and the trion had begun watching her closely, seeing how she led. How she made peace and forged people together.

"Cahan," said Furin, her smile warm. "I am glad you are back unharmed." Was he unharmed? No, he could feel an itching on his skin, a scar that could not be seen.

"We are no longer followed," he said. "I will ask the forest if we can have fires, small ones."

"That will be welcome," said Furin. Behind her Venn studied him, a strange look on their face. "I must ask your advice, on two things," said Furin.

"I will help how I can."

"Some of the villagers have had enough, Cahan; not that many, not even ten, but they wish to return to Harn."

"Are they fools—" She cut him off with a hand.

"They are cold, and frightened and long for what they know."

"If the hungry trees do not kill them then the Rai will, just like they did Dyon and those who went to Harnspire." Furin nodded.

"I know that, I think they know it too. I want you to speak with them, but not lecture them. Give them some hope." Hope? Out here in the Harnwood with the light slowly dying? He felt little enough himself. He was drained, empty. "And I want to know what you plan, Cahan, the villagers have been asking me and knowing no more than –" she once more approximated his voice "– 'we go into the forest' is not a help. They think Wyrdwood is death."

"The Forestals live in Wyrdwood," said Cahan, "so it is possible to live there." He looked over at the villagers. "We will find a way." She did not look convinced. "You said there was another problem?"

"Follow me." She led him into the camp past shivering groups of villagers.

"You have not had problems with the Harnwood?" said Cahan. "Orit or skinfetch?" Furin shook her head as they walked. The undergrowth had been trampled flat in a wide area between the looming trees and he wondered how long the villagers had been here. How long he had been away from them, but he could not ask. There would be questions.

"We saw orits but avoided them, and nothing else that would hurt us. Venn led us, they sense the forest." Cahan glanced at the trion who had clearly ignored his warning about using their cowl when he was not there to guide them. Maybe he was a poor guide, given the choices he had made. "It is not Venn, but the hunter, Sark, I need you to see."

He was about to ask why when he saw Sark, or the back of them. With him were two more villagers, Buris and Gafnar. Ont stood before them, saying something to Gart. Beyond them he saw a figure collapsed on the floor and the fire within him burned, the roaring temper that was always there leapt up. He almost forgot the guilt. The feeling of dirt in his veins from touching death.

The body of a rootling lay on the floor, still and slack. Its almost-but-not-human form curled up, the fur on its thin limbs lank and greasy. Sark was the villager's hunter and Cahan jumped to an immediate conclusion. Despite all he had told them, all he had said, they had gone out and hunted the creatures of the forest. Then the rootling moved, not much, a twitch of its legs at the same time Sark saw Cahan.

"Cowl-R—" began Sark, then stopped, remembering how the bearded forester hated the title. "Cahan," he began again, "I am glad you have come. We found this creature, sick and we're trying to help."

"A rootling," said Cahan. "I thought you villagers disliked them."

"After they brought us arrows at Harn," said Ont, "we thought it was the least we could do."

"It is wounded, all over its body see?" He pointed. Weals were risen over the skin beneath the light fur that covered it. The creature looked up at him with big frightened eyes, it did not even have the energy to bare its sharp teeth. "We are treating it with allbalm; Buris here is chewing it up so don't expect her to talk."

"Only one of us who likes the taste," said Gafnar. "Buris always was a bit wrong in the head." Buris punched him on the arm and Gafnar laughed. The rootling shrank away from them.

"It looked like it has tangled with a littercrawler," said Cahan, "you can see the circles from its tentacles. It was lucky to escape." He crouched. "Odd, littercrawlers do not often take rootlings."

"Littercrawlers are not big enough to take a rootling," said Ont with a laugh, a little of his old personality showing.

"Not the ones you are used to," said Cahan. Ont's eyes widened.

"Maybe it grabbed it and threw it away?" said Sark.

"Why is the rootling a problem?" asked Cahan.

"We do not know what to do with it," said Gart. "Ont thinks we should take it with us when we leave, to continue to administer it." The big man nodded.

"It is right," Ont said, "they protected us, so we should protect them." Odd, thought Cahan, how much a man can change in such a short time.

"And you, Sark?" The hunter looked up, plainly uncomfortable with talking to Cahan. In many ways Sark was the most like the forester, he kept his own counsel, enjoyed his own company.

"I think we leave it," he said. "It is of the forest, we do what we can for it and then it becomes the forest's decision."

Cahan's first instinct was to agree with the hunter, use it to put Ont in his place. The man had caused him much trouble; back in Harn his rabble-rousing had come close to killing Venn after an accident hurt another villager. But Cahan held his tongue. The man who had been a butcher was trying to change, he had been humbled by Udinny's sacrifice. Cahan took a deep breath.

"It is good, what you wish to do, Ont," said Cahan softly, "but Sark is right. What is of the forest must be left to the forest, and we frighten the rootling. To take it with us we would have to bind it."

"It will die," said Ont, looking confused.

"Maybe," said Cahan, standing. "But it may also be that other rootlings are out there, too scared by us to come for their friend. Or it may be its time." Ont licked his lips, thinking. Something within Cahan quivered at the thought of death.

"Your will, Cowl-Rai," Ont said. Cahan stepped forward, put a hand on Ont's arm, felt the man flinch at his touch. He wanted to tell Ont not to call him Cowl-Rai but now was not the time; though Ont tried to hide it, being wrong had hurt him. The man was trying his best to change, to follow Udinny's example and become a monk of Ranya. It would be a poor way for Cahan to remember his friend by making this man feel bad.

"There are those who think they should return to Harn, Ont," said Cahan. "Will you help me convince them otherwise?"

"Of course," he said, surprise rushing across his face. "Gladly. In fact I know who you mean, I will lead you to them." Ont took him through the camp, past small groups of survivors. The adults were quiet, still contemplating what they had been through, still healing wounds both physical and mental. The children were not. Issofur, the Leoric's son, ran past, shouting and playing some game with Gillet, the girl who had come to warn him when the Rai arrived. She still held the corn doll he had given her, and Issofur, he was no longer quite a boy. Something in his posture as he ran, in the sharpness of his features, reminded Cahan of a rootling. Other children were playing the same game, running round the adults. Finding joy, seeing this life-or-death trip as an adventure. It made Cahan a little happier.

He only wished he had some idea of where they were going, and what they would do when they got there. He had intended to ask the Forestal, Ania, for help but the Forestals had not stayed. The villagers were on their own, he was all they had to rely on.

"Cahan," said Venn, from behind him, "are you well?" Cahan turned, he had not noticed the trion following him. "I said are you well?"

"Of course," he replied. The trion studied him. Ont watching.

"You are different," said Venn. Cahan stared towards the Reborn at the edge of the clearing, watching the villagers. "Something about you is different."

"And you have been using your cowl, Venn, though I told you not to."

"I have learned much," said Venn. "I have learned things even you do not know."

"Learned, or only guessed?" It was a struggle to keep the anger out of his voice. Venn blinked. "Do you actually know what you do, or simply do it?"

"And do you know how you do what you do?" At Venn's words the feeling of touching the bluevein rushed back, bringing with it nausea. Had he ever known what he was doing?

"I trained for many years, Venn, I found discipline. You have not been trained and the power is . . ."

"Different for me," said Venn, lightly touching his arms. "I am not compelled to use it." Cahan did not know what to say, because he thought it was probably true. At the same time he knew how insidious the voice of the cowl – the call to any power – could be. It came to him as pain, but maybe it came to Venn as something else. "You should trust others more, Cahan." The forester grunted and nodded, a movement so slight most would have missed it.

"It is hard."

"We ran into orits in the forest. Had it not been for Sark the villagers would have attacked them, they are used to driving orits away."

"Impossible in Harnwood," said Cahan, "this is their home. The villagers have only come across small nests in Woodedge, barely established. Sark was right. The orits would have come for them in their hundreds."

"Sark said orits were the least of their worries and they should save their strength." Cahan nodded. "Look at them, Cahan," Venn glanced over at the villagers. "They are worn out." The trion was right, he could see it in the posture of each and every one of them. The elation of winning a battle was long past. Now they were only surviving. "I used my cowl to feel the creatures of the forest, steer us away from anything large or dangerous. That is all. It is passive, not aggressive." Cahan looked at them, shrugged.

"I suppose that may have saved lives." Venn smiled. "Now, Ont and I must speak to some of the villagers." He walked past, to where Ont waited. The big man led him through the villagers to a group stood on the edge of them. He counted nine, leading them was the tanner, Tirra.

"Ont," she said and the look she gave him was as frosty as the air. "I see you have run telling tales."

"The whole camp knows what you wish, Tirra, you have not been subtle about it."

"We are not outlaws, we are not Forestals. This place is not for us, we want to go back." Her voice, equal parts aggressive and defensive.

"You cannot go back," said Cahan. She was about to start arguing with him, he could see it in her face. "I mean only that Harn is gone, there is nowhere to go back to.

And the trees that grow there now, they will not welcome you home."

"I do not mean to Harn," said Tirra softly. Less aggressive now that Cahan had not mocked her. "We know Harn is lost. I mean back to Crua.

"We are not of the forest," she said. "We are people of villages and largers. They are for us. We will go back and find places that do not know us. Vanish into them, each of us will go to somewhere different. We will not be found." She sounded hopeful, those behind her were nodding. He had thought he would be angry, but he was not. He understood. They were frightened and in an unfamiliar land, looking for a way out.

"Tirra," said Ont softly, "they will find you." She shook her head.

"No, Ont, just because you have found solace in some new weak god does not mean we must. We will be clever, we will be hard."

"What do you do every morning, Tirra?" asked Ont softly. "Without even thinking?"

"What do you mean?" she said. "What does my morning routine have to do with this?"

"The clanpaint you put on the side of your face, Tirra," said Ont, "so much part of you that you do not even consider it."

"I will make new clanpaint." Her words coming quickly, defensively.

"And if you meet someone whose heritage you claim to share," said Ont, "what then?" She looked about, the eight with her now less sure than they had been. "Or if you slip, share a memory of Harn with the wrong person?"

"Well, I will forego clanpaint."

"Become clanless?" said Cahan. "If you think the forest is hard, then being alone and clanless is harder."

"And how would you know . . ." she began but her voice tailed off, as Cahan Du-Nahere had never worn clanpaint, and he knew more than any of them what it was to be clanless. Tirra knew how they had treated him, what they had thought of him. The sounds of the forest moved in to inhabit the silence between them.

"We are frightened, Cahan Du-Nahere. And we are cold and we are hungry," she said eventually.

"I understand, but it will become easier, I promise. When we find a place to stop, to live. I will teach you how to exist within the forest. To do only what it allows, so the trees will hide you and not resent you."

"So where do we go?" said Tirra.

"Wyrdwood," said Cahan, "we will become people of Wyrdwood."

Tirra stared at him, took a deep breath.

"Very well," she said, "I suppose we must follow you to Wyrdwood, it seems there is nowhere else to go."

9

Sorha

She did not know how old she was.

She had never even thought about it, or if she had she could not remember. Maybe age had been important when she was very young, counting down the days until they let her into the blooming rooms and she took on the mantle of her family, became Rai. That had been all she wanted, all she dreamed of as a child. No longer treated as less than her father and the others in the bottom of Storspire. No longer a child running round. A real person, someone who mattered. Let the trainers try and beat her then.

Had the blooming rooms been hard?

She didn't remember it being hard, only the rush of power like a cold sweet drink on a hot day. With power had come a new life; mortality had ceased to be something she thought about. She was Rai, she was eternal. She was strong and feared nothing but other Rai, and even then fear was the wrong word. Wariness was better, knowledge that there were some she could not go up against, not yet. She learned that sometimes it was better to scheme than confront head-on, though she had been glad to do that too. Enjoyed the rush of the fight.

She lived, those around her died. Those not blessed with cowls shrivelled up and passed on in what felt like the blink of an eye. One day they were there and the next another servant had taken their place and name – it was easier if all the servants had the same name, a waste learning new ones. Rai had no time for niceties, let others bend to their will, change for them. They were what mattered.

She thought that must have been how it was for the gods, before Iftal broke and Anjiin fell. Before they lost their power and had to use the people of Crua. She hadn't even been sure gods existed, even Cowl-Rai felt like stories told to scare and force obedience. None of it had felt real to her – gods, Ancient Anjiin, the stories of her childhood.

Then she met Cahan Du-Nahere.

She remained undecided about gods, but Cowl-Rai, they were real at least.

Because of him she was no longer Rai, but she knew Rai in a way no outsider could. She knew what they thought of her. She knew how they hated her and how they feared her for what she had become. A null spot that blocked their power.

But they did not hate, not really. They only thought they did.

They did not feel at all.

When Cahan Du-Nahere had burned out her cowl, robbed her of everything she was, she had wanted to die. She had seen no use for her existence, no point in her life. Then she had become consumed with the idea of regaining her cowl and the belief the man who took it away could give it back to her. He could not, and again she had grieved and she blamed that grief on her defeat at Harn. It had clouded her judgement. She should have killed him there and then, not waited, not kept alive a faint of hope returning to what she had been. Pining for what had been was weak, she knew that now.

She had become something else.

Something new.

With that realisation had come another. She may have been long-lived as Rai, but she had never really been alive. With the loss of her cowl had come emotions – grief, hope, the deep-seated need for revenge and she had experienced them all so intensely that she had interpreted them as pain. But they were not pain, they were something to be savoured. A pure and sparkling precious gem, each emotion a different facet of it. Oh, they could be scarifying, overwhelming; when Cahan Du-Nahere had raised the forest where Harn had been she had never felt anything like it. Something in her that was old and powerful, taking control of her. Forcing her to run over heaving land, shaking and shuddering in a way entirely unlike the usual tremors of Crua. Every step expecting to die, to feel the hard, piercing, branches erupt into her. Spearing her from below, thrusting her up to hang above the land. The life coming up was violent and vengeful. It was not random, it was targeted, the plants and trees waiting for someone to pass over them before they exploded from the soil, thrusting screaming bodies into the air.

She saw a man split apart by a tree. Saw a woman dragged down, entangled in viciously thorned briars that whipped and clawed at her as she begged for help.

But they did not touch her.

As Sorha had run, she had become more and more sure the forest did not see her. Amid the noise, the pain and the stink of ruptured bodies, she slowed to a walk. Strolling through death and destruction and all that touched her was dirt flying through the air as it was forced out from below.

That defeat she could not be blamed for, it sat firmly at the feet of Rai Galderin, though no doubt those feet were now high in the air and rotting. She could have stopped all the death at Harn. She understood Cahan Du-Nahere, you did not fight him as Rai. He knew how to fight Rai, how to use their own arrogance against them. But none would listen to her, the pariah. They banished her to the rear of the column to stand with the Hetton. Not even the High Leoric of Harnspire, Kirven, had bothered to ask her opinion.

Their arrogance had cost them all their lives.

Afterwards, she had found a few Rai and a small force who had been scouts, far away enough to escape the fury of the forest. She hid from them, sat and waited and watched. One of them looked like they were reaching out, feeling for life, for lost soldiers but they did not feel her. That was when things first began to make a little sense. When she first escaped Harn she had thought it odd that Cahan's Reborn did not bring her down with spears. Thought it even stranger when the forest did not attack her. But as the Rai before her counted off their assets and found a very few soldiers and Hetton to bring in, what she had been suspecting for a while became a truth, a reality. She found herself smiling.

"You cannot see me," she said to herself.

She had continued with her plan. It was not such a different one to the plan the Rai she was following had. Trail the survivors of Harn, find out where they went and report back to Harnspire on where they were. But Sorha had an advantage those Rai did not, she was invisible. She had no doubt Cahan and his Reborn would come for the Rai, but they would not know she was there. So the Rai followed the villagers, and Sorha followed the Rai and she listened to them and allowed herself to feel in a way she knew they never would. They were motivated only by one thing, self-preservation. She was motivated by something far more powerful.

Hate.

Of all the emotions she felt this was the easiest of them, the simplest and least confusing: the purest. She hated Cahan Du-Nahere, hated him for what he had done to her, for taking her cowl and for defeating her at Harn. She would end him.

She hated the Rai too, and especially the Rai she followed. They talked about her, about their plans to blame their loss here on "the Pariah". How they would enjoy her death when it came, if she was not dead already. More than once she was tempted to slip into their camp and cut a few throats. Once she would have; as Rai she would have burnt them alive. Not now. She could not do it of course, the power was gone from her. It forced her to think longer term. They thought only of surviving the now, how events here would impact on their power. She thought of surviving the now as well, but she thought of far more than that. Because she knew she had value, a walking, living and able to fight duller.

What a weapon she was for someone. The High Leoric of Harn had seen it – unfortunate that she died, though Sorha had never liked the woman, and who cared for a High Leoric of some forgotten county when there were far more powerful people in Crua: the generals of the Cowl-Rai, or the Skua-Rai of Tiltspire, or even the Cowl-Rai themselves. She would become invaluable.

Then, like a poorly trained garaur, she would turn on those that fed her and take their place.

So she followed, and she watched, and she hated.

When Du-Nahere and his Reborn came, she watched them destroy the small force. She did not feel pleasure in their deaths, not exactly – at some point screams of pain had started to bother her, and the strange fire Du-Nahere used set her on edge. But it was good to know she was right, that he would come back and deal with those who pursued him. Good to know she knew how he thought.

Once the Rai and their soldiers were dead he and his Reborn left, sure that they had eliminated the threat to them and their people. Wrong, of course. They had not, she was the real threat, the thorn that would cut and bleed him dry. When she finally had him at her mercy she would glory in his death, bathe in her hate. She would not kill him slowly, would not prolong his pain. She would just end him.

She would enjoy that. No chance for him to escape.

Then she would deal with the Rai.

So she followed Cahan Du-Nahere and the people of Harn towards Wyrdwood.

And she hated.

10
Udinny

I have been travelling, or not travelling, for a very long time. Or no time at all.

Being dead continues to be incredibly confusing and, if you can avoid it, I wholeheartedly recommend that you do. It is very dark. Which is tiring, saddening, and weighs upon you like a stone. I had never realised, when I was alive, how much light there is. Even at night there is light, the darkness is never complete – here there is nothing else. I travel through it, unsure of how, constantly hoping I move towards some respite but with every moment I become more certain I will not. It has always been said that I am a person of high spirits, it takes a lot to bring Udinny low, but if this is to be my eternity, if I will never have respite from the darkness and the nothing – well, it is frightening.

I am frightened.

And I am sad.

And I am scared.

I follow a hint of other Udinnys in the hope I will find some answers but that hope has begun to die. I begin to doubt the other Udinnys are any more than a fond invention of my lonely mind. As I move, I dredge my mind for the thought or act that could have condemned me to this nothingness, this strange misery. I cannot find a particular one, but maybe it is not one, maybe it is an accumulation of acts. I have been weighed and found wanting. But then where are the Osere? Where were those who fought against Iftal? The servants and their dark gods? Where were the cursed and furious monsters, ready to rend me limb from limb, to skin me and reskin me to start again for all eternity? Where are the searching tentacles of the monstrous creatures doomed to the underground? I would almost welcome pain, this constant nothingness is its own special torment.

I have never been a fan of torment. I avoid it whenever possible but in death, as in life, sometimes things cannot be avoided.

But also in death, as in life, sometimes the darkest time is just before the dawn.

For so long, or not long, maybe a moment, maybe an aeon, I float in the darkness. At first I thought the light I begin to see a trick of my mind. A hope made manifest as my sanity slowly disintegrated. A single bright point so small it could be nothing, but so alien to this place that it must be something. I changed the direction of my travel, and only then did I become aware of how fast I moved. Faster than any skyraft, gasmaw or even predatory spearmaw. A streak through the night, a burning star falling from above. At this thought terror gripped me. What if I was an arrow? What if that light was Crua and I was hurtling towards it only to burn up in the sky? Maybe Cahan or Venn would look up and see the flare and never know it was me and at that thought my heart broke a little, even though I do not have a heart any more.

I did not try to stop.

Even if this was my end, even if I did burn in the air anything was better than the darkness. Maybe in the last moment before the flash I would see my land once more:

the giant forests, the geysers of Tilt, the villages, largers, the fissures that cracked the land. It would be worth it.

Had I eyes I would close them, but I did not. I had no skin but felt a gentle warmth suffusing me. My travel slowing, not by my wish; all I want is to continue towards the light, feel the heat of it, the realness. I am like a starving person shown food, but no matter how I tried I could get no nearer. The golden light hovering in the distance, a glowing ball of gold that, swelled and shrank only to grow again, shooting out streams of fire that fell back into itself.

I came to a stop, again not of my own volition, denied the glowing ball of warmth and heat. Misery welled up within me, powerful, the pain far purer than it had ever been when I was physical, a cold lance and there was nothing here to mitigate it, no one to hold, no way to find comfort.

"Do not despair, Udinny Mac-Hereward."

The voice, pure warmth, melted the pain away as if I was taken up in the arms of a loving mother. Though not my mother, who was never loving.

"You know my name." Did I speak? Did I say those words? I must have as I received an answer in warmth, like sweet sap freshly tapped from the tree dripping onto my lips.

"I know much of you, Udinny Mac-Hereward. I am the path that turns, always leading back to itself." The ball of heat split, grew, became huge. A central ball surrounded by eight waving tentacles of fire, three thick and bright, five more ethereal, all waving around a bright core. I feel no threat from it, only awe in it. It is so bright I feel I can not look at it, though I have no way to look elsewhere, but I feel no pain. "I am the one that sees all, the watcher on the way, the gentle whisper that nudges you in the right direction. I touch upon all things, in the hope they may be directed. I am the small voice that allows the lost to find themselves."

"Ranya," and I said it only in awe, in love, in peace, in joy. Shocked by how close her words were to the way I described her. Clearly, I had been a very good monk of Ranya.

"One of many names, and one I will answer to for now."

"Do you come to walk me along the Star Path?" The tentacles pulsed and writhed in the darkness, the huge flaming star of Ranya slowly spun in the ether.

"You have been a good listener, Udinny, but your travail is not yet finished. Your path is not yet walked. Great creatures move beneath." I had the oddest sensation that what I heard was not what was said, that I was hearing words but behind them was far more than I could ever hope to understand. "A darkness approaches, the great towers fell and must rise or all is lost. The mistakes of the past haunt the future." A huge sadness, an unstoppable terror. A vision of the world I had grown up in dark and carbonised, as if fire had run wild through it. No life there, even the great cloudtrees fallen, burned and stunted.

"You are a god!" A cry into the darkness. "Surely you can do something to stop this."

"I am a remnant, Udinny Mac-Hereward, even gods can be cursed, and my curse is to see all but be unable to touch, to affect." A sudden pain, an overwhelming noise, the screams of a million past atrocities. "I help those few who hear my whispers act and act again."

"What of other gods? Can they not help?"

"Crua is not as simple as you think, gods are not gods, but not as you imagine. They are greater and they are less." A huge sadness. The whirling circle before me became brighter. "I give a choice, Udinny Mac-Hereward. What you call the Star Path is open, you may walk it if you wish. But if you are brave, Udinny Mac-Hereward, I see another path." A sense, a feeling of pain and loss and hope – not hope that the pain and loss would leave me, but that it could be averted for others.

"What will happen to me, Ranya, if I walk your path?"

"I cannot see the future with any clarity, Udinny Mac-Hereward. All possibilities exist together. Sometimes what is seen along the route is beautiful, and sometimes it is awful. One cannot exist without the other. All I know is, that without you, Crua's fate is darker than with. The walkers may walk again and again. We are nearer and further away than we have ever been."

For a moment I did not know what to do. The future scared me. What I had been through with Cahan Du-Nahere in Harn had been terrifying. The fights, the killing. I did not want more of it. I heard the sounds of past atrocities echoing through the darkness. I heard the crying of Udinny's past. The star of Ranya shivered. My choice was made then, how could I make any other?

"Show me the path."

"Brave Udinny," said the voice of my god, "you have never failed me." Something ran through me, a thrill, and a strange familiarity. "Behold my kingdom."

The darkness receded, and the light, the glorious, glorious golden light, engulfed me.

11

Cahan

He led them towards Wyrdwood. Venn felt the way out for them, steering the group in a way that had them twining through Harnwood, avoiding its more dangerous denizens. There were still wounds taken, from thorns, or wildlife. A wandering spearmaw, the vicious carnivorous cousin to the gasmaw, attacked one of the children, wounding the boy's leg before it was driven off. One of the villagers got an infected littercrawler bite, and had to be placed on travois and dragged through Harnwood, hard going as the undergrowth was thick and the paths few.

He watched Venn as they knelt, feeling the way.

"It is safe to go straight on," they said. Cahan nodded, motioning for the rest of the villagers to pass. Furin was at the front with Ont. When all the villagers had passed Cahan followed, he wanted to be at the back. There he felt a little solitude, unlike when he was at the front, where he could feel the eyes of the village upon him, their expectation.

"Cahan," said Venn, and the forester tried to slow so he did not catch up to the trion. "We must talk, Cahan."

"I am busy walking." Dead leaves rustled as Venn slowed, forcing the forester to catch up.

"We can walk and talk, Cahan, I am not so out of shape that it is a struggle."

"Maybe I am," he said. Venn paid no attention.

"It has been sixteen days since you went into the Harnwood to fight the Hetton and the Rai." The trion was studying him and Cahan did not like it.

"Not long enough for you to forget about it, I see."

"You hide something, Cahan," said Venn quietly, "something weighs on you."

"There is a lot of pressure on me, true, but I have strong shoulders." Cahan walked more quickly.

"A moment ago you said you may be so out of shape you could not walk and talk." Despite himself Cahan smiled, caught in a snare of his own words. "Sometimes, Cahan, a secret must be let free, or it will fester."

"That sounds like the sort of thing Udinny would have said."

"She did." Cahan almost tripped, his feet betrayed him as a trapvine found them. His mouth filled with that awful taste of death, sickness and loss.

"I have no secret." Even as he said it he felt something move within, like the black mud at the bottom of a pond, thick with leaf mulch and filth.

"Cahan," said Venn and put a hand on the forester's arm, slowing him. "Something is within you, I can feel it." Cahan wanted to shrug the trion off, push them away but instead he took a deep breath.

"I took energy from a rotting log. From the dissolution of life."

"I did not know that could be done." The trion was not looking at him, eyes on the trail. The roiling and waves of darkness inside him rose up, a burning in his stomach, acid in his mouth.

"It was a mistake, Venn, I know that now."

"So you will not do it again?" they asked. Cahan shook his head.

"I will find another way if the Rai come for us." Though he did not know how, and somewhere, in the back of his mind he was already wondering if it had really been that bad. Unpleasant, yes. But unbearable? Maybe not. Sacrifices had to be made, he had a village to protect.

"When they come," said the trion.

"If they come," said Cahan.

"Given that I am the youth," said Venn, "is it not my job to be the naive one."

"If we bury ourselves in Wyrdwood they will never find us."

"Really?"

"It is vast beyond understanding, Venn." He smiled at the trion, trying to reassure. "You will know when you see it."

"Have you thought . . ." began Venn, the words tailing off.

"Finish what you have to say," said Cahan. Above them something called out, a soft trill, and branches shook as a flock of tiny gasmaws darted from a branch heavy with moss. Each one a tiny version of the more familiar larger ones, eight tentacles at the front – six for grasping, two for poison – large eyes, behind them a streamlined gasbag that kept the creature floating and vents that propelled it through the air.

"The Forestals." Venn glanced over at Cahan. "They share power, give it as a gift almost."

"They told you this?" said Cahan.

"I felt it, I think." Silence, apart from the song of gasmaws and flyers, the hiss and crackle of people making their way through dense brush.

"The cowl," said Cahan after thinking on it, "it is hungry, all the time." Was this true? He had barely heard the voice of his cowl recently. In the time since he had touched death it had quietened and faded, leaving a gap, and when he thought of it he filled with nausea.

"Maybe I could . . ." The trion's voice faded.

"If someone shared with me, Venn, I would take and I am not sure I could stop." Worse, he thought they may feel something of the darkness settling in his stomach, soaking through him like liquid from a wetvine into dry ground. Venn nodded to themselves.

"Then you should continue training the villagers with weapons," said Venn. "In case they have to protect themselves. Maybe they will not need your power."

"I am just a forester, Venn. Furin is their leader and it is her decision."

"She is the leader of a village that no longer exists," said Venn. "And she will lead the new village when it is built. But you must get us there. They need to be bound together again, to have something more than fear to keep them going." Cahan sighed, decided that maybe he had liked Venn better when they were being a sullen child unwilling to help.

"I will think on it, if you give me some space to do so." Venn nodded, squeezed his arm and ran on to join the villagers, finding Issofur, the Leoric's son, where he was playing with Segur, who in some ways he thought the child resembled, and some other children. Cahan wished he could slough off the world as easily as Venn seemed to. Within moments the trion was running in and out of the thick undergrowth, engrossed in the imaginary world of the children as they chased "horned people" through the bushes. Cahan suppressed a shudder; horned people brought back images of the Boughry, and how Udinny had died for them.

He took a deep breath, trying not to lose his head in a cloud of troubled thoughts.

Cahan considered the villagers, what they had been through and what they may yet encounter. They thought him some forest savant, but the truth was he knew little enough of it, and especially of Wyrdwood where they headed. His visits there had been seldom. Now the villagers of Harn expected him to help them live there.

He had also noticed, during the long days of their walk, how more of the villagers were gathering around those who wished to return to Crua – a foolish thought. Venn was right, he had to find something to distract them, to focus them.

At the end of the early eight they came across a clearing in the Harnwood and Cahan bade them stop, rest and eat a little. While they did he walked among them, most were so tired they could barely speak. He found Ont, sitting alone chewing on some berries and staring out into the forest.

"I am glad I am not blind to this place any longer. It is beautiful in its own way, the Harnwood," said the butcher, "if deadly."

"Yes, it is both of those things," said Cahan.

"Well, we must trust to Ranya to lead us through it." He smiled, a shy delicate thing. Strange to see on such a big man. "And you of course, Forester." He tried to sound sure but Cahan knew he was looking for some reassurance. "Have we quietened those who would leave us?"

"We did, but I must do more and for that I need your help." He stared at the man, then added, "if you are willing." Ont looked surprised, and Cahan considered how he must still appear to these people, that they were surprised at a little politeness from him.

"Of course I am willing, just tell me what needs to be done."

"I need some rope, thick rope. And vines, preferably ones that have been allowed to dry a little."

"Anyone would give you these things, C . . ." He caught himself before he said "Cowl-Rai" . . . "Cahan."

"Yes, but they would feel they had to give me their best, Ont." He looked away. "I do not want that, I want only what they do not need."

"I understand," said Ont, pushing himself up.

"And send Sark to me, the hunter." Ont nodded and

walked away, stopping off where Sark was squatting and eating berries with a few others. They were not speaking, all too tired. Ont then went to another group as Sark came over to Cahan.

"You wanted me," said the man. He did not seem scared, not exactly, but he was not comfortable either.

"You know the forest, better than most of them."

"Aye," he nodded, "me, Retya, and Garha, we all hunted in Woodedge, but you've put the fear of the Osere into 'em, forester."

"Why?" said Cahan.

"They all think the forest is just waiting, to avenge itself on 'em like, for hunting." Cahan took a deep breath. He had been so eager to impress the dangers of the forest on them that he had gone too far. Made them fear everything.

"Nothing that happened in Woodedge will affect them here, tell them not to worry." Sark nodded. "And hunting is why I wished to speak to you. Maybe I have been overly cautious."

"What do you mean?" He cocked his head, his white make-up flaking, the clanpaint smudged. He had stopped shaving and had a scrappy beard.

"I worried people may kill thoughtlessly, but death is also part of life." Or was that what he had touched talking? No, he could not second guess himself. This was a thing he had always known. "We can hunt, but we must not be foolish about it."

"I try not to be."

"Of course," Cahan nodded. "I think we are safe to take male raniri."

"I always try for the weak or the old ones," said Sark, "and never the females."

"Good."

"I'll ask Retya to hunt with me, it's easier with more than one."

"And the third, Garha, you said?"

"Garha is frightened if a leaf falls since the battle," Sark shrugged. "I doubt I can convince him to hunt."

"What about if he showed the children how to check trapvines for histi caught within them? They could do it while we walk. Make it a game."

"Aye," Sark licked his lips, "he can do that. Meat will cheer people up a little, but they'll not want it raw."

"Small and careful remains the rule for fires, but they should be able to make them large enough to cook on." He looked up into the canopy. "And we are no longer followed. Smoke is not a worry."

"Are you sure?"

"You think we are?" Wise to listen to hunters, of all the villagers they were most attuned to the trees. Sark shrugged.

"On occasion, I have thought I saw something." He looked out into the trees. "But truthfully, could be rootlings, they get everywhere." He shrugged. "And this place makes me nervous, I will not lie."

"Well," said Cahan, and he scanned the wood, looking deep into the gloom between the trees, "keep watching."

"If I go now, maybe we will have meat by the evening."

"Yes. Thank you, Sark." The man started to walk away. "And Sark," he called after him. The hunter turned.

"Aye?"

"What you did for that rootling, the forest will not forget."

"I hope not," he smiled, "though there are a few here who still think we should have eaten it." With that he returned to his small group and started explaining what they were about. A moment later Ont returned with his arms full.

"It is mostly scraps of rope, Cahan," he said as he dropped them. "No great lengths, so if you wish to climb we have some work to do re-braiding it."

"It is not for climbing." He took a piece of rope, rolling it in his fingers. "Let me show you what I wish us to do."

He gave Ont back the small piece, then found some rope he judged long enough and coiled it until it was a large flat plate about as far across as his forearm. Then he used vines and thorns he had picked from a bush to secure the rope he had coiled, ignoring the inquisitive eyes that watched him until he was sure his construction would not fall apart. He lifted it up.

"There," he said, "what do you think?" Ont looked blankly at him.

"It is very nice?" he said slowly.

"Do you think you could make one? Well, a few?"

"Yes," said Ont, "I imagine so. It did not appear too hard."

"Good," said Cahan, as he lay it down. "You look a little confused, Ont."

"Aye," he said with a look of such puzzlement it almost caused Cahan to burst out laughing. "What is it?"

"Ah, I am fool," Cahan grinned. "I forget how little you know of bows. It is a target. We pin it to a tree, or lay it at the base of one. Then we loose arrows at it."

"Of course," said Ont, picking it up, "like the wooden ones we used in Harn."

"Exactly, but much lighter. They can be made from woven reeds as well." The butcher studied the target, and gradually his smile faded.

"Are we not done with bows and war, Cahan? Is that not why we run to Wyrdwood?"

"Bows are useful for many things," said Cahan, "I have spoken to Gart about hunting. He uses a spear now, but a bow will be easier when he is comfortable with it." He picked up his bowstaff. "And we hope not to fight again, Ont, it is my greatest desire. But better to be prepared than not, and the more we practise, the better prepared we are. Remember how much you ached when we first started."

"Aye," said Ont, "your name was black in the air, Cahan Du-Nahere, and I have never seen so many people cursing their own muscles."

"Well," said Cahan with a smile, "the best way to avoid that is to keep practising." He stood a little closer. "And it brings the people together, Ont. To do a thing, as a village."

"Of course," he bowed his head, "the Leoric will be pleased."

"She will be even more pleased soon, Ont."

"Why?" said the man as he leaned over to pick up another rope.

"Because I intend to teach your village how to safely make bigger fires, even in Wyrdwood."

12
Saradis

Saradis, Skua-Rai of Tarl-an-Gig and, outwardly, second most powerful person in the whole of Crua, knelt before the first. The Cowl-Rai had her back to Saradis, and was staring out of the window, the shutters pulled back to let a warm breeze blow into her room. This private throne room was behind the long hall, and from it the whole of Tilt could be seen, framed by two of the outer spires, which were in turn framed by the twisted wood of the Cowl-Rai's cage. The room was spare, a warrior's room, not a ruler's. A few chairs, a desk, armour on a rack, a bed that was more a campaign cot than something for comfort. The Cowl-Rai cared little for softness, she was barely aware of her surroundings most of the time. Once she would have gloried in expensive clothes and furniture, things she had been denied all her life and took an almost childish joy in.

That person was gone. Nahac, sister of Cahan Du-Nahere, had been a great warrior, a brilliant tactician, still was in many ways when she focused. Her ambition was driven by a rage at being overlooked for a brother she thought of as weak. She had faked her death, raised her own armies and even convinced Rai she was a person of power, such was her focus. Both ambition and focus were becoming rarer and rarer. Saradis was to blame for both her rise and her current position. She had seen the resentment Nahac felt for her little brother. It would have gone, eventually, and she would have stood at his side as his protector. Saradis had not wanted that, she wanted the Cowl-Rai to herself and fanned the flame of Nahac's resentment. Her plan to one day use her as a weapon if her brother could not be controlled.

She had fanned that flame too hard and the girl had turned on her. Used what she learned at the monastery to become something more.

"Do you remember, Saradis, what I was like before the god touched me?" These flashes, as if she could read Saradis's mind frightened her sometimes, but not as much as the rages which became more frequent, more uncontrollable. "I was a warrior without equal, Skua-Rai."

"You still are, Cowl-Rai," said Saradis.

"The geysers will leap soon," she said, "as high into the air as a cloudtree, then the water will fall as rain all over Crua, or flow in the rivers to the farthest edges of the land. It is unstoppable, the water. It cannot be held back, it gets everywhere. I am the water."

"You are, Cowl-Rai. None will stop you. They cannot, you bring the god Tarl-an-Gig to the world."

A silence then, a long one. Saradis remained kneeling, the cage of twigs around her clothing digging into her flesh. The Cowl-Rai remained staring out of the window.

"The trion. Where are they?"

"In the north."

"Were they lost at Harn?"

"I do not know, Cowl-Rai."

"We must have the trion."

"I have told you, the new ways—" Nahac turned, moved so quickly. One moment at the rear, then at the front at the bars, hands on the wood, facing Saradis.

"We must have the trion." Her words an urgent hiss, the blue stones set into her skin shone. "The people expect a trion so I can Tilt the world, bring warmth to the North. The Cowl-Rai needs a trion." An answer on the edge of Saradis' tongue, wishing to leave her mouth even though it would create a rage that lasted days: *But you are not Cowl-Rai*.

"You," she said, took a breath, steadied herself. Even caged, Nahac could still frighten her. Saradis did not know the extent of what the stones had done to her. Laha had been the first touched by them, but in him it had not engendered the same madness – or power. "You bring new ways, Cowl-Rai. Make new rules." The Cowl-Rai's gaze like a knife, cold against her skin.

"I want this. I am Cowl-Rai. We will do this properly. Tilt the world. Save the north. Do the things my brother was too weak for." Saradis took another deep breath. Told herself it did not matter what this woman thought, not in the end. Humour her for as long as was needed. The fire would consume Nahac as it would consume them all. Pressure built in the room, the stones above Nahac's eyes glowed. Lines of blue shimmered over her skin.

"Of course," said Saradis. "The trion will be found. We are sending a great force north to take hold of the Treefall. If the trion Venn cannot be found, then another will be provided." The Cowl-Rai stood back, brushing down her simple clothes, the pressure in the air bleeding away.

"Good," said Nahac, and in her voice was a lightness rarely heard. "Good." She turned, walked back to stare out of the window. "I want you to address the Rai for me; I will not be going North myself, I need to prepare for the journey southward to take the final counties. They have gods there that must be quietened."

"There is only one god, Cowl-Rai," said Saradis, a soft reminder of what they had agreed. The woman nodded.

"Of course, only one god." She said it offhandedly, as if

it was unimportant. "One god with many voices. I hear them." That was new, Saradis did not like it.

"And what do these voices say, Cowl-Rai?" Saradis did not know if the woman genuinely heard something, or was slowly sinking into a madness she would never return from. Not that Saradis did not hear voices. She heard Zorir-Who-Walks-In-Fire, had done since she was a child. But it was not a voice in the way the Cowl-Rai meant, not a direct communication, more like a feeling, a slow seep of knowledge. Or, when she touched the blue taffistones, an overwhelming surety, a hunger.

"They say Ancient Anjiin is rising." Saradis let out a breath – a child's story nothing more. "And that they long for freedom, Saradis. But it makes no sense, how could a god be imprisoned?" She found she was holding her breath. That did sound like Zorir. Nahac turned and there was confusion on her face as she walked up, put her hands on the bars. Examining them. Something ran through Saradis, part fear, part jealousy. Could it be Zorir the woman heard? Was Zorir demanding to be acknowledged, rather than hide behind the fiction of Tarl-an-Gig? "How can I hear gods, Saradis, when I invented Tarl-an-Gig as a child?" Saradis blinked.

"Maybe they were not invented, Cowl-Rai, maybe you heard their whisper even then."

"I wish they were still whispers," she said. Nahac wore no make-up, her face scarred from fighting, burnt from the backwash of cowlfire. Her eyes pale, not as pale as old Rai, but too pale to mark her as one of the people now, and across her forehead the chips of taffistone, blue taffistone that the Cowl-Rai herself had demanded be put there. She ran a hand down the bar. Then with the same hand touched the stones in her skin. "Can you take them out?" A real, sudden and intense desperation. "I want to be who I was before. I care nothing for all this." She waved a hand at the room, and the world beyond the window, voice wavering at the edge of tears. "If my brother rises in the north . . ." her eyes were wild, searching for something. Her voice moving from desperate to lost. "Can he not be your Cowl-Rai? You chose him first. I can be what I was meant to be, his protector. What if all this," she waved a hand behind her, towards the window, Tilt and Crua outside it, "is a mistake. What if I am a mistake?"

"I chose incorrectly in Cahan," said Saradis, though she was not sure, not any more.

"I was meant to protect him," a real desperation there, "I betrayed my brother."

"No," said Saradis, "you are strong and he is weak, you are what is needed." Nahac's eyes became unfocused.

"Sometimes I feel, like I no longer exist." Her voice, barely there.

"You are the bringer of great change, an avatar of great power."

"Take it from me," she said, touching the jagged stones in her skull with shaking fingers. "Take them away."

"I cannot, you know that. Without them you have no power. All would know you are not what we say you are."

"I do not care. They followed me when I did not have them." Grabbing the bars hard. Her hesitancy and worry vanishing. A fierceness returning. "Take them out."

"I cannot." The Cowl-Rai silent then, her chest rising and falling with each breath as she fought some battle Saradis could not see. The pressure building again, and Saradis was ready for the magic to erupt, black and wet, raging against the bars in her room. It did not happen, instead Nahac walked to her armour stand, put on the helmet and lowered the visor.

"Go about your work," she said, "I want to be alone."

Saradis gave a brief bow of her head and left. Outside the doors to the Cowl-Rai's chambers Laha, her second, waited. Like the Cowl-Rai he also had blue stones in his skin. Small, barely noticeable to most.

"The Rai and the commanders of the great army await you in the main hall, Skua-Rai," he said.

"Good."

"And how was our ruler?" Was there sarcasm in his voice? He was a hard man to read.

"We keep up the pretence, Laha, and never forget that. One slip and all we do is for naught." Laha bowed his head acknowledging her. "And she was –" a pause, before she decided on the truth "– not good. Erratic, more than usual."

"The spires can play tricks on the minds of all," he said as they walked.

"It is not that, it is the stones. What is useful for us also works against us."

"They do not affect me." He touched his face with his hand, the stones almost hidden by a layer of make-up.

"You are different." He nodded, and they walked on until he spoke again.

"Will you go south with the army?" For a moment she wondered if he planned something, then wanted to laugh at herself. No doubt he did, but not against her. Never against her. He was as loyal to Zorir and the great fire as she was. The only one she could really trust.

"No, the Rai will go alone. I will stay here and watch our Cowl-Rai." She stopped. Listening. The spires were excellent places for people to listen in as they had odd acoustic properties, the dark shiny materials bouncing sound around. Did she hear something? Maybe. She carried on walking, talking more quietly. "And I must know what happened at Harn. The Cowl-Rai is insistent on the trion for the tipping of Crua, fixated on it."

"We have had no luck making another, they all die."

"Well, that does not mean we can stop, Laha, have them keep trying." He nodded and made a mark on his wooden tablet. "But we must know everything that happened in the north, what Cahan Du-Nahere is doing."

"I have news from the south."

"Good news?"

"That is dependent on how you interpret it."

"Explain."

"Our spies confirm what we have long believed. The Cowl-Rai of the Red, chosen of Chyi and ruler of the south, is dead and has been for years." Laha glanced at her. "That is why they have never taken the field; our Cowl-Rai will not be needed to fight them." Saradis walked on, thinking about what he had said.

"Good and bad," she said. "Mostly good, I think. I have standing orders to execute all Rai and soldiers of the Red who try and defect. They will still not surrender easily when they know they will end up a head on a pole."

They were at the door that led into the great hall and now she must brief her army. Laha could listen, that would provide any answers he sought.

The great hall always took Saradis's breath away. The old ones in the time of Iftal created the spires, and after the one god, Iftal, broke themselves and destroyed the city of Anjiin to help the people and their gods banish the Osere, the people took these places for their own. When she was younger Saradis had wondered why the gods did not stay in Crua. She heard many stories, that once their purpose was finished they moved on. Or they had taken the Star Path, gone on to their own paradise where they built a new Anjiin, a new city of gods, where they watched and helped when they could. Some said that they were ashamed because both the gods and the Osere were born of Iftal and that made them kin, and no matter how right the cause it weighs on a soul to war against your own.

She did not believe any of it; she thought that the gods of Crua waxed and waned like the light at dawn and dusk. That they fed upon the belief of the people and there was their strength. What else explained it? The thousands of gods that had once been throughout Crua? In every grove of the forest another shrine, a hundred monasteries with monks all planning to raise their own Cowl-Rai? Constant warring and fighting. The strength of the people fed the cowls, so why would it not do the same for gods?

Only Zorir was different. Zorir asked for no followers, Zorir wanted the fire and to start all again and Saradis would bring their vision to fruition. This world was finished, she had seen that from a young age. Seen it in the decay of the spires and the tremors that cracked the land. The way they barely grew enough crops to feed the people. The cycle of violence and tilting of the world. It must be made anew so people could live in peace.

That was what Zorir promised. A cleansing fire that would send the unworthy to the Osere who had opposed Iftal, the rest along the Star Path where she, Saradis, Skua-Rai of Zorir, would reign as queen under the glory of Zorir-Who-Walks-in-Fire in a new Anjiin.

It would be a good world, no hunger, no death and no pain. It would be worth the sacrifice. A pity most would not understand, or make the journey.

The great hall was thick with hanging flags of the many gathered Rai, all streaked with the blue of Tarl-an-Gig and the north. Maybe a hundred Rai waited, foremost among them were the generals Dashan Ir-Vota and Istil Maf-Ren. Though they were meant to be allies the two Rai were always scheming against each other. They wore their dress armour, gorgeous, blue-black heartwood. Dashan's helm sculpted like a crownhead, great curling horns around the side of his face to protect and strengthen the armour: though this armour had never seen battle and was never meant to. The same with Istil's armour, ancient and made for followers of some forest god, plain on first glance but when you looked more closely you saw the willwood, the way the vines and flowers carved on it moved, writhed slowly across its surface. Flowers and leaves opened in response to the Light Above. Behind stood the Rai that served them; behind those Rai, their trunk commanders, and behind them a few select branch leaders who had been brought to witness what was said here.

Saradis took her place in front of a huge statue of Tarl-an-Gig, the balancing figure, woven of tree branches, hands clasped in front of its chest, one leg raised so the foot was against the knee, the leg sticking out to make a triangle. Behind the figure, the eight-rayed star of Broken Iftal.

"Rai and soldiers of the Rai! Loyal followers of the blue!" At her words the low hum of conversation in the room quietened. Her words were loud without effort, another clever trick of those who had built this place. "We have gathered a great army, ready to finish our assault on the lands to the south." A cheer at this, banging of hands against shields. "You are ready to take Mydal, and Jinneng, to banish the foul rule of Chyi from our land!" Another roar, only Dashan and Istil did not join. They watched her the way a predator watches prey but she did not fear them. They hungered for power and saw her as a way to it. "Well, warriors of Tarl-an-Gig, the one true god, the one who will restore the warmth . . ." She breathed, let the expectation mount. "I bring you great tidings. But as with all great news, there is a price. So do not be disappointed with what I have to say, for what follows it is greater than you will believe." Confusion in the crowd before her, as if a cold wind had blown through the great hall, carrying away their enthusiasm into the great vaulted roof where carvings whirled and twisted in ways uncomfortable to look upon. Their enthusiasm would return, and even if it did not then it did not really matter. Their purpose was not to agree with her, it was to do as she commanded.

"And what is this news, Skua-Rai?" said Istil. A glance exchanged between her and Dashan.

"It is that you, Istil, will march south to enact the Cowl-Rai's plans, but you will only take half our army to Seerspire." She felt the confusion deepen, a hum of conversation filled the hall.

"Skua-Rai, that will not be enough soldiers to lay siege to Mydalspire and take Jinnspire. Both are well defended, and Jinnspire is the strongest city outside of Tiltspire." Dashan spoke this time, his words condescending, talking to her as if she were a child in spite of him knowing exactly why it must be this way as they had discussed it many times.

"You are right, Rai Dashan, of course. But it will be enough to hold Seerstem county and push further into Mydal, that is all we require for now."

"What is so important," said Istil, "that you will lengthen the war against the followers of Chyi, that you will allow their corruption to fester in the south?" A general sound of agreement, an ugly undercurrent in the hall. From the corner of her eye she could see Laha at the door that led further into the spire.

"Tarl-an-Gig has blessed us, but we must move quickly to take advantage of this blessing." Quiet again, a palpable curiosity, all eyes focused on her. "We moved against the rebel village of Harn, you will have heard of it, you will have seen the corpses of the traitors that once lived there on the walls of Tilt." Silence, waiting. "Well, not all of Harn died and those people, those few who are left, fled to Wyrdwood like cowards. But by fleeing they showed us what had made them act so foolishly as to stand against the Cowl-Rai." She had them now, every eye on her, rapt, focused. "Greed, that is what possessed them. Common greed." She could almost hear it, could feel the question on the lips of them all – *greed for what?* Well she would tell them. She would glory in their excitement and she would use it. "Treefall!" A gasp of shock. "The great hand of Tarl-an-Gig has reached out and pushed over one of the giants of the forest. Proved their strength over the trees of the old gods!" A hiss, a chatter, men and women turning to one another to whisper of this great fortune. "Riches will flow to Tiltspire, to all of us." She held up her hands.

"Now quiet! Listen to me, listen!" Saradis waited until silence fell. "It is imperative we seize this great bounty, make it safe and begin the process of hewing this great treasure." She let her words sink in. "Dashan Ir-Vota will take half our forces to claim the tree." She looked around, let the beat of her heart count out a space and then smiled, raised her voice. "They will bring us plenty!" A roar, a huge shout of approval and she turned, walked off the stage and left the Rai to make arrangements on how to split their forces. Laha watched her return, his eyes bright.

"The tree, Skua-Rai, is not going anywhere. But it is a convenient way to slow down our advance south." He blinked. "Tarl-an-Gig smiles on you." She laughed. "Is that the only reason they go North, Skua-Rai?"

"No," she said. "I want you to go with them." He licked his lips, he missed the killing and she knew it. "Cahan Du-Nahere is still in the north."

"The weakling lives?"

"Yes," she said, "and I would have you change that."

13
Cahan

The days continued, seamless and sameful.

Their trek through the darkness of the Harnwood began to feel repetitious. He constantly thought that they should see Wyrdwood, but they did not. Tricks of the Harnwood slowed them or altered their direction of travel. There was nothing to do but accept it and keep walking.

They existed in a sameness and routine.

The same trees, the same shrubs, the same low-lying mist that came in with the light and went out with it. The same bow practice in morning and evening. The same spear drill at the end of the early eight. In the darkness they sat on cold ground and ate berries and histi around small fires. To break the monotony he had them fashion shields to replace those lost and damaged in the fight, making them from the leaves of tasint plants, which were wide and dark and could be worked like hide. New shields would make the villagers feel safer, though without half a season to treat them properly the safety was an illusion, they would stop no decent spear thrust. Still, the routine improved morale and at least the weather was warming.

"Once more," his words ringing through the clearing. A

groan from some of the villagers. One of the old soldiers, Aislinn, laughed.

"This is nothing, the forester is soft, try training under a real commander." She whirled her spear and then went into a crouch. "You would do this all day and half the night."

"Spears up!" They stood in a ragged line; a real soldier would laugh at them but Cahan felt a certain pride. Ragged, maybe that was true, but these people had defended their village against the might of the Rai. He had served in sell-spear groups that would have had them whipped for their lack of discipline, but he had served in none that had fought as hard as these people – or won so great a victory.

"They are doing better." He turned to find Furin. She stood very close to him.

"Yes," he replied.

"You could tell them that."

"Why?"

"If you had not lived in the forest with only Segur and a flock of crownheads for company you would know." She stepped even closer. He felt her presence as a warmth he was unused to. "It would lift them. Make them try harder." He pulled his hand down his beard. Then turned back to the villagers.

"Spears up!" Their spears came up. He glanced at Furin, she widened her eyes at him, nodded. "Well done," he said. A couple of spear-tips dipped in surprise at his words.

"They are feeling better, you know," she said softly, "some have even formed groups of lovers. Maybe you should find one." The Leoric smiled to herself at his expression and walked away.

"Lunge!" he shouted, filling his discomfort with noise and action. A messy forward lunge with their spears. He grinned at them, it felt strained and forced but he saw return smiles among the villagers. "Again, well done. Now, weapons away, pack to leave."

He watched them pack. Some still bearing wounds from

Harn, some bearing the marks of the forest's thorns. All tired, wilted like plants after the energy of flowering had passed. He felt the same, but unlike them he had a new temptation. Decay was everywhere and he was starting to feel an itch in his mind, not his cowl, not a voice, a longing. Fortunately the further they went into Harnwood the rarer bluevein became, and he needed it to find the power in death. As the villagers packed away their weapons and gear he went to a tree, to reach out and try and touch the clean power running through it. All he felt was bark. The energy of the tree was not there for him.

"Cahan?" He turned to find Venn.

"Is this tree dead?" It was a stupid question, he knew it was not.

"No, Cahan, why?"

"Nothing." He took his hand from the trunk. "I am tired is all." He waited a moment, expecting the voice of the cowl, the familiar *you need me*. But it did not come, and he felt a sense of panic bubbling up within. What had he done? He had always thought he would be pleased if he no longer had the cowl. That was not what he felt, not at all. Nearer to terror, to panic. It was part of him, always had been and he was only just coming to terms with that and now it was gone?

He felt a sudden deep and real pity for the Rai, Sorha. A sense of guilt for what he had done to her. An understanding, if not a will to forgive.

"Are you all right, Cahan?" said Venn.

"Yes." The word came out part cough, part clearing of his throat. "Go help Furin pack. I am fine." The trion looked him up and down, blinked, then nodded in a way that the forester knew meant he had not heard the last of this. He went to pack his own gear to find the two Reborn watching him, still as statues. How long they had been there he did not know. He was struck with an odd feeling that they may have been there for a long time, or they may have appeared that moment. The two grey women, statue-still amid the greenery. They did not come to him, only waited. One face uncovered, one swathed in scarves.

"You want me," he said. Nahac nodded.

"Something is coming," she said.

"What? More Rai?" She shook her head.

"The forest."

"What do you mean?"

"I know only that it is coming."

"When?"

A pause. Nahac turned, looked over her shoulder.

"Now," she said. "It is coming now."

He swallowed, his mouth dry. Then heard it, rustling far out in the brush, a crackling of branch and twig as if some massive beast ran towards them.

"To arms!" His voice as loud as he could make it. "To arms!" He grabbed spear and shield, no time for bows. Villagers dropped whatever they were doing and grabbed weapons, ran to join him. Those who could not fight pulled the travois into an arc that the line of spears could back on to.

"I will take the centre," he said. "Reborn, flank me!" Nahac shook her head. "You came to me to fight, Reborn."

"Not against the forest," she said.

"Then what use are you?" He turned from her and she stepped away, melting into the brush. A moment of despair, true and painful. If the Reborn would not fight then he was all the hope these people had. Even he could not stand against the forest.

He could not feel this place, to know what was coming. Touching death had robbed him of his connection to life. He wished he could find bluevein in the ground, a need for it gnawing inside him, a deep and dark desire. But for the best reasons. Power lay in the soil.

"Cahan?" It was Venn. "Cahan, what is wrong?" They were staring at him, confusion on their face. Behind them the villagers had formed into a line, facing the forest.

"Get behind the line, Venn." He pushed the trion towards the line and they ran. Cahan followed. Barely made the line before the forest erupted. "Raise spears!" The moment the words had left his mouth he knew it was useless. The forest was boiling, leaves and branches shaking as a solid line of howling screeching yipping and yapping rootlings smashed through the brush before them. "Brace!" he shouted, lifting his spear and ducking behind his shield. "Brace and get ready to hold them!"

Twenty paces from the line the rootlings stopped as if held by an invisible wall. Howling and growling against it, clawed arms reaching, sharp-toothed mouths snapping. The smell of them, part garaur, part forest loam, filled the air. Something within Cahan wanted them to come on. He wanted to stab with his spear, feel the bite of a weapon. Bring death. He needed it. The days of walking, the fear he had lost his cowl a ball of fire within him. He wanted to loose it in blood and fury.

The rootlings did not attack.

"Hold," he said, "hold!"

"Why do they not attack?" This from beside him, Furin; he barely recognised the Leoric, hidden beneath a hat made of leaves. With her was Sark, the hunter. The mass of rootlings split, creating corridors within the hoard of growling forest creatures.

Down the corridors came the true soldiers of the wood, the swarden.

"Spears up! Hold! Hold!" He could smell fear in the air. Spears were wavering. Someone cried out in fear.

The swarden advanced, creaking with every step, the grass that wrapped the human skeletons stretching and snapping. Some swarden held old weapons, some held sticks. They did not hurry and they did not slow. They advanced. Relentless. Cahan dropped his spear, took up one of his axes. Held it high.

"Lunge!" he shouted, throwing himself forward, cutting

the head from the nearest swarden. Hacking into the ribs of another. Spears coming forward, some pierced the grass muscles of the swarden. The creatures trapped the weapons within them, held them so others could get past. The swarden pushed forward. Villagers falling back around him. More and more swarden streaming from the mass of rootlings.

They were not attacking. Not using their weapons even when the villagers did.

All of this was wrong, strange. The swarden overwhelmed them in moments. Bone hands wrapping around arms. Those who ran found the swarden surrounded them, hemmed them in, but still they did not attack. They only came in greater and greater numbers until every villager was held still by figures of bone and grass. Only Cahan remained untouched, a circle of swarden around him who lowered their spears. Cahan turned on the spot, waiting for them to come at him but they did not attack.

"Come then!" He screamed it, holding his axes out to his sides. Within a darkness writhed, a coldness. The swarden he had beheaded bent over, picked up its skull and replaced its head, grass swirling around the neck to bind it where vertebrae had been severed. The air was silent, no rootling chittered or growled, the swarden never spoke and the villagers were too afraid to.

If Cahan could have brought fire, have it swirling round his axes, that would bring the swarden the true death. But he could not.

Hs cowl was silent. The only life here to feed it on was the villagers, and he would not do that. Could not do that.

"Cahan! Stop, Cahan!" Venn, he recognised the voice but could not find the trion. "They do not want to hurt us." Then he saw them – the swarden had them, they were dragging Venn to the edge of the circle growing around him. A swarden put a rusted blade to Venn's throat. Another pointed at Cahan.

"It does not look like that to me, Venn." The fire, if only he had the fire. He could burn these creatures to ash. In desperation he reached out, he could feel death, the power of it in the ground, the slow rot, but no bluevein here. No way to access it.

"Can't you hear them, Cahan?" shouted Venn. "They do not want you or me, or us. Stand down." Despite the blade at their throat, Venn looked calm.

"Hear what, Venn?" All he heard was the rush of the wind through the trees, the creak of grass as it moved over old bone.

"The swarden, Cahan. Can you not hear them?"

"No."

"Lay down your arms, Cahan," Venn said softly.

He did not want to. He wanted the fire. He wanted to consume these swarden, they would burn like twigs.

"Cahan." He felt the swarden about him moving. As if they knew his thoughts. "Cahan," said Venn again. "Look."

From the mass of furious rootlings came something else. The air changed, the sky took on the pink of dawn, the air white, opaque and mist-cold, everything hazy and unreal as if clouds had reached down to surround them. A figure from the haze, thin and brittle as twigs, tall as two people, cold like the iciest days of Harsh. Animal skull head topped with reaching branches. It did not walk but floated, its robes twisting around it as if caught in the currents of an unseen river.

One of the Boughry, the Woodhewn Nobles of the forest. The air so still and clear every movement chimed.

He felt the terror of those around him. The Boughry were more feared than any other creature of the forest. Cahan did not share their terror, he felt anger. They had taken Udinny from him. He wanted to fight it but the Boughry froze him in position as surely as Harsh froze water. His body no longer listened to his mind. The swarden closed around him, taking his weapons, pushing him to his knees, holding him down with a strength beyond nature. All around the people were forced to their knees.

Walking behind the Boughry came a rootling, the one Sark had saved, or one with very similar markings. It hopped forward, cradling one arm and coming right up to the line. It turned its head, left and right, huge eyes studying those held by the swarden.

It pointed at Sark. The Boughry twisted, a sharp motion, a blink-and-you-miss-it refocus of position and attention. The float of its robes swirling about it.

"No!" Sark screamed, both betrayed and terrified, struggling and fighting the heartwood hard grip of the swarden. They did not even notice his efforts as they dragged him forward.

"Take me!" Shouted from further down the line. "Take me!" Cahan turned his head, saw it was Ont, fighting against the grip of the swarden. "I offer myself! Take me rather than him. Take me!" The Boughry floated over to Ont, it studied him. A winter hand of bare twigs reached for him, it felt slow, but moved quickly. Hovering before Ont's face. "Take me, for Ranya." The words breathless with fear. A moment of complete stillness, a crystal pool within a clearing. The Boughry turned, as if checking with the rootling.

The rootling blinked again. Then it hopped backwards, lifted a hand and pointed at Sark. All but the hunter were released and the wall of rootlings and the army of swarden reversed into the forest, not walking, not running, barely moving, it was as if they were sucked back into the greenery along with the Boughry. And Sark went with them, screaming and begging but the forest did not care. He was taken to wherever it was they went, to exact whatever price the forest wanted of him.

No one moved, not for long time. Venn was first to stand, came over to Cahan. Offered him a hand and helped him up. Cahan's knees hurt, he felt like an old man.

"You really could not hear them talking, Cahan?" they said.

"I heard only the wind." He lowered his voice. "This is my fault."

"Why?" That from Furin as she came to join them.

"I told Sark it was safe to hunt but I was wrong. The forest came to take a price for my mistake." He looked to Furin, hoping for some comfort, found none. She was frightened, stunned. All around the villagers were moving to pick up their packs and they moved as if in a dream, slow and languid. He could not help noticing that each and every one of them was refusing to look at him.

14

Udinny

How to explain?

How to describe what Ranya showed me?

To see a thing you have no reference for. To feel a feeling that has no parallel in the life you lived, when you were alive. Presuming I am no longer alive. Which may not be the case but it may also be. It was entirely overwhelming, to be nothing and something and realise how very small you are and how utterly vast everything else is. I did not move to see these things, it was simply as if a new world blossomed around me. The shining eight-pointed star of Ranya willed it, and a new world appeared in light as gold as the finest Yannis blossom at the start of Least.

Coming into being like one of the geysers at Tilt, thrusting up through the darkness from below. Illuminating but not blinding. A gentle and kind light, formless but definite and with purpose. It flowered, up and out and around. It enveloped me in a bright cocoon. I felt it passing through me and for the first time I was sure there was a me for it to pass through. It kept growing. The only way I can explain it is with Wyrdwood – it had the same sense of scale as Wyrdwood, a massiveness that made it feel unreal.

Once that thought had occurred to me, and as the light grew around me; folding out and out and out, I began to understand why I thought of Wyrdwood. Vast pillars of light, reaching up from a golden floor and some new sense told me that below that floor vast pillars of light reached down. If up and down had meaning here, which I was quite sure they did not. There was only here and there. Past the pillars were smaller pillars, and then smaller, and after that a limitless golden horizon. I knew what I saw, Wyrdwood, Harnwood, Woodedge, then the plains of Harn and beyond that the other counties, the copses, the geysers, the far southern Woodedge, and Jinnwood and the southern Wyrdwood. The light slowly faded at the edges to what must be east and west where it met the Slowlands, as misty as a cold dawn. I felt their terrible weight upon me.

"This is Crua," I said. "I see the life of it?"

"Yes, Udinny." The circle of Ranya continued in slow revolutions. The three bright tentacles twitched while the others waved aimlessly.

"Are you the Light Above? Always there, always watching?" The circle brightened, for a moment.

"What you see is not me. It is Crua. It is me. I am in the Light Above. I am the trees. I am all things, Udinny, and I am none of them." These words that were not words were a warmth in my mind. For a moment the web of Ranya overlaid on the light, white on gold, and I saw how thin and fragile it was, how tattered and distorted. "Look closer at your world, Udinny. Understand."

I did, and yet did not. I saw more, I saw detail: how each vast pillar was made up of a million, million golden lines and all of these lines were moving, some up, some down, some linked across as if there was a constant exchange of energy, in among the pillars was movement – animals? Gasmaw and raniri and histi and a hundred thousand other living walking flying things. Connected and yet not. In among them darker areas where the gold was tarnished, the joyful brightness somehow sickly.

"What is that?" Perspective changing without movement. Understanding, shapes coming in to focus, bright plates of gold, in the centre areas that were dark and dead and lifeless, even while the gold and sickly yellow moved within. Familiar, circles and points. "Spires, it is spires? And the bright plates the towns? The strange colour . . ." It came to me. "Cowls? The Rai? They are not right."

"Much is wrong, Udinny Pathfinder."

"Why do you call me that?"

"It is your name, it has always been your name and your reason." Around me those other Udinny's shifted, a hundred thousand versions of me: male, female, trion. A rootling. A Rai. I did not understand. "I have lived so many times?"

"Yes, Udinny Pathfinder."

"But never walked the Star Path."

"You are needed."

"Why?" Silence, only the spinning lights, the slow pulse of Ranya before me. I thought about what I had been shown once more, as it seemed my question was not to be answered. "Crua is sick."

"Sick, broken, it has been so a long time. I am to fix it, yet I cannot."

"And I am part of this?"

The golden lights fluttered, blinked in and out of existence, Ranya included. In the count of a heartbeat while they were out I saw another set of lights. Blue, and a blue thread, twisting through the cities, thick in some places, thin in others. A web, not unlike Ranya's web though not as big. It pierced the land, twisting down deep beneath the surface. Then the light was back, the blue gone.

"What was that?"

"All things have an equal and an opposite, Udinny Pathfinder. So I seek to guide all, there are those who seek only travel for themselves." The light moved, it was as if I ran from it; in the darkness there were a thousand points of light, a million colours centred around Crua. I stood in the darkness. I was as nothing. I saw a golden line draw itself from Crua, dancing among blinding dots of light until it terminated at a shining dot at once familiar and brighter than I had ever seen it.

"The Cowl Star. You show me the Star Path."

"They seek to end it, Udinny Pathfinder."

"Is it not already ended for me?" A flash and once more we were within Crua. Looking down on a place that felt familiar. Dots of golden life moving together, at the head of it a light so bright and pure it was almost white, and I knew, without any doubt whatsoever, as clear if they had taken my hand, what that was. Venn. By them walked another, just as bright but the gold was touched with darkness, a sickness that filled me with foreboding.

"Pillars of Iftal."

"What?" I said.

"So much is forgotten, Iftal must be Reborn. The guide, the conduit and the strength. The forest and the path and one who never was. Without them, the world you know dies so one may live again."

"The Osere?"

"Take my gifts, Udinny Pathfinder." Before me appeared three objects, they coalesced from particles of golden light: a walknut that showed the way, a crownhead, fitted with what looked like a flat seat on its back, and a sewing kit with cord and needle.

"What are these?"

"A way to go, a way to move, and a way to fix." I reached out, and rather than pick them up I took them into myself, felt myself becoming more certain of existing, of being real within this unreal place.

"Has this happened before?"

"Of course."

"And how many times have we been successful?"

"Where there is life, Udinny Pathfinder, there is hope."

With that, Ranya vanished, leaving me alone and confused in a forest of light.

15

Cahan

They walked under a cloud. What morale, what acceptance of the forest had been slowly building up in the villagers had been destroyed when the Boughry took Sark. It was not only that he had been taken, but that in doing so the terrors of the forest, the creatures that Venn had carefully been steering the villagers around, had revealed themselves. Cahan had hoped to introduce the people of Harn to swarden gradually, explain how important it was to stay away from them. He had hoped they would never meet the Boughry, and that Forest Nobles could be forgotten, returned to being myths to scare children.

The forest thought otherwise.

Once again he was viewed with suspicion by the people of Harn. The group around Tirra, those who wished to go back to Crua and lose themselves in other counties, was growing once more. The effort put into bow practice and spear drill became noticeably less and it was a constant battle for him not to lose his temper. A fight to stop the cavalcade of small and annoying or foolish things the villagers did becoming a geyser of anger erupting from his mouth. Today Undir was not even trying to hit the target. Aldan barely put any strength into their spear thrust. He could feel the darkness in him, not a fire any more, something different – something he did not like. Sometimes when he closed his eyes he saw lines of blue against his eyelids.

The offer of power was there again. He did not need to take lives, only find a patch of bluevein. He could walk away from these people safely, leave them to their misery and foolishness. He would be safe, he would be strong.

But he did not, because Furin stood near him and it was as if she sensed his frustration. Sometimes she put a hand on his arm for no reason. Sometimes she stood closer than he expected anyone would and he felt a warmth from her. Sometimes she smiled and it eased what hurt within him a little. Sometimes she trusted him to watch Issofur. She did not speak of what had happened, not on the first day after losing Sark, or the second or third. She simply remained around him, as did Venn; though the trion hovered around like a worried flyer and Cahan wished they would not.

Ont avoided the forester too. Which worried and gnawed at Cahan; the man had been a rabble-rouser and almost turned the village against him once. Had the events with the rootling turned him back to his old ways? Cahan thought it likely, he barely saw the man now. If Cahan was at the front he was at the back. If he was at the back then Ont was at the front and the rare times their paths crossed the butcher-turned-monk would not look him in the eye.

"It was not your fault," said Furin. Cahan had been so lost in his own thoughts, in the forest around him, the flicker of light through branches, the noise of animals crashing through thick underbrush, beneath it the world rotting away and changing into different forms of energy. He struggled now to remember how sick and foul it had made him feel. More and more he remembered the power, and the feeling that somehow it was meant for him. "I said it was not your fault, Cahan." She walked with him, looking up at him.

"Then whose was it?"

"Sometimes a thing is no one's fault, it simply is."

"I told Sark it was safe to hunt, have fires and to raid the trapvines." He glanced at her. "We are lucky they did not take a child." She looked away, then back to him.

"Did you tell Sark what you did knowing the forest would turn on us for it?" Her make-up was not as thick as usual, and Cahan wondered if she was running out.

"No." The word came grudgingly.

"Have you had a fire yourself, Cahan Du-Nahere? Have you taken a raniri with that bow of yours?"

"Yes," he said. Why had the forest chosen Sark? It made no sense. There were some here he would have been glad for the Boughry to take.

"Then you acted without malice, put yourself in the same danger as the rest of us and acted in good faith."

"I am not sure the rest of the villagers are as charitable as you." Furin looked at the floor, shook her head.

"They are frightened, Cahan, and since Sark was taken you have barely said a word to them. They are cold and they are hungry, many of them are too scared now to even take the odd berry."

"Well they are fools," he said, surprised by his own vehemence, "the forest will not act against them simply for taking berries."

"Then tell them that, Cahan Du-Nahere."

"And what? Explain that the forest cannot be known? Even by me, who they expect to know it?" She did not reply, only listened and walked. "How will they ever trust again if I tell them I do not know why this thing with Sark happened?"

"Cahan –" his name came out as a sigh "– it is a mistake to think a leader must be infallible. Everyone fails, everyone makes mistakes."

"Then what? If I am not expected to know, what is expected of me?" He was fighting his anger, both with himself and with the way Furin looked at him, some strange expectation that he did not understand.

"All that is expected is that you do your best to do what is best for them." She walked away then, leaving him with his thoughts and a nagging sense of guilt, that he had been unfair to her. When they stopped in the evening he waited until people had quietened, and when they were wrapping themselves in blankets getting ready to sleep, he stood on a rock, looked round the small clearing.

"I do not know," he said, "why what happened to Sark happened." There was no reply but every set of eyes watched him, every set of ears listened. "We did not do anything I have not done before, and that has never brought the forest down on me." He wanted something back from them, some understanding.

"Maybe," came a voice – Aislinn, he thought, "it was something he did before we set off. He has always been the farthest-ranging hunter. I have heard the forest remembers past insults."

"It could be," said Cahan, though he did not think it was. "But I wanted you to know you have done nothing wrong. I think we should carry on as we were. Small fires. Take berries and fruits, the odd animal." He looked around, no reply. Then he added. "I will do the hunting. So if I am wrong, it will be me the forest takes." At this he heard a few affirmative noises, as if this was right, and he tried not to be angry with them for it. Tried to understand they were frightened and hungry and cold. "You may have noticed," he pointed north, "that if you look through the Harnwood, you can see the cloudtrees," he said. "No more than two or three days and we will be in Wyrdwood. We will find a home there." If he expected some clamour, some joyous outpouring he was disappointed. But he had not, so he was not. "I will try and make contact with the Forestals, they know more of the forest than any other and I hope they will help us." In response the odd groan, but mostly the villagers only wrapped themselves tighter. He stepped down from the rock and people lay down to sleep. He found his own blankets, wrapped himself up and as he lay down he felt a light touch on his shoulder and turned. Furin looked down on him.

"That was well said, Cahan," and she smiled.

Behind her, darkness fell, and the forest exploded into its night-time show of light, a million luminous creatures filling the air.

In the morning they continued to trek through the forest. It would not be true to say that spirits were raised by Cahan's speech, but the feeling among the group was not quite as dark as it had been. By the end of the second eight the thick brush, moss and vine had begun to thin and Wyrdwood, huge and quiet, was plain before them. No more than another day's walk. Cahan took a raniri with his bow and they had a fire while they camped, raising the spirits of some though he noticed not all took the meat. Some ate only berries or what they had in their packs and though he wished they did not, as it created a split in the group, he tried to understand their fear. Venn came to sit with him.

"Let me heal you, Cahan." He turned to the trion; they had grown in the time since Harn, changed. Their face was no longer as round as it had been, their eyes more serious and sombre.

"I am not wounded, Venn," he said and slid meat off a bone, dangling it in the air to try and tempt Segur to him, but the garaur hid behind Venn and would not come close.

"Not in body no, but something ails you."

"It is fine, Venn. I am well."

"You are more withdrawn than usual, you have barely spoken to me, or Furin or . . ."

"I have a lot on my mind, that is all. A whole village and a home to find for it."

"It is more than that, Cahan, I think it is to do with what you did, the rotting log and—"

"It is not!" His outburst made them recoil. Silenced the conversation among villagers. He took a deep breath. When he spoke again he did so more quietly. "If I feel I cannot cope I will come to you, Venn. But I am fine." The trion stared at him, then stood.

"If that is what you think," they said and walked away, leaving Cahan alone with his thoughts and a gnawing within that he knew was unnatural but told himself was slowly dying away. To distract himself he concentrated on a flower, a single white bloom of sharp petals. It was beautiful, though small. He knelt, to look more closer and as he came near the leaves begin to wilt and curl up, the white of the petals became brown and the flower died as he watched. At first he did not understand. Not until he looked down and saw the grass around him, brown and wilting. Nausea and fear and an icy coldness flooded through him. It was him, he was doing it, leeching from the world around him, killing what was near. He stood. Backed away, looking around hoping no one was near enough to see. Thankfully none were. He found a fallen tree branch and dragged it over the scar on the ground where he had been sitting. Never had he so wished to hear the voice of his cowl – at least that was a thing he knew. Whatever sat within him now frightened him in ways he could not put into words.

The Reborn had warned him; maybe they knew something of this. He tried to find them but as was often the way when he wanted them, they were nowhere to be seen. Scouting, maybe, or simply avoiding the villagers who they made uncomfortable.

Someone else he did not find among the villagers was Ont. He expected he was rabble-rousing again with a group of conspirators, had been sure the man had turned against him once more but he counted the heads of the villagers and none were missing. None except Ont.

Curious, he began to walk around the outskirts of the small camp. Once, twice, each time he widened his search and still did not find the butcher. Not until the third circle. Ont sat on a tree stump, his head in his hands, his position one of utter dejection. Cahan did not understand. He walked over, close but not too close.

"Ont?" he said. The man turned quickly, as if caught doing something he should not be. Tracks ran through the white make-up of his face. "What is the matter, Ont? Why do you weep?"

"I . . ." His words died away, he looked at the floor.

"Ont?"

"I am not good enough."

"What?"

"I thought I could be the monk of Ranya for the village, like Udinny." He looked up, eyes limpid with yet-to-be-shed tears. "You told me how Udinny offered themselves to the Boughry, and they took her. I tried to do the same and was rejected. I am fool to think I could ever be a monk."

Cahan stood, words whirling in his mind while he searched for a way to make the man feel better – was surprised that he wanted the man to feel better.

"Udinny came with me unasked, followed me when I did not wish it. Offered herself instead of me against my instruction. Gave her life for me, for the people of Harn." Ont nodded, not looking at Cahan. "And all the while, she always said that Ranya put her feet on the path, but she must choose to walk it. Every decision she made, she told me was a branch on the path. When it did not go her way, it was the path. When it did, it was the path." He laughed. "Her talk of Ranya almost drove me mad, Ont." He paused again. "But I think if she was here, she would tell you that you have only just started your journey along the path, and maybe it would be a pity to leave it so quickly." Ont's brow furrowed.

"You mean, the Boughry did not take me because something else is planned for me?"

"Or that something was planned for Sark." Cahan crouched so he was at Ont's eye level. It was good to forget his own fears and think of his old friend. He missed her. "Udinny would say, you will never know if you give up. She never gave up, on herself or me." He stood. Put out a hand, "Now, will you walk with me? Furin wants me to lead your people to Wyrdwood and Iftal knows I could do with the help." Ont looked up at him, nodded. Took his hand and Cahan pulled him up.

"I will do my best."

"Good, first thing is to get the villagers packed. I hope to make Wyrdwood by last light."

They did not, in the end, make Wyrdwood by the fall of light. Camping out once more in the bright darkness of the Harnwood, he sat with Venn, Furin and the two Reborn, Segur curled at Venn's feet eyeing Cahan warily. He made sure he sat on a rock, not touching the ground at all.

"Wyrdwood tomorrow, Cahan," said Venn.

"Aye," said Furin, "and then we will need to start some hard thinking on what comes next."

Cahan barely slept that night. He did not know what to do, he did not know how to make a home in Wyrdwood or how to keep these people safe.

Something dark lived in him, he was not sure he could keep anyone safe.

In the morning they woke to a thick mist. Only the walknut let them know they went in the right direction and after some hours – how long Cahan did not know as the Light Above was entirely obscured – he felt a change in the air around him. Smelled it too, something strong and animal. The same smell that had filled the forest before the rootlings had appeared. He made sure he was the one at the head of their column, walking towards whatever waited – he was sure something did, some new obstacle for the forest to put before him. He found Ont by his side.

"We walk the path, forester," he said.

"Yes." From the other side, Furin smiled at him. Then the smile fell away. "Look!"

In the mist ahead were figures – not the growling wall of rootlings as before, only two. One tall, one small. They came forward as if they had nothing to fear. A mismatched pair. And not two rootlings, as Cahan had first thought. A man, with a rootling trotting along beside him. It was Ont who was the first to recognise the man and he called out in great joy.

"Sark!"

"Aye!" said the hunter, jogging towards them with a smile upon his face. "I thought myself dead when they came for me, but it was not so. My friend here." He pointed at the rootling and it chuckled and whistled back at him. "I think it wanted to thank me for saving it in the Harnwood. It had something to show me."

"What?" said Furin.

"A home," he said. "It is not far from here, they have found a place for us to make our home." He glanced at the ground, smiled shyly, then grinned, a big beaming smile. "I hope it was not too presumptuous, but I have called it New Harnwood."

16

Cahan

New Harnwood, at the start, was little more than a clearing with a few muddy huts in it. Though huts was maybe too strong a word to use. The buildings had been made by rootlings, and they were built on a rootling scale and with a rootling's idea of what a house should be. As forest creatures they were used to living outside; ideas like roofs and walls were alien to them, and the huts were of little use if what you wanted from them was shelter. Nonetheless, the buildings had been treated with a sense of wonder by the villagers as Sark walked them through New Harnwood.

Sark too had changed. His skin was lightly furred with a silvery down that caught the dim light filtering in from above, and when he moved his long hair out of his face there was a subtle point to his ear. It reminded Cahan of the way Udinny had changed after meeting the Boughry. When the rootling accompanying Sark spoke in its burbling, gentle language, the hunter understood it. He was not the only one who noticed, the boy, Issofur was constantly following the hunter. Ont too – though the look of pain upon his face could not be missed. It hurt the man that the forest had passed him over for another. Then he pushed out his shoulders, and stood taller, as if centring himself and fixing his mind and coming to terms with what was. Ont reached out to touch the branches that made up the hut nearest to him.

"These look freshly cut," he said. The rootling chittered something.

"There is a small copse of a few thousand trees of many ages to the north of here," said Sark.

"And we can cut them?" said Ont.

"Yes," said Sark, and as if sensing something in the other man he added, "and your great strength will be needed to move them, even with all the floatvine growing in Wyrdwood." Ont nodded, smiled.

"I will gladly help," said Ont.

"We must take these down," said Furin, pointing at a hut, "and start again. They are built a little small for us. Tell your friend," she pointed at the rootling by Sark, uncertainty on her face, "that I do not mean any insult."

"They do not mind, firstmother," said Issofur.

"They do not," said the hunter – he sounded a little vague, as if he were half asleep. "They do not think like us." What he said was true, and as the makeshift village was taken down more rootlings appeared, first at the edges of the forest and then slowly coming a little closer. The villagers were nervous at first, but as the work went on they accepted the rootlings. Even finding them amusing, with their constant curiosity and mischief. Some of the braver ones they gave names to.

Good days followed, good weeks and good months. The seasons changed and the people of New Harnwood grew a proper village. The nearby copse was more akin to a large wood, grown in the ghost of some ancient fallen cloudtree The people, at first awed by the strangeness of Wyrdwood, the massive size of the cloudtrees, the strange creatures the like of which they had never seen, slowly became used to this new place. They hunted sparely, did their best to use every part of the trees they took down. Firepits were made and charcoal burners set up. A large wetvine was found and diverted to make tanning pits which were situated far from the village, downwind so as not to fill New Harnwood with their stink. Wild crownheads were penned, soon to become tame when they realised they would be fed regularly. Fields were marked out, ploughed and planted and the villagers were pleased to find no sign of bluevein here, none at all.

Though Cahan already knew that.

In the square a shrine to Ranya was built. Ont questioned Cahan about the god, and he told Ont what he knew, how he had made his own shrine as simple as he could, not knowing what Ranya looked like. For a time the shrine was only a large rock and a wicker Star of Iftal, though that did not last. Soon it was a cleared area with a raised stage where Ont stood and talked to the villagers each morning. Encouraging them to look out for signs and find their own way. That he did not ask for any form of sacrifice seemed to confuse them, so he started to ask what they could give back to the forest. Small offerings of food were made, and Ont took them out into the wood. Soon after this started Cahan began to see signs of shyun, the forest children, mostly their structures of sticks and stones. He warned Ont and the villagers not to be frightened of them, but to remain wary and had Ont place their food offerings in the structures. Though the forest children themselves were rarely seen, Venn said they watched and regarded the village with curiosity rather than animosity.

After they had been there long enough for moss to begin growing on the roofs of the buildings, Ont finally told Cahan he had found what he believed was a good place for their shrine and that he needed some help.

Intrigued, the forester followed. He had become more and more desperate for distraction the quieter their lives had become. It seemed without something for him to concentrate on, the gnawing within – the constant knowledge that all around him in the decay of the leaf litter and once-living things there was power that he was denied – only grew. He had to be careful only to sit on rocks, never on the ground and he knew Venn had noticed. The trion had many questions but Cahan either headed them off or avoided them. The same with Furin, and he knew that hurt her. He had felt himself growing nearer to her and, though he had little experience of people, he felt it was mutual. She needed someone too, her son was slowly becoming distant, more and more comfortable among the rootlings or in the forest than with people. Cahan's sleep was haunted by thoughts of her dying, of her lying down beside him and him waking to a corpse, sucked dry. Not by his cowl, but by the darkness within, the quiet hunger that had silenced it.

Ont's request to go into the forest was a welcome one. They walked away from the village and towards the copse of trees they had been gifted, or Woodedge, as the villagers now called it. Cahan offered Ont some of the dried meat from his pack.

"No thank you, Cahan," he said, "I have stopped eating flesh."

"Odd choice from a man that was once a butcher," said the forester as he chewed on tough meat.

"Yes, but I noticed that, though Sark hunts for us, he never eats meat. Not any more." He paused, looking about himself in the wood, along the many meandering paths made by the forest creatures that lived there, until he found the one he recognised. "He only eats what he can forage – berries, roots and mushrooms mostly."

"You think it will make you closer to the forest?" Ont shrugged.

"I think it cannot hurt." He paused, looking around. "West here, I think."

"What are we looking for, Ont?"

"A shade tree," he said.

"We can barely move for shade trees."

"Not like this one," he said, and led them forward. Cahan could not deny he was intrigued. The land began to rise, gently at first, then more steeply. At the top there was what looked like a natural wall, or a very old fortification. It was made of huge smooth stones with many years' worth of earth and growth forming gently sloping banks against them. Ont led Cahan around them until they found a way in, an arch made by placing one stone atop another. Leaning against it was one of the strange statues found throughout Wyrdwood, the Forest Men. This one held a spear and its other arm ended in a round hand with vicious-looking hooks for fingers. It looked liked it could get up and walk at any moment, and would have been frightening if it was not covered in moss and vines and had clearly been there for many lifetimes. "That scares most of the villagers. I think it is why they have not come in here before."

"I always wonder who made them," said Cahan.

"Maybe those who fought the Osere, or the Osere themselves," said Ont. "Come, look inside."

Within was Ont's shade tree. Some oddity in its make-up had meant the branches did not grow straight as they did on most shade trees, instead they looped and twirled around themselves, growing into a huge tangle. Despite this it looked healthy; though it was not much taller than the butcher himself it was clearly very old.

"Your tree," said Cahan.

"Yes, see, it is like Ranya's paths." He looked like a child waiting for a parent to tell them they had done well. "It looks like something you already know, but it is not. It goes in many directions but still reaches the light. It is different to what we know but not wrong." He looked frustrated, like he would like to smash something with his huge hands and he let out an exasperated breath of air. "Gah, I do not have the words, I am not good at this."

"No," said Cahan. "I am sorry you think that. I did not speak because you made me think. They are good words, Ont. It is a good tree."

"At first I thought to dig it up, bring to the village."

"We probably could but—"

"No, Cahan, no." He walked to the tree and knelt down, carefully moving aside the curling branches so Cahan could see what was there. A stone, almost as tall as the butcher and twice as wide. "It is a taffistone, a real one, not like the fake one we had in Harn. I think the villagers should come here. I think we should call it Ranya's Grove, and bring them here."

"A good idea, Ont," said Cahan.

"I intend to live here, I will build a hut outside the grove. Care for it."

"The people will miss—"

"I will still go to the village. But I need to get closer to Ranya." He clasped his hands, wringing them in front of him. "What do you think?"

"I think it is a good idea. But do not become too fond of being alone. It can be hard habit to break."

"I know," said Ont, "I have seen how you still push away those that become close."

"Yes," said Cahan, and he had to fight to keep his temper in check. Not that he was angry with Ont, he was angry with himself. "I should get back."

"I will stay awhile," said Ont. "Make a start on my hut. Would you bring the villagers here in the morning?"

"Will you be safe alone here, Ont?" The monk nodded.

"Yes, and I am not really alone. I have been coming into the forest for a while now. Getting to know it. I feel like I have friends here." As Cahan walked away he noticed a few shyun stick shrines around the grove. Some with food on them, some without. He glimpsed one of the forest children, only for a moment, as it vanished into the thick undergrowth. The childlike figure, the long black eyes like stripes on either side of its smooth head, and one on top. He heard its voice, the sound of wind through leaves. He wondered if these were Ont's friends.

In the village all were busy and he hurried to tell Furin of the grove in the wood and what Ont had found. When he had news he always sought her out first; he was happy to be in her company but if she moved to touch him he moved away, the cold ghost of bad dreams wafting across his skin. It could not be long before she asked him about it, and as he explained about Ont's tree and the taffistone he wondered if today would be the day, but she did not get the chance. A shout went up from one of the lookouts on the squat wooden towers built to support the walls they were yet to finish.

"Intruders!" came the shout. "Intruders coming!" Cahan felt himself wilt. A war inside him: he was glad something was happening, a distraction from the gnawing within, though a gentler part of him had been enjoying the peace.

17

Sorha

She had, and no one could be more surprised than her, started to like the forest. This place had a viciousness she understood. It was always killing: fungus parasitised plants, slowly dragging them down, spearmaws hunted gasmaws, packs of garaur hunted raniri, and littercrawlers – of all sizes – hunted smaller versions of themselves. They were the most like the people, they preyed on their own. It pleased her.

Everything here hated.

She hated more. She hated better.

The people of Harn had been making their new village. At first only a pathetic bunch of huts made by rootlings. Little more than branches leant against each other. The huts slowly became roundhouses and then the whole village pitched in to build a longhouse. They planned the place, where to plant crops, have tanning pits, a meeting square and a market. She had done so much to bring these people low, paid such a high price and here they were carrying on as if it had never happened. As if she was simply a bump in their lives they had stepped over. Even their spear and bow drill was no longer quite as laughable, their lines tighter, their target shooting better.

She hated each and every one of them. Spent her time daydreaming of killing, of taking one into the forest. Leaving their corpse for the rest to find, mutilated. She dreamed of standing, bathed in golden light, and watching Cahan and the trion die.

One morning she woke to find a rootling staring at her, huge solemn eyes considering her, and she had to shoo the creature away hoping that it did not alert the villagers to her presence. The strange relationship between the rootlings and the villagers upset her. It did not fit with her idea of the forest as an engine of violence. She told herself the rootlings were unnatural, and tried not to think past that.

But she made no attempt to kill them.

She stayed longer than she needed to and did not know why. Watching, identifying each member of the village, committing them to memory and telling herself it was important because she intended each and every single one of them to pay. She told herself she could not trust them, that she stayed because they had proved themselves tricky in the past. What if this entire village was simply a ruse? What if they, somehow, despite her invisibility to the cowled among them, knew she was there? It was a feeling she couldn't shake and so she stayed far longer than she needed to, watching, seething. Every time she saw some small act of gentleness between them it made her itch inside. All that made her feel better was to watch the way the forester failed to connect with the woman, Furin. How his actions confused and hurt her. She hoped that would cause dissent, come back to haunt them when they most needed it.

When Least began to wane, and the trees and bushes she used for cover began to shed their leaves, she knew she had to leave and put the final part of her plan into action. To stay any longer would be too risky. She left knowing her information was valuable, her abilities too – to the right person. Finding them was the trick. Being among the Rai was not that different to the forest, make a mistake and you were dead.

She walked towards Harnwood, through the vast spaces of Wyrdwood, millions of dry cloudtree pins crunching beneath her feet. Strange and uncomfortable-looking fungal towers twisted upwards, and she used them as distance markers on her path because they grew so regularly. She had no doubt she travelled in the right direction, and yet she did not know why. It felt as though there was a way she should go and she did. Twisting round great walls of thorns, around the vast trunks of cloudtrees. Even she could not deny the magnificence of this place, the only rival to it she had ever seen was in the central spire of Tiltspire.

She stopped by a large meadow of pale mushrooms, a break in the trees letting in the Light Above to glint off their pale caps and show the paths that ran through them left by countless small animals. The mushrooms smelled of dead things; everything in Wyrdwood was strongly scented, sometimes pleasantly and often not. Tiny flying things buzzed over the meadow and the grey discs of the mushroom tops teetered on slender white stalks. They came up to her waist and disintegrated the moment she touched them, becoming a fine yellow mist that hung in the air around her. She forged a path through the mushrooms marked by clouds of the powder, as if an artist painted a line of pale yellow across the grey field. These plants were weak, barely existing, their grip on life tenuous. She slapped at one with her hand and it fell apart in a puff of yellow, covering her hand in dust. She raised her hand, looking at the dusting of yellow, brought it nearer her face as to sniff it. Something turned her foot as she did, almost tripping her and she looked down.

Bones.

Bones and matted fur covered the floor. Small bodies littered the earth. The half-rotted skull of a rootling looked up at her from empty eye sockets. She looked again at the paths running through the mushroom field, saw how they ran in, but none ran out. As the paths cut deeper into the mushroom meadow they became more erratic, weaving from side to side and round in aimless, confused circles.

"Osere below," she spat, "poison." And she struggled to focus. Colours became at once brighter and less sharp. The edges of the world closed in. She pulled at the sash she used for a belt, wrapped it round her nose and mouth and began to run, making more yellow dust shoot into the air as she disturbed the fruiting bodies of the mushrooms. Her hands were coated in the dust. Her sash must be as well. Her mind was not working so she did not take it off. Instead she ran on, weaving through the field, finding it hard to see the edge. Legs weakening, bones crunching beneath her feet.

Where was she going?

Sorha aimed at the edge of the mushroom field. Knowing only that out of the billowing clouds of spores was her only chance of safety. There she would find relief and joy. Fighting her way forward, staggering and coughing as her legs gave way beneath her, limbs refusing to move.

Was she out?

Not even her hate could save her from the darkness.

She came to in the night, after strange and torrid dreams of branch-headed creatures, standing over her. She had felt utter fear in front of them. It had been as if they stripped her down to her component parts, armour gone, clothes gone, skin and flesh and bones removed and considered. She trembled before their power and feared what they would find in among the bloody remnants of who she was. They considered her for what seemed like an aeon – trees bent around them, the world changed colour, day to night and night to day as the eighths flew by. They could crush her without effort. She trembled before them but they did not move against her, only watched, then faded away as she returned to consciousness in the mist of a fresh morning.

Words she did not recognise hanging in the mist around her like an echo. "*Nevawaas*".

When she moved her head ached like she had been beaten. She was desperately thirsty, her mouth as dry as old crownhead leather, and she crawled through leaf litter and clinging ferns and shrubs as she sought out a wetvine. Found one. Cut it and drank. Let bitter water fill her mouth and cleanse her of the poisons of the mushroom field.

Thirst slaked, she washed her hands and soaked her sash to remove the last of the mushroom spores that had laid her low. She turned to the field, followed her tracks through it. They started straight and then meandered, eventually stopping. From where she stood it looked as if she had fallen within the field, not out of it. That made no sense. If she had fallen in the field she would be dead.

Sorha turned away, unwilling to look more closely. Telling herself she did not know how far the fungal spores drifted and did not want to fall under their spell again. Setting her course southwards, and her mind against the tracks in the mushroom field.

Her way became harder when she entered Harnwood, and rather than continuing southwards as she wished she was forced to turn and head east along the border between the two great forests. After three days' journey she started to hear noise. A rhythmic hammering that she at first thought was some unknown animal, then she began to suspect it was the work of people. It was too consistent for nature and she had, in the long weeks and months following the people of Harn, become used to nature. Come to know it. She moved forward carefully, using thinner paths as she approached the noise. Staying away from where she thought it likely people would be.

The hammering grew, one becoming many until the noise was almost constant, a din ringing through the trees. She heard a cry, a shout, and then the unmistakeable splintering and crashing of a tree coming down followed by a cheer.

Forestals, maybe? How near were they? It was hard to accurately assess distance in the forest, the trees bounced sound around and played tricks with it. She headed carefully towards the sound. The nearer she got the more she began to think it was not Forestals, they crept around like thieves, they did not fill the forest with noise.

This was Rai and their servants.

Later in the day, at the midway of the second eight, she saw a break in the forest before her. Ever careful, she made a slow approach and went up a ridge thick with ferns, clinging on in the crevices of jagged grey rocks.

A logging camp. Hundreds of people milling around, about various tasks she had little interest in. Rootling heads had been stuck on poles around the edges of the camp. Behind them tents, small ragged ones of troops and the grand tents of the Rai. The camp was busy. Soldiers patrolled around it while the loggers worked with axes to bring the trees down. They did not cut for wood, she thought. They brought everything before them down, not choosing the best and most valuable trees. So no, not a logging camp. They were building a path through the forest, heading north towards Wyrdwood. The trees were being taken down, stripped of branches, split and placed in the ground to make a wide road that would not be easily overgrown. Roads were rare in Crua, but she had seen such things in Tilt, where the land became muddy because of the geysers. Never in the north. Such paths were expensive and needed maintaining and as it was so easy to make goods float they were not needed.

"Treefall," she said to herself and smiled. The Rai were coming to Wyrdwood. This meant the forester's village doom was even closer than she had thought.

She would like to see that.

She would see that.

A group of guards passed her hiding place and she listened to them talk.

"I don't like it here," said one.

"It is not up to us to like it, think about the bounties instead." They would pass below her hiding place. Maybe she would appear to them, tell them who she was. Have them take her to whoever led this expedition.

"Rootlings are getting wise, hard to catch them now. Osere-cursed thieves."

"I'm not talking about them," said the first guard. "I mean the traitors." Sorha smiled, she could give them the traitors. It would provide her great pleasure. She began to stand.

"I still can't believe our own Rai turned against us." Sorha stopped. Their own? She could not imagine Rai turning against the forces of the north.

"How else could a Woodedge village stand against so many Rai and soldiers?"

"But why turn, Fonire?"

"Treefall," said Fonire, "riches enough even to tempt a High Leoric, never mind some fallen Rai without their cowl." Sorha felt ill at the words, sickened within. They meant her. She must have been blamed for the loss of Harn.

She could not approach the forest camp now. As if to seal it the soldier kept on talking. "When they catch her, that'll be an execution to watch. Osere themselves will tremble at her death. And the rest of the village going to the Osere with her. Be a right party." Sorha remained in hiding, waiting while the soldiers moved on. One of her hands was shaking; involuntarily she grabbed her sword. Used the familiarity of the grip to stop the tremor.

Harnspire then, she must find the High Leoric's second, the trion who had served Kirven Ban-Rhun. What were they called?

Falnist? If they still ruled they would know the value of her information. Or would they betray her? Maybe she should go all the way to Tiltspire? She turned and, slowly and quietly, made her way from the forest camp.

Her journey was not over yet.

18
Dassit

Dassit Gan-Brinor walked a tightrope. She had walked it for many years and the act of balance never became any easier.

The war was lost, the Red was beaten and everyone knew it, they also knew there was nothing they could do. Surrender was not an option. The last Rai who had tried had been skinned and hauled up on a pole just outside a spearthrow's reach from the border; it took them a long time to die.

Strangely, it had given Gan-Brinor hope. She had the oddest idea squatting in the back of her head, one that felt like a madness and yet she could think of no better way of explaining the way the war was going. She could not give voice to it, the Rai would laugh at her, but it at least let her believe she could walk the tightrope a little longer.

But first she must live through this meeting of the Rai, the warrior lords of Chyi.

They were losing, but could not admit it to themselves. They had brought her back from menial duties because they knew she was skilled. At the same time they looked for someone to blame and she knew, every time they met, at least one of them would try and put that blame on her. Fortunately she had allies, for now at least, in the two oldest and strongest Rai, though she did not doubt that at some point they would also turn against her.

Until then, she walked the tightrope.

Still, she thought as she looked over the table, at least she was not one of them.

Not for Rai to fall into a drunken stupor around a table of soldiers, revelling in good company and forgetfulness of an evening. Not for them to lose themselves in the abandonment of loving arms, husbands and wives all a-tumble in the bed.

They only knew cruelty.

She had come to realise a long time ago that was how worry and fear manifested in them.

"We should look to Gan-Brinor," said one of the older Rai, Dealish, his voice as much a gurgle as speech. He had a scar across his throat, taken when he was young and before the cowl had set in. She knew that his words were really those of Uter sat by him, she was the clever one. Dealish was the hammer coming from the front while Uter slipped round the back to slide a dagger between your ribs. "Gan-Brinor is the reason for all of our turnarounds. She ran like a coward at Seerspire. Gave ground to them without even a battle and drew right back to Mydal. The whole of Seerstem given up to the enemy."

Incorrect of course. Her supposed cowardice had been voiced many times by Dealish. She was almost bored of it, but to get bored of the Rai and their constant probing attacks was to guarantee your death.

It was tiring. She was tired.

"The truth has not changed, Rai Dealish," she said. "Maybe one of your fellows could explain if you are unwilling to hear it from me?" The Rai's mouth hung open, he had not expected her to have allies.

"Trunk commander Gan-Brinor has explained before, Rai

Dealish," said the oldest of them, Das-Inlier, as a halo of glowing flame grew around his head. "She was ordered to retreat. Seerstem is too wide a front to hold. She would have been surrounded and her forces destroyed." Dassit did not actually agree, Hallick-Larger could have been a lynchpin in a new defence, but she knew better than to say anything. "Our forces burned the crops and the villages of Seerstem, left the traitors nothing. You seemed to enjoy that at the time but now you complain."

"I enjoy war, as is right." He did not, thought Gan-Brinor, he enjoyed massacring the defenceless when there was no threat to him. "But to retreat so far with not even a battle, that is the act of a coward, not a Rai. I do not think Gan-Brinor understands that." Silence then. A heavy silence around the table as everyone but Dealish realised what he had said. "What?" said the Rai. "Why are you all so silent?"

"Trunk commander Gan-Brinor only advises," said Das-Inlier and his words were all the more menacing for their softness, "the decisions are mine. Do you call me a coward?" It was a fight for Gan-Brinor to keep the smile from her face at the way Dealish's face contorted upon realising what he had said. Das-Inlier smiled. "But let us not dwell on the past." The look of dismay melted away. "The armies of the Blue hoist the flag of Tarl-an-Gig and march again. A force is coming from Tiltspire, a strong one. The fighting will be fierce and now I know how much you despise cowards, Dealish, you will march in the front lines." Dealish was stricken, but unable to back down, they had walked the tightrope and fallen. Despite that, the Rai had a much thicker rope to walk upon than she did.

"How many?" asked Uter from beside Dealish, more to take attention off her ally than because she needed to know.

"They are overconfident," said Das-Inlier. "Our spies tell me they gathered a great army and then split it in two. Half goes north, half comes to fight us."

"We will make them pay for that foolishness," said Dealish, eager for his insult to be forgotten.

"Why do they go north, why split their forces, it makes no sense?" said Gan-Brinor, though she had her own ideas. This made her suspicions about the Blue's plans even more likely, though she would not share them with anyone here. If she was right they might help keep her balance on the rope, despite what may come.

"We have heard reports of Treefall in the northern Wyrdwood, they seek to secure it."

"A cloudtree is not going anywhere," said Rai Uter.

"No," said Das-Inlier, "but if another Rai managed to fortify it they could make a real problem for their Cowl-Rai."

"The false Cowl-Rai," said Dealish quickly.

"I have heard the false Cowl-Rai is dead," said a Rai from further down the table.

"It is best not to base tactics on rumour," said Uter.

"Securing Treefall makes sense," said Gan-Brinor, aware of the dark looks cast her way by Dealish and Uter. "It is too valuable to take risks with."

"Yes," said Das-Inlier. "Our spies have provided some interesting information. Talk of a fight at a village in Harn county. More than three hundred lost, including the Rai that led them."

"Beaten by villagers? The northern army is weak." Everyone ignored Dealish, they knew the northern army was not.

"There is talk it was Forestals, also talk that some of their own Rai turned on them. A cowl was used," Das-Inlier shrugged, "details are difficult to come by. The villagers fled to the northern Wyrdwood."

"The skyrafters tell of hundreds of traitors hanging from the walls of northern largers and spire cities," said Gan-Brinor.

"Our enemies are riven by strife," said Uter.

"They are riven by something, and it is kept a tight

secret. The move they made three seasons back against a skyraft family was a mistake. The Archeons of the other families no longer allow the north to move soldiers on their rafts. The Hostiene raft they took is small, and they struggled to crew it." Das-Inlier looked around the table. "There are cowards out there who say we are already beaten but we are not. Our enemy acts rashly. We should be ready to take advantage of that."

"Be better if they all came at once," said Dealish, "then the Cowl-Rai could take the field, raise the power of Chyi and crush them all."

"Of course," said Das-Inlier, and Gan-Brinor wondered if Dealish was the only person in the entire land who knew the Cowl-Rai of Chyi was never coming, that the time for them to intervene was long past. "But they will not all come at once, so we will split our forces across Mydal and what we still control of Seerstem. I will take the largest part and garrison Mydalspire. Rai Carnaf will garrison Stem-Larger, both those towns should be easily held. Dealish, you will take a force of five hundred, and rove the lands between Stem-Larger and Mydalspire. You are to skirmish and withdraw, your job is to slow any advance and send skippers to let us know where they are. Rai Uter, you will have a larger force ready to come to Dealish's aid if he meets enemy forces of any great size." Gan-Brinor tried not to show any discomfort at being last, at her assignment coming after the two younger Rai. At where that put her in the command order. "You should go and prepare," said Das-Inlier and watched the three other Rai go, waiting until it was only him and Gan-Brinor.

"What do you want me to do that you could not say in front of them?" she said.

"Talk to me." Das-Inlier picked up his cup and took a sip. "What do you think about my orders?" She took a breath; it would have helped her standing had Das-Inlier asked this before the others left. Of course, that was why he had not. He trusted her counsel but at the same time could not afford to be seen listening too much to one who was not Rai. She understood it, did not like it but there were many things about life in Crua she did not like.

Crua did not care.

"I think it is brave to put Uter and Dealish together." She pushed her own cup from one hand to the other but did not drink. Rai Das-Inlier smiled, a strange thing to see on his face, with the skin dry and stretched tight, eyes pale and inhuman.

"I agree." He put his cup down. The candlelight made it look like his face twitched. "But it is less risky than giving one of them somewhere that can be fortified; they may get ideas. This way their troops will be first to meet the forces of the Blue. With any luck either Dealish or Uter will be killed and their troops will become mine." He waved a hand in the air to encompass the room, them, the whole situation, "But the way things have been going I see little likelihood of luck for us. We have had precious little so far."

"Yes." Gan-Brinor took a breath. "I suppose it was the best choice out of few good ones." Das-Inlier nodded. "What do you want me to do?" Rai Das-Inlier leaned forward, leather creaking as he did. The strange smell of him enveloped her, dry like stone parched by the Light Above.

"Do you know why I like you, Dassit Gan-Brinor?"

"No," she said. "In my experience Rai rarely like those of us who aren't them." He laughed, as dry and arid as the scent that surrounded him.

"True. Very true." He sat back. "But you are not proud. Not like Rai are proud. It makes you pragmatic." He turned the map of the south around so she could see it. The spire cities and the largers. The border with Mydal to the east and Jinneng to the south. "Here," he tapped the map, "this town Fin-Larger. Mydal may well fall this season if they push hard, we cannot hold it so we will withdraw, but you knew that." Gan-Brinor nodded. "This is the first town within the corridor of Seerstem that we control that could conceivably be held. It commands the plain around it and will stop an assault on our eastern flank."

"And you give it to me? A lot of responsibility for one who is not Rai."

"It is." He stared at her, cold eyes locking with hers. "You must hold it, Trunk Commander, I will send two hundred troops with you to fortify the place."

"How many Rai?"

"No Rai." A coldness settled within Gan-Brinor.

"Then what you hand me is a death sentence." His stare continued, looking her up and down.

"You are clever, Gan-Brinor, in a way most Rai are not. Cleverness will hold Fin-Larger better than Rai. If I send a Rai with you they will want to take control." She nodded, but felt like this was another punishment for being good at what she did. "I trust in you, the Skua-Rai of Chyi trusts in you, he is very impressed. You have won battles many others would have lost, we know it is often your voice whispering in the ear of successful Rai. That is why I give you this most important of tasks." She took a drink; all became clear to her now. Das-Inlier was no different to the others. Important people have noticed me, she thought, and now you want me dead. "One other thing," he said, just as she had begun to rise. She stopped, half stood, half sat. Uncomfortable. "Why do you really think they have split their forces? Treefall can wait, traitor Rai or not, we both know that."

Should she tell him the truth? Maybe she would have if he had asked earlier, before assigning her orders sure to get her killed.

"Overconfidence," she said. "They are too sure of themselves." He nodded at her.

"That's what I had decided."

And it is what you are, she thought as she stood fully and left. Feeling like the rope she walked had just become a little thinner.

19
Laha

In another world or another life Laha may have been a gentle soul. A man who devoted himself to a garden or to healing or to the general wellbeing of others. But this was not another world and another life, this was Crua and Crua was not gentle.

Laha was a man who desired certainty, who struggled to understand the world he walked through, who found the thoughts and wishes of others confusing. Certainty provided him comfort and his certainty came from Saradis; in her he felt assured. If he was capable of love then what he felt for her was as near to it as he ever came, and it manifested as a fierce loyalty, an absolute devotion. She knew how the world should be and the route it should take and followed the route like a gasmaw to food. So he followed her.

Did he believe in Zorir? This was not a question he asked. It did not matter to him. He believed in Saradis, in her will, and in the fulfilment of her will he had found purpose, and he strove to be the best he could be for her.

He had barely noticed, on the trip from Tiltspire to Harnspire, following the circle winds on a long journey, the way the skyrafters looked at him. Their barely disguised hatred did not matter to Laha, *they* did not matter to Laha. They were simply bodies carrying out work. He had watched the skyrafters' cook prepare his food to make sure they did not poison it. He had studied the wind dials and the schedules to make sure the archeon was making the best possible time. When he was not doing those things he had stayed in his cabin, practising the martial forms he had been taught as a child in the monastery of Zorir. Dancing with the paired, curved blades he wore strapped across his belly hidden from all. It did not do for a priest to be seen carrying weapons.

Though Laha was no priest.

He knew the words to say, how to go through the act and convince anyone who met him that he worshipped just as hard as any, but it was not true. There was a gap within him where faith should be, there was a gap within him where many things should be. Only Saradis mattered.

It was a mixture of his fierce devotion, his lack of empathy and his single-mindedness that made him so good in his chosen profession. Assassin and killer. Like all good assassins he was clever. He understood tactics and he understood politics in a detached, cold way. He made decisions well and quickly and with absolutely no regard for others.

He was a blade. A blade did not care who it cut.

But Laha did not enjoy confusion and he did not enjoy what he did not understand. In general this was not a problem for him. Saradis walked the grey areas, she made up his mind for him – but here, at Harnspire, it was not as simple. He had met with Falnist, the trion and de facto High Leoric. Listened to their report. How a Rai had stumbled into town with tales of the fall of Harn. Saying she needed to get a message to Tiltspire. Falnist had recognised her as Sorha, a woman who had already failed the previous High Leoric, and immediately had her imprisoned. The trion High Leoric had been too timid to deal with her, frightened about having the blood of Rai on their hands.

So Laha had come down to the dungeon to see the prisoner.

She had recounted what had happened at Harn. The way the Rai's confidence had led them to destruction. Bad decisions had been made, the enemy had been underestimated.

Laha would not have done that.

He knew punishment must be seen to be done. He knew Saradis's preferred method of execution for the Rai who failed her and he enjoyed killing Rai. He enjoyed the moment they touched the bluestone and found they could not let go, the look of confusion, then pain and anger then fear, as the stone changed them.

He did not enjoy the way this woman smiled as he began the punishment.

"You smile," he said, standing five paces from the bars and trying to work out what possible plan this fallen Rai could have that meant she was not frightened, "but your life is forfeit." Maybe her mind had cracked? Falnist said when she appeared she was filthy, armour broken and scratched, telling them she had spent time in Wyrdwood. Few escaped Wyrdwood unscathed.

"Of course it is. Failure cannot be countenanced," she said. "But what if I swear allegiance again? What if I give my whole self to Tarl-an-Gig once more? Can you find it in yourself to show mercy then?" Those words, they were what he wanted to hear, what he wished her to say. He wanted her to walk forward, put her hand on the stone in her cage and be removed from this world as anything but a useful tool. Somewhere, in the back of his mind, he thought she may be mocking him.

"Will you swear on the taffistone, in your cell?" She nodded. He stared at her, another body to fall for Saradis, to bring her god's will into being and bathe Crua in the fire of rebirth. Laha pointed at the stone, the other hand he ran across his head, feeling the rough stubble and wondering when he would get time to shave it. "Swear then, Rai Sorha."

"Any particular words?" He shook his head, watching as she stretched out her hand, placed it on the stone.

"I swear allegiance to Tarl-an-Gig, I give myself to him and the Cowl-Rai in Tiltspire."

He waited. He watched.

Nothing happened.

She began to laugh, her hand never left the stone. Something broken in that laughter that even he recognised, something of a mind that had been stretched too far.

"I have done this before," she said, "the High Leoric demanded my loyalty in exactly the same way. But your stone cannot touch me." She took her hand away, the look she gave him a challenge.

"It seems I will need a spear." He turned away from her and to the silent guards sent from Tiltspire by Saradis. Water ran down the black stone in the back of the room; the guard held out a spear for him.

"You need me."

"I need no one." He took the spear, weighed it. Deciding if he liked the feel of it and no, he did not. He put it down, and turned to where more were leant against the wall. Chose another. Better. Heavier.

"I know where he is." Laha turned, spear in hand. "Cahan Du-Nahere. He raised a forest."

"We will find him ourselves."

"And how long will it take you?" She showed no fear as he altered his grip on the spear. "I know exactly where he is, and the villagers. I can walk you to them." Laha leaned on the spear.

"People," he said, "always they think they can hide but they cannot. They make smoke, they build. They want to trade. They fall out and leave their communities. They go looking for family. I will find them, given time."

"Given time. Do you have time?" Laha took a deep breath. "And what if he comes after you, or the Cowl-Rai at Tiltspire? What if he disrupts the plans you have to take hold of Treefall? What then? You will wish you had let me lead you to him." He stared at the woman, low cunning, like an animal in a trap.

She was an animal in a trap.

But the stone did not affect her. That was interesting.

He stepped closer, using the haft of the spear as crutch, thudding it against the stone of the floor. "Maybe we do need your information. Fortunately, I am adept at getting people to tell me what I want to know."

"Not me," she said.

"Everyone thinks they can hold out." Laha enjoyed thoughts of what he could do to her. The many ways a human body could be broken. "But when the process starts, no one does. They beg for death."

"You need me to fight him."

"I need no one to fight anyone."

"He brought the forest to life, it fought for him. It killed for him."

"And how would you stop that?" said Laha to her.

"For the same reason that stone does not work on me." She pointed at the bluestone. "Cahan Du-Nahere took my cowl from me. Turned me into a walking duller." Laha felt his eyes widen in surprise. Another, he had thought he was the only one. "Confronted by me he is just a man, less than man because like all Rai he relies on his cowl for power. I can best him." Laha stared at her.

"Dullers do not walk. They lie in a pod until they die."

"I am different. If you do not believe me, bring down any of the Rai and see how they recoil. I am a weapon like no other." He tilted his head; she was a weapon that he understood. She would be useful to Saradis. For a moment he felt jealousy, but he swiftly put it aside. He served, that was his essence. Two like him, Saradis would want that. He stepped closer to the bars, inspected her. She was different to him, no stones in her skin, no subtle blue lines.

"How near must you be?" he asked.

'I can dull Rai from across a room, from a spearsthrow away.' She exaggerated, Laha was sure of it but even so she could affect Rai from distance like a true duller, that was interesting. Laha needed to be almost able to touch them. "Cahan Du-Nahere is nothing before me."

"You hate him," he said.

"Yes. I hate him," she replied. Laha nodded to himself and turned, placed the spear against the wall. He understood hate. Saradis always said hate was useful. "His ruination is all that keeps me living." Revenge. Another simple emotion that spoke to him. A need he trusted.

"I must think on you," he said. "I must think long and hard."

"The trion Venn is with him," she said as he stepped back. He blinked.

"As I said, I will think long and hard."

20
Cahan

The intruders came from the forest.

Appearing on the edge of New Harnwood like spirits. One moment their Woodedge was empty, only the dark bushes, the wide flat spaces of Wyrdwood and the shadow of the small forest: then they were there. Forestals, clothing laced with twigs, branches and leaves so they appeared as much part of the landscape as they were people. Hybrids, thought Cahan, neither one nor the other.

The dark place within him twisted and squirmed.

Each Forestal held a forestbow. At the front of their formation their leader, Tall Sera. Behind him was Ania, who had stood with him and the villagers at Harn before the Rai and the forest destroyed it. The villagers gathered around Cahan, holding spears and bows. He felt their trepidation and the anger within him kindled, the fire that burned dark and damp, choking his airways with thick smoke.

"What do they want?" A hand on his arm. Furin's voice as she came to stand with him. He could breathe again. She wore a different make-up on her face, not as white, not as stark. It softened her but did not lessen the strength that ran through her. Venn stood by her, taller and more sure of themselves. They had stopped cropping their hair, as was common of trion, and had a thatch of dark, tight curls. Venn also grew in confidence, the building of the village had brought this to them and unlike in old Harn they had been eager to help. Venn had found a freedom in Wyrdwood. Gone was the child who wished to be left alone, replaced with someone who had a curiosity, who wished nothing more than to learn and would put their hand to anything. Not always successfully, and to Cahan's annoyance they still refused to carry any weapon but a staff, and refused to stop harrying him about the thing within. Behind them Cahan's silent sentinels, the Reborn, spears in hand, faces hidden behind their helms. he touched Furin's hand, only briefly.

"There is only one way to find out." He turned to the figures gathering in the early morning mist of Wyrdwood, among the fading lights of the night creatures.

The Forestals did not approach, they waited and Cahan wondered whether it was because they disliked the village or sensed some boundary where the domain of Wyrdwood, their domain, ended and his began. No, not his, the villagers. He had led them here, taught them to fight and taught them tactics. He had told them of the forest, but more and more this place within Wyrdwood had become theirs. Furin led here, he did not, and that was right, though it gnawed at him and he suspected that was another symptom of the darkness within.

He bit down on that thought. Walked away from the village and towards the Forestals. As he did the air became clearer. The forest had a freshness the places of people lacked. A solitude that he still yearned for.

"Cahan Du-Nahere." Tall Sera stepped forward. "Chosen of the Woodhewn Nobles, settler of Wyrdwood." Was the man mocking him? It was hard to tell when his face was hidden beneath a hood.

"Show your face if you wish to speak with me."

"Is that any way to talk to the ruler of your realm?" Laughter in his voice. A hard edge behind it.

"The forest has no ruler, Tall Sera," said Cahan. The man laughed in reply, pushed the hood from his head. Beneath it his skin was painted with greens and browns, the better to hide him among the trees and bushes.

"True, the forest has no ruler." He nodded and leant on his bow, a slow and relaxed action. "But like all places, it has its fiefdoms and it has its cantons and counties and you know, Cahan Du-Nahere –" he pointed, smiled "– that it requires tribute. You pay it to small things like the shyun, to much larger like the Boughry." He stretched his neck, lifting his chin and sighing as he got out some crick before bringing his gaze back to Cahan. "The forest brought you here, into my realm. We have let you stay, we have let you hunt on our paths and caused you no mischief or grief."

"That is true, and we thank you." He could feel the villagers closing, trying to hear what was said.

"What do you want," said Furin, "some sacrifice of us? We have little enough as it is, our houses are no more than huts. What food we have is barely enough to feed our children." Tall Sera turned to her, gave her a small bow of his head.

"Furin, trunk of your people, strength of them. It is a pleasure to meet you. I have heard only good things about you, and I know your child is beloved of the trees." Did she blanche at that, step back a little? Not for long.

"Then you know I will fight for my people, and my child."

"And so you should." He smiled at her. "But we want no sacrifice, such things are for towns and villages and Rai. We are not of them." But you have cowls, thought Cahan, or at least some of you do. "We have a more . . ." he bit his bottom lip as if searching for a word, "collective, approach to tribute."

"What is it you want?" said Cahan, the words came out a growl.

"You," said Tall Sera. "We want you. And the trion; we wish to take them to our home."

"Why?"

"The trion? Because they have much to learn that only we can teach them."

"You would take me away?" said Venn. Tall Sera nodded. Venn shook their head. "My place is here, these are my people now." The Forestal cocked his head, considering it. Then shrugged.

"I am told it is the will of the forest you learn with us," said Tall Sera and there was a shuffling among the villagers. A subtle change that frightened Cahan as it promised violence, and the villagers were not ready to take on the Forestals. At the same time it warmed him, that they considered Venn one of them. Behind Tall Sera, Ania took an arrow from the quiver at her hip. Tall Sera raised a hand. "We will not force you to come, Trion," said Tall Sera genially. "If it is the will of the forest you will find your way to us anyway." He gave them a nod. "May the Boughry stay off your path until then."

"What of me?" said Cahan.

"You we do need."

"Why?"

"To cause trouble," he said. "The Rai have come for Treefall."

"I do not see why it is my problem." Cahan dug his staff into the ground. "It is what you wanted, in order to rob them."

"What we wanted, yes." A nod of acknowledgement. "The forest wants its price from them, we are to exact it."

"You have plenty of experience of that." Tall Sera nodded.

"That we have. But they bring Rai, and a bow is good from a distance, but sometimes we need to get in close." A smile. "We have no fancy armour like you wear, no special friends." He nodded towards the Reborn.

"But you have cowls," said Cahan.

"Of a sort." He felt Venn behind him. The trion may not want to go with them but their interest was like a buzz in the air, the shared awareness of cowls. Strangely, he felt nothing from the Forestals, though he had seen Ania who stood silently behind Tall Sera work with hers. "We are not as quick, or as strong in close up work as you. Help us."

"I have no wish to—"

"You will share in what we take," said Tall Sera. "I bring you a gift in lieu of whatever that will be. Given in good will." He raised a hand, made a clicking noise and some unseen hand, out in the small wood, acted; a herd of crownheads trotted out and past Cahan into the village.

"I have no wish to become a bandit."

"Ania has made a list. The Reborn and five others who can fight," he said. "We wish them to come also."

"I said, I have no wish to become a bandit. Nor do the people of New Harnwood." Tall Sera sighed.

"But you wish your people to prosper." Cahan almost denied they were his people, old habits, words leaping into his mouth, but the lie died before it reached his lips. So much had changed. Instead Cahan nodded. "If we prosper, Cahan Du-Nahere, then you prosper."

"If we attack them, they will come for us."

"They will come for you anyway." It felt like the breath in Cahan's throat caught, he wanted to cough. To hear that truth so plainly expressed was hard. "To put it bluntly, Cahan, we can help your people hide better than you or they can, but you must be prepared to give back. You, they, are all of the forest now."

"Maybe I should come with you," said Venn. "To heal if anyone is hurt." Tall Sera smiled, though he tried to hide it.

"The Forestals have healers, Venn. The village needs you," said Cahan. He did not want to join the Forestals in violence, but at the thought of it his armour creaked as a hundred thousand cilia tightened, as if its wood grew layer after layer. The hilts of his axes emanated a warmth and he wanted to take them in his hands. The darkness inside moved.

"Cahan," said Venn softly, coming to stand by him. "Are you well, you seem—"

"I am fine." He breathed out, feeling the armour loosen. The axes cool. "Fine." He looked around, aware all eyes were focused on him, even those without cowls and he wondered if he had emanated some threat that was so stark all could pick it up. "I only worry about this place." He nodded back towards New Harnwood. "Who will protect it if the Reborn and some of our best fighters follow me?" So he was going then, he had made the decision and not even realised.

"You have trained us well," said Furin; he heard an edge of pain in her words. "We are hardly helpless."

"No, you are not." He tried to find the words, to explain without insulting, sounding like he was dismissing all the hard work the villagers had put in. "But the Rai are . . ."

"We will not leave you helpless," said Tall Sera, "from now on your strength is our strength. A shared power. One tree falls in a storm and it is gone. A few trees fall in the forest and it remains. So we remain." He nodded his head at Furin. "So you will remain." Cahan said nothing, weighing what the leader of the Forestals said. Part of him did not want to go, he wanted to stay here in the shade of the cloudtrees building a village. He wanted to herd the crownheads with Segur and fall back into the cycle of shearing and sloughing that marked the turn of the year. He wanted to help Sengui farm gasmaws, to watch the weavers as they created cloth from tangled fleeces, to help the woodcarver, to hunt and to forage for the people of New Harnwood. Even to witness the stink and strange magic of the tanning which turned hides to leather. He wanted to forget the thing within him and the lives he had taken.

But he understood what Tall Sera said, and life here would be easier for all if they had the Forestals as allies, rather than bystanders; and, deep down inside, he wanted the axes in his hands. He wanted the heat of the fight, the blood, the respite from the turmoil within that action brought.

For a moment he longed for the voice, the knowledge of his cowl and the power it gave him.

But the voice was missing.

The voice that had been with him for so long, that surfaced whenever there was the threat or thought of violence, sometimes a whisper, sometimes a shout. *You need me.*

Not there. The strength was there. The power, the ability, all remained in the back of his mind but changed, not as hot, not burning. Now it was turmoil, not fire. Something slower and darker and it may have freed him from the desire to kill for power, but he suspected it bound him to something worse.

"I will go," he said. "But Venn stays here." Tall Sera cocked his head to one side and a smile breezed across his face.

"Surely that is Venn's choice, not yours."

"I am going with you, Cahan," said Venn. "I will not leave New Harnwood for where the Forestals live, but maybe I can learn something of my cowl on the way." Cahan turned to the trion.

"This will be killing, and death. All that you say you hate and . . ."

"I will heal. And learn."

"What of Furin?" said Cahan, aware he sounded desperate. At the same time he was unsure why. Surely it was good for Venn to get out, to learn more? Their ability to heal was invaluable and, if he was truthful, he was beginning to enjoy being around the trion. Mostly. When Venn was not pushing him on the darkness within.

Was that why Venn wanted to come?

"I survived by myself before, Cahan," said Furin. "I do not need my hand held."

"Very well," he said. "Venn can come. But they stay away from any fighting." Tall Sera gave him that nod again. "And you must ensure their safety."

"We will do all we can," said Tall Sera. "Now my people will rest in the small copse over there. Pack what you need to bring with you. We will be gone a while and I want to leave tomorrow morning."

That night, Cahan could not sleep, he lay in his blankets in the small hut he had built, alert to the world around him. He heard footsteps outside, his door opening but he sensed no threat. Did not move. The weight of a body lay down by him and he recognised who it was by her scent: Furin. She put an arm around him.

"I am cold, Cahan Du-Nahere," she said softly, "warm me," and for a while, he forgot all of his troubles.

21

Udinny

I had, from the moment I first heard the voice of Ranya when I was young and wild, lived with the belief I was chosen by a god. Sometimes I had gloried in it, when my journey had taken me across great vistas. When I watched the geysers at Tilt or saw a river of water fall into a chasm in Seerstem. When I was fed by the kindness of strangers. Other times I had cursed it, when my feet blistered for want of good shoes, when I walked alone along freezing roads, when I begged for shelter and found all doors shut against me.

Yet, to believe yourself a thing is very different to finding out you really are that thing, and not only chosen in this life, but chosen in death and many lives before. Spinning round and round and round through endless lifetimes trying to right some wrong I can neither understand nor remember.

Though moaning about it will not help, I suppose. Even if it does make me feel a little better.

Let me look at the good in my current existence: I have a body, that is a good start, or at least an awareness of a body though it has no true substance to it. Still, it is better than nothing and I have missed my body. I can look down and see myself, though I am not flesh as I understand it. I am not solid, but I have legs that walk if I think *walk* and arms that move if I think *move*. This is all a great improvement. I can also pass my hand through my body, something I found out by accident and did not enjoy. That is not an improvement at all.

Before me were the three gifts given to me by Ranya, glowing gently in the darkness. A walknut to find the way, a crownhead to travel on and a sewing kit to fix things. I have never been much for sewing, and I have never heard of anyone riding a crownhead, and though a walknut would be useful I had no pockets and would probably lose it. Gods are strange creatures, giving unto us gifts without so much as an instruction on what they are for or why or how to use them. Or maybe Ranya had told me before how to use them, many times and simply thought I knew. Or maybe Ranya was bored of telling me and of me still getting whatever I was meant to do wrong.

There was a noise, as if a hundred thousand people sighed. No one there. Only the ghosts of myself and they were poor company as they insisted on being barely seen. The walknut, the strange triangle, rocked slightly where it lay on the nothing in this nowhere. I picked it up.

"I wish I had pockets," I told it, "or I will lose you." A shiver. A shimmer and a twist and my shadow body was clothed, a jerkin and a long skirt with pockets. "You grant wishes?" I held up the walknut. "What a fine thing you are. I wish for a feast of rare raniri meat and forest vegetables, roasted over an open fire." I lifted the walknut high, as if to expose it to the Light Above, although that did not exist here.

Nothing happened.

"So, you only grant some wishes?" It did not answer, magic nuts are not great conversationalists. Next I picked up the sewing kit, a simple thing of needle, thread and pins in a folded cloth. I took out the needle and it grew in to a glowing spear that vibrated softly in my grip. "I hope I am not expected to fight with you, I am not much of a fighter. Not that I have met anyone here to fight." I looked around, hoping I was not wrong and hordes of soldiers bent on murder were about to appear, but nothing came from the darkness, no dark creatures intent on killing me.

Again.

What will happen if I die again? Another question I will ask Ranya if the great glowing star ever reappears.

I replaced the needle in the wrapping and put it in my pocket. Then approached the crownhead. It eyed me warily and apart from a gentle golden glow around its horns, and an ornate and beautiful leather pad on its back, no doubt for sitting on when riding, it was no different to any other crownhead.

"Hello," I said to it. It blinked at me, the pupils of its eyes like tiny black stars in the whites. I wondered if this was normal for crownheads or if this one was special. Cahan would know, I wished he was here to ask. Though I suppose that was wishing him dead, which I did not. "You are to take me places," I told it. "And as you appear to be the only other living thing here, we should be friends." The crownhead bleated gently and I put out my hand towards its muzzle. In return it immediately snapped at me. It had a set of extremely pointed teeth. That was definitely not normal for a crownhead. "Is our relationship to be adversarial then?" It blinked at me. "I had hoped not, though I suppose I would want to bite someone if I knew they were about to ride on my back." It let out a low bleat again and looked away. I noticed very thin chains ran from the riding pad and through the crownhead's ears, no doubt to steer it with. "Maybe you would be friendlier if I gave you a name?" I reached out once more and it let out a warning hiss. "Cahan would be a good name for you. He is someone I knew when I was alive and a lot like you, personality wise." It hissed again. "I agree, Crownhead, I would not want to be named after him either, though he was a good friend. And you are definitely not a Venn or a Furin. Maybe you are an Ont?" Again, a hiss. "Possibly, a name can be thought of later." I stepped round the creature's vicious mouth and towards its mid-quarters, where a loop of leather hung to help the rider ascend. It was definitely larger than most crownheads. As I neared, the creature shied away.

I tried again.

The same.

And again. And again. And again until I was quite exasperated.

"Now listen to me, beast," I said to it. "You were given to me by a god, and it would no doubt be a good idea to consider what such a creature will do to you if you continue to deny their will and refuse to let me ride." It turned away and showed me its behind. I decided that, gift from a god or not, I did not like this creature much and made a wide circle around its rear as crownheads can give a vicious kick.

It definitely did not want to be ridden.

Whenever I approached it skipped away, bucking its hind legs and making a quite unpleasant screeching sound. Eventually it calmed down and stood a good distance away from me, watching me with its starry eyes.

"You are a bad creature," I told it. The crownhead did not seem to care and began to eat invisible grass. I could not help thinking this may be some sort of test. Though why my god would test me if it also wanted me to carry out some task for it, I did not understand; it seemed unfair and annoyed me. Instead of chasing the beast I sat on the ground, which existed without being there. I could not see it but I could not pass my hands through it, which I suppose is important for something that wants to call itself ground. Though I would say it is also important for something that intends to be a body but I am not a god in charge of a strange realm beyond life, so maybe there are things I am unaware of.

Why a crownhead? This realm was not flat like the world I came from. It was left and right and forward and back as well as being up and down. A gasmaw would be far more useful. Though I knew less about gasmaws than I knew about crownheads I had never heard of them being ridden either.

A small light in my mind. I had once had a crownhead. When I was very young. Not a real one – a toy, and I played with it when I was alone. When my older brothers and sisters mocked me for being the youngest and a dreamer, when my family had no time for me. My father had burned it, told me it was a crutch to lean upon that made me weak. That I should get used to being alone and become strong, as I was from a strong family.

I did get used to being alone of course. Though he had not intended me to become an outcast. Careful what you wish for, I say. I had not thought about that toy crownhead in all the years I was alive. Even though I still remembered the pain of losing it. The way I had cried when my father put it on the fire. The beatings I got for my tears.

My crownhead had a name. A silly childish name, no more than a sound I enjoyed saying, but it had been a comfort to me and even when it had gone I had kept its feel in my mind with that name. I stood.

"Syerfu." I shouted it into the unmaterial of this place. The crownhead lifted its great horned face and turned it towards me. "I shall name you Syerfu!" It considered this, bleated, then ran towards me, skipping and kicking out its back legs in a way that was joyful and made me want to laugh out loud. It stopped and let me use its thick fur to pull myself up onto the leather seat. I burrowed my face in its fur and found it smelled familiar, safe and soft and warm like my bed when I had been very young. "You are a link, are you not? To my past, to the world of the living." The crownhead shivered and I felt us come closer together, become part of one another. I had thought the golden chains through its ears looked cruel but I did not need to pull on them. I held them lightly in one hand. With the other I took out the walknut and held it aloft. "Show me where to go," I said. A light, bright and blinding grew from the walknut in my hand. It slowly became a line, pointing far ahead of me. "Go Syerfu, go!" I shouted.

We moved.

So different to how I had moved before. Such speed. The air rushed past and despite the sensation of going faster than any person ever had, I felt safe on Syerfu's back, I felt cared for as we streaked into the darkness.

22

Dassit

She marched a troop of four hundred towards Fin-Larger under the unrelenting heat of the Light Above. The grasslands were golden, waving in the circle winds which brought a little blessed cool for her and her troops. They had given her three branches of soldiers, not enough, and of the commanders she knew only Vir. She was glad to have him with her, he was a soldier's soldier, living for each day, never wondering about the future or the past.

The other two were new to her, younger. A woman named Tirin Har-Barich who wore clan marks so long they almost covered the entire side of her face, and she wore her long hair wrapped up in a bun. She was quiet and her branch seemed to respect her. They did what she asked at least. The other was a man named Cavan Har-Gollust who was the type of commander she disliked, considered himself above his troops and got his way by shouting or having his second lay about them with the whip. She did not get the feeling he liked her much, but a few dark looks from her subordinates were simply something a commander had to get used to. Besides, he did not matter, not really. She had already won over their troops.

Every night she had done the same thing. Gone around the fires, sat with the people she would fight with. Talked with them, asked about them. Reminisced about actions past with old hands, reassured those who were new. Drank too much and regretted it the next morning. Shared commiserating looks with those also hungover.

Another thing she did was let the entire column march past her, waiting until the parade of floating rafts caught up. Talking to passing soldiers, commenting on their kit, sometimes a compliment, sometimes picking them up on failings. Enough for them to know she was there for them and that she was in charge. Then she would talk to the rafters and camp followers, listen to their worries and their woes because they were the true barometer of an army's feelings. That done, she would jog back to the front. Careful to make sure everyone saw her, their trunk commander, in full armour, running the whole column.

They might complain about the heat and the time she was forcing them to make, but they could never complain that she was unwilling to put herself through the same rigours. She had known Rai and Trunks who had themselves carried, or rode on carts, and she knew exactly what the common soldier thought of them for it.

First lesson of command, be part of the army, not above it.

She heard shouting from the rear, Cavan Har-Gollust berating his troops again.

"You'll have to do something about that." She turned to find Vir approaching. He was a thick, heavyset man, wearing only a tunic and skirts, his armour on a raft at the rear. By him was Tryu, one of his "sticks" as he called them. Rai armies had few ranks. Branch, Trunk and then Rai. Below that everything was more informal and Vir had a few that served as his seconds. The others were back with his troops. Dassit was reasonably sure Tryu had taken her place in Vir's bed, though no one was indelicate enough to mention it. She hoped they were happy.

"I thought, if I led by example he would start to follow. Instead his resentment only grows," she said and Vir nodded.

"Him and the other." She felt the day get a little more chill at his words. She had thought she got along fine with Tirin Har-Barich.

"Don't look like a whipped garaur, Trunk," he said. "She is all smiles and readiness to your face but I've seen the ways she looks at you when you're not looking at her. She hides her resentment behind that smile the way a spearmaw hides in a canopy."

"Well, that has brought the clouds to my light," she said.

"How far are we from Fin-Larger?"

"If I have read the maps correctly, it should be on the horizon today." Vir wiped sweat from his brow with his forearm, using the action not to meet her gaze. "Out with it, Vir; even if what you have to say is unpleasant, better I hear it."

"Not unpleasant, Trunk," he said. "Just that I think you should make Tryu here branch of your personal troops." She almost tripped. It was not usual for a trunk commander to directly command their troops, she knew that. Hers had been with her for a long time; she had offered Vir command but he had his own people. Vir marched a little closer. "I know why you have not done this before, Dass," he said – no one else ever called her that but him, "so listen. Those other two, if they gang up together can stalemate any decisions made. Make Tryu a branch, she gets a say and she is as loyal to you as I am." The Light Above burned down on her armour and she wished she could take it off like Vir did. The helmet felt heavy, the wood felt like it sapped the strength from her bones. Command, it slowly took everything from you.

"You are right," she said. "Tryu has more than earned it." Vir nodded at her, wiped sweat from his face then beckoned Tryu forward.

"Tryu," he said, "the trunk commander wishes you to be the branch of her personal troops." From the look on Tryu's face Vir had not discussed it with her.

"You will answer directly to me, Tryu," she said. "Vir can give you some paint for your armour, some red stripes will look good on it. If you want your own sticks, Bakal and Marif are dependable soldiers, if not imaginative."

"Thank you, Trunk Commander," she saluted, hand across her chest, "I will not let you down."

"I know that," she said. "I'll introduce you to my guard when we camp." Vir smiled at her, then nodded Tryu back towards his troops and she left. He watched her go, almost tripping over something hidden in the grass as a result.

"Osere take trapvines," he spat. "Nearly broke my ankle."

"It'd get you out of the fight," said Dassit. He looked at her, a twisted smile on his face.

"I don't like any of this." He scratched his head. "I don't like where we're being sent or what we are meant to do. I don't like all these fields either, nowhere to hide."

"Have you ever been anywhere you did like, Vir?"

"Tiltspire was all right," he said, "what it was under the Red."

"Only all right?"

"Too many Rai; you never knew if someone was going to burn you up for kicks." He looked up at the light, as if he could wish it less hot. "Anyway, now the Blue have got it they'll have turned it into an open sewer. You know what they're like. Filth."

"No, Vir," she said. "They're just like us." Vir laughed.

"I doubt it. And don't let Tirin or Cavan hear you saying that, they'll have you reported as treasonous."

"I am very careful about who I trust," she said.

"That you are," he looked forward. "I think I see our destination on the horizon, like you promised. Maybe we'll get there by lightfall."

*

The town of Fin-Larger was further away than they thought, some trick of the endless fields of Seerstem, and they slept that night with the walls of the town a squatting gap-toothed shadow before them.

In the morning, as the light rose, Dassit left her troops and took Vir into the town with her. She had left notice that the column could spend the morning relaxing, they had marched hard to get here and some rest would do them good. Besides, she wanted to speak freely with Vir as she surveyed the town.

There was no embassy to greet them, which she thought strange. It was usual for the Leorics of towns like this to come out and meet an approaching army, especially when they had been sent to defend them. She saw a few figures as she approached – fleeting shapes vanishing between houses in the early morning mist – but she was less concerned with the figures as to the fact she could see them through the walls.

"It's a ruin," said Vir, staring up at the wall. It had been huge once, thick dirt walls twice as high as a person and topped by a wooden palisade. Time and lack of care had worn them away. Where the palisade still stood the wood was rotten and the dirt walls had begun to crumble, ravaged by plants that had grown in and loosened the hard packing of the steep ramps. In places the town had outgrown the walls and they had been removed, replaced with a flimsy wooden barrier barely higher than Vir's head.

"Osere," spat Vir. "Should burn it down, give all those in it over as traitors like we did at that last place. There's a war on and they let it get like this?"

"It could definitely do with a little work," said Dassit. She tried to ignore Vir's enthusiasm for punishment.

"More chance going up against the Osere with shovels than defending this place from a determined army." Dassit smiled to herself. "I'm glad someone's amused," he said.

"It won't be easy, you're right, Vir, but I begin to wonder if our enemy actually are that determined."

"What's that mean?" Vir kicked a stone across the parched and cracked mud in front of the town.

"I have a theory," she said. He raised an eyebrow. "I'm not sure the Blue want to win." Vir laughed.

"All these years of being a soldier, Dass, and somehow you missed that the whole point of war." He looked up at the broken walls and let out a sigh. "I may have to rethink my high opinion of you."

"Yes," she said. Beyond the wall she could see the gables of houses, built tall and sharp. "It is just that the Blue have made so many poor decisions, and I'm struggling to think of it is accidental. They should have rolled over us a long time ago."

"That ain't true," said Vir. "We're in the right. Besides, they're scared of our Cowl-Rai." Those last words died away, stolen by the circle winds. They had both fought a long retreat across Crua, and both at times cried out for their Cowl-Rai, the living embodiment of Chyi to come to their aid. They never had.

So many had died.

"Maybe they are scared," said Dassit; she found her own rock, rolled it under the sole of her boot rather than argue with Vir. "They have split their army this year, sent half to secure Treefall in the Northern Wyrdwood."

"Treefall's valuable," said Vir. "Makes sense."

"Yes, but it's not going anywhere." She kicked the stone across the ground. "Let's go in, see who is home to greet us."

"We should kill a few," said Vir, hand on his blade, "teach them a bit of respect."

"No one gets killed today." Vir shrugged. She wondered if he had always been so hard, she didn't remember him being that way.

They walked around Fin-Larger until they came to the gates, large, with a walkway above. The gates were wide open, the same grasses that were growing out in the fields tall around them.

"These haven't been shut in years," said Vir and spat. "I hate civilians."

"You used to be one." Vir shook his head.

"Don't think so. I was born with a spear in my hand."

They walked through the gates unopposed, Dassit uncomfortably aware of the sweat trickling down her back. She hated fighting in the southlands, the heat was worse than the cold of the north. She hated the cold too, but at least when you were fighting you warmed up, or you could have a fire if you needed it. There was no escape from the heat. If Fin-Larger had a chimney house she would claim it for her officers. That at least would be cool as its shape convected the heat up and out, making a welcome breeze run through it.

The town felt deserted as they walked through it, the main street was wide, the houses large and well kept. Red flags gently fluttered everywhere in a breeze she barely felt.

"Do you think this is a trap?" said Vir. She stopped, looked around. Imagined for a moment soldiers appearing in the houses around her, spears being thrown. Rai burning the air.

"No," she said. "Makes no sense, you couldn't hide enough people in here to fight our army, or defend this place from us. And you couldn't hide an army out on the plains." She looked around, wondering if she was right. The grass was tall, could you lay a whole army down? Sneak it close in the night?

Why would they?

This place couldn't be defended as it was. A trap felt like a lot of effort for little gain and she knew the Rai were rarely given to effort, or smarts. Their way was to throw lives at a problem.

"People," Vir pointed down the street towards what looked like the town square. A gallows stood in the middle of it, and below the gallows stood four people dressed in fine garments. Vir started towards them.

"Stop," said Dassit. "Let them come to us, I want no doubt about who is in charge." Vir stopped and they waited, dripping with sweat as they watched the four fail to approach. It did not appear to be a powerplay, but only because they were involved in some sort of argument.

"Osere's feet, I'm going to melt if we stand here, Dassit," said Vir. She waited a little longer then shook her head and strode forward into the square. It was like many town squares, a number of wooden market stalls had been set up, though all were empty. Opposite the gallows stood a shrine to Chyi, a garlanded taffistone, though the statues of the god that should be there, head bowed and hands held before his eyes, appeared to have been removed. A star of Iftal had been raised behind it. The four nobles of the town still didn't notice them, their argument was all-consuming.

"You!" she shouted. "I am Dassit Gan-Brinor of the Red. My army has come to your town on the word of the Cowl-Rai and in service to great Chyi. Who is in charge here?" The four turned to her, expressions of surprise on their faces. Each wore ribbon gowns, deep reds and purple strips of wool that ran over their bodies, exposing as much flesh as they covered and good for the hot weather. The skin beneath was tanned and leathery with exposure to the light. The oldest of them stared at her, then raised himself up. His crested hat, lined with gasmaw pearls that gleamed in the early morning light, made him look far taller than he really was.

"I am Leoric Ghorle," he said, his voice wavering. "And I welcome you to—"

"Have you come to evacuate us?" said the woman stood by him.

"No," said Dassit. The woman appeared to deflate. "I am here—"

"I told you," said the third of the finely dressed nobles, "this Rai has come for the prisoner. We were right to keep them." The bickering broke out again.

"Quiet!" She used the same shout she used to cut through the sound of battle and it shut them up. "I am no Rai, but I am sent by them to defend this town. To rebuild your walls, to make Fin-Larger a fortress against the foul lies of the traitors from the north." The words came easily, though she knew they were a lie. She had been sent here to die.

"Not to take us away?" said the man who had hoped they were to be evacuated. She shook her head.

"But what about the prisoner?" said the woman, tiny and older than Dassit believed anyone had a right to be in Crua. "Surely they will interest you, Rai?"

"What prisoner?" She did not bother to correct the woman again.

"A spy, they appeared here one morning, in the square, and we caught them." She smiled at her. "Jurant wanted to hang her but I said no, save her for the Rai, to question and feed from."

"A spy? That interests me, take me to them. And you," she pointed at the Leoric, "Vir here is my second. Take him to a chimney house so we can set up a command base." The four nobles gave small bows and Vir leaned in so he could whisper to her.

"We're dead if the enemy come here, whether they want to lose or not, aren't we?"

"Where there's life, there's hope, Branch Commander," she said.

23
Ont

Ont was a very confused man, but also happier than he could ever remember being. He had spent his entire life terrified of Wyrdwood, terrified of Harnwood too and even frightened of Woodedge. Now, when he knelt before the taffistone of the tangled tree and spoke to Ranya, he found himself considering his life, and how he had been scared for a long time. Maybe it was his great size, and the expectation of others that with a great size and strength came some inherent greatness. His firstfather had been well-respected, a harsh man who looked down – quite literally – on everyone around him, including his son. Nothing Ont had ever done had been good enough and despite his size he had always felt small compared to others.

Back in Harn he had played a part, he had been who he was expected to be, the shadow of his firstfather who had worn the bloody apron of the butcher before him. He supposed now that if you stood in someone's shadow the world was always darker. He smiled to himself. He must remember that next time he addressed New Harnwood, he would use that.

New Harnwood.

Was that what it was? Had he really needed his entire life destroyed before he could see the truth of himself? He did not wish to dominate like his firstfather had, he did not wish to force his will on others. He had seen Udinny, priest of Ranya, penniless and filthy with mud, give her all for people who barely even liked her and that had struck some chord within him. Then he had travelled the forests, and he had seen terrors. The huge littercrawlers, the hordes of rootlings, the swarden and the Boughry. His fear had cleansed him and washed away his worries, it had brought a greater knowledge and a calmness. He wondered if Udinny had felt this, if it was what had brought her to Harn and to her sacrifice. To realise there was no greater service than to serve your fellow people. He would not force his will on any of the villagers, he would only guide and if they ignored his guidance and fell he would pick them up without recrimination.

He opened his eyes and let out a laugh.

What would his firstfather say? Nothing, probably, he would have taken out his strap and decide to teach Ont a Lesson. But his firstmother – that quieter voice, always in the shadow of his father? He felt they would be smiling down on him from the Cowl Star where they were free of firstfather's tyranny, no longer forced to hide in the background.

He stood, using his forestbow to help him up and grunting as his knees complained. It was hard to be tall, your body did not like it. He stepped forward and put his hand on the taffistone; as always he thought he felt something, but was not sure enough to swear on it. It was so small it could have been a wish as much as it was a vibration in the fingers touching the smooth rock. It felt like there should be something there, almost like a memory but not. He ran his hand along the twisted boughs of the tree. In places they had died, not from disease, but because they were no longer of any use to the tree and Ont had decided he would shear off these dead branches, make himself a headdress of twisted wood.

"I give myself to your path, Ranya," he said softly. "I travel where it takes me." He waited, hoping to hear a reply. Udinny had heard the voice of her god but he did not. He pursed his lips, nodded and tried not to show his sadness before her shrine. He had met many monks, and very few spoke of hearing the voices of those they worshipped. They existed on faith and faith alone. That and the generosity of worshippers, so that was what Ont must also exist on. He must be satisfied with that.

He walked out of the grove, past the huge Forest Man, slumped against the entrance to the grove as if asleep. He put his hand on the great leg of the statue.

"Good morning, friend," he said. Looking up at the bearded face of the wooden man. Sometimes he imagined the thing had moved slightly during the night. On windy nights when he lay awake in his wooden house he imagined the creaking of the trees was the creaking of the Forest Man, getting up and stretching his legs. He never looked, of course; if the Forest Man chose to do such things in privacy that was his decision.

He nodded at it; something of it struck a strange chord in him, again that almost familiarity.

He walked to where he had set up his target, leaving a little food at the shyun shrines as he passed. Then he strung his bow. Took an arrow from the holder he had set up there and loosed. Watched the arrow fly. He hit the target, but only the outer rim, and sighed. He had watched Cahan loose, his quick and fluid way of doing it, how the bow was almost part of him. Ont aimed at not only the target but at that level of skill. He loosed again, trying for the same fluid action the forester had.

A better hit this time, though he knew it was partly luck, not skill.

In the corner of his eye he caught a movement and turned,

lowering the bow. Two of the shyun stood in front of one of the huge bushes that grew thickly around New Harnwood.

"Hello friends," he said. Their answer was lost to him. They spoke in the rustle of leaves at the touch of a breeze. "I put out food for you, I hope it is to your liking." One of them spoke again, strange mouthparts moving inside a nest of tentacles, then it used its feet to kick up the pin litter of the cloudtrees. He understood little of the shyun's language, but had come to see that particular action as friendly. They made more noise. They were not frightened of him in the least and it made him happy. He was about to say more when the shyun froze, sensing something he could not, then they were gone, vanishing into the thick brush and it was as if they never were.

"Shy, the forest children are. Always have been." He turned to find it was the Forestal, Ania, who had spoken. She held her bow loosely in her hand, her long cloak pushed back over the hilt of a small axe that she rested one hand on. She frightened him. She held no love for him after the way he had acted towards the Forestals back in Harn. He wanted to tell her he had changed, but saw no reason she would believe him. Instead he unstrung his bow.

"Can I help you?" She looked past him, at his bower.

"They tell me you have a shrine here, to your god Ranya?" He nodded. "And a taffistone?" He nodded again. "Are you going to start bleeding your people so you can live in luxury, have them leave you food while they starve?" He shook his head.

"It is just a place for people to come, when they need to."

"Can I look?" He had the distinct feeling that whether he said yes or not did not matter.

"All are welcome." She walked past, barely looking at him. Her face was distorted by the forest colours she wore, they made her unknowable, hid whoever was underneath them from those around her. He followed her into the bower and she walked straight up to the taffistone and knelt before it. He watched her with the oddest feeling, as if she studied it for some particular reason but he dared not ask her what. She reached out and touched it then, as if this decided something for her, she stood. "Do you worship your gods at these stones?" he asked.

"Our gods need no worship, all we do and are is for them." She looked around, not really paying attention. He was not sure what she meant.

"The trees," he said eventually. "Your god is the trees?"

"It is everything, the trees, the floor, all of it," said Ania and she walked over to the wall of the bower, examining the huge stones and the thick trailing plants and vines growing between them.

"Even the Boughry?" Her hand slowed.

"Even them." She turned to him. "We do not name them often, it is best they do not notice us." She laughed to herself. "But surely you know that."

"Yes," he said, "of course." She nodded at his words. Her attention turned back to the taffistone.

"When they come," she said, "this is the last line, it is the most defensible place you have."

"If they come." She shook her head and shuffled a little closer to the stone.

"They will come. It is not in them to let you alone. They hate the forester. And the trion, Venn? They value them." She spat on the floor. "They cannot bear anyone else to have something they value." Ont swallowed – did she speak of some old hurt? He had no intention of asking. She was not the type to share, and definitely not with him. She stood and walked past him. He followed her out of the bower, back into Wyrdwood. She glanced at the Forest Man as she passed. "I watched you loose," she said.

"I practise every day, it calms me. I wish I was better."

"You are trying to be Cahan," she said. Her words as gruff as the forester ever was. "You are not him."

"I know that." He tried not to sound disappointed but knew he failed.

"No, you do not." She took a step towards him and it took all he had not to step back. "I mean he is not something for you to aim for. Neither am I. I have loosed arrows since I was young, so has he. You have not."

"No," said Ont, he felt himself wilting beneath her words. "I know I will never—"

"That is not me saying you are a bad archer, Butcher."

"I am not that anymore." Ania studied him, her eyes as fierce as any spearmaw.

"No," she said eventually, "you are not are you?" A nod. "What matters, with the bow, is that you hit the target. That is all. I watched you loose, you draw quickly and hit a target well enough. You can probably do enough on the move to make your enemy keep their head down." He felt Osere-cursed with faint praise. "Good and useful skills . . ." she paused, searching for something. Then she walked over to him and took his bow, studied it. The Forestal strung it and held it out to him. "Loose for me." He took the bow. Strung an arrow, bringing it up quickly, some part of him determined to prove her wrong but she stopped him before he let the arrow go. Her hand coming out. Touching the bow. "Slow," she said. "Take your time." He took a breath. Pushed away his annoyance at being told what to do. Lifted the bow again and drew it, feeling the strain in his shoulders, across his chest. The world blurring around everything but the target. He let the string go. Watched the arrow streak towards the target, hit it dead centre. The Forestal made a noise, a sort of satisfied grunt. "See the shade tree," she said, "about a hundred paces behind the target? Hit the third branch up on the left." He turned to her.

"That is too far for me."

"Show me, don't tell me."

He drew again, taking his time, pulling the string back even further, muscles burning in a ring around his chest.

He tried to imagine the breeze, the way the arrow would drop off. Loosed.

Missed.

Again that satisfied grunt from Ania, despite him missing.

"I fell short," he said. "I told you I would."

"Nonetheless," she said, "that should be your target."

"Why?" She stood a little closer, took her bow off and put an arrow on the string. Pulled it to full stretch, sighting on the branch. He noticed notches on the inside of her bow. Then she loosed, the arrow flew and they watched. It fell short too. She turned to him.

"You shot further than I did," he said.

"But neither of us hit the target."

"I don't understand." The bow felt useless in his hand, foreign to him.

"I will never hit that target," she said, "but you could, one day. You have the eye of a sharpshooter, monk, Skua, whatever you wish to be called. And you have the strength and build for range." She unstrung her bow and put it back in the holder on her back. Put out her hand for his bow and he passed it across. "This is a good enough bow, for most." She turned it over, examining it then gave it back. "I am going to be here a while and I am already bored. You and I, we will make a bow more worthy of a man your size."

"Thank you," he said, unsure whether he wanted to spend more time with the Forestal. Uncomfortable with the way she looked at him, and in the back of his mind, the oddest sensation that this conversation was familiar, like the stone and the Forest Man. "The notches on your bow," he said to change the subject, "do they mark out your kills?" She laughed, a short and sharp thing like a knife blade shimmering in the air.

"If the notches were kills my bow would be nothing but splinters. They are to help me with distance. I will show you that. But first I must finish my rounds." She walked away, stopping just before she entered the wood. "The shyun," she said, "they don't show themselves to many." Then she turned and was gone and Ont wondered at the strange turns his life took.

He took up his bow, strung an arrow and sighted for the branch of a tree that looked impossibly far away.

24

Cahan

They walked for four days; Tall Sera, his Forestals, Venn, the Reborn sisters, chosen villagers and him. The forest around them never anything less than vast. He had thought of Wyrdwood as a whole, as one thing: a never-changing landscape of brown dead needles with occasional stands of bushes or shade trees and the great punctuation of cloudtree trunks, like cliffs: immovable and eternal, exclamations of the forest's power.

But it was not true, he had simply not spent enough time in Wyrdwood to really know it. The forest was its own land, with all the things a land needed. It had its own ecosystems and plants: eruptions of rocks, grey and angular and many times taller than a person, leafy bushes and trees he did not know the names of, fungi, in all forms, wide caps, teetering towers and branching colourful forms. Some so small he barely noticed them, some towering above him. Beneath it all he felt the second system of the forest, Ranya's web, that touched upon everything, a massive net of fungal cilia that linked everything in Crua. It would have been easy, once, for him to reach out and touch it but since he had touched the bluevein he could only feel the web, not touch it. Beneath Ranya's web he could feel the other, the net of dead things, of slow decay, part of nature, he knew that. Ranya's web ran through it but in many places it was wrong, twisted by outcroppings of bluevein that called to him.

He was distracted by thoughts of Furin, her softness in the night. Her fearlessness of what he was.

They stopped to fill their gourds at wetvines and sometimes at streams where Cahan marvelled at the clarity of the water. It was a long time since he had seen water that had come from anything but a wetvine. Tiny creatures darted backwards and forwards in the liquid and Cahan was transfixed; he closed his eyes and felt for the tiny dots of life. Abruptly, they winked out of existence. When he opened his eyes they were dead, being carried away on the current and he looked around, glad to find no one was watching. His guts as icy cold as the stream but this feeling did not flow away, it stayed within.

The Forestals rarely spoke. They communicated with hand gestures: stop, go forward, go left, go right. The rest was simply walking and staying alert. Stop for gasmaws, go around a littercrawler nest. At one point they picked up a trail but it turned out to be rootlings and the Forestals quickly lost interest. The carpet of cloudtree needles changed to a thick, dark grass. Cahan knelt and touched it: soft, slightly fuzzy like fur. He wondered if Segur had followed them. Probably not, the garaur had taken to the villagers and seemed to prefer having people around.

The grass became thicker and they skirted a swarden tower. A huge one, rickety and strewn with the skeletal grass people. The Forestals told them to stay low as they went around it and Cahan's back ached by the time they were finally walking upright again. He stayed at the back of the line, rubbing his lower back.

"Are you all right, Cahan?" asked Venn.

"My back aches." That gruff voice, the same one he had

used so long ago when he felt like an invader every time he went into Harn.

"It does?" He tried not to look at Venn, the ruff of hair around their face, the light dusting of powder on their skin. Easier to pretend he didn't hear the surprise in their voice.

"I do not think the Forestals want us to talk, Venn." The trion stared at him, then nodded, falling back so they walked behind but Cahan knew why he heard surprise in their voice. Aches and pains were not part of him. The cowl fixed him; the only time he was aware of how much weaker he would be without it was when the duller, Sorha, had been near him. What he felt now was not as bad. Not as complete as her presence.

But he ached. He told himself that thoughts of Furin made him careless, but it was not. It was thoughts of what dwelt within him.

They stopped that night with the same ritual as every night. The Forestals had some way of knowing darkness was coming. A clever trick, as there was no twilight here, only the sudden curtain of night falling, as complete and irrevocable as death. Tall Sera would raise his hand and the Forestals would stop, then they would collect rocks, make a small pyramid of them. After that they would stand behind Tall Sera, all touching, and Tall Sera would place his hand against the rocks. Cahan would feel a discomfort as some power passed between them and the rocks began to glow with heat. Venn was transfixed by it.

Then night would fall and they would sit quietly around the heated rocks and eat while the lights of the night creatures threw a wash of colour over them.

Usually Venn would try and talk to the Forestals then, ask about what they did: how they made the rocks hot? Why did they not need to steal life? Where did the power come from? But the Forestals did not answer and Venn would eventually quieten, or Tall Sera would tell Venn that now was not the time and he was not a teacher. It annoyed Cahan, that they were so transparent in trying to tempt the trion away from him with promises of knowledge.

On the edge of sleep, thoughts of her. Of Furin.

In the morning they walked again and each day was the same as the last one, until the day they heard the screaming. A woman's voice, ringing out in the wood. Cahan's first thought was to help but the Forestals did not move. Instead they crouched in the litter. Venn did not. They started to run but Cahan reached out and caught them by the arm.

"Someone needs help!" hissed Venn.

"This is the Forestals' place," said Cahan, "and we follow their lead." Tall Sera moved forward in a crouch and his archers slowly spread out around him. Cahan and Venn followed. A sign was made by Tall Sera, bows were taken from backs, strung in quick and practised motions. Step by step they moved on, moving into a meadow of black grass that was high enough Cahan could barely see over it when crouched. They stopped at the edge of the grass, in a clearing; before them there were trees with wide spreading mushroom-shaped canopies of red leaves, their green and mossy trunks covered in gnarled bracket fungus.

In the middle of the clearing lay a Forestal, moaning in pain. A hand to their stomach to staunch the blood flowing into a pool below them.

"Help me, please."

Venn stood, Cahan grabbed them.

"They need healing. I can—"

"No, Trion," said Tall Sera quietly. "They do not need healing. These are hareft trees, often the habitat of skinfetch. It is trying to lure us in."

"Why?"

"To eat you. Now be quiet. Our best hope is to stay together and go around it. They are Osere-cursed hard to kill but not a threat if we stay together."

"Why come so close then?" said Cahan.

"Because it may have been one of our people, we had to check."

"How do you know it isn't?" said Venn.

"We do not travel alone through Wyrdwood," said Tall Sera, "and if you take your time, concentrate, you will feel it." Venn blinked, then closed their eyes. Their breathing slowed. They opened their eyes, nodded.

"The skinfetch is dangerous but hunts by surprise and stealth," said Tall Sera. "It takes on the skin of others, to let it get near. In the light, and as long as we can always see each other, we should be safe." He looked from Venn to Cahan, made sure they understood. "Now, let us move on and stay close."

They did, and the creature did not follow though they heard the screaming for long hours.

They carried on, moving by day, sleeping at night until Tall Sera stopped them one early morning and gathered them around.

"We are near, and this evening," he said, "we will scout. Tomorrow we will strike. I have steered us for the centre of the fallen cloudtree, away from the branches."

"Why?" said Venn. The Forestals looked at them. Tall Sera smiled.

"The roots will be tangled and must be cleaned of soil. The trunk gets thinner as it nears the top, and the branches must be cleared away and sorted. At the centre of the tree the trunk is not as massive as lower down and branches do not need to be cleared, the mining can start straight away."

"How do you know so much about it?"

"I know many things, Trion." He turned away from Venn. "Now, come, we must scout, we must see how far on they are in the mining and plan our attack."

"What do you do with it?" said Venn.

"With what?" Tall Sera turned back to them.

"The cloudtree, what use is it? You cannot sell it to the

Blue. They will know you stole it." Tall Sera smiled at them, his face a mass of creases.

"We sell in the Largers and the Spiretowns. In the north and the south. There is always someone willing to buy things they should not have."

"Oh," said Venn.

"You look disappointed," said Tall Sera.

"I thought that . . ." Their words tailed off.

"That we were more than thieves? Is that what you were going to say?"

"Well," Venn looked away and Cahan could almost feel the disappointment burning in the trion.

"Treefall, Venn," said Tall Sera, "is a gift to those of the forest, to us. Part of the cycle of life and death. We lose one of our great gods, that is true. But its body is there to bring about new life. Riches and plenty. There is more than enough for everyone. It is the Rai who are the thieves, they who wish to keep it for themselves. They live in fear of what others may do if they are not held underfoot." The trion blinked. "We only reclaim a part of what should belong to everyone." Venn nodded, stepped back. "Now," said Tall Sera, "let us continue, I would approach the tree at night."

Cahan could not imagine what it would be, to see one of the great cloudtrees of the forest, immovable and eternal, a vast exclamation of its power, fallen. But of course, nothing was truly eternal, and even gods may die.

25

Saradis

Seven hours she had knelt alone in the hot room halfway up Tiltspire. Her stomach ached from fasting.

She was rarely truly alone, it had been that way all her life. Even when she was not surrounded by others she was always aware they were there for her to call on. As Skua-Rai of Zorir she had been surrounded by acolytes, and when she had been an acolyte herself she had been with her siblings under the god. All living together in the dormitories, like a great family of first, second, third and fourth wives and husbands. The hardship of life under a god allayed a little by the softness of shared bodies.

That small comfort vanished when she started to rise in the ranks. The monastery wanted those who were hard, so she pushed others away to prove she was. With her commitment had come a wall within that she allowed none over – they stood at the bottom of it or they broke against it but none passed it. When she had craved silence she found it within herself and it was in that silence where she first heard the voice of Zorir-Who-Walks-In-Fire, though voice was not the right explanation for it then. It was more a feeling, a memory or compulsion. A knowledge of their presence that made her furious with those around her who were monks only because it was expected of them.

She had heard others say that with power you became more alone but it was not true. You became more isolated, but you were never truly alone. There was always someone who wanted something, who would use you for their own purposes. Even now, as powerful as she had ever been, she must answer to the Cowl-Rai, but that was a rod of her own making – one she fully intended to break. For now, being unable to relax because of the Cowl-Rai's moods was a small price, compared to others she had paid. She would be called to her and find a woman who wanted to die, or a woman who raged at the world or a woman overcome with energy, desperate to talk through a long list of plans that verged between cunning and insane. She had found that the focus of battle and campaign planning seemed to reign in the Cowl-Rai's worst attributes, gave her mind something to focus on.

Without her Saradis would not have taken Crua.

Though lately, the Cowl-Rai had become more focused on Tilt, and the trion, and her obsession with doing what a thousand Cowl-Rai had done before. Somewhere along the way Nahac Du-Nahere had forgotten that she was a lie, that she was a construct as much as her imaginary god, Tarl-an-Gig, was. That the stone in her skull gave her power, but not the power of a Cowl-Rai. The Tilt, where the land shifted and brought heat back to the north, and cold to the south was not something she could ever do. It had to be delayed and delayed and delayed again until Saradis's great work was finished. Then the Cowl-Rai would cease to matter, and she, Saradis, would stand before the great taffistone and the fire would come and the land would be cleansed. All born again in the Paradise at the end of the Star Path. Zorir would look down on her and know she had done its bidding.

She took a deep breath.

Time alone. No. She was never alone, her task was too great. The pressure too much and the nearest she knew to peace was this, kneeling naked before Zorir's taffistone. Not as big as the huge one before the Spire, but larger than the ones she sent out to the Spiretowns. This one though, it was hers, it was peculiar to her. It had been in the monastery where she had made her greatest mistake, though it had not fulfilled its true potential until many years later. After she had journeyed to the north and found them, Cahan and Nahac, playing in the dirt of some filthy clanless farm. There she had chosen the wrong one. She had felt so sure, even felt the seed of strength within the boy, the simmering of power the stones had attuned her to. Nothing from the sister.

Nothing.

Yet here she was.

The boy had been weak.

The sister had been strong.

She had found out too late, blinded by her surety. Zorir had punished her for it and she had learned not to fail.

Saradis leant forward from the waist, the heels of her feet digging into the tops of her thighs, sweat beading her skin. The stone before her was warm and it, not the heat from outside, gave the room its warmth. Her stone was not warm like fire, not warm like the Light Above, but warm like when the gaze of another fell upon you. A feeling, the prickle across her flesh that she knew was the eye of Zorir. She felt it now, Zorir was finally looking upon their servant and she felt a flush akin to arousal. Years ago she had been able to stay knelt like this for days if needed. Now her back burned after only a few hours and she was forced to sit upright to ease it. But as Zorir was here she would not move until she felt they allowed it. So she knelt and she waited as the awareness grew in increments. She could hear the rasp of creatures moving across the wall, the sound of the people of Tiltspire far below, going about their business unaware that a god manifested above them, not just a Cowl-Rai, an actual god of their land. Shadows lengthened as the Light Above moved across the sky and as it moved the sound of the people below was replaced by a slow and gradual hum that filled her mind with a deep, deep blue, almost purple. A vast field of flowers blooming in her mind, a thousand tiny flying littercrawlers buzzing in her ears. Out of the corner of her eye she saw the blue glow around the stone brighten.

Now was the time. She sat straight, wanted to stretch to rid herself of the cramps in her muscles but did not. To do anything but pay full attention to Zorir when they manifested was to risk losing the attention of the god.

Hands on the top of her thighs, she let the tension flow out of her body with her breath. Then reached out and placed her hands on the stone. Cold against her skin, despite the heat radiating from it.

Sometimes there was no contact and she was left disappointed, unfulfilled. Sometimes she thought there was no contact and then later, in her daily tasks, or in her dreams she would get a gradual feeling, a desire to do something.

It had been like that with Cahan and Nahac, a slowly growing desire to go north, to take a train of her people and travel until she found the Cowl-Rai of Zorir. Every monastery searched for the Cowl-Rai, but she had felt no need to until that point. That was before she had purified the stone, or even knew she needed to, when she had taken sweat baths, heating a room up until water ran from her skin like the geysers outside of Tilt in full flow. Filling her stomach with teas made from flycaps and visionhoods in search of her god.

Very rarely she was gifted with a definite – not vision, vision was not the right word, a compulsion. That was how she had found the first stone. When she was in the wilderness, when her monastery was lost, sacked by the woman she now served and her furious army. In her misery and her failure she had found a grove of visionhoods and taken enough to kill ten people. Yet she had not died. She had felt death, felt its creeping tendrils around her, felt it touch upon her skin, move into her body, but it had not taken her.

She had woken desperately thirsty and with a mania upon her, a madness. To go back to the north, to Harn, through Harnwood and into Wyrdwood. She was barely lucid, a filthy madwoman marching half-alive and hoping only for a release from the failure that was her life.

She remembered digging, clawed hands pushing through the layers of brown, dead cloudtree leaves. She saw none of the magnificence around her. Only felt the sting of the sharp, dry leaves breaking her skin. The coolness of the dead earth as she broke through a thousand season's worth of fall. Bluevein thick in the ground. Barely hearing her own ragged breathing, the strange, animal noises she made as she dug.

Until she found the stone. Disappointment at first, an old taffistone buried in the dirt. Like so many others.

Until she touched it. Until it touched her.

All that mattered then was getting it out of the ground.

Days of work and increasing frustration as it seemed immovable. Laha appeared. He must have been following her, watching, staying close enough to protect her. Unsure whether to show himself or not until she tried and failed and tried and failed to move the stone from where it lay beneath earth thick with blue threads. The most loyal of her subjects spoke no words, only added his strength to hers so they could lift the stone.

It did not glow, not at first. Not until they had righted it, so it stood as a taffistone should, the rounded point facing up towards the sky. Then she saw the faint blue glow around it. Laha too. He reached out before she could say anything, put his hand on the stone.

He felt nothing when he touched it.

But when she touched it?

She was overwhelmed.

That was the first, the only time she saw what she had come to think of as Zorir's loom. In the briefest moment she understood some of what it must be to be Cowl-Rai. The whole of Skua stretched out below her, Wyrdwood to north and south, Slowlands to east and west. Below it all a pulsing, spinning web of bright white and with it came a feeling, a visceral, awful hatred that radiated from her bones, though at the same time she knew it was not of her. It was from the stone. It was from something else. Within that hatred were other feelings: a deep loneliness, a raging fury and a pure and true purpose that put hers to shame. Within the mass of white was, not a web, but a framework of something that was slowly growing, that could be but was not quite yet. This was the loom of Zorir in icy blue, the colour she had always associated with her god. It was weak, built of something long dead and broken, little more than thin threads beneath the blinding, painful whiteness. But she found enough in it, enough to know it must grow for her god to prosper. That this loom was the key to the great fire, and she was the key to it growing. All this in a single searing flash. Burning away all her doubt and her pride. Shame covering her like a shroud. She had given up, run away, doubted when strength was required. Zorir was waiting. Zorir needed her.

She was within the stone for a moment, with Zorir for a moment, she suffered with them. A million seasons of confinement. Panic rising, that she was stuck, would never escape.

Then she let go.

The stone cracked and eight shards fell to the floor, each little more than the length of her middle finger. Each heavy with purpose she did not yet know, though she felt sure she would one day. Pins for the web. Around the eight shards, more tiny pieces of the stone, hundreds and hundreds of them. Behind her Laha was touching his face, blood running down it. Shards of rock embedded in his skin.

Saradis groaned.

The memories were so strong. She looked at her hands, confused as to why there was no dirt beneath her fingernails before remembering she was not there. She was here. The shards had been used to create more blue taffistones, the first one used on this stone before her. Each new stone breaking off its own shards and some of those shards were hidden within the headdress she wore, jewels more precious than any knew. Laha had changed after the stone joined with him, subtly but importantly. And some of the small stones, in a night of blood and screams, had been slowly driven into the skull of the Cowl-Rai.

"Saradis."

Her name, said over aeons. Whispered in a voice she had rarely heard before but one she knew better than her own body. Zorir. The god spoke. They knew her name.

"I am here." An echo, her own voice magnified eight thousand times. Surrounding her, suffusing the air with sound.

Vision. Bursting in her mind. The same as all those years ago. But now Zorir's loom, the blue framework growing beneath the bright white one, was much stronger, and somehow fixed to the web of light in a way it had not been before.

"Close." A flash. A figure. The boy, Cahan? With him came a desperate sense of need. Why? Then it was swept away.

The voice. So ancient and wise, full of longing.

The two frameworks and the web merged fully. The brightness increasing until she knew that if she had she seen it with anything but her mind she would have been blinded. A wave of heat, the fire burning Crua. All light becoming a single point in the darkness, a concentration of energy and from it leapt a line, out and through the darkness, reaching along the Star Path, touching it and linking two bright points. One Crua, one the new paradise of the Cowl Star. She saw again, two figures, standing at the start of the path.

"Soon."

Was she even breathing? She did not know. This was a direct communication. A prophecy from her god. Following it came a wave of pleasure, a pool of darkness she fell into. Every nerve in her body lit up, something beyond the physical. She could not speak, moan, do anything. It was all. It was everything. A reward for her good work.

And the darkness swallowed her.

26

Dassit

There had been two quakes since they'd arrived, the land shaking beneath her feet, and she tried to ignore them. The quakes came more and more often now, something to do with the passing of one Cowl-Rai and rising of the next no doubt. Dassit put it out of her mind, she had other things to think about.

The town was not as empty as she had first thought. Most of the populace was hiding, though when they appeared they did not give her any great hope of creating a defence force. They were either children or very old. All the strongest had already been taken for the armies of the Red, it was the same everywhere. Any that had not been taken had most likely been sent away the moment she was seen approaching. It annoyed her on a professional level, but on a personal level she understood. If she was a Leoric it was what she would do.

That did not make her any kinder.

She had Vir sort through the townspeople, finding any strong enough to rebuild the walls. Tiran and Cavan she had commanded to take their troops and reap the grasses around the walls. Partly because they would need them for food, and partly because she could not get that Osere-cursed image of an army sneaking up on her through them out of her head. The two branch commanders were not pleased, so she had Tryu take her personal guard and join them, then none could claim she played favourites. After that she had walked the walls, or what there was of them. Spitting and cursing to herself with every step. This place had been rich, but it had never thought it would need defending. Its Tanside walls were in the best condition, no one knocked down defensive walls to build poor housing; though it was not that poor, the tannery pits were long since gone from Fin-Larger. On Grasside the walls were almost entirely gone to make way for the tall thin houses. One good shot from a Rai and the entire town would burn. She started making notes on a map as she moved round, becoming more and more morose as she did.

Dassit was not the type to give up, but she could not stop thinking that if someone asked her to design a town that was indefensible then she would have drawn something very much like Fin-Larger.

To take her mind away from the state of the town, she decided she would go and see the spy the Leoric said they had caught. The one currently languishing beneath the guardhouse on the town square. That a spy had come here seemed unlikely to Dassit.

The watchhouse was an ugly, blocky building of mud and straw bricks around a wooden frame. Small windows, sturdy, difficult to storm and difficult to burn. This would be where they made their last stand if the armies of the Blue came here in force.

She wondered who she would find in the basement. Some poor outlander no doubt.

Inside two soldiers sat; they gave her a salute.

"Prisoner?"

"Two of them, downstairs."

"Two?" The nearer of the two guards nodded.

"A woman and an old man."

"Which do they say is the spy?"

"The woman," said the other guard. "The old man is a vagrant." She nodded.

"I'll be downstairs, come if I shout. Come if it sounds too quiet."

The prison room was surprisingly bright, light holes had been cut into the wall to let the sun in. The heat was oppressive, the smell of the buckets given to the prisoners as latrines powerful. She ignored it, she'd smelled much worse. She made a mental note to have the light holes filled with rubble. Someone could get in, or pour burning oil through them and bring the building down in flames.

The prisoners were asleep, or pretending to be. Their beds had once been next to each other, separated by bars – she could see old marks on the floor – but they had been moved as far away from each other as was possible in the cells. There was not much else in the room. A desk, a chair and a long stick, tapered at both ends, leaning against the wall. She smiled to herself, walked over and picked it up. The smooth wood was weighty, at the centre notches had been cut into it.

"Forestbow," she said to herself and put it back.

"Few recognise that, Rai." The words were quiet, but said with venom. Dassit turned to find the woman sat up on her bed, her clothes the green of new fields, her face discoloured by old bruises.

"I am not Rai," said Dassit. She picked up the bowstaff again. "I've never seen an unbroken one of these before." It was beautiful, in its own way. And lethal.

"Few Rai live to say they've seen one at all." Dassit let out a short laugh, little humour in it as the woman stood, she was in pain and had to lean against the wooden bars.

"I was on a patrol, sent to escort two Rai near a Jinneng village called Murtast." She carefully put the bow back and picked up the quiver of arrows from under the desk.

"Forestals had been attacking, taking willwood from the Treefall site. These bows did a lot of damage but we fought them off in the end. Soldiers found one of the Forestals wounded." She put the arrows down. "They impaled him on his bow. Broke it in the process." The woman stared at her from her cell.

"Is that what you will do to me?" Dassit shook her head.

"Not my way. Death should be quick. A knife to the throat, a rope round the neck."

"So that is what you will do to me?" Dassit laughed again, more real this time. The woman sounded entirely unconcerned, conversational even.

"No, at least not yet." She walked over to the cage. "I am curious to what a Forestal is doing here, and having fought some of you in the past, even more curious as to how the fools that run this place subdued you. They are hardly warriors." The woman behind the bars only stared at her. "Do you have a name? Mine is Dassit." She did not really expect an answer.

"You are very polite for a servant of the Rai, Dassit." The Forestal cocked her head to one side.

"Why are you here, Forestal?"

"To die, of course. Just like we all are. Her, me, and you." This from the old man, he had sat up on his bed, a halo of frizzy white hair around his skull. At his voice the Forestal sneered, she tried to hide it but failed. More going on here than it appears thought Dassit. She hated a mystery. Mysteries got you killed. "My name is Fandrai," said the old man. "I am not as impolite as the Forestal." The old man laughed to himself and the Forestal turned from him.

"Why would you say we are here to die?" asked Dassit.

"The paint on your armour," he said, "tells me you're a trunk commander. Probably at least two branches under you from the noise outside."

"You seem to know a lot, old man, are you a soldier?"

"I've fought," he said. Grinned at her, showing his teeth

were painted black, some filed into points. No clan paint on him. "That many troops must just be passing through, I thought. But you haven't passed, which means you're here to defend this place." The Forestal made a noise, a mixture of a laugh and a grunt.

"You must have really upset someone if you're meant to defend here," she said, "the old man is right. You've been sent to die." It annoyed her that it was so obvious, even to a Forestal.

"I believe you have still not explained how you come to be here, Forestal." The woman stared at her, turned away and sat down on her cot.

"We are not only bandits, Trunk Dassit," she said softly. "We are also traders."

"Traders of what you have stolen." The Forestal turned back to her.

"Isn't everything in our land stolen from someone?" she said. The old man laughed.

"She's got you there, soldier. She's got you there." The Forestal ignored him and continued talking.

"Fin-Larger is famed for its flour. The finest bread in all Crua, I am told. I was sent to find out what price they wanted for it."

"I know the Forestals trade," said Dassit, "but they don't usually come to do it with a bow and looking, well, as much like a Forestal as you do."

"I mis-calculated," said the woman. "Did not think rich and comfortable townspeople would even know what I was." The old man watched them both, bright-eyed and amused. Dassit stepped closer to the bars.

"I do not know, Forestal," she said, "whether to think you are stupid, or whether you think I am?" The Forestal did not reply. "How were you were subdued by a bunch of old people and children?"

"I slipped and fell, hit my head. When I came to I was bound and they were beating me."

"Even so . . ."

"And I am a little past my prime, though it kills me to say so." Dassit stared at her; now she had mentioned it Dassit saw that, beneath the make-up and the bruises, the woman was far older than she had first assumed. Older than Dassit, but not as old as the man.

"You're lying to me," she said. "And much as I have nothing against you personally, I may have to fight a war here, and I have no time for mysteries that may bite me from behind when I least expect it." She turned away from her and to the old man. "What's your story?" Beneath his white hair she could see tattoos, strange lines and shapes weaving across his skull beneath flaking white make-up.

"Just an old man, Rai," he said, looking at the floor, "looking for somewhere to beg, and a dry place to sleep." The Forestal snorted, a derisive sound. Dassit let out a breath.

"You're both lying to me," said Dassit, "so you'll both hang today." With that she turned, walking towards the door.

"I can help you!" She stopped. The old man had called out and she turned back to his cell. He stood with his hands on the bars, his long dirty robe covering his feet. "You have a fight coming, and I can help. I am a healer." She stared at him. A healer she could use but she had no reason to believe him.

"Don't listen to him," said the Forestal, her voice dead, "and don't hang him either. Spear him in his cell but make sure you don't get too close." Dassit closed her eyes, rubbed her forehead.

"I do not have time for this. I was of half a mind simply to set you both on your way." She looked from one to the other. "Either tell me the truth or the next voice you hear will be my executioner." She didn't have one, but Vir would gladly step up.

"He is a criminal," said the Forestal, nodding towards the old man.

"I have paid my price," he said, there was bitterness and

pain in his voice. "All has been taken from me." Something in him changed as he spoke. A darkness on his face, a personality he had hidden behind the laughter emerging.

"Explain," said Dassit. The old man sat down heavily, as though his strength abruptly fled. The Forestal stood.

"Have you ever heard the name 'Hirsal-Who-Is-In-The-Shadows'?" Dassit shook her head.

"Sounds like some grove god; I heard the new Cowl-Rai has been eradicating them. We still have them in the south, but there are far too many to know them all. My family followed Yua-Who-Brings-Bread and I swear we were the only ones." No reaction to her joke from the Forestal.

"Even among the myriad forest gods," said the Forestal, "Hirsal was mostly unknown. They had a grove right in Wyrdwood, hidden in the depths and none knew of it."

"A hundred other gods do," said Dassit.

"Hirsal is a god of murder," said the Forestal.

"Death is necessary." The old man bit the words out, as though compelled to. When she looked over at him he had his head in his hands, staring at the floor. When he spoke there was a desperation there. "Without death there is no life. The bodies decay, the great canopy breaks them down and they rise anew. In Hirsal's name the swarden rise and—"

"Shut up, old man," said the Forestal, her tongue sharp with anger. "Bleat about the circle of life all you wish but you murdered families, you murdered innocent travellers, you killed for the pleasure of it."

"No!" he stood. "Never for pleasure." There was a power in his words then, anger. Dassit no longer felt he was a foolish old man. "It was for the balance of life and death."

"Put two monks together and let them name a god and they try to raise a Cowl-Rai." The Forestal looked across at the old man. "He is Hirsal's."

Dassit felt fear then. The same gut-churning fear as when she stood in the spearline, watching the enemy advance. She took a deep breath, swallowed. Wished she had a weapon in her hand. "Why is he still in there?" She pointed at the cage. "Even a normal Rai wouldn't be held by that cell, they would burn through the bars."

"Something happened to him," said the Forestal. "Maybe he is weak now, I do not know. We found his grove, wiped them out."

"And you call me a murderer," spat the old man.

"You had been preying on us for centuries." Anger like the first flash of lightning in a storm. "And what we did was not murder, it was a battle. One that you ran from like a coward."

"That is why you are here then?" said Dassit. "You were chasing him." The Forestal nodded.

"Kill him, now. Before whatever has made him weak and unable to access his cowl wears off." The old man sighed – it was the sound of a true ancient, like it came from the depths of somewhere dry and desiccated.

"Think what you want of what we believe. Lie to yourself about the inevitability of death if you must, but do not call me a coward." He stood. Dassit reached for a sword she was not wearing. "Something is wrong in Crua, death itself is corrupted. Had you come across us any other time, Forestal, every one of my people would still live to worship in blood. To feed the mother forest. The fungus beneath your feet would have reached out and rotted you where you stood. I have lived two hundred years, seen Cowl-Rai die, and Cowl-Rai rise." To Dassit, it was like the room shook, she expected dust to rain down, and brick and shattered wood to follow.

It did not.

The old man sat. The feeling of power ebbed away. "My power is in death, the strongest and most inevitable of all of Iftal's gifts. But to touch it now will destroy me. I am reduced to being just a man." He turned to Dassit. "But I meant what I said, Trunk Commander, to destroy a body you must know it. And I know all the secrets of the flesh. I will heal your warriors."

She was about to answer when a horn blew outside. The alarm. Dassit made to leave; if the cages had held them this long they would continue to hold them.

"Tanhir," shouted the Forestal; Dassit stopped at the door, turned. "My name is Tanhir." Dassit gave her a nod.

Outside she found Vir waiting.

"The Blue are here?" she said. He shook his head.

"Not yet. It's the Army of Rai Dealish, they have sent a messenger to us. The enemy have been spotted. They go to intercept them." She took Vir over to one of the remaining wall towers to watch the tail of Dealish's army. Over a thousand troops, far more than she had been told he would get, palanquins carrying the Rai, siege engines being pulled by crownheads.

"Wish we had a catapult," said Vir. "I like a catapult."

"Don't know why he has them, he's meant to be mobile." She shook her head; the catapults would be more use here. "He's not leaving anyone or -thing behind to help us fortify this place then?" Vir shook his head.

"Messenger barely stayed long enough to deliver the message." She shook her head, then turned away from the army and handed Vir her map of the town.

"Anything marked with an X, bring it down. I want spikes all along whatever walls we can make. Firebreaks within the town. If there's enough wood you can even build yourself a catapult." He laughed. She wanted to, but it wouldn't come.

"You all right, Trunk?" he asked, a line of worry on his forehead. "You seem distracted."

"Just something the prisoners said."

"Don't worry about it." He spat and coughed, the dust of Fin-Larger got everywhere. "People like that never tell the truth." She turned back to watch the army as it moved away, hoping that Vir was right because the words of the old man, they frightened her in a way nothing else had in her life.

Death itself is corrupted.

And the land shook beneath their feet.

27
Cahan

It was difficult for Cahan to understand what he looked at. He knew that the cloudtrees were giants, the greatest living things on Crua. He'd walked around the base of them and looked into canopies like vast roofs, seen them from a distance vanishing into the clouds: an immovable wall against the circle winds. But here, staring from the cover of bushes at the trunk of a fallen forest god his mind rebelled at the size of it.

They had found a place where the land undulated, creating a great crest above the fallen tree. It was hard not to think of these undulations as a shockwave, a ripple of the land frozen in time, an eternal scar on the forest, a hard reminder of the moment a forest god fell.

There were no branches on the trunk, not at this point. Only the trunk, heading away in either direction as far as he could see, bathed in the Light Above as there was no canopy here to shade it; the giant tree had brought everything down, crushed all in its path.

It was good to feel the light on his skin. Just like it had felt good to be touched, to be held by Furin back in New Harnwood. His mind wandered away to thoughts of Furin.

He was not poison, not to her. He wanted all of this over, wanted what was in him gone, wanted to be back in New Harnwood with her.

He tried to distract himself by estimating the width of the trunk, the height of it. The tallest thing he had ever seen was the central spire of Tiltspire, that was long ago but he thought the width of the trunk may be even taller. How could a living thing grow so vast? It made his head ache to think of it.

People swarmed over the cloudtree, hundreds of them on a slowly growing scaffold. The clearing around Treefall rang with voices and the sound of hammering. Some were building the scaffold, others worked on the trunk below them using long tools. It looked to Cahan as if they were scraping at the thick, whorled bark. Further up another group were using axes to cut into a huge bracket fungus. Away from the trunk a camp had grown: tents and a few houses of wood. There were soldiers too, a lot of them. Standing about with spear and shield. Fires burned in the camps, and the air was bitter with the scent of woodsmoke. He saw a gasmaw cage with about fifty of the creatures crammed into it, by that was another cage, full of bladderweed and floatvine. Both weed and gasmaws were being used to lift people and materials up the scaffolding.

"What are they doing?" asked Venn from behind him. Cahan expected Tall Sera to shush the trion, but the Forestal did not.

"Starting the harvest of it," the Forestal whispered. "The platform fungus you see them working on over there?" Tall Sera crept a little closer, crouching between Cahan and Venn, pointing at the clearing. "Valuable. The material of the outer skin can be split into many layers, good for armour. I wear it," he tapped his chest, something hard beneath the cloak, "soft, pliable enough for movement but will stop most spear strikes. The skin of the fungus is as thick as I am tall. Beneath the skin is the flesh; the first lengths of it, they are not much good for anything. We use it in the walls of buildings as it keeps the heat in and the cold out. Beneath that is the real value."

"What is that?" asked Venn.

"The heart, it is good to eat. So good it's unlikely you've ever tasted it, only the Rai get to eat it." Tall Sera smiled. "And the Forestals of course."

"They are not all working on the fungus," said Venn.

"No, some will be harvesting willwood vine."

"I thought it was a tree," said Cahan.

"The vines on cloudtrees are thicker than any forest tree." Tall Sera pointed. "See what looks like black veins on the bark?" Venn nodded. "That is willwood, dangerous work harvesting it as it resists." As if the wood heard him, a scream rang out and a body fell from the scaffold, landing with a crash. Tall Sera nodded, more to himself than anything. "As I said, it resists. The forest will have its price."

"I have heard it scars the hands of the carvers," said Venn.

"It will kill them, given the chance, but with skill they can create miracles." He held up a hand to show that the third and fourth finger on his drawing hand were willwood. He turned away, looked down into the camp and was about to say more when the land trembled, a low moan of the earth, the complaint of rock against rock, the shivering of the great trees. The scaffold below shook – people grabbed hold of the uprights, clinging on as their aerial world swayed. Some fell but were tied on with long vines and remained, swaying like pendulums and shouting for help if they were lucky, screaming out in pain if they were not.

"It pains the land to lose such a giant as cloudtree," said Tall Sera. "It complains."

"We cannot attack here," said Cahan, and despite the tremor he did not take his eyes from the soldiers.

"Why not?" This from the Reborn; he had almost forgotten they were there.

"Because there must be five hundred or more down there, and some of us can die." Cahan's eyes never rested on one place for long, his gaze moving, searching.

"And the same amount on the other side," said Tall Sera, calmly. "Orits nest in the platform fungus. They drive them off with smoke, kill as many as they can but they always come back, and with other orits. They are drawn to their own dead. So they need an army to protect the workers. And the swarden come too, that is what the fires are for."

"They fear fire?" said Venn.

"Swarden do not fear anything." He lifted up his hand, showed his willwood fingers. "As I know. But fire burns away the grass that powers them. Then they burn the bones."

"That kills them?"

"There are always more swarden," said Tall Sera quietly. "But you are right, we cannot attack the camp. Now look down there." He nodded with his head towards one of the clumps of tents. Cahan tore his eyes away from the soldiers, still unsure why he was so fascinated with them. They were only standing around on guard. There was no sense of danger up here on the ridge as he, Venn and the Forestals were well hidden. He looked where Tall Sera pointed: near a fire were a number of rafts, suspended from vacant-looking gasmaw, their huge eyes blind and lacking intelligence, the tentacles around their beaks aimlessly searching the air and the gasbags behind the heads looked sickly, deflated. So different to the quick, and sometimes vicious, wild gasmaw of the forest. A rafter was pushing bladderweed and floatvine beneath a raft to balance out the weight of new cargo as it was added.

"Soon," said Tall Sera, "they will take those carts into Wyrdwood. Farmed maws don't last long, and they have to stop and gather floatvine from the trees. Right now the main track is not finished. There is plenty of Wyrdwood and Harnwood to hide us."

"We will ambush it?" Tall Sera nodded.

"It will get harder later," he said, "when they have the tracks finished, guard posts set up. This is the best time for it, we will give back to the forest what belongs to the forest and may the Boughry look away from us as we do."

"How do you know?" Cahan turned – Venn was studying Tall Sera, their face a picture of puzzlement as they spoke. "There has been no treefall in the north for hundreds of years. How do you know how all of this works?"

"Forestals travel, Trion. We have seen Treefall in the south. How it is processed." He moved back, keeping low, pushing branches out of the way slowly so the foliage did not shudder and attract attention. They followed, Cahan the last to leave. His eyes still searching the camp for something. His guts burning as if with acid. It was only as he stepped back that he realised what he was looking for and it struck him with the force of a hammer blow. He searched for her, for Sorha. Looking for a flash of red hair, a certain walk, elaborate armour, a beautiful sword and the foul stench of the Hetton about her. She must have been in the back of his head ever since Harn. He should have taken for granted that she died there, with the rest of the Rai's forces, but he could not. Something within him would not let him believe that and somewhere inside he knew at any moment his strength could fall away, his ability to sense the world around him vanish as she appeared, sword in hand and a burning need for vengeance in her eye.

He felt vulnerable and it was not a feeling he was used to, and for the first time in his life there was another, someone in his life. He did not want to die so soon after finding Furin.

As if in answer to his vulnerability he felt the presence of bluevein in the earth, reaching for him, as if he called to it. A need threatening to engulf him, it became a yawning void and within that void the power of death called to him. Offered him strength but at a cost he was unwilling to pay, not only the natural process of death there, it carried corruption with it. He found himself longing to hear a voice he had pushed away for most of his life. His cowl.

I need you.

But he did not.

28
Udinny

Oh, to fly through the sky on the back of a crownhead, to weave between golden trees, to dance over golden streams, to blast across a fractured land of the imagination, to feel the wind in your hair and for none of these things to be real.

What a strange life it is to be Udinny.

Syerfu, my loyal crownhead, moves at speeds unimaginable and has no foolish affection for sensible things such as ground and the rightful place of a crownhead upon it. She leaps, great and glorious leaps, goes faster than any message skipper could even dream. In my left hand I hold the walknut, in the right the needle grown into a great spear and I feel as strong and powerful as the warrior I have never been.

But one cannot simply bound about in glory for ever, no, I am on a mission for a god.

We land, coming to rest upon a hill of glowing green. Ever since Ranya showed me this world it is no longer dark, though it is not as real as actual land for living people. No, not at all. It feels as if the land coalesces around me, as if I travel through a landscape beyond my understanding in a bubble of my perception that makes the land change and become something I can understand. Even the distances, the huge distances I can see, they – and I appreciate how difficult this is to understand – only seem to exist when I am looking at them. I never remember them not being there, but I feel sure that, without my concentration, they do not exist.

A strange life and a strange world for Udinny Pathfinder.

This world is not solid, like the land of the living. Instead it is a world constructed of Ranya's web, sketched in lines, with spaces between them and it is bizarre, but my mind fills in the spaces and I see the land for what it is. A tree, a hill, a building, a person and the lines I barely even notice now. What is bizarre quickly becomes normal when there is no normal to measure it against.

Ranya's needle burns with golden light in my hand, the walknut pulls me forward with great energy and Syerfu leaps again. We arc through the air, we transition from one place to another and it is the most joyful feeling. If this is death then it is far greater than life. It is exhilarating.

But what is my purpose? A god brought me here and gifted me with three great gifts, and a phrase in my mind. "The pillars of Iftal." Which sounded very important, though I was not quite sure what the pillars of Iftal were.

I did begin to think, or maybe one of the hundreds of thousands of other Udinnys that hangs around in the periphery of my vision thought, that bounding from hill to hill is all well and good and the most wondrous and exciting adventure, but it is not exactly useful. I let Syerfu rest, she bleats in a good natured manner. I holster my spear-needle and once more it shrinks to something tiny. I hold up the walknut.

Where should I go?

If I expected some great revelation, or some instruction I was to be disappointed. It did not arrive. But to be fair, even though the nut was a gift put into my hand by a god, it is still only a nut.

Syerfu bleats at me.

"You are right, perhaps I expected too much of it, Syerfu. We cannot all be as clever as you." The crownhead nodded her whole head and neck enthusiastically. Then shook it, making the rings in her ears jingle. "Maybe I should ask it in more detail?" Syerfu had little to say about that. I wondered what the best way to address a nut was. "Left?" I said, and made ready to throw it but before I did I felt a pull, a definite pull towards the left and it became stronger until I turned my whole body. Then it stopped. I waited, wondered. "Right?" The same again. I did not need to throw this walknut for it to show me direction, it was far stronger than a normal one. Clearly, a nut given by a god is better than the one given by a forest outlaw, and this nut seemed to react to me. But what did I want from it? What did I really want?

A wave of sadness rolled over me.

What did I want?

"Walknut," I say softly. "Take me to Cahan Du-Nahere."

The pull was strong, fierce. Syerfu reacts to it, calling out, holding her head up, opening her mouth and shouting into the world. We moved. A great leap, a blur, landing in a wooded glade. A great leap, a blur. Landing in a spire city at market time, ghostly figures move around us. A great leap, a blur. Landing in the middle of a plain with grasses waving, the broken walls of a larger above us. A great leap, a blur. Landing in the forest.

Wyrdwood.

Deep in the forest.

Cloudtrees, vast pillars of gold, something flows down through them and into the below of the land. I had not thought about the below. Could I go there? Could I walk unseen among the Osere? Or would they see me?

Ranya had spoken of others.

Interesting.

Figures, moving through the brush, tore me from these

thoughts. Two were strange, true ghosts. There and not there and yet it felt as though something hovered above them. Some thread that went into a world hidden from me, a realm beyond this?

The Reborn? It must be. Did that thread link them to the Star Path? Or the land of the Cowl Star at the end of it? I did not know, could not know.

The other figures. Something within them, a different brightness and as they moved it touched the lines of power around them, as if assisting their movement, pulling them, steadying them, checking for them. Cowls. I found Venn, recognised the hesitancy, and the curiosity. Their cowl reached for more, tested everything. The others, I did not know who they were, Forestals? I had seen them do things in Harn that spoke of cowls.

But the last figure, oh, I knew him. Larger than the others, walking with an unmistakeable gait, a weariness but also with a determination to continue that would not be denied. I slip off Syerfu's saddle and leave her to graze on unreal grass so I can walk with Cahan. Nearer, I see he is different in other ways, his cowl brighter but within him, something else. Something the rest did not have. A blue glow, a faint web of it, sitting within and to see it is to shiver. The needle in its pouch dances and rattles, Syerfu cries out.

"Oh, Cahan, what is wrong?" I reach out to him, foolish, for I is not there and he is not here. My hand simply passes through him as he doggedly continues on his path. He stops. Pauses. Glances over his shoulder and I can imagine him shaking his shaggy great head and brushing off whatever he feels as a fancy, a side effect of walking in Wyrdwood where there is always danger.

Cahan continues on and I watch him go.

How could this be? I was the servant of a god, but if those I cared for, my friends, were in some sort of trouble, I could not help.

Though, Cahan, he had felt something, Maybe there was a—

Syerfu bleats and butts me gently.

"You are right, Syerfu, I have something important but also oddly nebulous to do. Maybe by doing that, I can help him." I pointed at the ghostly figures as they pushed on, then mounted up. Held the walknut above me.

"Take me where I need to go." An explosion in my palm. A beam of light streaking out before me. I felt warmth within and with a cry, Syerfu leaps once more into the air and we streaked across the un-sky of this un-place, about the business of gods.

29
Ont

The arrow fell, twisting in flight. Ont imagined the fletching, wind rushing over it, and the head of fire-hardened wood streaking towards the target. This time.

But it was not.

"Anjiin's ruins, missed." He laughed to himself. Segur, Cahan's garaur, sneezed in commiseration from where it lay by his leg. One day he would hit the target. One day but not today. He had the distance now, the Forestal had been right about that. If anything he had too much distance. He shook his head and picked up the bag of arrows – no, the quiver. Ania called it a quiver. All these new words that had come into his life. He unstrung the bow, removed the tension from the shaft and put the string into his pouch. He slipped Segur a little dried meat and hoped no arrows had broken in the loosing: he had little to trade for more and felt an odd guilt when people gave out of generosity. They had a new community here, new ways and the wooden coins and splinters of Crua were of no use in New Harnwood. The people traded by barter, the trappers and hunters had skins and meat. Guan, the new butcher, would soon have cured raniri meat. A thing he had showed her how to do.

The spinners and the menders and the tailors, the fletchers, the weapon makers. They all had things to barter.

But not him.

He offered his brute strength for labour, though most of that was done now. The village was built. Walls put up around it. Ditches dug around them. Plenty of his sweat had gone into that but now he had no work. Not yet harvest, the time for planting past. All was done and he had little choice but to rely on the generosity of the village. Every morning he woke to find food left out for him. A kindness, and he did not know by who. He never looked for who brought it and never asked. He spent his days brushing out the shrine, keeping it clean. Talked with any who would come; often he was helped by the Leoric's boy, Issofur, who some found strange now, no longer quite one of the people since he had been foreststruck, but still so obviously a child. Ont found him comforting – though the boy had not been here for a while. Odd in itself. Every eightday Ont walked into New Harnwood and spoke of Ranya, of the forest, of the path and of the gentle way, as he had begun to call it. Move through life as you move through the forest, softly, breaking as few branches as you can.

He had the distinct feeling there was a better way of putting that. He would work on it.

He loved his new life, but it left him with little to trade and these arrows were a luxury. The village kept a communal supply for morning practice, which he joined every day, but he had found he preferred a longer arrow to the rest of the villagers. His draw was longer than most. Those arrows had to be made specially for him, no one else had the draw he had. The fletcher, Ilda, always made a few but she had the village to supply as well, so his arrows were precious.

"Come on then, Segur," he said to the garaur. It stood, making a happy hissing noise. "Let us see how many arrows survived the flight." He walked through Woodedge; odd he often thought, to discover that Wyrdwood had woods within the greater wood. He recognised some of the plants and trees from Harn's Woodedge, though they were much smaller there. Maybe everything grew larger in Wyrdwood. He did not know.

That odd feeling of being watched would not leave him. An itch between his shoulders.

Segur streaking ahead, knowing from weeks of this where to go. What to do – which was not to try and retrieve the arrows. The garaur had proved too excitable to do this safely and more often than not chewed them in two. So now Segur knew not to pick up the arrows, though it had become excellent at finding them, then it stood above the wooden shaft, whining and drooling until he gave it a treat.

In the bushes behind his tree he followed the sound of the garaur and found his first arrow.

"Broken, Segur," he said, "we are down to eight now."

He had shot a total of five of his nine arrows, and after searching, two more were broken and, most annoyingly, one was lost. Neither him nor Segur could find the final arrow no matter how much they looked. He had found this, sometimes arrows simply vanished. He smiled. It was not lost on him that his arrows were just the right size for a shyun spear, he did not begrudge the forest children for taking them.

"Monk!" A shout from the clearing.

"I am here, one moment. I am retrieving my arrows." He pushed his way through the foliage and back to the clearing. Ania stood before the grove dressed, as ever, like a living bit of Wyrdwood. Part of it, in a way he never would be.

"You have found your range then," she said.

"Aye, and one day I may even hit my target." He lifted his two found arrows. "If I do not run out of arrows first. Maybe Ilda has some more for me but she has much to do. I do not like to ask." The Forestal walked over and took one of his arrows. Segur growled and bounded away, it was wary of the Forestal but Ont was glad she was here, he liked her company, gruff as she was, and he had questions for her.

"They are longer than the ones you used before," she said. He nodded.

"I draw the bow further." She studied the arrow.

"Any longer than this and they will flex too much, not fly as well."

"Oh," he said. "I did not know."

"You need a stiffer bow, but these arrows are a good length for you." She pushed her cloak back, at her hip she wore three quivers in a clever arrangement of belts so they did not impede movement. From the bottom one she drew half the arrows. "Here, have these, ten there are, not quite as long as yours but they should do you."

"Thank you, Ania." He took the arrows and placed them carefully with his others, picked up his quiver. "I have to ask something, and hope not to offend."

"Ask," she said, and he wished he could see her eyes below the hood.

"Have any of your people been in my grove, at night when I am not there?" She was barely moving, and he was sure her eyes skewered him from beneath the shade of her cape. "I do not mind, the grove is for all. It is just, things have been moved, and it bothered me, that and . . ."

"And?" she said.

"I have a strange feeling there is something out there in the forest," he said. "I cannot shake it."

"There is always something out there in the forest," she said softly.

"True," he tried to laugh. But giving voice to his feelings had not lessened his worry, If anything he felt it more and in her reply he found no comfort. It was almost like she attempted to deflect him.

"It may be," she said, "that my people come to the grove in the night. It is a good place. A comforting place."

"You lead them?" he said. He had not meant to. Did not know why that had come out and more words fell from his mouth in a rush. "It is hard to be a leader, I know. People come to my grove to speak. If you ever need to speak then . . . I keep many secrets and . . ." He let the words tail off. What was he thinking? She was like a female Cahan, gruff, hard. Happy to advise but he could no more imagine Cahan sharing of himself than he could imagine a gasmaw talking. It was the same for Ania. She did not move, not at first. Then she shrugged, walked towards his house. Sat on the tree stump he used to cut wood. He followed. Sat by her on the step before the doorway. "Two of my people vanished recently." She did not sound like Ania then, she sounded like someone letting out a great pressure from within. "I have checked the golwyrd pits, I have looked for signs of spearmaws, though my people would not be surprised by spearmaws and they rarely attack us. My people should fall to very little of this forest." She took a deep breath, and Ont found himself surprised she shared anything with him. "They may have been surprised by something else. I am a good tracker, but I found no sign. I brought in more trackers. And I brought in more of my people."

"Is it them I sense in the forest?" She stared at him.

"Does it feel like Forestals?" She pushed back her hood, her eyes locked on him while he thought on that. Slowly, he shook his head.

"It does not. Another thing – small, but odd. The boy, Issofur, the Leoric's son. He has not been to see me recently. Usually he cannot be kept away." Ania took a slow deep breath and her gaze returned to his Woodedge.

"The boy was foreststruck, he is attuned to this place like few others."

"You think something is out there?" said Ont. "or someone is out there?" he looked out into Wyrdwood, unquiet within.

"I am sorry," she stood. "I should not burden you with my worries. It may well be nothing."

"I have wide shoulders," he said. She bowed her head, he heard her expel a breath. She placed a hand on his shoulder.

"Thank you, Ont." Ania looked up and out, past him. "It is not so strange, to lose people. That is a truth of living in Wyrdwood. The forest takes its due and sometimes it is never explained. It is simply Wyrdwood; the Boughry take what the Boughry take, may they always look away from you."

"That is what you think has happened?" He unwound a little within.

"Most likely," she said, "our cowls, they are not like the thing within Cahan. The power is not as strong. But I sense the forest."

"And you do not sense anyone out there? Anyone who wants to hurt us?"

"I reach out for the forest, Ont, and I sense nothing."

"And that is how it always is?" He expected a nod, a reassurance. Instead her eyes widened and she looked stricken, like she had been confronted with a truth as horrific as it was obvious.

"No," she said, "it is not."

And that was when the screaming started.

30
Sorha

She hated.

She hated them all and she had worked on that hate all the way from Harnspire to the Treefall site. They had left her in her cell until she was sure she was to die. Then the man, Laha, had taken her out, given her armour and put her under the command of a Rai named Sco Tak-Arndew. She had treated Sorha with such obvious revulsion Sorha wished to do nothing more than run the woman through on the spot.

But she did not. She listened, she meekly put herself at the back of the column with ten Hetton, caged on rafts, and the rear guard and baggage train. She walked and she seethed and she planned.

Odd, she thought, that once she had felt so much of the world, once her cowl had been constantly testing the environment about her, telling her about people, about things, about what was there. Now that was gone. Unless she concentrated she walked in a bubble, completely alone, even the voices of the people around her vanished, the colours of the land began to blur. She was truly apart from the world.

It was his fault.

Cahan Du-Nahere. Three times he had escaped her. Three. He would not again. The advantage was hers now. She knew where he was. He would not expect her. He would never know she was coming until it was too late.

Or would he?

He could feel the forest, like she had once been able to feel those around her. So could the trion – oh, a knife in that one's gut would be a pleasure. But that was the only rule Laha had given her. She must not kill the trion. The trion must be kept safe. The monk had said it many times as he watched her put on her armour, like he thought she could not remember a simple order. Even stopping her as she left the room.

"If the trion dies, so do you."

Her sword at her hip, she had almost drawn on him. But she did not. Partly because she wanted Cahan too much, but also, and this she was only aware of afterwards, something that crept up on her fingerbreadths through the night – the monk disquieted her. She was not used to such a feeling, she did not like it or accept it. Instead she buried it deep within and told herself it was anger.

While she walked with the column she tested herself: how far did this bubble where Rai power died reach from her? How near did she have to get to Rai to affect them? Each day she concentrated on where she thought it stopped. Imagined pushing it out, just like she would have done with the awareness of her cowl. Did it move? She was not sure.

In the third week of the walk, one of the Rai, a young one she did not know the name of, came to the back of the column. She watched them pass the dullers on the carts. Saw them grimace as their power winked out, then smile when they passed out of their influence. The Rai walked with one of the rafters with the supply train. Sorha was not near enough to know what they talked of, but they talked for a long time and the rafter pointed up into the trees more than once. Probably discussing harvests of floatvine to keep the rafts up, they had not brought any gasmaws. Maybe they planned to farm them at the site, she did not know. Did not care. What she cared about was the Rai.

She walked forward to a point where she knew the Rai would not be affected by her, but was not too far from the edge of her power. Then she concentrated on pushing the imaginary line of her own dulling field out. Nothing, not at first.

She kept trying, and was rewarded by the Rai missing a step, almost falling, looking round in confusion, and she slipped behind a knot of soldiers to remain unseen. The next day the Rai was back, and she tried the same thing from further back. And each day this was repeated as the Rai came to get reports on floatweed for those above them. Sorha waiting for the look of comical confusion, smiling to herself.

This was good.

This was useful.

This was power in a way – oh, not throwing fire or drowning of people in water pulled from the air, this was the power of the shadows and if she could have nothing else she would take that.

By the time they were approaching Treefall she was sure she could hide herself and her Hetton from anyone who was not looking at them. She asked permission of the Rai to leave and scout the area. Was granted it, she was sure they felt relief that she was going.

She took her Hetton, which she despised as much as the Rai, maybe more, and travelled towards the village in Wyrdwood. Something in her swelling as she did, not joy, or relief. A new emotion she was unfamiliar with, maybe a sense of completion. Was that it? A feeling this would be an end to it. She would kill Cahan Du-Nahere. Maybe even kill the trion despite Laha's threats, though she was not sure the Hetton would accept that. They accepted her commands, but this was because they thought her in service of the Cowl-Rai. If she tried to go against their standing orders then the Hetton were not like soldiers who could be suborned by fear or bribery. They were animals, following instinct and that instinct was to submit to the most powerful, the Cowl-Rai. Or Laha, their representative here.

The Hetton were poor company on the long journey to the Wyrdwood village, but Sorha did not mind poor company, she preferred to plan and seethe within herself. Hetton were easy like that; they followed, they acted on her will. She liked that sense of control, though she liked their constant whispering less; they sounded like wind slithering through tree branches. She knew most were revolted by them but they did not really affect her, only their voices made her skin itch and they could not be told to be quiet. They spoke to each other constantly, it was part of them. The volume might go up and down depending on the situation, but the noise never stopped.

At least it kept the forest creatures away; even the small, flying biting things avoided the Hetton. They were inimical to nature. It would not have shocked her to see their footsteps marked out in dead grass. That did not happen, the grass only bent and sprung back as it did with any other. The only real strangeness she noticed was how attracted they were to fungus – sometimes one would stop, staring intently at the ground and she would go over to look to find a small patch of mushrooms growing on something dead, more often than not thick with bluevein. They would also stop to stare at huge bracket fungus growing on the cloudwoods, or put a hand on the spongy trunks of the tall shadecaps that sprouted everywhere at this time of year, pale and flake-skinned like the Hetton, though the gills beneath their caps were a bright and livid red, like blood. The Hetton never stopped for long but they did stop and Sorha folded that bit of knowledge away, in case it was ever of use.

The Hetton needed no rest and she did not need much either. The explosive colourful illumination of Wyrdwood at night gave them enough light to see by. Not quite enough it turned out: one of the Hetton fell into a golwyrd pit, mewing piteously as it lay impaled on the spikes. Its companions only stared down at it.

"Pull it out," she told them and they did – it screamed as they were not gentle, and that was how Sorha found out golwyrd spikes grew barbs when they snared pray. Half the Hetton's innards were left behind. It continued to mewl and hiss as they lay it on the ground. Where the spikes had entered it looked burned, another thing Sorha mentally marked down. The wounded Hetton's companions stared at it and Sorha knew that even a Rai would not survive such injuries. "End its pain," she told the lead Hetton and it nodded, taking its spear and striking through the head of its injured comrade. If it felt anything at such an act Sorha could not tell.

After that she used a stick to test the ground before her when they walked at night.

She heard the new village before she saw it. Had the Hetton move away so she could scout it alone.

They had built a wall, not much of one, but they had also built on a slight hill, and dug a pit around it. Rudimentary but effective. Well, effective if they were not fools and not overly confident. They had left both gates open and people wandered in and out at will. Hunters went into the forest, farmers went out to the fields they had created around their village. A tanner had pits right on the edge of their clearing. A few gasmaws hung in nets outside the walls. They were living life as if they were not fugitives, as if they believed the Rai of Tiltspire would simply leave them alone for their crimes. As if they would put up with the insult done to them by these commoners.

Sorha spat into the grass. Then found a place in a tree where she could watch and remain hidden by foliage.

They did not do much.

They practised with their weapons, they went about their lives. But she did not care about them. She cared about him. The false Cowl-Rai.

And she could not find him.

She saw Forestals come and go. Staying mostly hidden from the villagers but plainly keeping watch, patrolling the forest. At one point they went right below her tree but they did not notice her, she was invisible. Sorha spent a day and a night in that tree, expecting the forester to return in the evening, maybe he hunted.

But he did not appear.

Had he sensed her?

No, she was sure he could not. If he had been able to sense her she would have died when he raised the forest in Harn, along with all the others.

She followed the butcher, Ont, one of the worst traitors, to his place in the forest. What he did there she had no idea but she did not trust it. Strange forest creatures kept watch on him and she stayed well back, but marked his place. She would have the butcher.

Three more days she waited. Three days when she saw nothing.

That was when she decided to take a Forestal. She could have taken a villager, easier to take a villager, but she remembered the Forestals from the battle, how deadly and accurate their arrows were. There was a score to settle there. For two days she followed their patrols. Marking out the furthest points they went from the village. Noting how relaxed they were, listening to them. Both them and the villagers considered themselves safe. Thought the village well-hidden, and that any attack would come from an army they would hear coming long before they saw them.

Fools. So sure of themselves.

The Hetton took the Forestals quickly and easily, rising from the foliage. Too close for the cowards' bows to be of any use and the Hetton were too strong for them to fight, too surprising, and they spirited them away to a glade where she could cover them with her shadow and none could find them. Then she questioned them, long and hard and painful, until she was sure they knew nothing more than she had wrung from them. Sure they had nothing to tell her and every word spoken was in desperation, in the hope it was what she wanted to hear so the pain would stop. The strangest thing, she did not enjoy it the way she had when she was Rai.

The bodies they threw in a littercrawler pit.

The whole trip was a waste. The forester was away from here, preying on the rafters coming from the Treefall. The trion too. She should go back, better chance of catching them by following the rafters. But that would bring questions, and Rai, and soldiers, and they would take Cahan instead of her. They would claim it was their work. She would not get him.

She wanted him.

For herself.

She needed to win.

She waited for him to return, waited for a long time but he did not.

Back in her tree, she watched the village and tried to think of a different plan. She watched the people. In among them the Leoric. Easy to see, she stood taller than the rest. Held herself differently. A woman used to power. A woman who had worked closely with the forester to defend her village, to bring them here, and she already knew the man was weak. That he cared for the villagers. That he was close to her.

Sorha found herself smiling.

He is loyal, she thought.

He will come for you, woman.

She was sure of it.

That morning, they waited for the Forestal patrols and

surprised them and six Forestals lay dead in Wyrdwood. She moved closer to the village and waited in the bushes, surrounded by Hetton ready for blood.

"Her," she said, pointing out the Leoric. "Kill as many of the others as you wish." The sound of air seeping from ruptured lungs in reply. "But we take her alive."

A hissing passed between them; did they feel pleasure? If so, then killing was where they found it, she was sure of that.

"Alive," she spat at them. "And take out the remaining Forestals, the ones with the bows, first." A nod, an affirmation. Then the Hetton attacked. Running through the gates, the villagers surprised, barely aware before the Hetton were among them , swords and spears reaching out to carve a wet, red path to the village gates.

And the screaming started.

31
Saradis

She woke on the cold floor of the hot room.

Zorir's stone inert before her, the smell of urine and stale sweat on the air. It was always this way when she spoke to Zorir and the reward was given. She lost control of her body, one of the reasons she communed naked.

She took her time, letting herself return to her senses, going from lying to sitting. Slowly stretching her muscles. When she felt able, she stood. There was a small ante-room off the hot room and in there she kept a table, a mop, bucket and ewer of water. She cleaned the floor first; she did not think Zorir cared if the floor was clean but it felt disrespectful to leave it awash with urine. If those that followed could see her now, Skua-Rai of all Crua mopping the floor, what would they think? When that was done she washed, the cold water blissful against her skin. Then she dressed, and all the time her stomach ached and reminded her of how long she had been fasting for.

She only ate when she was fully dressed, and then sparingly. Sometimes bouts of nausea followed her communion with the god, and the more she ate afterwards the more likely they were. A moment of dizziness. She grabbed the table and it passed. Only after did she realise it was not because of her communion. The spire still swayed a little and she heard thin shouts from the city below. Another tremor wracking Crua. She imagined the spire coming down, cracks running up the ancient material, the darkness coming apart, the tower shivering, sliding and destroying everything in its path, crushing everything within.

She took a deep breath.

"It is Zorir's work," she said to herself. "I am safe, I am their hand upon Crua." The shaking subsided and she took another bite of dry bread. As she finished there was a gentle knock on her door. She almost said "Come, Laha," from force of habit, but of course Laha was far away in the north. Instead she went to the door, opened it a little. "I am in communion," she said, her voice had not quite returned, she sounded hoarse.

"I am sorry to interrupt, Skua-Rai." One of her monks, head bowed. "A message has arrived by skyraft from the north, and another from the army in the south came by skipper this morning."

"Why was I not told?"

"You were communing with Tarl-an-Gig," they said. So soon after touching Zorir it was hard for her not to snap at the name of the made-up god, to put them right about who they really worshipped. She could not, of course. She knew that. Names did not matter, the effects did. "Laha waits for you in your rooms."

"Laha is here?" A momentary flare of anger. She had told him to stay in the north, to find Du-Nahere and oversee Treefall. Did he have him? Something jumped inside her. Du-Nahere was her only real problem, the only one with the power to hurt her. There were other pretenders out there but they were weak, frightened, hiding. In every monastery they had taken in the name of Tarl-an-Gig she had made sure the Skua-Rai was kept alive, brought to her to be questioned. It was never pleasant, but it was necessary.

She caught herself – she had thought Du-Nahere weak, she had been wrong. She could not take chances. They must double their efforts to find other false Cowl-Rai.

"Skua-Rai?" The voice from the other side of the door. She had drifted off. So easy to do after communion. It did odd things to her. A shiver of pleasure ran through her, an aftershock.

"I will be down presently, have food taken to Laha, he will not have eaten and will not ask."

"Yes Skua-Rai." She listened to them leave, footsteps echoing oddly round the strange passages of the Spire. She finished her food and went to Laha.

He was eating, slowly chewing on raniri meat and staring off into space.

"You are not meant to be here," she said. He dropped the food back on the plate, put the plate on the table and went down on his knees, bending at the waist so his head touched the floor.

"Forgive me, Skua-rai."

"I was not scolding you, Laha," she said; it was easy to forget how literal he could be with her words. Like a garaur in many ways, eager to please, sad when he did anything wrong. "Continue your meal. When did you last eat?"

"Before I set off."

"The rafters did not feed you?"

"They do not like us," said Laha.

"They need us," she said, sitting opposite him, a soft breeze billowed out the tan curtain that covered the balcony. From outside she could hear the noise of Tiltspire as its people went about their business. "They need our trade and our anchor points for their rafts. They will accede to anything we ask." She leaned forward, smiling. "They will feed you."

"And spit in it when they do," said Laha. She laughed.

"Yes, probably. But it will not matter when the time comes. They will pay. We already have one skyraft." Laha took a bite of Raniri. "What brings you here from the north? Have you captured Du-Nahere?" Laha shook his head.

"No, but we will. I thought you may want to be there when we do."

"What do you mean?" He swallowed the meat he was chewing.

"I met a Rai, but not a Rai. She had failed to capture Du-Nahere three times and burns with hatred."

"And you trusted her?" He nodded. A slow nod, she could almost see the thoughts going through his head. She had noticed this before with Laha, he made decisions seemingly without thinking, but when challenged was able to work back, understand his thought process. He simply trusted who he was and she was sometimes jealous of that. She often thought too much.

"Her failures, she learns from," he said. "First time she failed, she was unaware of what he was, any would have fallen. Second, she wished more than anything for him to give back what was taken. Her desire betrayed her."

"What was taken?"

"We will come to that." She nodded. Best to let him tell this at his own pace. "Last, she was commanded by Rai, they hated her but if they had let her be in charge Du-Nahere may already be dead."

"I am not sure I want him dead now," she said. "My communion has revealed something to me, I believe Zorir wants him. So I want him. Caged and surrounded by dullers. He is needed." Laha took that in as if it was unimportant.

"It may be too late. I put this Sorha in charge of bringing him from the forest village. She hates him." Saradis took a deep breath. If he died then they would find another way.

"You mentioned something being taken from her?"

"Her cowl," said Laha. "He did something; she is like me. No." He chewed thoughtfully. "No, she has no stone," he tapped the stones in his skin. "She is like one of your dullers, but can walk and talk." Saradis smiled.

"A useful tool."

"And a clever one. She knew where the new Harn was, where they had all gone. After the destruction of the army, she followed them."

"Resourceful," said Saradis.

"If he is there she will kill him and destroy the village." Saradis smiled.

"What if he is not there?"

"She believes he is fond of these villagers. Maybe she will use that?"

"Play on his weakness, well done. What of this Harn built in Wyrdwood?"

"It will be gone," said Laha. "If Sorha fails I will have the Rai take care of it. I commanded they follow her but stay well back."

"Well, that is one less thing to worry about." She stretched, her muscles were still wound tight. "But as I said, I want him alive. I communed with Zorir, he is something to us. He is needed." Laha only nodded.

"I will return as quickly as I can, make sure all know." Saradis gave him a small nod.

"I will assign you a marant and you can fly directly."

"How is our Cowl-Rai?" he said.

"Worse." Laha nodded.

"She is weak, like her brother." Saradis thought on that.

"The south lost their Cowl-Rai and no one even noticed." She looked up, "If it looks like she may get in our way, I will end her."

Laha smiled and she let him eat a little more before speaking again. "How goes Treefall?"

"The Forestals prey on the caravans, but once the raftway is finished that will be harder for them. One soldier said they thought a trion was with them." Saradis tapped her teeth with a nail.

"Could it be our trion, this Venn?" Laha shrugged and fear ran through her, even now, Cahan could be dying. The trion could be dying and both were needed. That thought was deep in her, implanted by her communion. "Go back now, Laha," she said. "If the trion is with the Forestals then Cahan Du-Nahere may be as well. Leave now." Laha nodded and stood. "And remember, I want them both alive." As she spoke, some hazy thought. Some memory, some message from her god. It puzzled her but she did not question it.

"Du-Nahere may be hard to cage," said Laha. She thought on that. Whispers in her mind on currents of blue.

"Make him use his power."

"His power?" said Laha, even faithful Laha questioning that, but she felt it was right. The urging of Zorir in the back of her mind. Tendrils of blue.

"It is . . ." Certainty growing as she spoke. "It is a trap, Laha. That is what Zorir tells me."

"Then I will set a trap," said Laha and bowed to her.

32
Cahan

The first attack was easy. They were not expected and no one even died.

The three rafts only had a small escort of soldiers. They recognised forestbows and had no wish to try their luck against them; even if they had, the presence of the Reborn terrified them even more than the bows. The guards and rafters were roughed up a bit, on the request of their branch commander so it did not look like they gave up without a fight. Then they were tied and left. The rafts taken by five of the Forestals. Cahan never even drew his axes.

The rafts and their escort vanished.

New Forestals arrived soon after.

The second attack was nearly as easy. There was one death.

This time they had sent one of their Rai with the rafts – they marched at the head of the column, haughty and confident in splendid armour that was bright with paint that glowed in the gloom of Wyrdwood. The Forestals did not give them the opportunity to surrender. Four arrows found them, loosed simultaneously from either side of the track. Their impact made the Rai spin once before they fell to the forest floor, dead. The troops gave up immediately.

Two rafts this time, their contents once more vanishing into Wyrdwood. Cahan thought it odd they only sent five with them. Surely it would be better for the whole troop of Forestals, fifteen of them now, to guard them on their way back to their home? Tall Sera only smiled when he suggested it. Soon after five new Forestals arrived, the same five who had left with the first raft.

The third and fourth and fifth column of carts were well guarded, and Tall Sera let them pass unmolested.

"Leave them, hope they get complacent," he said that night as they cooked raniri over heated stones.

The sixth column of carts almost killed him.

The design of the rafts had changed after the second attack, a box of thick wood now covered the place where the driver sat to control the crownheads. They had also added two extra rafts, one at the front, one at the back, that were covered and held more troops. Thirty soldiers marched together with trunk and branch commanders to make sure they did not simply give up when threatened. The soldiers held thick shields to protect against arrows. Two Rai, these ones having learned their lesson about forestbows, walked within the cover of the soldiers.

"This one we have to earn," said Tall Sera.

They had already begun working for it. Forestals had weakened some of the huge bushes either side of the track the rafters used to transport their cargo. Now all that held them up was rope, tied to one of their sibling plants and ready to be cut with a well-aimed arrow. They had to stay well back from the track, as the Rai would be reaching out with their cowls for what they could feel of the forest. Cahan would have done the same, if he could. At the thought of it something twitched within him and he felt vertigo, a sense of the death around him, the slowly rotting mulch of the forest floor, the gradual consumption of it by the weave of Ranya's web, and behind that the other web, the one he had taken from. The one that lived within him now, promising much but within that promise a price, and one he thought too expensive.

For now.

The thought unbidden, and not from outside of him like the voice of the cowl had been, the voice he heard no longer. Once he would have rejoiced at that.

"Ready yourself, Forester," said Tall Sera, "We will need your axes."

"What of me?" said Venn. Tall Sera turned to the trion, a twist to his smile and somehow it betrayed his age. The light struck the man so Cahan saw the wrinkles and furrows on his face and knew him for much older than he had thought. The make-up hid much and as the man also had a cowl, though of a different sort, Cahan thought he may be a hundred, possibly even older.

"Hide, and make sure you do it well," said the Forestal. Then he turned back to watch the path. Waiting until the rafts reached a point he had marked in his mind. The Forestals were well practised, professional. In the early morning gloaming of the emerald canopy, Cahan wondered how many innocent merchants had fallen to them. Then wondered when they had become so adept at taking down Rai. They showed no fear of them, but Rai rarely, if ever, went into the northern Wyrdwood where the Forestals ruled.

The Forestals had secrets, but then again they all did. Apart from Venn, who was as open as the Light Above was bright.

A whistle from Tall Sera. A moment later, an unearthly sound, like souls dragged down by the Osere. Tall Sera smiled.

"The rope cutting arrows scream," he said.

A wave of fear and confusion passed along the column, soldiers turning, looking around for what horror of Wyrdwood had arrived. Shouting to each other, angry, confused, frightened voices echoing through the glade. A creak, a groan of splintering wood and the bushes, tall as trees came crashing down between the covered rafts with troops in and the cargo rafts and their guards. Fire sputtered around the Rai, shields were raised. More arrows cut through the air and one of the Rai fell, an arrow sticking out of their helmet. The other was quicker getting behind the shields. Shouting came from beyond the fallen bushes. "A trap!", "It's a trap!", called again and again from many throats.

"Wait here," said Tall Sera; he pulled himself up one of the bushes lining the raftway until he could look down on the panic he had wrought. "Good morning, Rai," shouted the Forestal. "I would say I am sorry to spoil it for you but I am not. Instead I make you an offer: leave here, and leave those rafts, and you may take your lives with you. Fight and you will not survive, and though we will be sad to kill the soldiers around you, we will not hesitate if they get in our way."

"Quiet!" This voice roared out from the Rai amid her troops. She stood behind five stout shields, though Cahan did not think they would protect her as well as she thought. There were Forestals up high in the bushes who could shoot down on her. "We have expected you, filth," she shouted. Her soldiers arrayed themselves behind thick, long shields. "We are prepared for you!"

"Pull back," said Cahan.

"No," said Tall Sera, and was there the gleam of obsession in his eye? "They haul willwood. It is too valuable." He whistled again. Once more the sound of screaming arrows cut the air and the third tree the Forestals had prepared fell.

The huge trunk came crashing down amid the soldiers, causing chaos, killing many.

"Into them, Cahan," shouted Tall Sera, and he began to loose arrows. "Go for the left raft, we will protect you." Cahan's axes were in his hands, warm and familiar. With him came the Reborn, cold and strange. The wall of shields had come apart with the fall of the tree. Before him two guards tried to protect each other, one fell to an arrow in the throat. The other thrust at Cahan with a spear and he danced around it, bringing his right axe across and into the guard's neck.

"With me! Get the raft," he shouted at the Harn villagers who had come with him. "Reborn. Protect them." Fighting, axes rising and falling. Bloody trails in the air. Grunts and screams. The impact of sharp wood on shield, on bone and flesh. Within him something rejoiced, something desired. The Reborn flanked him as he cut his way to the raft, they danced, spinning and twisting, spears finding flesh, small buckler shields deflecting attacks. Behind them the villagers formed a wedge. There was a beauty to the Reborn that Cahan lacked – he was brute force, skilled, no doubt, but he was all strength and fury. A boulder barrelling down a hill, destructive and unstoppable. The Reborn were light, like water. Moving around their targets, not always a killing blow, spear rattling off a shield, off armour. One Reborn pulling attention to her and the other taking advantage, a stab in the back, the side. They worked like one person split in two. Behind them the people of Harn, terrified and fighting despite the fear. Faces drawn, spattered with blood. Spears and shields up. Protecting each other as they headed for the raft.

The Rai before him, fire dancing round her hands. She launched it at him, burning, reaching. He responded. A fire of his own, dark, purple and blue and it hurt, it felt like a scream within him. The Rai fire held at bay, the Rai surprised for just long enough. Cahan's axe coming down. She was shocked when death found her.

He felt strong. Around him men and women were dying, and he felt it. It he wanted it. This chaos fed him. A hunger within, the purple flame licking blood from his armour.

"Cahan," shouted a villager, "we have the raft." They did, and all from Harn had survived. Half were already beginning to push it back towards the forest. The other three fighting to guard them, Reborn dancing among them.

"Protect them!" shouted Cahan, his voice loud enough to cut through the shouting and fighting. "Protect the raft!" It was moving, floating through the air while all around it was blood and fury. The soldiers, incensed by the death of their fellows renewed their attack. A villager fell, spear in the gut and Reborn cut down the attacker. Then Cahan was there, joining those around the raft. Axes rising and falling, thrilling to it. The gut churning nausea of what was within him no longer alien, or painful and miserable. It felt right, like this was who he was meant to be. He felt the bluevein beneath the ground, in the wooden track. It energised him even without reaching for it. He cut a soldier down, his axe biting straight through their shield. His armour was no longer smooth, subtly spiked lines running along his forearm.

"Look right!" called from the forest. He turned, soldiers scrambling over the fallen tree.

"Hurry!" Cahan's voice unnaturally loud, more hoarse than usual. Arrows raining down on the troops coming over the fallen tree. "Push!" he shouted. "Push the rafts!" He cut down a woman with his left axe. Cut down a man with his right. Blood sprayed over his armour and he felt like a giant, a god. This was him, what he was for. War and destruction. "Come to me!" he shouted, axes held out from his body, "come to me for I am death!" Bluevein, seeping through the rotting logs of the pathway, connecting with him. The attack faltered; it seemed the forest paused around him and he could feel a hundred, thousand million tiny lines of blue beneath the causeway, the ground here thick with it. Tendrils digging into bodies, feeding him.

"Quickly!" shouted from the forest. "Bring the raft." Ropes, thrown out of Wyrdwood, the villagers attaching them and the raft with them was pulled away.

Cahan, and the Reborn took up the rear, protecting the

raft's retreat. Holding the soldiers here on the raftway. A slow fighting withdrawal that was not too hard, they had taken the heart from the enemy. When Cahan and Venn left the path the Rai's soldiers stopped at the edge as if it was some form of invisible barrier. Cahan expected a shout, some branch or trunk officer to demand they pursue the thieves of their precious willwood, but none came. As the trees covered him the exultation he felt within died away, the feeling of power ebbing to be replaced with revulsion, not as bad as it had been before. Something of the power clung to him, the way a nettile web clung to skin after passing through it; invisible and uncomfortable, something that he could not see but knew was on him. The villagers and the forestals were already gone. They made to follow them and Cahan was so distracted, he did not notice Venn, considering him. Watching.

Shouts, out in the forest. Coming from either side of them.

"Now!" Movement. All around them.

"Cahan," said Venn, pointing at the groups of soldiers running toward them. No sign of the raft, no sign of the forestals.

The Forester took hold of his axes and readied himself.

"We have been betrayed," he said.

33

Udinny

Am I made of light, to travel so fast and so swift?

Am I born of the glow from above, once set there by Broken Iftal to kiss the cloudtrees and show our way? That is how it feels to fly with Syerfu.

Am I all knowing? Am I blessed with the knowledge of a god? That is how it feels to be drawn in the wake of the walknut, pulled through the sky over an ever-changing landscape that both is and is not Crua.

What the needle makes me feel I do not know as I have yet to use it, though within me grows the certainty that I will, and soon. A leap, a drift, and Syerfu is careening towards the ground, a blur of speed, a shift of scenery and I am there.

Stood by a crevasse, like many that exist on Crua, and like more which appeared all the time when I was alive. A breach in the land and to stare into it is like looking into a deep and creatureless night. Syerfu bleating as I slide from the saddle, taking out the needle and feeling it twist and move in my hand as it becomes a spear.

"Why am I here?" Syerfu has no answer, only crops at unseen grass as if she has not a care in the world. Do crownheads know to care? Maybe, though Syerfu seems to know more than many people have met, I half suspect she knows more than me.

The land growls.

It shook and I stumbled. All thoughts of the crownhead's intelligence chased away by a quake running through the ground. From the crevasse came something like the tentacles of a gasmaw but a dark and icy blue. Writhing and reaching up for the sky and then, though it had no eye or ear or nose to sense me with, it became aware of me and more appeared. Six darted towards me while two stayed on the edge of the crevasse, as if providing purchase as the rest reared to attack.

A moment, I knew I had a moment only.

In my ear the whispering of a thousand Udinnys past grew; my hands shook and another took control. I fought it, became paralysed. Tentacles shot towards me. Knowledge, passing before my eyes, the voices of all the me who had been before, male, female, trion, Rai and not Rai.

I gave up the fight.

Became a warrior – long dead or living within me, I do not know, do not care and it does not matter. My hands knew what to do. Pull back, arc my body like the forestbow beloved of Cahan. Release the energy. Throw the needle.

A golden streak from my hand to the nearest tentacle, trailing behind it a thread that dances in the air. The needle spear circles, returns to my hand. The tentacles shiver in fury. Smash down on the ground and I leap, strength in my legs like I have never known. Reaction times far quicker than they have ever been. Throw the spear again. Another tentacle punctured. Once more we dance and I jump and spin and twist and throw until the tentacles are bound within a web of bright gold.

"Pull!" A voice or a compulsion? I do not know and it does not matter. I am already pulling on the golden string and the tentacles writhe and fight against me, I feel strain in the muscles I do not, and have never had.

Something calls out, in frustration and fury. The tentacles put in one last effort to escape me, nearly pulling me from my feet but failing. They began to shrink, withering away to nothing. Breaking apart to become flakes on the air that in turn become ash that leaves no sign it has ever existed. The crack in the ground closes as if it has never been.

"Well then, Syerfu," I said, pulling myself into the saddle, "it seems I have found my purpose here. To stitch and to fix." I lift the walknut, "Take us where we need to be."

We become a streak across a strange sky. An arrow headed for a target I could not see but knew existed as surely as I knew I existed. Another rift, another set of tentacles waving angrily in the sky. I watch and am sure they push at the break in the land around them, widening it. Again I throw the spear, I dance the spearholder's dance. I thrust and twist and throw and tie the tentacles, holding them and breaking them, reducing them to ash.

And we fly on and we fight and we win and we do it again, and again.

Later, after four or five or ten or twenty fights I find something new, something I have not seen before. Two rifts close to one another, and rather than the tentacles waving above them, alert to any threat, the tentacles from each have found one another and joined together to lay flat across the ground. Occasionally they shine, as if with some inner light, and they pulse and pull and the land around them shakes.

Syerfu will not go near, forcing me to dismount for my approach. More tentacles erupted from the mass, smaller and capped with sharp and shining ends. This fight is harder, though I do not need to bind these ones. One hit and they fall as if dead, but more constantly erupt around them. I fight for hours, and make no headway. I do not tire, not exactly, but begin to slow and the tentacles begin to mark me and bite. It is not pain I feel, but a wrongness, and know within myself that should they stab me too much, I will end as surely as if my blood flowed from my body in life. Something of the tentacles will flow into me to replace it and I will no longer be Udinny. I will be someone, some*thing* else.

How or why I knew this? Well, only Ranya can say for sure.

I retreated beyond the area the tentacles grew in to look and think.

At first I was confused. How could anyone win against this? How did one fight an enemy who returned from the dead? How did they return from the dead? How was such a thing possible? It seemed that of all people, this really should be a thing that I understood. Yet I did not. I stared at the thick rope joined across the land, slick and blue and wet. The needle shook in my hands, its form changing, the end no longer pointed but wide and spatulate with a sharp edge.

"Of course, Syerfu," I said, "what a fool I have been, they fight me to protect what matters to them." Once more I stand, weapon at my side and this time I did not engage the smaller, stabbing tentacles. I dance between them avoiding their vicious sting until I find myself in a position over the bridge of blue flesh. Then I throw. The spear leaping out, slicing through but not cutting the bridge completely. Like leaves caught in a whirling wind the attacking tentacles renew their fury towards me. Hundreds of them, more than I could fight one-on-one. But I am one Udinny of many Udinnys now, their pasts and fates swirl around me and are part of me. A pressure in my mind, I let go of my body and give it to an older Udinny.

We leap like a raniri, up and out of the clutches of the spiny tentacles, over the bridge of flesh to land on the other side. Casting the needle spear and it flashes again through the bridge of flesh, severing it entirely.

The stinging tentacles fall slack and dead and the air is

filled with a great shriek as the thick ropes wither and become as nothing, the land healing and closing.

"Truly, Syerfu," I say, "I did not know I had it in me to be such a warrior." Pulling myself once more on to the back of the crownhead and lifting the walknut. "I think we have worked this out, Syerfu," I shout into the land. "Walknut, take us to our next conquest!"

With that we leap across the land, drawn by the inexorable pull of the walknut, strong and capable and powerful and on Ranya's mission. Never have I felt so sure and strong, so purposeful. Syerfu bunches her muscles and carries me, great and true and loyal. We know our purpose, we warriors of Ranya. We have faced our foes and we have their measure now. Five more times we come across the rope crevasses, linked by writhing blue tentacles, ten more times we fight tentacles leaping from the land and each time our victories are more sure and more quick.

I would free Ranya's web in a day if this continued.

In life, it is often the way that when you feel most confident the cruellest blow is struck. It is the same outside of life as well. This time when we land it is not a small crevasse with a few tentacles. Or even a rope of them lying across the land.

A canyon, one so wide I cannot see the other side, the air above filled with a haze of blue, like water hanging in the moments after the great geysers at Tilt have spouted. Below me, the land falls away, deep and dark and filled with the same sparkling lights as I have seen before. The walls of the crevasse move, alive with tentacles, some thin and spiky, some as thick as a cloudtree trunk. Always shifting, and if they were aware, or cared about me at all, I got no sense of it. But on seeing them I am filled with a strange and upsetting sense of purpose.

"Well, Syerfu," I told her. "It seems it will not be as easy to vanquish Ranya's enemies as we had hoped."

34

Dassit

They had, much to the chagrin of the Leoric of Fin-Larger, demolished a large part of the town. Buildings had been brought crashing down and their remains piled up into makeshift walls. Killing grounds were created. Spikes were everywhere, an entire branch of troops had been doing nothing but sharpening stakes for days which had left them and their commander out of sorts. Her small army had definitely become two camps, though as long as they followed her orders they could hate her as much as they wished.

She did her rounds of the defences with Vir: it was plain they were too hurriedly built, they had not even managed to create decent wooden walls. The wood used in the building of houses was not the right size or thickness and they did not have the right tools. Fin-Larger once had a carpenter, but they had left and taken everything with them. What defensible walls they had built were full of holes – they would stop an army, right enough, but not for long.

"Good walls," said Vir, looking up at them; the mound of rubble and old building material came up to his waist, the wall on it was half again as tall as him. "Considering what we have to work with." He didn't look at her, and though he tried to sound upbeat he couldn't fool Dassit.

"Movement!" Shouted from one of the roofs, a house left standing for lookouts to use.

"Where, soldier?"

"To the north, looks like an army."

"I better get up there, Vir," she said, "you continue the inspection of the walls, find some way we can shore them up a bit more, make sure the walkways don't collapse."

She left Vir and went up through the interior of the house, it had been beautiful once, but now it was a wreck. Holes punched in walls to allow spears to be thrown from them. Half the roof gone and replaced with a platform built on it for lookouts; similar posts had been made at all the compass points. From here she could see the other three soldiers, looking out in opposite directions, occasionally glancing at the troops approaching.

"Look like ours, Trunk," said the lookout. Dassit squinted, her eyes were not what they had once been.

"It's Rai Dealish," she said. "Doesn't look like he's still got his catapults."

"Are they coming to help us?" She shook her head.

"No, looks like they will pass by, their route will not bring them here unless they change course." She stayed at the lookout post, watching the army approach and when it was at its nearest point – an hour's walk away, she thought – and the Light Above was at its highest, a message skipper left the army and came to them. She climbed down, went to their makeshift gates to meet the messenger, trying to ignore the sweat trickling down the inside of her armour.

The skipper stopped before her, the earthy smell of the dying gasmaw tethered above them stinging Dassit's nostrils.

"You have a message for me?" she said. The messenger nodded, beneath their wide-brimmed hat their face paint was cracked and veined with sweat.

"The great Rai, Dealish Mat-Brumar has encountered the armies of the false Cowl-Rai." He spoke the message with a sense of importance she did not think Rai Dealish deserved. "They are marching this way. You are ordered to hold them here."

"Has the great Rai, Dealish Mat-Brumar actually seen this place?" she said, waving a hand at the makeshift walls and piles of rubble. "It was not built to be defended. Unless he brings his troops here and joins us we will barely hold them for a day."

"The great Rai orders you to hold this place," the skipper repeated. Dassit said nothing in reply, only watched the snake of the Rai's army making its way across the plain in the distance.

"And what will he do?" she said eventually.

"He will meet up with the second army of the Red under Rai Uter Gan-Hilsen, and they will plan a defence. You must give them time to do that." She nodded.

"So the order is to buy him time?" she said.

"Yes. You are to hold the enemy." Dassit swallowed; a death sentence if she had to stay here.

"Return to Dealish, tell him I will buy as much time as I can." The message skipper nodded.

"May I get a drink first?"

"Of course," she said, "try the chimney house in the centre, or the guardhouse by it. One of my branch commanders will provide you a drink and something to eat." She nodded and turned away. Vir stood behind her.

"What plan do you think the great Rai, Dealish Mat-Brumar, will come up with while we're dying?" he said.

"I don't know." She looked over the defences again, trying not to despair.

"I do," he spat, "run back to Jinnspire and hope the Cowl-Rai will hold his hand."

"Careful how you talk, Vir," she hissed. Vir only shrugged.

"What does it matter? Not like we'll survive to get

reported; this place, with us in it, will end up as flat as ruined Anjiin."

"It's not Rai ears I'm worried about." She glanced over at a group of soldiers on patrol, saw Vir realise his foolishness, bow his head.

"Well," he sniffed, "I'll put more troops to strengthening the walls, and get more spikes out there." She looked around the larger; it was a shambles, they could never hold it.

"Get them working," she said, "and bring the branch leaders to the guardhouse. I want to talk to them."

She sat and watched her branch leaders as they made themselves comfortable, Vir as laconic as ever, Tryu, looking uncomfortable with her new rank but proud of it as well. Tirin Har-Barich and Cavan Har-Gollust sat separately. The woman, Tirin, had been here when she entered, passing over a package of food to the message skipper and sending them on their way.

"We should do this in the chimney house," said Cavan sullenly, wiping sweat from his face.

Part of Dassit agreed. The chimney house was blessedly cool. However, the walls were thin and she knew she would have to move her command to the guardhouse at some point anyway. Nowhere else would stand against an army. Besides, the chimney house was a good place to rest soldiers, a way of rewarding them. Finding officers there was no reward.

"Better use that place for soldiers to rest," she said. "Now, pay attention." On the table in front of them she had used some scavenged building materials to make a rough approximation of Fin-Larger. "We have to hold for as long as we can," she said. "No surrender." She looked at the others around the table. "So we at least have to put on a good show before we leave."

"Leave?" said Cavan, leaning forward, voice and manner gruff. He styled himself on the Rai in his demeanour and she thought the reality of such officers was that they were weak, having to borrow another's authority. "We hold this place. The Cowl-Rai and Chyi are with us." Privately, Dassit wondered if the man was stupid, deluded or both.

"As the Cowl-Rai is not here we cannot hold this place," she said.

"That is defeatist, treasonous talk," said Cavan. Dassit stared at him for a moment, a big man in cheap armour polished to a shine. Did he believe what he was saying? Was he prepared to die here?

"Branch Har-Barich?" she asked, turning to Tirin. The woman scratched her cheek with the long nail on her little finger, something many affected so they did not mar their make-up.

"As Cavan says, we have been told to stand so we must stand." Dassit took a breath. The woman had not struck her as the type to throw her life away.

"We have not quite been ordered to stand," said Dassit. "We have been told to buy time and not surrender."

"There is a difference?" said Cavan. She saw Vir smiling from the corner of her eye.

"Yes." She stood. "We can only hold Fin-Larger for maybe a few days at most before we are overrun. Our orders are to buy time. Surrendering is giving up to the enemy. A fighting retreat is different. That is escaping so our forces can be of use later." Tirin Har-Barich was watching her, Dassit wondered what she was thinking. Across from her Cavan Har-Gollust looked like he was wrestling with what she had said. Good, she thought, let him wrestle, it would keep him quiet. "I think we can buy more time by splitting our forces." She looked over at Vir who was nodding. "Some of us will leave Fin-Larger and attack their convoy, using the fields as cover." She looked around the table: Tryu was staring intently at her, drinking in her words. Cavan looked confused and Tirin remained unreadable

"Our order is to hold them here," said Cavan again.

"Well, no plan survives contact with the enemy," said

Dassit. "We cannot hold them here. So we will split up, half to make hit-and-run attacks. Slow them down that way. Tryu, you will take my chosen and lead that force." She knew her chosen wouldn't like that, but better they grumble and have a chance than die here. "The rest of us will continue to fortify this place, make it look like it's important but we're not staying. With any luck they will split their forces, some to lay siege here, some to follow our harrying forces. By the time they realise this place is empty they'll be days behind the rest of their army. Tryu, do your best to lead the enemy to Rai Dealish and Rai Uter who will find it much easier to crush a smaller force. Then they can come back for the rest which we'll hold in a fighting retreat." She knew it was a plan that probably wouldn't work. No guarantee the army would split. Even if it did she would likely be overrun. But it stood more chance than trying to hold Fin-Larger.

"No," said Tirin. "That is not the order. The order is hold here. I ask that we vote, it is the way." Dassit nodded, though inside she was seething that this woman would question her.

"Very well," said Dassit, "I vote for my plan."

"As do I," said Vir.

"And me," said Tryu.

"Then it is decided, Branch Har-Barich," Dassit stood. "Even if Har-Gollust votes with you. Get your people ready. You and your branch will accompany Tryu while the rest of us make this place look more impressive than it really is."

"Me?" Her surprise plain, but it suited Dassit to have the cleverer of her two rivals out of the town. The woman stared at her. If looks could kill, thought Dassit. Har-Barich bit her lip, plainly desperate for some way to save face after losing the vote. "What about the prisoners?" she said.

Har-Gollust chimed in. "You should execute them now. I'll do it, it'll raise morale. Everyone likes an execution."

"I will deal with the prisoners," said Dassit. "You and Vir can organise the troops, make sure they know we intend a fighting retreat and will not have to hold this place. That will improve morale better than any execution." She watched them leave, Vir hung back.

"I don't like Har-Gollust and Har-Barich much," he said.

"As long as they fight, Vir, that's all that matters." He nodded. "Get out there and keep an eye on them, make sure they're doing as they're told." With that she went downstairs, trying to decide what to do with the people in the cells.

The Forestal and the murder priest seemed no fonder of each other than they had been when she first visited.

"Have you decided to use me as a healer, yet, Trunk Commander?" said Fandrai, standing as she entered. Was he really a Cowl-Rai? Or did the Forestal, Tanhir, play some game?

"Sooner let a spearmaw out among sleeping children," said Tanhir.

"I have decided not to use you as a healer," said Dassit.

"Then surely you have better things to do than bother with us?" said Fandrai. She did and she knew it. But here she could escape her responsibilities and there was still something about these two that did not ring true. She hated that. Besides, the Forestal and the monk – if that was what he was – knew nothing of what was happening above. They had their own fight, and Dassit could be free from thoughts of the coming army while she was down here.

"The armies of the false Cowl-Rai are coming."

"And you cannot defend this place," said Tanhir, "and we are a drain on your resources so are to be executed." Dassit stared at the Forestal; the woman seemed resigned to her fate. "I wonder how long the murderer's promise not to kill will last when you put a noose around his neck."

"I have not decided what to do with you yet," said Dassit, wondering at how callous they thought she must be.

"One of your officers has made a decision though," said Tanhir, "we hear everything down here."

"I can be of help, as a healer," offered Fandrai again. He sounded tired.

"My bow would be more use to you than his hands."

"And what of when you run out of arrows?" asked the monk. "How many do you have, five? Ten?"

"I can fight with a spear as well as a bow," said the Forestal.

"No one is being executed today," said Dassit.

"Then why are you here?" said the monk, sitting on his bed. "This is what, your fourth visit in as many days? An odd way for an officer to spend her time."

"As I have said before, how you are here does not make sense. I do not like mysteries." Upstairs a door opened. Vir coming back, no doubt.

"We are not a mystery," said Fandrai.

"That is true, it is very simple," said Tanhir, "he is a murderer, I am his justice."

"No," said Fandrai, "she is a woman driven by revenge. I am merely a man obeying the tenets of my god." Dassit stared at him. Her world had always been full of gods, every week the processions of different groves coming through her village. In Tiltspire, as a soldier she had seen less of them, Chyi was everything there. But leave the city and once more you would walk among a hundred different religions, all paying fealty to Chyi while scheming to be the strongest. Each had their own customs, some quite foul. The less acceptable ones tended to be wiped out, just like Fandrai's had been, but she could not hate him for it; she could hate what he did, yes, but it was likely he had been raised in his religion since a child and knew nothing else. At the same time, the Forestal's desire for revenge made sense to her. This was Crua, it was the way of things, or it had been. She had heard that in the north, Crua was no longer the land of a thousand gods, that Tarl-an-Gig was a jealous god and had driven out all others.

Dassit found that worse than the idea of a god of murder. It upset her that the northerners were changing the world in such a definite way.

"You say you were a travelling trader and just happened to recognise Fandrai?" The Forestal stared at her, nodded. Fandrai let out a small laugh. "Such things happen," said Dassit, "but look at you, dressed like a Forestal and carrying a forestbow?"

"You would be surprised how few people recognise those things," said Tanhir. Fandrai laughed again.

"I do not think you rise to trunk commander by being stupid, Tanhir," he said.

"Take my name from your mouth," said the Forestal.

Dassit heard footsteps, getting louder as they came down the stairs and she turned, expecting to find Vir. Instead she found herself looking at Tirin Har-Barich. She was not wearing her helmet, her hair long and dark, flowing over her armour. Her entire genealogy written down the side of her face which Dassit thought odd; it was not a particularly auspicious one. Har-Barich stared at her, then looked over her shoulder at the two prisoners.

"If you have come to try and convince me to die defending this place, Har-Barich, then you are going to fail. My decision is made."

The branch commander nodded.

"Oh, decisions have indeed been made," giggled Fandrai. Dassit ignored him.

"What about them?" Har-Barich pointed at the prisoners. "Have you told them they are to be executed?"

"No," said Dassit, and she turned back to Fandrai and Tanhir. "I have not decided what to—"

Words stopped.

Pain. A blade sinking into her side like a lance of fire. Thrust between the plates of her armour as an arm came around her neck. Har-Barich hissing in her ear.

"You were meant to die here," she said. "The skipper

brought orders, and they are to make sure you never leave." Another stab. A wash of pain. Dassit groaned. For a moment she was overwhelmed, not by pain but by anger at her own stupidity. Should have seen this. What sort of message skipper needed a drink and food after such a short trip? He had plainly been delivering another message.

The urge to live rising up in her. Overwhelming her. Years of training and instinct kicked in. Survive. Survive at all costs. She twisted her body, flesh ripping around the knife, feeling it cut deeper but she could not let the woman stab her again. Trying to put armour between the knife and her. The move took Har-Barich by surprise, spinning the woman round. Dassit, with her strength quickly ebbing, pushed backwards, smashing the branch commander against the bars of the cage behind her. Pain radiating through her at the impact. Lights flashing in her vision. Her attacker grunting.

"You die," hissed into her ear. "You die here." Dassit struggled but the woman had her tight, no escape. Strength ebbing. Her life would end in a cell, stabbed from behind by one of her own. It was not how she imagined it. The arm around her throat tightened. She felt Har-Barich moving to thrust the knife into her side again. Here it comes, she thought. Hot blood flowed down her legs. Movement, a grunt, readying for the blade. About to bite again.

The blade about to bite.

Again?

Har-Barich struggling. No longer hissing in her ear. The grip around her neck loosening. Letting go. Dassit fell forward. Landed heavily on her knees. Falling onto her side. Rolling over. The Forestal had Har-Barich, her arms through the bars. One around the officer's neck, the other holding her knife hand. Har-Barich's face slowly turning purple as the bandit woman squeezed, a look of pure concentration on her face. Next door the murder priest was dancing from foot to foot, chanting.

"Death! A death for Hirsal of the Shadows!"

The Forestal continue to squeeze until Har-Barich went limp. She let go and the branch commander slipped to the floor.

"You saved me," said Dassit, the words coming out slowly.

"And you me, from the sound of it," said the Forestal; in her hand she had the key to her cell.

"Help me," said Dassit. She had been wounded before. Knew it was bad this time. Could feel blood pooling around her. Hear the sucking sound when she moved. The Forestal unlocked the cage, used the door to push the body of Har-Barich out the way. She knelt to look at Dassit's wounds, her face told Dassit everything she needed to know.

"I'm sorry, Trunk Commander," she said, "it is too late for you." She stood, walked across and picked up her bow and arrows. Strung the bow, bending the wood to fit the string, all the time staring at the other prisoner.

"I can save her," said the monk, all levity fled from him. His face serious. "Let me out, I can save her. I know the workings of a body, she is not beyond my help. You know this is true." The Forestal nocked an arrow. Dassit watched, it all felt very far away. She was cold. What a place to die.

Tanhir pulled on the bow, bringing it to full draw and aiming the arrow at Fandrai.

"This is for my family, last monk of the god of murder."

"My death is her death," said the priest with a nod towards Dassit. She did not mind dying, not really, it would be good to rest. Fandrai stood, to meet his fate. "Is that not also the murder of an innocent?"

"Be quiet," said the Forestal, her voice low and full of threat, "and prepare to meet your god." Dassit closed her eyes.

She never saw the arrow leave the bow.

35
Ont

Running, as fast as he could and, despite his legs being far longer than the Forestal's, Ania far outstripped him. She wove between trees and thick bushes, was aware of the trapvines and small obstacles of the forest floor in a way Ont knew he never would be. Nevertheless, he still ran. Once, he would have run away from screaming, been desperate to hide. The thought of violence would have weakened his muscles. He still felt fear. It was still there. Fear was strong, powerful, it grabbed at every breath he took, caught in his throat.

He would not give in.

A flash.

He stumbled.

Huge, plunging through the forest, crushing bushes beneath his feet. Strength flowing through him, arms and legs like trunks, body as thick as a cloudtree branch. Smashing obstacles out of the way. No fear, no worry of damage, no knowledge of weak flesh.

He stumbled.

A trapvine had his foot and it was all he could do not to turn an ankle as he sprawled on the forest floor, dropping his arrows, his mind awash with the strange feelings of the vision. What did that mean? Where did it come from? He did not know. Screams among the trees. No time for this. Hands covered in dirt, dry pinleaves sticking in his skin as he gathered up fallen arrows, pushing them hurriedly into the quiver at his hip. Up and running again. The wall of green that surrounded the village clearing, almost as if the forest had put it there to hide the village. He ran towards it, slowed, pushed through. Found Ania knelt among the leaves. She held up a hand to stop him. Screaming filled the air.

"We need to help them." He tried to push past but she grabbed him.

"No, we run in without knowledge, we may as well join them."

"But they are my—"

"My people are in there also, Ont." She turned to him. "I have been a warrior all my life." In her eyes he saw a pain he would have never expected, years of loss revealed in a moment, quickly hidden again. "We must find a place where we can see in through the gate." Screaming. She went maddeningly slowly through the undergrowth, pushing aside branches and keeping low. He followed, not as silent as her, never going to be as silent as her. They stopped when they could see through the gate. Chaos. Screaming.

Death.

The majority of the village had formed a line of spears and shields with their back to the gate. They were slowly retreating towards it. Past the line Ont could see a Rai, and with them those creatures that had attacked them before, Hetton? They made Ont shiver, filled him with a feeling past fear. Bodies on the ground, awkward with death. Poor Harn, its people had been through so much. They did not deserve this, not again. Another scream. Forestals had arrayed themselves along the spearline, and were loosing arrows at the Hetton but the creatures moved so quickly.

More quickly than they had before he was sure, and when an arrow did catch them they ignored it or it bounced off their armour.

"They are different, faster," said Ania. She took out an arrow, licked the flights. One of the Hetton dragged a man from a longhouse by his hair, raised their sword. The Rai stepped forward. Stopped them. The Hetton froze, the arrows stopped. The spearline halted.

"What are they doing?" said Ont.

"She wants to talk," said Ania.

"We should . . ." He began to stand but Ania stopped him.

"Watch," she said quietly. "If we need to act we will act. But for now we watch. They are only eleven, even if they are Hetton."

"The one called Furin," shouted the Rai. "Where is the one called Furin?"

"I am here!" came the reply, and Ont smiled to himself. His leader. Right in the middle of the spearline. "Why have you come to our village?"

"You defied the Rai. You must be punished."

"We are no threat." The Rai laughed at that.

"True, you are no threat. But I have come for Cahan Du-Nahere and the trion, Venn."

"They are not here," shouted Furin. "They left a long time ago."

"I know," said the Rai, and she stepped forward. "But we have met before, Leoric Furin." She lifted her visor. "Do you remember me?"

"I remember you." Only scorn there, only hate. "Rai Sorha."

"Cahan is flawed, he cares." She took another step forward. "He cares about these people, though he tries to hide it. I was in the forest when you built this hovel," she waved at the buildings around her. "I saw him. And I saw you. If I take you, he will come to me. For you."

"No," said Furin. The Rai flicked her hand at the Hetton

holding the man by his hair and the sword came down; the man had no chance to scream. Bows were drawn tighter. "There is no reason for more of your people to die. I want you. And you only."

"Do not," said Ont under his breath.

"She will," said Ania. "Her life for theirs, she is a leader."

"But . . ." Before Ont could say any more Furin stepped out of the line.

"What guarantee do I have that you will not come back here with an army?" Sorha shrugged.

"You cannot stand against my Hetton, you know that. The Forestals with you know it. I offer your people one chance to live." She waited. The forest held its breath. Then Furin knelt, putting her shield and spear on the floor. Ont and Ania watched as Sorha bound the Leoric's hands and pulled her up. Then she began to back away, using Furin as a shield. "When Du-Nahere returns," she shouted at the villagers, "tell him if he values this woman's life he is to come to me. Find me in forty days at the western Slowlands execution stand." She continued backing away, her sword at Furin's throat. "His life for hers, that is the deal. His life for hers." Then she was moving more hurriedly and Ont found himself sobbing. Overcome with emotion. Unable to understand why. He felt Ania's hand on his shoulder.

"She had no choice."

"I know," said Ont. "I know."

"We must empty the village, New Harnwood can no longer stand."

"But she said that—"

"She lied," said Ania, standing, "and you know it, and the people of New Harnwood know it if they are truthful with themselves. The Rai do not forgive, they know where you are now. You must convince your people to leave this place."

"Me?" said Ont. She looked at him, her eyes were deep like dark pools.

"You are their Skua, their monk, they will look to you with their Leoric gone."

"Will you help me?"

"I will, but there is something I must do first."

"Take your Forestals and bring back the Leoric?" Even before he had finished the sentence he knew the truth: that he spoke with hope, not good sense. Ania shook her head.

"No, I am sorry, Ont. You saw the Hetton, I am tasked to protect your village. I cannot take my Forestals after them and leave the rest undefended. Even if we bested her Hetton, she would kill Furin."

"Where are you going?"

"To get more help." She smiled, a true smile, and he had never seen her do that before. Then she leaned in close. "If they come while I am gone, if all seems lost, make for the grove and I will find you there. Do not doubt me." Then she was gone, within a few steps vanishing as surely as if she had never been, and Ont was alone.

He stood. Walked towards New Harnwood and though he was tall and strong he felt he was neither. He felt as if he withered under the eyes of the villagers, frightened, scared. Once more they were thrown into a fight they thought they had escaped. Ania had been right, they were looking to him. Some villagers wept, others huddled together. The dead man, Ganfa, was being wrapped in cloth. He heard a scream of misery from one of the houses and a woman came out, falling to her knees and saying "She's dead, she's dead," over and over again.

"What now?" asked Manha, the weaver.

"We leave here," said Ont.

"But she said she would not come back." He turned to find Tilla looking at him. "She promised us."

"You would trust Rai?" said Ont.

"But it is so far for them to come," said Manha, "and we are no threat. We have walls, if we keep the gate shut then . . ."

"Have you forgotten what happened at old Harn?" said Ont softly. Villagers gathered around him, the light was dying, the constant gloom of Wyrdwood taking on a subtle sepia tint he had learned to recognise as a warning of night coming, black and solid. Others felt it, torches were lit and the night, the utter blackness, came into being. Then silence. Followed by an explosion of light and sound as the nocturnal creatures woke. This was usually a moment of wonder for him, a reminder of the beauty of Iftal's creation, but he felt desolate as he looked around at the villagers, his friends, faces bathed in the lights of Wyrdwood. "At old Harn," he said, "we had walls, we had deep pits. We had Venn who could heal wounds, we had Udinny, who spoke with Ranya. We had Cahan, who brought the forest to life around us." All watched him, eyes locked on him. "Even with them so many died. We came close to ruin and we lost everything. If you think that we can stand against the Rai alone, even with the Forestals," he nodded at the remaining warriors, "then you are too quick to forget the horror."

"Is this our life now? To do nothing but run?" He did not see who spoke in the dark, their voice masked by sorrow.

"We walk Ranya's path," said Ont. "The way may be hard, but look at how far we have come." Too dark to gauge their reaction. Why would they trust him? He was just a butcher.

"They need us alive." That voice would have been him once. So confident sounding in their fear. Did they even know it was fear that spoke through their mouth? "They want Cahan to go after the Leoric. She said so. They need us alive. They will not come after us."

Ont stood, thinking. There was a sense to what was said. He wondered what Ania would say; the sharp-tongued Forestal would have an answer. Cahan would have an answer. Furin would have an answer.

"They are right," said another, "Hunla is right. They

need us alive." A flash of anger within Ont, the man he had once been resurfacing, and in that anger he found the answer he sought.

"No," he said. "They only need one of us alive. That is all." He looked around the circle of villagers. "Think like Rai. What is more likely to bring the man you want into your trap, angry and not thinking clearly? The news Furin has been taken? Or the news Furin has been taken, delivered by one survivor in a forest of bodies hung from trees?" He heard sharp intakes of breath. "They will make old Harn of us, repeat what was done to them with us and they will see it as sport. They will see it as deserved, as justice." He let his words sink in.

"We will need rafts," said a voice.

"And somewhere to go."

"Rafts we can do," said Ont, "the forest provides. Somewhere to go, well, we will have to trust to Ranya for that."

They packed through the night. Gates closed, the Forestals vanished into the darkness to keep watch. By the morning they were ready, tired, wary, unsure, but ready and they looked to Ont.

"Where do we go?" asked Ilda. "You want us to leave, Ont, tell us where to go."

"I have given it much thought," he said. "I have communed with the night and with the spirit of Ranya. And—"

"To arms! To arms!" This a cry from beyond the walls, and Ont ran towards it. Scaling a ladder to stand atop the flimsy wall of New Harnwood. Forestals were running towards them.

"Gates!" shouted Ont. "Open the Forestgate for them." Villagers opened the gate, standing behind it ready to slam it shut when the Forestals were in. From the surrounding green wall of their Woodedge a ball of fire seared across the ground, spinning and leaving a trail of dark smoke before it engulfed the rearmost Forestal who screamed and dropped, tried to roll, tried to smother a magical flame that would not go out.

They had come.

The Rai had come and Ont watched their army coming forward, at least two full branches spreading out to surround the village of New Harnwood. The final Forestal pushed through the gates and they closed it after them, though Ont knew it would do little good. The Rai would burn it down. They would burn it all down.

"What do we do now?" said Ilda. Ont took a deep breath, looked upwards into the mist that hid the branches of the great forest gods, the cloudtrees.

"We get ready to fight," he said. "What else can we do?" He felt a touch, looked down to see Issofur, Furin's child. He could not imagine how the boy felt having just lost his mother.

"Do not worry, Issofur," said Ont, "I will take care of you." The boy looked up at him and put out a hand. Ont took it, feeling a downy coat of fur on the boy's skin. The child smiled.

"This was all meant to be," said the boy.

36
Cahan

A running battle.

He had to protect Venn. Tall Sera must have prepared for this, won Cahan's trust then sold him to the Rai. Even so, something in his blood made the fight a thrill. He and the Reborn had cut them free of the first ambush and now they ran. He didn't want to run. The forest was full of death. Death to come. Death that had been. Death from very long ago. It spoke to him in cobalt language.

"Cahan." Venn in front of him. "Stay with me, Cahan."

"What?"

The trion grabbed his hand, pulled him on. "You keep stopping. We have to run—"

A flash behind Venn, a soldier with a spear.

"He's here! I have him!"

Cahan pushed the trion out of the way. No choice but to put himself between them and the spear. The weapon scraping across his armour, catching on a whorl that had become a vicious hook. An axe in his hand. Into the neck of the attacker. More soldiers. Heard them coming. He wanted power. None in the dying soldier he held. Not yet. Not for him. Not until he was dead. But there was power below. In the earth, the bluevein, in the slow dissolution of the—

"Cahan!"

Another soldier, two, three. More coming through the undergrowth. He pushed Venn to the ground. Met the first soldier. Spear coming in. He grabbed it, pulled it away, lifted the axe. A spear hit him from behind, staggering him. A spear from the side, he stumbled. More soldiers coming out of the clearing. A spear raised above Venn in a two-handed grip. A gleeful look on the soldier's face as it came down. Cahan threw an axe, spinning through the air into the smile. Another hit. This one he felt in his flesh, they had found a gap. Searing pain. Another hit, a club on his back. Another and another. All he could do was throw his body over Venn to protect the trion.

Power. There. Below them.

"No!" a desperate shout from Venn, though whether it was because Cahan was reaching out for the threads of bluevein or because of the attack the forester did not know.

A storm of blows. A scream. More screams. Being pulled up. The Reborn. One helping, one spinning and whirling through the soldiers, every spear thrust a killing blow. As he was pulled up a soldier ran at Nahac from behind. Without looking she reversed her spear, holding it out behind her and the soldier ran onto it.

"Venn," said Cahan, standing, not looking at the trion, everything aching. "Help Venn." The Reborn pulled the trion up.

"That way," she pointed with her spear. Cahan pulled his axe from the fallen soldier. Then they were running again. Pursed again. A spear thrust at him. All was chaos. The Reborn protected Venn, pulling the trion forward. Cahan following. Wyrdwood thick with the enemy. Running. Fighting. No time to draw power, only fed by what splatters of blood gave him.

Blood and pain and the luxuriant green of the wood.

A scream. A slash. Agony. Their agony. His agony. Blood inside his armour.

He should be healing.

Why wasn't he healing?

A sword, he blocked it with an axe. Brought his other axe in and under the blow, into his attacker's stomach. Strike, strike, strike. Push on.

Forwards. Fighting. Never knowing where the next attack would come from.

"Where are we going?" Struggling to get the words out. Protecting Venn from a spear. Killing. Pushing through branches. Running over needles. Axes striking out. "Where are we going?" The sure feeling of being overrun.

"Follow," said Nahac. He looked around, breathing hard. A soldier running after them. Falling, a spear through his gut. The second Reborn running over him as he fell. Taking the spear from the soldier's dying hand and leaping, throwing the spear past Cahan. It cut the air, felled another soldier.

And they were clear.

They had either killed their pursuers or lost them. The sound of pursuit falling behind. They broke from the bushes into a clearing. In the centre a half-fallen taffistone.

Before it, a man. Tall, thin, his head shaved and something sparkled on his brow. His skin was very pale, almost no need for make-up and despite the cold he wore only a kilt that fell to his knees. A wrapping of thin woollen bands around his chest held two knives. The Reborn came to a stop either side of Cahan. He let go of Venn who fell to their knees, breathing heavily. He found himself frozen. No words. No thoughts. What he saw could not be. Cahan knew this man. He had felt this man's fury, his lash, many times. He had watched this man light a fire that burned to death the only kindness Cahan remembered in the monastery of Zorir.

"Laha," he said, unable to understand how, or why he would be here.

"I wanted to see you, again, Cowl-Rai. You are not as impressive as I imagined after hearing about Harn." He approached. The Reborn moved to block him. Cahan looked for the Forestals. Gone. Sold him out. The Reborn must have been following the Forestals and that had led him straight to Laha. The anger within him, roiling, burning in his stomach like sickness. "But you let these women do most of the work." The world spun, a weakness came upon him. Cahan put a hand to his side, grunted. "You are wounded, interesting. Healing was the one thing you were good at." Cahan went down on one knee in a controlled fall, grinding his knee into the carpet of dried pinleaves, the smell of forest loam surrounding him. Not going down by choice, his body demanded it of him. "On your knees. That is where Zorir will want you." He needed the strength, but here, around the taffistone there was no bluevein.

Venn slowly backed away from Laha. Though the trion did not know him, they could feel the danger the man radiated, a violent confidence. Venn placed their hand on the back of Cahan's neck and he wanted to tear it away. The trion was healing him but it felt like another battle happening, a war within. He wanted to vomit as he felt his strength returning, he wanted to weep in thanks to the trion as his pain fled. He could feel himself healing. Could feel his body fighting Venn.

Sweat on Venn's face.

Sweat on Cahan's.

"It wants you to sicken," Venn said, grunted. Laha drew his knives and advanced.

"Come back, Cahan Du-Nahere," said Laha, "you will be welcomed."

He shook his head but could not speak.

The Reborn went into fighting crouches, the yellow wraps around their armour brushing the forest floor, armour creaking, small shields coming up, spears out.

"Stop now, Venn," said Cahan, the words little more than

a disturbance of the thick forest air. He pulled the trion's hand away. "I am healed." Not enough, he knew it, but he would live. "Escape if you can, we will buy you time." He struggled, forcing himself to stand.

"I have heard of Reborn," said Laha, the air of a man assessing a curiosity. "They say you are great warriors." Now he was nearer Cahan could see what flashed on his forehead: it was as if he wore a ring of sparkling stones, not centred but scattered across his skin. "Let us see if it is true."

Nahac moved first, a thrust of her spear, and Laha deflected it with a knife. The second Reborn, the silent one, thrust at where Laha should be but he was already dancing out of the way. They circled, he circled.

Was he smiling?

It looked like he was smiling.

The silent Reborn closed, she was fast. A strike that surely must connect.

It did not.

Laha contorted his body, rolling himself down the haft of her spear and struck. His knife piercing the eyehole in her visor. The Reborn shuddered and fell, dead. Or as dead as they ever were. Nahac moved in. Strike, deflection. Laha made no move to attack her. Only defended himself from a flurry of furious and incredibly quick blows. He remained calm. It was like watching two dancers who had spent their lives rehearsing only one dance. A spinning, twisting, ever-changing set of movements. Laha smiling as he fought. There was something in the way Nahac fought too, he could not see her face but he thought she relished this challenge.

Cahan felt only fear.

And weakness.

The nearer he was to Laha the weaker he felt. It was not as strong as when Sorha was near, but a cousin to that feeling. He needed power, but there was none. Not here.

He could not tear his eyes away from their battle.

Laha danced away from Nahac, close to the taffistone then stopped, one knife forward, the other reversed, held by his hip.

"You are everything I have heard," he said.

"You are very skilled," she replied.

"Yes. But this must end now. I want Cahan and the trion."

"True, it must end. But you cannot have them."

They closed, a flurry of blows that were almost too fast to follow. Then Nahac thrust with her spear. Laha swayed, trapped her thrusting arm between his body and his left arm. Brought the right hand down in a short, powerful blow with the hilt of his knife, breaking her arm with an audible crack. Brought his knife up under her chin, through the bottom of her jaw and into her brain. He held her close for a moment, one hand wrapped around her helmet. They could have been lovers, he could have been consoling her.

He let her fall, looking down at the yellow wrapped corpse.

"Is it true," he said, as Cahan forced himself to stand, every muscle aching, the wound in his side throbbing, "that they will rise again?"

"Yes," said Cahan, he moved in front of Venn.

"What if I burned them?"

"Even then." Laha nodded to himself, made a sound in the back of his throat as if intrigued, as if this required further study.

"I am taking you and the trion, Cahan Du-Nahere."

"Over my corpse," said Cahan. Though he had no intention of dying, he had something to return to New Harnwood for. He would fight. He would find a way.

"There are ways to incapacitate without killing." He stepped forward and within Cahan fear grew. Laha had stood at the side of Saradis when Cahan was a youth. He was the priest of weapons. The one who enforced her will and the one who frightened him the most as a child. "You were always weak," he said. Cahan wanted to hear the voice inside. His strength.

You need me.

But it was gone, driven away by a bad decision. Sometimes there was no other type. He stepped back and back and back until he was far enough from the stone to feel thin tendrils of bluevein in the ground. He knelt, put a hand down, feeling for the power he feared and needed, the layer of rot below the layer of needles.

"Yes," said Laha.

There was nothing there, not for Cahan. The bluevein was there, but Venn's healing sat like a barrier between the power and him. Not only that but Laha affected him, stopped Cahan focusing, stopped him connecting and even if he had not, something in the way the monk had sounded like he welcomed Cahan's use of his power would have made him pause.

"When the fight begins, Venn," he said quietly. "Run."

"Stand, Cahan Du-Nahere. If you do not struggle I will make your defeat quick and painless," said Laha. Cahan stood. Took a breath. Hands at his sides. He stared at Laha, Laha stared back, amused. "Take up your weapons, Cahan; if you think you are able to best me I will let you try. There is a first time for all things."

"What happened to your head?" said Cahan. He wanted to distract him, wanted to put this off. Wanted to run with Venn, wanted to get back to Furin.

"My god blessed me." As he finished speaking Cahan took hold of his axes.

He launched himself at Laha with a roar. The man swayed out of the way. Cahan passed and Laha grabbed one of his arms. Twisting it. Bending it. Making the joint work against itself and forcing Cahan to drop the axe in that hand. Laha swung him round. Pushed him to his knees, all in one motion. Cahan brought the other axe round, trying to cut Laha's legs from under him but the man was already behind him. Arm locked around Cahan's throat, blocking the air, suffocating him slowly.

But not completely.

"Without power, you are nothing." Laha held him between life and death. Not acting to kill, as if he was weighing something up. "Take it if you wish to live."

"No," said in desperation, not because Laha wanted him to draw power. Not because he could not. But in the hope Venn was running. That every moment he held Laha here, Venn was getting further away.

"You have changed," whispered in his ear. Then a blow to the back of his neck and it was like his mind was cut off from his body. A numbness ran through him. Laha let go of him and he crumpled to the floor. He could still see, the world was on its side, floor and land bisected. Feet walked up towards a sky, and down towards a sky. Such a strange view. He wanted to say sorry to Furin, say it out loud here and hope the forest took his last words to her.

Laha bent over, looking at him. He rubbed the shining stone just off-centre of his forehead

"Who are you?" Laha said. "Why are you needed?" He took up one of Cahan's axes and the forester watched. His heart beat faster. His wound ached. He could feel the power below the land, the strangeness of it. He could feel it within the man before him as well, like a halo around the stone embedded in his head. "Something has changed in you, Cahan Du-Nahere." He took a step back. "You are lucky she wants you alive." Cahan did not understand. The angles were wrong. The world was swimming. "I will take both you and the trion to her. She will be pleased." For a moment he could not see anything of Laha. Then he returned. Holding Venn by the neck and Cahan wanted to scream at them. "I told you to run!" Venn looked so helpless. He hoped, somewhere inside, that the trion would use their power to push away Laha, to protect themselves but they did not. They bowed their head. Let themselves be pulled close to the monk.

A sound.

Not of the forest. Not natural. Like nothing Cahan had ever heard.

Like ripping fabric. Pressure in his ears as if he ascended to a great height. Laha's head turned. A look of alarm. He pushed the trion to the floor and swayed to the right. An arrow cut through the air. Another and another, making the priest dance across the ground. Tall Sera and three Forestals. Stood by the taffistone, drawing and loosing at Laha who was nearly at the Woodedge, about to escape their bows and flee into the lush green shrubbery. As he was vanishing there was a shout, the sound of an impact. Laha tumbled head over heels into the forest, an arrow in his shoulder. Then the Forestals were around Cahan, helping him up. One ran to the trees where Laha had been hit. Tall Sera pulled Cahan up, helped steady him. The feeling in his body slowly coming back.

"He is not here," shouted the Forestal from the undergrowth, "but we hit him, there is blood, but he is not here."

"We can't stay," said Tall Sera, "more of them will come. This was a trap well sprung."

"The Reborn," said Venn, "get their corpses, we can't leave them." One of the Forestals looked to Tall Sera, confused. The man nodded.

"Do as they say." Something warm in Cahan. They had not betrayed him. That was good.

"Leave me," said Cahan. "I cannot run. Can barely move. Will slow you down." The Forestal smiled at him.

"You do not need to run, Cahan Du-Nahere, Wyrdwood has many secrets you do not know. Let me show you one."

37

Dassit

She awoke to heat and to pain and a desperate thirst. Tried to sit. Felt like she was being stabbed again. A grating agony in her back and side.

"No, you must not move, the stitches will tear." The face of the old man, the priest of murder. His name escaped her.

"Fandrai," she said eventually. Speaking scorched her mouth.

"Get her water," said the old man. Vir appeared, a mug of water in his hand and Fandrai supported her head. Helped her to sit up. Every movement searing.

"Good to have you back," said Vir.

"Is it?" she said, a wince, and then the cooling water in her mouth, a gift. "I'm not sure. Being dead hurt less."

"The monk didn't know if you'd make it, we didn't have half the stuff he wanted."

"You are very badly equipped," said Fandrai.

"When he started burning you, I almost did for him meself."

"I had to cauterise the wounds," said the monk. "Stop the bleeding."

"How long?" she said.

"It is not the time to bother with that."

"There is an army coming," she said, hissing as she pushed herself more upright. "How long?" Fandrai stared down at her, shrugged.

"I can heal a body," he said, "the strangeness of a mind remains a mystery to me." He stepped back. "I suspect your mind is far more likely to kill you than your body."

"Vir," said Dassit, "come closer." She took another sip of water. Looked around the room. It was the guardhouse. Something was wrong. She didn't know what. But something. She could see it in the way Vir approached, trying not to look at her.

"Trunk Commander," said Vir.

"Closer." He leant in so she only had to whisper.

"Tell me the truth, Vir, am I dying?" His eyebrows almost met in confusion, the white make-up of his face cracking.

"No, I don't think so. The monk said that if you woke then you would probably live." She stared, looking for any hint of lie in his brown eyes, seeing nothing except worry.

"The army of the Blue?"

"It's here," he said.

"Then why are we?" Did he look wounded at her anger. "I gave orders, I told you that . . ." Her words died away. A slow realisation of what was bothering her growing. "Why is it so quiet, Vir?"

"We obeyed your orders – Har-Gollust, Tryu and my own stick, Lafan. We split up Har-Barich's troops after her betrayal. They left to carry out your orders. To harry the army as it marched. Try and split them."

"And yet," she said softly, but there was ice in her voice, "you are here." Vir nodded then smiled. She did not expect a smile.

"Yes, me, the monk, the Forestal, and fifty of your personal guard."

"Why?" she said. Vir laughed, a quiet laugh, as if he saw some joke she could not.

"Because you wanted them to believe this place was still a threat." She stared at him. "And the monk said you could not be moved." She closed her eyes.

"You fool, Vir, my life is not worth . . ."

"You were not here to make that judgement. So I had to send everyone else away, few of us stayed."

"Well we must leave," she said, struggling to push herself up, "whether I am ready or not." Vir put out a hand, not actually touching her, just stopping her.

"We're not going anywhere," he said. "Fin-Larger is surrounded."

"By how many?"

"Looks like every soldier from the north is camped on our doorstep. I think we may have made this place look too inviting, maybe. They've been here a fourday."

"And not attacked?" He shook his head.

"Or even approached us. I keep what soldiers we have on the walls, and that Osere-cursed bandit has been out and about too, looking the enemy over. We should have strung her up."

"The Forestal is still here?" Vir nodded.

"And wants to talk with you. I've been keeping her away, you can't trust 'em." She wondered if he knew what the monk was, had to hide a smile.

"I know about the monk," he said, "so don't you laugh at me."

"But you trust him?"

"Kept you alive didn't he?" She nodded, Vir's logic was difficult to argue with.

"Yes, though it hardly matters with the army of the Blue camped on our doorstep." She tried to move, groaned. "Help me sit properly, then send the Forestal in." He did, gently lifting her, taking her weight in his arms and sliding her back so she sat more upright. The wounds in her back and side throbbed gently. Then Vir stood back.

"Are you going to demote me for staying?" he said. She coughed, tried not to laugh.

"It hardly matters now does it?" He left; soon after the Forestal, Tanhir, came in. "Why are you still here?" said Dassit.

"Because the monk is." She took a chair and turned it, sitting legs wide, arms resting on the back. "I will not let him escape again."

"But you have let him live," said Dassit.

"To look after you," she said.

"Thank you then," said Dassit, "though I do not understand why I matter to you, I kept you in that cell."

"But you did not put a noose around my neck."

"And now I am awake you will do what? Kill the monk?" She shook her head.

"That will happen, Trunk Commander, but that woman sorely hurt you and his skills may still be needed." Dassit stared at her. She was amazed by how calm the Forestal was. Vir had been the same. An army camped outside and yet they did not seem to care. She was not surprised by Vir, he had been a soldier a long time, but the Forestal was only a bandit. She had fought in no wars, not had the time to resign herself to death on a spear being the inevitable end point of her life.

"I think my healing matters little. When that army comes, we cannot stop it."

"Your people did a pretty good job following your plans for this place," said the Forestal. "I have walked it. The piles of rubble with spikes. The way you sculpted fallen houses into killing grounds. Paths that funnel soldiers into dead ends. I particularly liked the catapult – up close you can see it will not work but from a distance it is convincing. The enemy put scouts on a platform floating on gasmaws, so they could have a good look at us."

"When?"

"This morning."

"Then they are getting ready to come." Dassit let out a long breath. "They will know how small our numbers are now."

"I don't know, I don't think they like what they saw. Your man, Vir? He does a good job of having people look busy."

"It will not be enough." The Forestal stared at her, something piercing there. Something searching.

"You are an excellent tactician, Dassit, I see it in the way you have set this place up."

"What would a bandit know of tactics?"

"I have not always been a bandit." She tapped the back of the chair. "Is that why they wanted you to die here? Some Rai saw you as a threat?"

"Probably," said Dassit, as she shifted, trying to take a little pressure off her wounds, "and Har-Barich has succeeded in her mission; she may not have killed me in the cell, and I thank you for helping, but we are stuck now." The Forestal was staring at her, ever more intently.

"So you are going to fight them?"

"I don't have much of a choice, do I?" Tanhir leaned in closer.

"Have you ever thought of fighting all of them?" she whispered.

"What do you mean?"

"The whole system – Rai, Skua-Rai, Spire cities, all of it."

Dassit found herself laughing until it hurt. "Fight the Rai? What would be the point? Knock one down the rest come for you, they are like orits. Happy to kill each other but full of fury and vengeance towards any threat that comes from outside." The Forestal said nothing, not at first.

"As I said, Dassit," she replied at last, "we were not all born Forestals. My people welcome those with talent."

"It is a kind offer, but unless you have somehow missed it we are surrounded by an army. I doubt you can simply sneak out carrying me on your shoulders." She winced as a pain shot through her. "By choosing to stay you have doomed yourself."

"If there was a way," said Tanhir, "would you take it? Would you wear the green of Wyrdwood?"

"If it saved the life of Vir and my soldiers?" Would she? Would she leave everything she had ever known? Why not? The Rai had shown what they really thought of her. "Yes," she said. "If there was a way I would." The Forestal was about to say more, a smile on her face, but was interrupted by the bellow of a horn. "But it doesn't really matter, does it?" Dassit began to struggle towards the edge of the bed, pain washing through her. "That means they are coming, it's been nice knowing you, Tanhir. Escape if you can."

She pushed herself up, every muscle in her body protesting.

"No!" shouted the monk. "You cannot move. You are not right, not yet."

The horn sounded.

"Sadly, monk, I do not think the armies of the Blue care."

"Wait then," said Fandrai, "one moment." He scuttled to the rear of the room and a table covered in gourds. Picking up one then another, lifting them to the light and staring through the thin skin.

"Do not put me to sleep, monk." She tried to get off the bed but her body betrayed her. The horn sounded a third time. "I do not want to die in my sleep."

"You will not," said the monk; he sounded resigned, bored, one hand played idly with long white hair as he sorted through the table's contents. He put down one bottle, swapped it for another. Mixed this with that and nodded to himself. "No, you will not." He turned and brought the gourd to her. "Pinnock juice, they grow well round here, mixed with sperrion extract."

"They are poisons," said the Forestal.

"Everything is a poison if you take too much," the monk snapped back. "In the right amounts sperrion extract numbs pain, better even than allbalm. Pinnock juice gives energy. A mouthful of this and the Trunk Commander will be able to command, for an hour, maybe. Then she will need rest. A lot of it." The horn sounded again as Fandrai passed the gourd over.

"An hour is probably more time than we need," said Dassit. She took a drink, it was surprisingly pleasant, sweet. "And soon we will have all the rest we could ever want."

She stood atop a wall that was not a wall, only a loose mound of hard mud brick and shattered wood, pierced with sharpened stakes. On one side stood Vir, on the other the Forestal with her bow and eight arrows. Before them the army of the north, flapping flags of blue and the many colours of the counties they had conquered. She saw the flags of Seerstem and it made her laugh, they had not conquered it entirely, not yet. She was not sure if it was really funny or if it was a side effect of the drug Fandrai had given her. In the end she had taken the gourd from him, despite his warnings that too much would kill her.

The attackers were taking their time, letting the Light Above get well past its zenith, she imagined. No one wanted to fight in the heat of midday, mouth dry with dust and fear. Late afternoon was a much more civilised time to kill each other. She fought to keep another laugh down. "Tactics, Dassit," she told herself, she had to think about how to meet them. They would struggle to get up the heap of rubble and wood. The loose material would give way under feet and turn ankles. It might buy her troops a few minutes.

Funny, she thought, when death is certain how precious every moment becomes. She could hear a small flyer chirping. The sky was very blue and lines of white clouds were being dragged south by the circle winds. She thought she could make out a black dot among them that must be a skyraft. She wished she was on a skyraft.

She had made a speech to the remaining troops. Vir called them the Foolish Fifty but he said it with a pride that she envied. He found some worth in dying here in this small town for no reason other than that she, Dassit Gan-Brinor, hadn't been clever enough to see a threat that was standing right by her. Too busy looking at the one that was far away.

She'd given many eve-of-battle speeches. Knew all the tricks. Put the bad news in early, end on stressing their commitment to each other. Heroes would be made this day, etc. All the nonsense they said to cover the filth of it, the blood and struggle and pain, the tears and the waste. She'd seen a woman who had served under her begging on the streets of Tiltspire once, missing a hand and half of one leg. Dassit knew it was the fate of plenty of her soldiers, hers too she suspected, if she escaped death. She'd passed her old comrade and pretended not to see them. Not because she didn't care, but because she couldn't bear to acknowledge the truth of her. At the end of her speech she had said something shocking. She told them they could throw off their armour, dress as civilians and pretend they lived here. That no honour would be lost. It had confused them but she had not backed down, not sweetened their sacrifice because she did not want it.

Though they must have known it gave them a better chance than fighting, they had refused. All of them. Sent her a message through Vir, saying they understood why she had said what she said, but that they were soldiers, her soldiers, and they would fight. All she had left to say then was, "For Iftal's sake, tell them not to get taken alive."

Half an hour had passed since her second hit of the monk's drugs. She wondered if she would run out before the fighting even started.

"Here they come," said Vir. "Looks like the Rai are going to soften us up first." She squinted, her eyesight was not what it had been. The enemy soldiers were beating their spears against their shields, setting up a racket meant to scare. It worked, Dassit's stomach was churning, but she had been in this place so many times the feeling was more like an old friend than something likely to send her running or turn her legs to water. Two Rai had come forward from their lines, soldiers around them holding up an awning of blue material to shield them from the early afternoon light. "Time to get under something, before they start chucking fire." Dassit began to turn but the Forestal did not. She bent her bow, put on the string and took out one of her arrows.

"They're pretty far away," said Vir to her.

"Not far enough," said the Forestal. She nocked the arrow, drew back the bow. Dassit could see her musculature tensing, the way her entire body arced, it was almost as if the woman had not been truly alive until this moment. Tanhir sighted along the arrow, lifted the bow a little and took a deep breath. Then let fly. The crack of the wood as the tension left it. The hiss of the arrow cutting through the air. The bow hanging loose in the Forestal's hand, horizontal to the ground and gently swinging as she watched the flight of her arrow.

As they all watched it.

It was as if the Rai on the left was swatted by an invisible hand. Knocked, sprawling to the floor. The other Rai stared down at them. The Forestal began to draw again and then the Rai, almost comical in their hurry, ran back into their lines.

"I can see why they don't like those bows," said Vir, and Dassit smiled to herself. The enemy horn blew, three quick blasts. The army started to advance.

"How many, do you think?" she said to Vir, looking past him at her soldiers on the rubble walls. The "Foolish Fifty".

"Three or four hundred coming at this wall," said the Forestal, "probably the same on each side."

"They've underestimated us," said Vir. "Should have brought double that number." He was trying to make his voice light, carefree, but it was a struggle.

"Forestal," said Dassit, "take out their trunk commanders and branch leaders with what arrows you have left." Tanhir nodded and Dassit raised her voice. "My Fifty!" Heads turning towards her. "Make your throwing spears count! Then leave the wall, head back into the larger and find the centre. We will stand there." Shouts of affirmation. Dassit turned; it saddened her to retreat so quickly, but they could not hold the wall against these numbers, and she didn't want to get caught here by the enemy coming from behind. She had four throwing spears of her own, then it would be sword and shield until they got to the guardhouse and fought to the end.

If they got to the guardhouse.

The Forestal began loosing arrows, soldiers falling. Small victories.

Dassit was ready now, the waiting had been the worst bit, false hope building. Up until the enemy started to advance you could pretend it was never going to happen. But it was happening. She looked behind her. The monk stood at the bottom of the wall, a bag full of bandages and unguents and she wondered what he thought he would be able to do in the heat of battle.

She looked along the wall.

"Ready?" she shouted. Cries of "ready" came back along the line but she knew the truth, even as she pulled back her arm and prepared to throw.

You were never ready. Not really.

With a roar they came at her. She didn't pick targets, only threw spears into the mass of them as they approached. Soldiers fell, trampled underfoot by their comrades, then they were at the bottom of the wall. Throwing spears up at her. Most falling short but from the corner of her eye she saw one of her Fifty fall, a spear in the chest.

"Back!" she shouted. "Back!"

Scrabbling down makeshift ladders on the other side of the mound. Pulling them down behind them. The enemy appearing above. Someone pushed her aside and a spear clattered to the ground where she had been. She bent to grab it but was being pulled away by Vir. Into the narrow maze of alleys they had created. Following signals and signs they had put up to direct them to the centre of the larger. Unbearable heat, light radiating off the wall and the floor. Her mouth dry. Enemy soldiers everywhere. They had overrun the walls on all sides with no trouble and were streaming into the larger. The maze had confused them, split them into small groups as Dassit had planned. Sometimes the two sides ran into each other, both surprised, and Dassit and her people pushed past them without a fight if they could, quickly losing themselves in the switchback passageways they had made. Other times they came upon the enemy from behind and showed no mercy, swords and axes and spears doing their filthy work.

And sometimes there was no choice but to fight. In close, grunting and swearing, the smell of armour worn too long, the smell of filthy bodies and rotten teeth. Blade against shield, spear against shield, axe against shield. Always searching for flesh. There had been ten with her when they left the walls, now there were seven and she did not know where she had lost three. She saw the Forestal go down, a spear through her thigh. Dassit's spear taking down the attacker as she fell. Then the monk was there. He ripped the spear from Tanhir's leg and she screamed. He bound her wound, hands moving so fast they were a blur. Behind him a soldier raised an axe and Dassit threw her fighting spear, not made for throwing but the range was short. Took the man down. Then they were free again. The monk half carrying the woman who had sworn to kill him.

"Not long now," shouted Dassit, drawing her sword, an old and ugly thing but it did the job. "We're nearly there."

Vir grinned at her, a cut on his face, blood dripping from his hand. Nearly where? she thought.

The place where we have chosen to die.

They burst into the town square. Something joyous in Dassit, that they had made it this far. She had never expected it, but this was where it ended. And it would come quicker than she had imagined. The enemy were coming from every side street, her people running before them. A shield wall of the Blue ran along one side of the square, neatly blocking off the guardhouse.

"To me!" shouted Vir. "To the Trunk!" and her people ran to her, and she to them and what good would any of it do? They were stuck, surrounded. Barely twenty of them left. Backing towards the taffistone while the enemy jeered and laughed.

"Dassit." A voice so quiet she barely heard it. She turned, the Forestal, her make-up run, lines of pain on her face as she hung on to the monk she hated. "You have saved my life twice now."

"It matters little," said Dassit.

"Let me repay you." So much pain in her voice. Pain and worry.

"How?"

"Trust me."

Dassit found herself laughing because, really, what other choice did she have?

38
Ont

There was no time. The Rai were approaching and the people of New Harnwood were on the edge of panic. Their rafts forgotten, their possessions forgotten. The Forestals who had made it back were bent over, shattered from running. Shocked at the death of their compatriots. The forest had fallen silent. To Ont it felt as if Wyrdwood was waiting, holding its breath for a decision to be made but there was no one here to make it.

There was only him.

His mouth dry. His legs, though strong as tree trunks, felt like they would give way beneath him.

"Ranya," he said under his breath, "guide your servant." No answer, only the drumming of spears on shields and the hiss of fire. Ont opened his eyes; for a moment he was back in Old Harn as fire was launched from Woodedge, a horrible brightness in the dark. But it was not Old Harn, the fire launched from the forest edge did not light up that village. It hissed into the sky, a bright spot in the complete black of Wyrdwood. A terrible repetition of what had gone before but without any of the protection they had then. "Forestals!" shouted Ont. "Protect us from the fire!" But they did not. Instead the leader of the Forestals, Binor, shouted back.

"We cannot, our focus died out there." He pointed towards Wyrdwood, beyond the walls; Ont did not understand what he meant. "Find shelter!" The first fireball hit the centre of the village. A splash of fire, incandescent liquid arms reaching out. Burning anyone it touched with a fire that could not be extinguished. The air full of screaming. The hiss of another fireball being launched. Ont paralysed. No help from his god, no whisper in his mind.

Beneath his feet the land trembled.

Running through the forest, pushing trees out of his way with huge arms. Unstoppable, strong. In the distance three, tall, thin and terrifying, sat on thrones of black glass.

He was down on one knee. Head spinning. Was this a message from Ranya? Or was his mind disintegrating, faced with his own lack of power? Was he falling into dreams of being able to do something? What could it mean? What did it mean?

Issofur appeared in front of him, grabbing his hand.

"Come on," said the boy. "It's time."

Time?

"Listen!" Ont shouted. "Listen!" Faces turning to him, the fire coming down, landing on a hut and exploding into flames. Sweat on his face. Listen? Listen to what? To him? What would he say? He had retreated from this place. Hidden in his grove. Why should the people trust him?

They brought him food.

They talked with him.

"We must still leave here, it has not changed."

"But the walls—"

"Will not protect us from the fire. Ranya has sent night to protect us, we walk under her black cloak." Ania had told him where to go when all seemed lost. "We must go to her grove."

"It has no walls." Shouted a villager.

"Ania instructed me that if New Harnwood was to fall, then we must make for the grove."

"We are surrounded," said a Forestal. Binor put a hand on their shoulder.

"If that is what Ania said, that is what we do." The Forestal nodded. Binor turned to Ont. "It will be hard. They will have moved to surround us." Binor looked around, at the villagers. "Do you know how to make a wedge with your shields?" Outside the walls of New Harnwood, the drumming and shouting of the Rai's forces continued. The hiss of another fireball. Nods from the villagers. "Then make a wedge, put the children in the centre. The best archers in the village must provide close cover from the back of the wedge. We will assist, you may not see us, but we will be there." Ont nodded, glad the Forestal had taken over. "And understand this," said the Forestal, "not everyone will survive, but you cannot stop. No matter what, you must keep going. When you are into the trees, split up, make for the grove on your own and in small groups. It will make you harder to find."

"Sengui!" shouted Ont. "Form the wedge and lead it." His hand was sweating, the grip of his bow slick in his hand. Movement all round, parents grabbing children, pushing them into the middle of the wedge of spears and shields.

"Why aren't you leading?" asked Manha.

"Sengui has the most battle experience of those here. I will be with the archers at the rear." He sounded so confident when he spoke. As if this was normal, as if there was no hint of the terror within him, as if he had done this before. It almost felt as though he had.

He tried to conjure up the feeling from his vision, of being massive and unstoppable.

"Wedge is formed," shouted Sengui. Ont felt the pressure of their expectation. All looking to him and he did not know why. Not until it was spoken. "Should we open the gate now, Ont?" He stared into darkness lit by the flames of the Rai's fire. It would be darker out there. They would not be able to see much at all, would not be able to use torches. Some would get lost on the way to the grove. There may even be soldiers at the grove already.

He could not know that. He could not know anything except that when he opened the gate, his people would start dying. How did Furin cope? How did Cahan cope?

"If we stay, more will die." He turned to find the Forestal Binor at his side. "Sometimes there is no choice, monk," said the Forestal, "not really." Ont nodded, at the same time feeling a strange sense of pride that the Forestal had called him "monk".

"The sooner we go the better," he said, and he raised his voice, took up his bow and breathed in, deep and long. He strung the bow and the Forestals and villagers around him did the same. "We make for the grove. As soon as we are free of the Rai's soldiers split up. Now, open the gate!" Forestals pushed the gate open and slipped through, the wedge moved after them like some great spiked beast and Ont watched as it vanished into the darkness, fire reflecting off the rearmost. It was eerie, in the darkness, knowing that soldiers must be out there but not where. The light-show of the forest was almost entirely absent, as if it had fled the violence.

"How can we shoot at what we cannot see?" said one of the villagers.

"They'll come round the village and through it, and they'll be in the forest," said Binor, "there'll be plenty to loose at then."

"I see them!" said a Forestal as they ran towards the gate. Ont could just make out the same. A flare where a Rai was beginning to call fire to them and the wedge headed straight for it. A big fireball would destroy the villagers formation before it got anywhere near the enemy troops.

"Out of my range," said Binor. More fire in the darkness.

"Nothing we can do," said a Forestal.

"Poor souls," said Binor, "get ready to run."

"No," said Ont. It felt like Ranya talking, like she had put his feet on the path and now he understood why. He took one of his long arrows, licked the flights. Drew. Sighted on the sparks and growing flames so very far away. Used the notches cut in the bow just as Ania had taught him. Aware of the Forestals watching, then not. The gentle kiss of wind on his damp skin. The cold bite of the air. The way the arrow would climb and fall, unseen in the darkness. The burn of the muscles across his shoulders and chest. Then aware of nothing but the brightness as it swelled in the distance.

Release.

The bow loose in his hand. Shouting and screaming. The intent way the Forestals watched and he was only faintly aware of it all, he saw nothing but the fire among the trees. Knew nothing but the death that would rain down on his people if he had missed.

He held his breath without realising.

Counted without realising.

Knowing exactly how long the arrow should take to cover the distance. Tried not to think about the terrible price if he missed the Rai.

Three.

Growing flame . . .

Two.

. . . a roiling incandescent ball . . .

One.

. . . that flickered out of existence.

He breathed again.

"Good shot," said Binor softly, but Ont could not relax or congratulate himself. The crash of shield on shield. Sounds of battle rushing in. Screaming. Shouting.

"Behind us!"

"To the sides!"

He turned. Coming through the village were soldiers, made monstrous by firelight. More, coming round the village. The whistle of an arrow and a soldier fell.

"Go!" shouted Ont, and he turned. Ran for twenty paces then stopped. Began loosing arrows together with Binor as the rest of the Forestals ran past them then stopped. They began loosing as Ont and Binor ran past. Twice they did this until it became clear the arrows were not stopping the pursuers. In the day they were terror weapons, but it now was too dark and their effect could not be seen well enough by the enemy to scare them.

"Just run!" shouted Ont.

Running. Ragged breath loud in the darkness. Bodies looming up. He almost tripped over a corpse, a child. A man came at him. Axe raised, screaming. Ont smashed him in the face with the thickness of his bow. Did not stop. Running on, tripped over a spear. Rolling, coming to stop against the corpse of a woman, face a deathly rictus, a wound where an eye should be. He felt he should know her, was not sure. His hand found a spear and he used it to push himself up. Running once more. A screaming soldier came at him and was peppered with tiny darts. Shyun vanished into the darkness as the soldier dropped, convulsing. A falling sword, he tried to dodge, felt it bite his arm. Kept going. Warm blood dripping from his hand. Knew, on some deep level he'd passed from the cleared area around New Harnwood and into trees, the thickly leaved bushes that filled this area hid people well. He stopped. Gave himself a moment. Heard people all around. Screams in the night. Shouts. Excitement. Pain. Terror.

He waited. Given time he knew he would begin to see a little better; even though the darkness appeared complete it never really was. He wondered where the night creatures were? Slowly, he began to make out a glow from the bushes around him, a barely perceptible green. It took time to see it but once he did he could make his way. He found another body. Definitely one of the Rai's soldiers. Her face contorted as if death had brought her a vision of terror, the Osere rising up to claim her, the Star Path forever denied. In her neck a slender dart. The shyun were still here, still hunting.

"Thank you, forest friends," he said quietly and continued on. At one point he found himself lost, everything unfamiliar.

"Ont!" he turned at the voice, Issofur, Furin's boy. There among the trees then gone but Ont went toward where he had been and found himself somewhere familiar. Knew which way to go then. He wondered how many had made it. Had the wedge even broken through the Rai's forces? He did not know. Had barely been able to see. The death of the Rai should have helped them. What if only he was left?

No. That could not be. Ranya had brought them here. Surely not to die. Surely not.

He continued moving slowly through the forest. The silence broken by echoes of pain and fear, but more occasional now. He heard the enemy around him. Call and response. Finding each other. Homing in.

"What is attacking us?" shouted a voice with the harsh rasp of a Rai.

He smiled at the thought of the shyun, slipping through the undergrowth unseen with their poisoned spears and darts.

When he found the grove he could sense his people, knew they were there, hidden. So he broke cover. If he was wrong and they were the enemy then his end would be quick. But they were not. His people were here, and more were coming, turning up in ones and twos. He stood and waited, watched with his bow ready while they ran past him and into the grove.

Sengui appeared from the dark, shepherding a gaggle of children, Issofur amongst them as they ran past him. Sengui was still holding her spear and shield. She stopped, turned and stood in front of him.

"We did it," she said. "But they followed us." He saw torches in the wood. Hundreds of them. Enough that they did not care if it made them targets for arrows or Shyun. He backed up, followed by Sengui until they were in the grove. So many people, he could not count them they were packed so tightly.

"There's too many out there," said Sengui. "We can hold the entrance against all but Rai, but the sides of the grove, they can just climb them and rain spears down on us."

"Where is Ania?" He pushed his way through the crowd, down to the twisted tree that held a taffistone in the tortuous grasp of its wood. "Ania!" he shouted. His people moved aside. "Ania!"

"It will be all right." He looked down to see Issofur, smiling up at him: sharp teeth, bright eyes. "The forest likes you."

"I am here, Ont." He turned from Issofur to find Ania, stood by the taffistone. How? He had just passed it and she was not there then.

"You said to come here but the Rai have followed us, there are hundreds out there in the wood."

"Do not worry," she said.

"How can I not worry?"

"Because as the boy said, the forest likes you." She smiled at him. "You are all about to become Forestals, and the Forestals protect their own." With that she turned and put her hands on the taffistone, said something in a language he did not know, did not understand and yet he felt the words resonate deep within him as if they were familiar. The material of the stone changed, twisted, bent, folded in upon itself.

What appeared within the taffistone he had no words for, it was like looking into a pool of water that stood on its end, taller and wider than him. But it was not water, because if it was he would see himself in the reflection, his face and body distorted by the ripples and he did not. He saw another place, a strange city illuminated by the explosive light of the forest and cages holding luminescent creatures. He saw people, walking around in the long green robes of the Forestals. A group were gathered on the other side.

"What is this?" he asked.

"It is an older magic than throwing fire or water," said Ania, "and a secret we have long guarded. Pass through, Ont. Lead your people to safety." He did not know what to say. The pool in the stone frightened him. He turned, saw the faces of his village, tired, scared, dirty. Only death awaited them here. They had lost everything. New Harnwood was gone, Furin was gone. Cahan was lost somewhere. He turned back to the taffistone. Frozen, he could not move.

But something else could, it came running past him, weaving through his feet, stopped to bark and chitter at him as if telling him not to be foolish. Then Segur, the garaur, jumped into the arms of Issofur, and the boy ran laughing with it through the pool, and, though he could not understand how or why, they appeared on the other side. The child still laughing, the garaur's bright, sharp mouth scolding his cowardice though he could no longer hear it.

"Follow me!" he shouted, his voice as loud as he could make it.

And he stepped into another world.

39

Sorha

The woman, Furin, refused to be scared. She had not been weak as Sorha had imagined. She had not been cowed as they travelled through Wyrdwood. No shouting or screaming for help, but a glowering presence behind her, not even wincing when Sorha bound her hands tighter than needed.

When that did not work and the woman did not react Sorha leaned in close.

"I promised I would not destroy your village." Furin only stared at her. "But soldiers followed me, and they are not under my command. Your village will be gone by now. Those who survive will be executed by the Rai. Their deaths will be slow and painful." The woman, Leoric of a dead village, stared at her. Sorha had been ready to strike her, she wanted her pain. Then the Leoric spoke.

"Cahan Du-Nahere will destroy you. He is the master of the trees, the forest comes to his call." Utter belief in the Leoric's eyes.

"He will come to my call, and bow before me," said Sorha. "That is what I have you for."

"You will regret taking me."

"I doubt that." Sorha stood, finishing off retying a lead to the bindings around Furin's hands. "And you will be in no state to care; I have heard death in the Slowlands is hard and that is what is planned for you." That got a reaction. Fear. All had heard of the Slowlands, where time was not the same, the impassable barrier that surrounded Crua on the western and eastern side. Sorha stood, pulling on the lead and dragging the woman through Wyrdwood, towards Treefall.

She was hard on the Leoric but the woman refused to complain, or moan or show pain. In revenge Sorha refused the woman food and water, stripped her of her warm coat and wore it herself. Regretted it quickly, the coat was too warm and made her sweat even in the cold of the north, but she could not give it up. When they rested the woman only stared at her. Not speaking at all, not asking for food or water. Only when they stood to set off again did the woman speak.

"If you do not feed me, give me water and my coat back, I will be dead before you can use me for anything."

Sorha wanted to hit her, feel the sting in her hand of another's pain but the woman was right. She needed her and the cold in the north would kill. So she gave the woman dried meat and water, put the coat around her shoulders. As she leaned in to wrap the thick wool around her Furin whispered in her ear.

"Cahan will kill you for this." All Sorha could do was pretend she had not heard, and keep in mind that no matter what the woman may say, she was her prisoner and it was Sorha who was in command here. Brooding silences and dark looks would not change that.

Now even that was gone.

On return to Treefall there was no sign of Laha, instead she met with a Rai she did not know, and would not even give her name. The Rai looked her up and down, her wooden armour so dark as to be almost black, and carved with spearmaws that danced around her chest piece and over the helmet, long tentacles making a basket over her powdered face.

"Is the false Cowl-Rai dead?"

"No," said Sorha. The Rai looked over her prisoner.

"This is not the trion Venn," the sneer as apparent in her voice as it was on her face. Around them Wyrdwood was filled with the sound of axe on wood.

"No, she is the Leoric of the village they called New Harnwood."

"You were meant to kill the false Cowl-Rai and bring back the trion." She turned away, to the trunk commander stood behind her, his armour well-worn and scarred. "Take this village woman to my tent, I'll have half her life, then have her impaled on the raftway. Make sure she lives long enough to set an example." The man stepped forward but Sorha put herself between the man and the Leoric.

"No." The Rai turned back to her.

"You think to deny me?" She looked amused. "In case you have forgotten you are far from what you were, now let my man do his job or join this woman on a stake." Sorha almost drew her blade. She could strike this Rai down, here and now, and the woman would deserve it for discounting her so easily. The woman was denied her cowl so near to Sorha, she would be easy prey. Pain and blood would drown out her anger. The trunk commander had his hand on his blade. Behind him his soldiers had lowered their spears as if they could sense the fury about to burst from Sorha. She bit down on her tongue, feeling blood flow into her mouth. Only blood drowned her anger, and if it could not be another's then it must be hers.

"Laha," she said, her tongue feeling too large for her mouth, already bruising, her teeth red, "second only to Saradis, Skua-Rai of Tarl-an-Gig and right hand of the Cowl-Rai, is who I answer to. The false Cowl-Rai was not there but my prisoner is precious to him. I have left word she is to be executed in the Slowlands. It will bring him out of the forest."

"Laha did not tell me this," said the Rai.

"Well maybe you are not that important?" The Rai stared at her.

"Laha went into the forest, with a raft caravan. There were reports in earlier attacks of a man with them who may be the false Cowl-Rai." Did Sorha show the shock she felt on her face? She did not think so, but it ran through her the way tremors ran through the ground of Crua. The Rai took a breath, looked around. "We will cage this woman," said the Rai, "until Laha returns. And you, Sorha, go put your Hetton back in their pens, we do not want them wandering around. They make the workers nervous."

She did as asked, spent the rest of the day with the simmering anger inside as her only companion. Furious with Laha for striking out on his own, and somewhere deep within scared he would be successful. That she would cease to matter, her plan would become irrelevant and all Furin would be worth was a lesson, a body on a stake at the edges of the camp. She hoped Laha failed, that he would come back and be glad she had the Leoric.

In the end she got neither.

Laha was dragged into the camp by a small group of his soldiers, wild tales of the havoc the false Cowl-Rai had wreaked upon them. Of men and women vanishing into thin air. Laha said nothing, an arrow had pierced his shoulder and he was feverish, sickly.

No one knew what to do. Eventually it was decided Laha must go back to Tiltspire, the prisoner as well and Sorha was sent as her guard. Dismissed as worth nothing more than a jailer.

She was not allowed near Laha on the journey to Harnspire, he was cared for by healers. She was unwanted, relegated once more to the back of the column, seething and hissing and swearing to herself, laying all her misery at the feet of Cahan Du-Nahere. She would make him pay.

Then she would make the Rai pay.

She did not know how but she would.

For now she walked, in the stink at the rear of the column. Moving through the night, the air thick with the scent of vegetation and the light and calls of the creatures that lived within it. She wondered if the Forestals would strike this caravan, she would like that. To wet her blade. They may even bring Cahan Du-Nahere and she could finally finish what she had started in these same woods so long ago. That thought kept her going in the days and nights they trudged through Wyrdwood, Harnwood, then Woodedge but apart from a small amount of excitement when they had to burn an orit nest to pass, there was no sign of the Forestals, no attacks and no arrows.

In the end, the journey was uneventful, boring even. They stopped briefly at the Hungry Forest where Harn had once stood. Her sleep that night was disturbed by dreams of the night Cahan Du-Nahere had brought the forest in to being against them. The trees rising from the ground like great snakes, branches reaching out quick as whips in the night, taking lives, impaling bodies and her standing among it, untouched, as if the trees could not see her. As if she did not exist.

Then the dreams changed.

She stood alone in a darkness. Something moved around her; like the trees of the hungry forest it writhed, it reached, it searched and she felt such a terror as she had never known. A conviction grew within her that she stood before the Osere. Just out of her sight was something impossible and inhuman, more gasmaw than of the people. It hungered and it longed and it wanted.

But it did not find her, could not, and although she knew she dreamed, that she was not in the real world, she found she could not wake. She could only stand, her body frozen in a place of darkness, while something huge and terrifying moved out in the shadows. It sounded like porcelain clinking against itself, it sounded like water dripping from leaves, it sounded like rotten flesh sloughing from bones.

It was terrifying, to be so helpless. She had never been utterly helpless before but this creature, this vast and bulky presence outside of her knowing, stripped away her anger, made her useless.

When she woke it was with the most profound relief she had ever felt, and she did not understand why. It was only a dream. She was no stranger to bad dreams. As she stood she found thin roots of bluevein had grown over her armour and she pulled them off, they stuck to her fingers and she had to rub them off on a tree to clean herself of them. They made her feel wrong, reminded her of the dream.

They left part of the caravan at the Hungry Forest to help fell it. The woodcutters who were attempting to remove the trees kept falling to them as the forest resisted them. They had to work in groups. If a woodcutter worked alone their friends would come back and find them strung up on trees. The smallest wound they took would turn poisonous. Lots had been drawn for which soldiers would stay, as no one wanted to.

The entire caravan was uncomfortably quiet and Sorha could not escape the fear the dream had left her with.

Between Woodedge and Harnspire the circle winds pushed the grass of the plains almost flat and bit into her, cutting through her clothes as if it had discovered a spite lacking when she had travelled before. She wrapped herself tightly in a crownhead wool shawl of green and walked on. The landscape was riven, the grass plains cut across by new fault lines and deep crevasses spanned by spindly, makeshift bridges. Each bridge festooned with small flags and charms that rattled and chimed in the wind. Statues of Tarl-an-Gig, in the guise of the balancing man, dotted the fields, some were so old they were falling apart. She could not help thinking this was a forlorn landscape and no matter how much she told herself it was only the dream echoing within her she knew it was a lie. Crua was worn down by the reaching tentacles of war. It could not last much longer.

She tried to pull herself up, banish this strange malaise that had fallen over her. If the war could not last much longer then that meant she must work all the more quickly to avenge herself upon Cahan Du-Nahere. Be all the more determined.

Their welcome in Harnspire was subdued. The trion, Falnist, who ran the place after the death of Kirven Ban-Ruhn greeted them with a small group of guards. Laha in his litter was spirited away into the spire and the rest of them left to fend for themselves, given directions to the cheapest boarding houses. She made herself as comfortable as possible, given the smell and the noise. She was almost asleep where was a knock on her door.

"Sorha Mac-Hean?" Her hand went to her knife.

"Yes? Who asks?"

"I am Brilla, I assist Falnist in the running of Harnspire. The monk Laha is asking for you." She let go of the knife and opened the door. The woman there, a monk, bowed her head. "I will have someone bring your belongings to the spire." Sorha peered into the gloom beyond her and the rickety wooden stairs that led down to where poor food and worse drink was served.

"The skyraft comes tomorrow, Laha wishes you to travel with him," said the woman. Sorha nodded.

Brilla led her through Harnspire; it was different to the place she had visited before. There was no joy here. The beginnings of the market were being set up in preparation of the skyraft's arrival, but it was meagre looking and she saw no sign of performers, or a stage – though there was a gallows, and pikes with the remains of rotting bodies on them.

Laha was in the central spire, low down as befitted a man of his stature. Brilla led Sorha through the tunnels of the spire, not as disturbing low down as they became further up, but the dark walls put her in mind of her dream and she could not lose that feeling that she was being dragged down, into a dark place where she no longer had control.

Laha lay on a bed, the sheets pure white and his skin grey against it, unnatural looking. His breath came in gasps as if the air fought him, not wanting to become part of his body. There was a terrible smell in the room, the stink of sickness, of a body slowly breaking down even while the spirit within it fought for every moment of life. The arrow had struck him in the shoulder, shattered the joint. The wound was raised and black with rot. Sorha knew he was doomed. Once the rot had started in a wound then the only chance of life was amputation, but where the wound was made that impossible.

"Sorha." Her name an exhalation of pain. Laha's hand, the one on the opposite side of the wound moved, the fingers curling as if to draw her to him. She approached. Knelt. "See what they have done to me." The words coming hard, each one a struggle. His eyes opened, locked with hers. "I would have liked to have fought you." The hint of a smile.

"You are dying," she said. No point lying to him, surely he knew.

"Wrong." Spittle fell from dry lips. "I am becoming." Becoming dead, she thought, but did not say. "You must. You . . ." He coughed, spittle laced with a web of blood and something blue-black and foul looking. When the coughing subsided he looked back at her. "You must ensure my body goes back to Tiltspire." Sorha nodded. "In my pack is a willwood rosette, it gives you authority in the name of Saradis. I put you in command of making sure Cahan Du-Nahere dies. And of taking my body to Tiltspire; tell Saradis to lay me upon the stone."

"What?"

A long gap, as if the words had taken most of his energy. Eventually he spoke again, little more than a whisper.

"Saradis knows."

She found herself smiling.

"Then I will attend to your wishes, Laha," she said and bowed. With that his mouth twisted, breath rattled in his throat and the life went out of his eyes. Sorha turned to find Brilla behind her. "You heard what he said?" She nodded. "Then make sure Falnist is aware, now I must find this rosette he spoke of."

40
Udinny

I stare at the rift in the landscape for a long time. Or a short time. I do not think time in the strange world Ranya had brought me into works in the same way as it does in the lands of the living. Syerfu waits patiently but is of little help. I pull the needle from my back, hoping it will grow into some weapon capable of sewing up the massive tear before me.

It stays a spear.

"That did not work, Syerfu." The crownhead bleats and begins to crop grass that is not grass. I take the walknut from my pouch, hold it aloft. "Show me where to go!" The walknut does nothing. No pull, no movement from it. Below tentacles wave in the blue-black of the rift. As I watch they find one another, form thick ropes and solidify.

"It is a mystery," I say to myself. Syerfu nods her great heavy head, up and down and down and up. "And you are still no help." The crownhead lets out a hiss. A bridge of tentacles breaks up and reforms below. Part of me wants to attack the tentacles nearest to me, my hand itches for the spear and the ghost of warrior Udinny whispers words that are more compulsion than sound in the back of my mind.

But there are other whispers, other Udinnys. I do not know them but how can I not listen? They are me. Or I am them?

The more I listen, the more frightened I begin to feel. They want me to go *down*.

Do they really say it? I do not want to hear it. All my life I have thought of down as something to be avoided. Down is the Osere, the dark creatures who once ruled Crua. Though why should it be the same in the lands of Ranya? Even if it is not, the tentacles are thick as a forest, waving and ready to snatch and tear at me. Staying away from them feels like a much better decision to make.

Are the tentacles the Osere? It makes a terrible kind of sense.

They frighten me.

Down.

There is only darkness below, the weight of the lands above squeezes out the light. Down is wreathed in Osere tentacles. How can I, small, scared, dead Udinny, drifter and wastrel – albeit the chosen drifter and wastrel of a god – hope to combat creatures that fought gods?

Fought gods and almost beat them.

Caused the breaking of great Iftal.

Down.

On the other hand, what else can I do? Stay here on the edge of the rift and watch the tentacles for ever? The land beneath my feet shivers as the rift becomes larger, pushed apart by the tentacles below.

If the answer is there, if there is some way of helping Ranya, as the voices of me that had once been appeared to think, then the longer I wait surely the stronger the Osere tentacles become?

I have to act. What I look upon must be the Osere, their darkness come to life, the destruction of our world, the absolute opposite of the glowing star that is Ranya. I draw my needle spear.

"Syerfu! We are needed in the darkness below, I do not

know what calls us, but called we are! Forward!" With that the crownhead bleats and leaps into the air and we fall. It is not a true fall, it is controlled as if Syerfu is a gasmaw and can jet from side to side. As we fall, the writhing tentacles reach out for us, some I pierce with my spear, but most we simply avoid. Syerfu twists and bucks and dances around them and never once do I feel like I may be unseated. It is as if we are one body with two minds and she leaps, left and right in great arcs through the growing darkness until, eventually, we can fall no further.

What a strange world we stop in.

Like a cave. Complete darkness that is not darkness. Where in life I was used to light, gilding every edge, and picking out the world in brightness and shadow, here I look on darkness, in deep purple gilding, and shadows so dark they swallow up my gaze. The land above me is lost, I can no longer see the tentacles. Was I too deep for them? Do they concentrate on the land above? I do not know, could not know.

But I also felt a certainty, now I was here there was no doubt it was where I should be. In this darkness, far below – why, or why not had not been revealed, but that is the nature of Ranya's path. You walk it and have faith it will take you where is right for you to go.

In the walls around me I can make out tunnels, six, or seven or maybe eight, heaving off in different directions. Some are huge, as high as shade trees, others are not much taller than I am, sat upon Syerfu.

Now must be the time for the walknut. I lift it.

Ask, "Which way?"

A definite pull toward one of the smaller tunnels. I slide off Syerfu and begin to walk. She follows and as we enter the tunnel I notice lines of blue, so dark they are almost black; running along the lines are pulsing lights that vanish into the distance of the tunnel, drawing me on.

"Where do we go, Syerfu?" I say softly, "where will this

take us?" Syerfu says nothing. It seems she knows no more than I do.

So we go on, into the unknown, into the darkness and yet, just for a fleeting moment, I have the strangest feeling, as if those I have known and loved in my life are with me, and then it is gone.

Still, even if it is only my imagination, it is a much-needed comfort in this darkness.

41
Ont

How to explain the impossible?

The feeling of stepping through stone. One minute to be in fear of your life, surrounded by the shouting and screaming of war. The next to be in silence and quiet and between those states. A moment of eternity that lasted no time at all. As a child he had fallen in a pool, one of those rare, deep bodies of water seldom seen in Crua. Ont still remembered the feeling of falling but not falling, how he was completely enclosed by the water, at once aware this was an entirely alien element for him, but at the same time he was relaxed, he felt protected from the world and safe. That was what it was like passing through the taffistone.

Now he stood somewhere entirely different, Wyrdwood he was sure, he recognised the smell, the flashing lights of a thousand tiny creatures in the air. But there was more light here than there should be, flickering floating torches, spiralling up and round, above him and across from him. It was as if someone had taken fire and scattered it through the air. And the air was different, almost stinging his nose it was so fresh, and warm, not cold. Warmer than he had ever known, like the body of another was pushed up against his skin. He was sweating like if he had worked hard, or run a long way.

He had done both, of course. Moments ago he had been running, fighting for his life and the life of those around him, but he was used to the sweat on his skin becoming cold quickly, turning to a thin sheen of ice in Harsh, or making the winds of Least cut his skin like knives. Here it was as if the air was sweating. He pulled off the thick woollen cloak he wore, though it brought little relief from the heat.

"What is this place?" he said.

"This is Woodhome." He turned to find Ania peeling off her cloak as she walked towards him, behind her his people, equally as bewildered as him, and behind them the taffi stone, as solid and tall as any other. He wondered if he had dreamed the journey here. If he still dreamed. Or if he had passed along the Star Path into some wooded paradise and none of this was real. "You are in the tree city of the Forestals."

"It is warm," he said, and felt stupid saying something so obvious.

"We are in the southern Wyrdwood."

"How?" He barely said the word, it slipped from his mouth.

"All will be explained in good time."

"Good," said Ont as she passed him, then he hurried after her. "Why did you keep this place secret from us?"

"It is secret from everyone; even new Forestals usually wait years before they are told of Woodhome." As Ania spoke more Forestals appeared, they held garlands of leaves and placed them over the heads of confused villagers before taking their hands and leading them away. Some would not go. Pulling their hands away, gripping their spears tight, ready to fight. The Forestals held up their hands, to show they held no weapons. "We will not hurt them, Ont," said Ania, "we will see to their wounds, give them rest, water and food." Ont's head was spinning, this still had the air of a dream.

"Go with them," he said, his voice a croak, and he cleared his throat. "They have brought us to their secret city. It is an act of trust. We must trust in return."

"He is right," said Ania. "You are accepted."

"Why?" It was Sengui who asked this, stood in a small knot of people, dressed for winter and sweating in the humidity.

"We have watched," said Ania. "You have tried to live within our rules, with thought and honour to the forest." Ont watched as more of the villagers let themselves be garlanded. "And we are partly responsible for what has happened. Your protector was with us when you were attacked. We took him away."

"We must find Cahan, tell him about Furin . . ."

"He will be here soon."

"Cahan?" Ont could not hide his confusion. Ania nodded.

"Tall Sera leads the raids, soon the Rai will move against him in force and he will return here with Cahan. If he has not already. I have had messages sent to call him home." She walked away. "Now, come with me. Let me show you this place." He felt a tugging on his clothes, Segur scaled him to lie around his neck.

"I must see to my people."

"They will be cared for, Ont." Her voice was different, still harsh – it was her nature to be harsh – but something was within it now. It was the same voice he had heard her use when she taught him to shoot, when they had been alone. "You have come to Woodhome, you are of us now."

He followed her across the carpet of needles, caressed by warm air. Usually Segur against his neck would be a blessing, protecting him from the cold, here the creature was stifling but he did not move it, he found comfort in the garaur's nearness. As he walked he stared in wonder at his new surroundings; she called it a city yet he saw no houses or huts. Only lights that hung in the air and the great branches of the tree they walked on. The more he looked, the more he began to see patterns in the lights. They were arrayed in strings, lines of light through the darkness: was that a stair? A bridge?

The Forestals had a city in the sky.

They walked past three great carved statues, tall thin figures in long robes with branches growing from the long skulls of their heads. They disturbed him on a level he did not understand. It was not that he thought they meant him harm, more that they seemed to embody something that was at once familiar and too large for him to understand. He stopped and stared up at them.

"What are these?"

"The Boughry," said Ania, "The Woodhewn Nobles of Wyrdwood."

"You worship them? They are monsters, they . . ." Ania was staring at him. His words froze in his mouth.

"They are cruel sometimes, yes," she turned to the carvings, made a short sign over her chest, "but they can also be kind, and they can be generous. They are the great trees of the forest made flesh and cannot be judged by the standards of people." She nodded to the statues. "And we do not worship them."

"You don't?" She shook her head.

"We acknowledge them. Sometimes we do their work, and sometimes we fight against their desires as we put our own above them. But Wyrdwood is their world, we live within it on sufferance. For all things we desire, there is sacrifice."

"They took Udinny." Ania nodded as he spoke. "And I think something like that came for Sark, I only half saw it."

"Yes," she nodded, "Sark, the woodling who brought you to New Harnwood. As I said, for all things there is sacrifice."

"Woodling?"

"Those who stand between. Not a rootling of the forest, but not one of the people. The hunter Sark is one, he is changed physically and you see him less and less, you must have noticed?" Ont nodded. "One day he will simply vanish into the forest and become a rootling. The boy, Issofur is another."

She walked on and he stayed for a moment, staring at the Boughry and thinking on what she had said. He had noticed the changes in Issofur, and Sark, but somehow they had not seemed important. He scratched the head of the garaur and followed Ania through the gloom of Wyrdwood, going towards the trunk of a massive cloudtree. As they neared it Ont saw steps had been tacked to the side, zigzagging up and down the trunk. He followed Ania to the stairs, touching the thick, gnarled bark of the tree as he did. Wondering at it, he could feel the strength of life beneath. Was that what it was like for a cowl user?

As he put his foot on the first step he glanced back at the carvings of the Boughry, and had the oddest feeling that he was being watched, judged and weighed by something beyond his understanding. Was it something floating and flying in the air, or did the eyes of the nearest statue glow? A momentary flare meant just for him? He did not like it, it felt like a cold chill running down his back.

Running through the forest, huge and powerful. Smashing branches and trees and soldiers out of the way.

Segur whined.

"Ont? Are you well? You stumbled. The stairs can be dangerous." The Forestal was looking at him, concerned.

"It is just . . . a lot to take in. New Harnwood is attacked, then you open a door in the stone and then, well, this." She nodded, smiled.

"Yes. I suppose it is. I hope Tall Sera waits below. All will be explained then."

"All?" he said as they descended toward a huge bracket fungus.

"Well," he could hear amusement in her voice. "Part of it at least."

The stairs went down a long way, but remained so high that Ont was never comfortable looking down. They twisted back around themselves as they descended the trunk, occasional platforms giving a small respite from their journey. They stopped at the top of yet another stairway, a junction where another stair led off into the darkness and a door at the end opened into one of the huge bracket fungus that grew on the cloudtrees. Ania gave him a gentle push towards it.

He expected it to be stifling within but it was not, it was cooler inside than outside; tiny glowing creatures in cages lit the room and he could see channels had been carved into the fungus so the walls were not smooth. The channels led up to holes in the ceiling where arrangements of seeds, the large, finned ones that spiralled down from trees in Harsh, had been put and they spun lazily, moving the air in the room and creating a breeze. Sat around the edges of the room were people, though he did not know them: another Forestal, by her an old man – who was bound, though he did not look displeased about it. By him another man, a warrior from the look of them, but not a Forestal, he looked as confused as Ont felt. With him was a woman, also clearly a soldier, her face drawn with pain and she held her side as if wounded. A tall man stood by the wall, looking out into the darkness and with him was a figure Ont recognised.

"Venn!" said Ont. The trion turned, smiled and came forward.

"Ont," said Venn, "have you looked around this place? It is full of amazing things."

"Is Cahan here?" Something passed across the trion's face, something dark. "He is not dead?"

"No," said Venn. "He is not. When we arrived here he was angry, he thinks the Forestals have been lying to us. He has gone to cool off."

"He may have a point," said the tall man, "but I was not ready to discuss the whys and wherefores." He stepped forward, intelligent eyes in a thin face. "You are Ont, priest of Ranya to the people of New Harnwood?" Ont nodded. "I am Tall Sera. I lead the Forestals and you are not the only new arrival here." He motioned towards the people sat around the room with an elegant hand. "Venn you know, the others are Tanhir, one of my people. By her is Fandrai—"

"Why is he bound?"

"He is dangerous," said Tanhir.

"No longer," said the old man, he sounded quite happy, despite the bindings.

"I have brought him here for justice," said Tanhir.

"And it will be done," said Tall Sera before Tanhir could say any more. "Next to them is Vir," the soldier nodded, "and by Vir is Dassit, a Trunk Commander of the armies of the Red. There are some of her soldiers here, but they have not been allowed fully into Woodhome, not yet." Ont's thoughts must have shown on his face, and Tall Sera smiled to himself. "You are not betrayed, Ont, do not worry. Even if you were, Dassit is in little state to fight." The woman tried to give him a nod but it became a sharp intake of breath and a grimace. Vir, by her, turned to help but she pushed him away. "You probably wonder what you are all doing here?" Ont nodded, as did the trunk commander and the Forestal, Tanhir.

"I should not be here," she said. "I should be taking Fandrai to the hanging bough and—"

"You go nowhere," said Tall Sera. There was no mistaking the threat in his voice, the displeasure. "You left without permission, you brought back strangers." Ont felt sure he saw Vir swallow. Tanhir sat back, folded her arms.

"I have explained that."

"You owed them your life, you paid a debt," said Tall Sera. "But you were only there because you disobeyed me."

Ont could almost feel the Forestal woman's desire to argue, but instead she looked at the floor. "Now," said Tall Sera, "we all have much to discuss. But first I must find Cahan. In the meantime meet each other, become familiar with one another."

"Thank you," said the old man, a big grin on his face. "Truly, when I saw where Tanhir had brought me to I expected to be already swinging from a tree. Every extra second is sweet as sap."

"Do not thank me," said Tall Sera. "As the world changes around us some things do not, our hospitality has a cost."

"Oh," said Ont, and he sat by the Forestal, Tanhir, this new, warm world suddenly feeling less magical.

42
Cahan

He climbed.

This wooden town of the Forestals felt as if it went up for ever. When he thought there could be no more stairs there was always more stairs. He passed whole villages suspended on thick ropes of woven vines, bladderweed and floatvine growing through the buildings to help hold them up. Thousands of glowing cages lit the night. As he climbed he found more communities, built on platforms around the huge trunk of the cloudtree. The size of this one, like all of the cloudtrees, was almost too much for him to take in. The fact people could live in and on one of the forest giants had never occurred to him.

No one questioned his presence, no one bothered him.

There were lifts, arrangements of vines, gasmaws and people working together to trundle cages of Forestals up and down, or across between the villages. He did not feel comfortable taking one, were there rituals? Was barter expected? He did not know.

The heights of the forest rang with the sounds of happy voices, flocks of children ran, laughing and shouting, splitting to pass him like water round a rock. Groups of adults watched over their play, sat around talking and laughing while they cooked food over glowing rocks. Rootlings were everywhere and no one seemed to care. There was a sense of relaxation and happiness here. In Harn, and even in New Harnwood, the people had always been tired, there had never been quite enough to eat and the work was constant. In Woodhome that did not seem to be the case. The people here were relaxed, gentle even. They had long, shining hair of all colours and wore face paint of white and light green stripes, like a dappled forest floor.

He turned away, his mood sour. These people were bandits, living off the backs of others. It was easy to be wealthy when you did not have to work for it. They were happy but he was angry, the Forestals had been here all the time, living in plenty and yet they had left him and his people to struggle. He turned his back on the laughing adults and their squealing children. Lies. He thought it all lies. They were no better than the Rai who lorded power over the people – the Forestals had riches and chose to hide them.

He needed sleep, or rest at least but when he closed his eyes he felt the moment when Laha had paralysed him. Felt his muscles freeze. Felt his helplessness and so he did not close his eyes. He climbed and he looked around him at the city built in and around a cloudtree. He did not let himself marvel at the platform villages, or marvel at rows of houses floating in the air. He did not stare in wonder at the pathways built around the body of the tree. He did not admire the engineering as the lifts went up and down and across. He only climbed. Felt his breath start to shorten and did not know why. His head ached and his heart beat faster. He felt nauseous. He did not stop climbing. He was drawn to climb and the more he climbed the more he felt drawn. It was as if he followed a walknut, going up and up, struggling to breathe until he came to the first massive branch of the cloudtree. A thing so thick and heavy it was hard to understand how it could remain attached to the trunk, another branch just like it was on the other side. When he reached the top of the branch he saw a town, the branch had been flattened out and was large enough to have not only wooden buildings, but streets and a market. Placed along the streets he saw ominous statues of the Boughry, Forest Nobles all tall, thin and branch-horned. Among them walked Forestals and he realised there must be thousands of them here. Hiding, living well while the rest of Crua struggled. He turned around, walked to the other branch.

This one was different.

It was dark.

In many ways it was the same as the other town: the flat branch, the buildings. But it was silent and walled off, the buildings broken down or destroyed entirely.

Decay, even here.

It called to him.

"You have come higher than most do on their first visit." He turned to find Tall Sera, the Forestal came to stand by him. "You should be careful if you are not used to it. The height can make you dizzy and sick. The air is thin here."

"I am fine."

"You sound like you are struggling to breathe."

"I am fine."

"You are stubborn," said Tall Sera. Was there mockery in his voice?

"And you are a liar, a liar and a secret keeper." Cahan turned away and stared into the dark village.

"Well," Tall Sera shrugged, "we are definitely the second, but we are not the only ones. You kept yourself secret for many years."

"That was different." He did not look at the Forestal. "If people knew about me they would find me and kill me."

"It is exactly the same."

"You can travel from one side of Crua to another in the blink of an eye. Escape the Rai at will." Cahan could not keep the betrayal from his voice, though he did not quite understand why he felt that way. Or if he really felt that way; somewhere deep within he suspected he did not and that if Udinny were here she would see through him, see his real worry. That he had taken death and sickness within himself and its slow creep was overtaking him in a way more definite and inevitable than his cowl had ever threatened to do.

"Yes we travel," said Tall Sera, "the taffistone network is an ancient thing. Forgotten by all but us." He put something in his mouth and chewed it. "We may even be able to teach you to use it. You have a cowl, if you know the right words the stones may open for you." The idea frightened Cahan, because what if they did not? What if he was too changed?

"But you did not tell me about this before?" Cahan wanted a fight, he wanted to bait Tall Sera and at the same time he hated himself for it. "Harn need not have died, you could have taken them all out of the village, brought them here to your land of plenty."

"Does that look like plenty?" Tall Sera pointed at the darkened branch village before them.

"You could have saved so many lives," said Cahan.

"Would you have? If your people had kept a secret for generations? Would you have given it up for those who hated you?"

"You use your secrets to rob and to kill." Cahan made the words a challenge because he did not want to reply to Tall Sera's question and be forced to lie.

"Aye, on occasion we do that." Tall Sera's voice sounded as though he was drifting, and Cahan wondered if he chewed on some forest drug. "But our enemies are the Rai, they always have been. They are everyone's enemy if only they would see it, and it is them we rob and them we kill."

"My enemy too, and yet you left me to defend a village that was indefensible. And what of New Harnwood, when the Rai finally come for them? Will you let them die?" He expected an answer at least, but instead Tall Sera was silent and something sank within Cahan. "They have already come? What happened to . . ."

"Your people are here," said Tall Sera. "And before you say anything you regret, I lost people defending your village and getting the villagers to the taffistone." Cahan wanted to ask about Furin but he dared not. His mouth was dry, his heart beating fast. Tall Sera took his silence for continued anger. "And the first time, yes, maybe we could have taken you all away. But what were you to us then? More servants of the Rai? Cutting your wrists to feed the next in a long line of false gods?" Cahan stared at him, knowing the Forestal was right but not wanting to give an inch. Besides, he could not speak, her name was waiting in his mouth. *Furin*. He breathed, calming himself.

"Many died that need not," he said eventually. What would he do if Furin was dead? The dark sea within churned.

"And that is unfortunate, but you know what those people thought of us then. How long do you think the secret of the taffistones and Woodhome would have lasted?" Cahan glanced at Tall Sera, looked away. "You do not think there was at least one who would have betrayed us?" Tall Sera left a gap in the conversation but all that filled it was the warm night air, though it did not warm Cahan. "All who come to the Forestals do so through trial, and are only let in among us when they have proved themselves. Nothing good is won easily. The Woodhewn Nobles are hard, and you as much as any other know the truth of that." He took another bite of his narcotic. "But you are here now, and your people are welcome to become my people. There is enough here for all if we work together."

Cahan did not look at the Forestal, it annoyed him that he knew Tall Sera spoke the truth. He should ask about Furin. How she would fit in. But if she was gone then how would he react? He did not want Tall Sera to see him weak. Instead he stared into the dead village.

"It is not all happy families here then." He nodded at the silent branch.

"It is not families here at all. That is not our way." Cahan looked at the Forestal, confused.

"How do you raise your children?"

"The Rai kill, wars destroy villages, children are orphaned. That is how Woodhome started. Once, long ago, the Forestals were a small group of people hiding in Wyrdwood. As the Rai warred we found those who wandered lost and without a place, brought them in." He smiled at the forester's confusion. "We raise children as a village, Cahan, we have no first or second husbands or first and second wives, we love as we will. We share everything."

"Even your houses?"

"People have favoured houses, that is respected. If someone needs somewhere to live we build together. That is what we have learned, if none want, there is little strife."

"Who taught you this?" Cahan tried to scoff but could not quite manage it. The way of life might sound alien to him, bizarre. But he could not deny the calmness of the forest city in the trees, it felt like nowhere he had ever been.

"Our cowls taught us, Cahan. You have seen how they work for us. We work together to accomplish all things." Now, he thought, he had found the thorn in the flower.

"So you throw your children into blooming rooms among the dead, just like the Rai do." It made it easier for Cahan to discount Tall Sera and the apparent happiness of his people. He was still haunted by the nightmare of the blooming rooms. He still woke in terror some nights, his senses overwhelmed by the scent of rot. Though recently, not as much.

"We are not barbaric, Cahan Du-Nahere. We do not need blooming rooms, just like you did not need a blooming room."

"What do you mean?" Did the night air get thicker? Did the heat became suffocating?

"The cowl was always in you, Cahan, because you spent time in Wyrdwood as a child." Did he? He remembered forest trips. Hunting. He even thought he remembered being in Wyrdwood sometimes, but was never sure. Tall Sera put a hand on his armoured arm. "Whether you remember it or not, Cahan, you were in Wyrdwood. The seeds of true cowls are set there, the strong ones. What the Rai do? Forcing children among the dead? It is unnatural, twisted. That is why they must steal life. What they have is a dark mirror of what should be. The Rai call us bandits and outlaws, but it is them that steal, we share."

"But I had to kill . . ."

"They twisted you." Tall Sera spat the words. "The cowl is a gift, it brings us together. You have seen how we use it. We lend each other strength. Alone, me against a Rai?" Tall Sera shook his head. "They would break me like a twig. But if they came upon a group of us, we would fight together. Then we are strong. We are like the forest, when one falls, another rises. The Rai stand like a single tree in a field – it may look strong but it is alone, weak. One alone may not fell it, but a people working together can dig out the roots and send it tumbling." Cahan turned away from Tall Sera, looking into the darkness of the ruined village.

"Not always together," he said, and pointed at the broken houses.

"That was the mushroom grower's village," said Tall Sera softly.

"Did they offend you? Did they want their own houses, or to claim a lover for their own and not wish to be forced to share?"

"No one is forced to share," said Tall Sera softly. "We only say no one owns another." He turned to stare at Cahan, his eyes dark pools. "Were you drawn here, Cahan Du-Nahere?" Cahan did not answer. "The mushroom growers were always popular among us. They grew many types of fruiting mushroom and like all here, they gave away what was needed and received what they required. Some of their mushrooms tasted good, some made you giddy, others induced visions." Tall Sera's words hung in the air, slowly dying before he began to speak again. "Then the growers started dying."

"Why?"

"Something wrong with the mushrooms, what they grew changed, twisted." He took a breath. "Something they brought in from the forest, it caused a euphoria in those that ate it to start with."

"A drug?"

"In a way. But the euphoria was short-lived, larger and larger doses were needed to find it. Then people began vanishing, it was a mystery we could not solve. There was no sign of foul play, it appeared they just up and left. Which was unusual, and worrying."

"Can people not leave here if they wish?" Tall Sera did not answer, only kept talking.

"One day we saw fire up here. You can imagine, living in the trees, how much we fear fire. We found the mushroom growers' village closed off, fire raging well beyond a barricade they had built to deny entry. When we tried to pass they loosed arrows, not at us. Not directly. But near enough to warn us off." Tall Sera sounded different, sadder. "You must understand, we have disagreements but we work to overcome them, war among us is unheard of."

"What happened here?"

"No one would answer us from the mushroom growers village, it lasted three eightdays. We approached, they sent arrows. But the fires were contained. Then one day they did not stop us approaching."

"Why?"

"They were all dead." Tall Sera stood straighter. "They had split into two factions, fought among themselves. One group was shot full of arrows. The other had done the shooting, then the shooters had taken their own lives." He ran a hand through his long hair. "The drug, it had changed those who took it, and many of those who grew the mushrooms."

"How?" Cahan found he was holding his breath, a terrible certainty growing within him that he did not want to examine.

"The drug made them strong; though there were few of them they had been terribly destructive." Tall Sera stared into the gloom, seeing past events and his jaw tightened, muscles bunched. "They had ripped some of those who did not take it limb from limb, destroyed their houses. It was remarkable that the defenders had held them. The final ones to fall had left a message for us."

"What message?" Cahan had forgotten to be angry, forgotten to feel sorry for himself. Despite the heat, his skin felt cold.

"It said, 'We did not know. Forgive us.'" Tall Sera still stared into the dark village. "The mushroom beds were all dead, burned out. The bodies of those who had been shot down with arrows, they were strange, not like usual corpses, withered rather than rotted."

"A cowl will do anything to survive, it sucks the life from the user." Cahan said it almost by rote, because he did not think this was the work of cowls. Tall Sera looked at him, shook his head and made a clicking sound with his mouth.

"Your cowl, maybe. Not ours, they are part of nature and they live and die with us." He let out a sigh. "Further back, in the rear of the village, we found our missing. Not all the buildings had burned. Our missing had been used as food for fungi. Some were still alive despite the flames."

"You put them out of their misery," said Cahan.

"They were not miserable, they rejoiced. They babbled endlessly, bodies thick with bright blue fruit that glowed in the darkness." Cahan's breath felt like it solidified in his lungs. "I could feel where the seed of these mushrooms had attached to their cowls, it fed on them, changed them. The strength they had was a lie, parasitic, not shared." A tight band across Cahan's chest, crushing him. "They kept babbling, saying the fire was coming even though they were half burned." A coldness within. Those words an echo of a life left behind long ago, but if Tall Sera noticed his shock and his fear the Forestal gave no sign of it. "The roots of the fungus had run from them and into the tree branch below." He looked up. "This cloudtree has been our home, our true firstmother and father for as long as there have been Forestals. They had infected it, you could see where it had eaten into the wood, the bark peeled back and blackened. Beneath, what should be stone hard was spongy and it pulsed in a way that was unnatural. Lines of blue and deep purple. Like wounds. We had to cut the branch away. We mutilated one of the great old gods of the forest." Tall Sera let out a breath. "That was my doing, and though I did it for the best reasons I do not doubt the Boughry will take their price for it." A silence, a breath, and when Tall Sera spoke again his pain was as true as if he had cut off his own arm instead of a branch of the great tree. "Something is very wrong, Cahan Du-Nahere. The fungi, they are the return of life from death, they are rebirth. That is the cycle of Iftal, the proof of the Star Path and the world beyond this. Something is poisoning it. And it is not just them. The taffistones . . . little by little, the network is changing."

Cahan could not speak, could not think. He knew what Tall Sera said was right, because he had touched that corruption and it lived within him. It gnawed at him and made promises that sounded sweet and real. But what those here, struck down by the fungus had said: *the fire is coming*. Those were the words in the prophecy of Zorir. Cahan's god, once.

It could not be a coincidence.

The two men stood together in the darkness for a long time. Listening to the night sounds, the creatures chirping, people laughing and playing music.

"Did you track me all the way up this huge tree, Tall Sera, to tell me the story of your village, and your worries? Do you think I can help somehow? I cannot." Cahan sounded more gruff than he meant, to mask his fear.

"You do not know that, Cahan Du-Nahere," said Tall Sera, "but you strike me as man who must find his way himself, even though the path may be harder to walk." He shrugged. "There is saying among us for those like you, we say they'd sooner the Boughry's Horns than Ranya's path."

"You know of Ranya?" Tall Sera nodded.

"We know many things, but the saying means some, when shown the way, will jump into a thornbank rather than take instruction. You are one of those people, I feel." Cahan had no answer to that, it was a difficult thing to deny.

"That is why you are here? To show me the way?"

"I am here to ask you something. I will ask you once," said Tall Sera, "and never again." His eyes searched Cahan's face, and the forester wanted to look away. He still carried within him the life of the clanless, and such direct eye contact was difficult. "Stay with us, Cahan Du-Nahere, help us find what ails Crua. Do not leave here and take your own path. No matter what has happened. The world is bigger than just one person."

"Why do you say that?" Tall Sera bowed his head.

"As I said, your people arrived earlier today. Ania has been among them for the whole time you were with me, and before. She is not blind to your feelings. Even if you are sometimes." He felt horror. Felt like a hammer blow was falling towards his forehead, unstoppable, lethal.

"Furin," he said. "She is gone." Something crossed Tall Sera's face, then he shook his head.

"You do not know how tempted I am to tell you she is dead." Cahan did not understand, why would the Forestal be so cruel? "It would save you much pain, but you will find out the truth from your people anyway. She lives." The relief was like seeing rain on a dry field, knowing the crops would grow and you would not starve that season. "But the Rai have her." The relief drained away, the crops withered.

"Then she is as good as dead."

"No, though it would be better, I think. A Rai named Sorha took her. The Rai say they will exchange Furin for you, in the Slowlands. Otherwise, she will be executed there."

"She will die in agony in the Slowlands," said Cahan. The words stung his mouth, the thought of it a fire more painful than the darkness within.

"Yes," Tall Sera did not look at him, "she will. But it is you they really want. You and the trion, I imagine they think it will be easy to take them once you are out of the way."

"You could help me free her."

"I will not let my people walk into a trap for you."

Cahan wanted to rage. Wanted to claim betrayal, to claim they owed him. He had fought for them in the forest. He had watched the people of Harn die needlessly when the Forestals could have saved them.

But Forestals had died too.

"Furin sent a message with her people, telling you not to come." Cahan nodded, of course she had.

"I am going to get her back," said Cahan. Tall Sera nodded again, staring at the remnants of the mushroom growers' village.

"I am not surprised to hear that," he said. "You are stubborn, but you have a code and when the two come together I doubted you could be argued with." Cahan was about to speak but Tall Sera raised a slender hand. "Though you are determined to jump into the thorns, Cahan Du-Nahere, it seems Ranya still looks over your path, and I think she may have sent others to hold the briars back for you." He smiled, though it was a small, sad thing. "Come with me."

43

Saradis

It had been a poor day.

The first report she had expected and it did not dismay her too much. Her forces in the south were making better speed than Saradis wished. Already they had taken a fortified larger and killed everyone in it. Now the army moved forward and it was not impossible that the entire south would be conquered in a season. That was not for the best, but it was not a tragedy. The Rai often became enthusiastic when the killing was easy, but Saradis could manage her Rai. She was used to that.

Not so easy to face the note in her hand, or the monk of Tarl-an-Gig who stood before her, their head bowed and hidden beneath a pale hood. What it said felt impossible, still filtering through her consciousness and the words swam before her, becoming meaningless.

Laha was dead.

How could that be? Laha had been with her for ever; even when she had sent him away he had refused to leave. He had followed her through her disgrace and her madness. She had been sure that Laha would be the one who stood at her side when the world burned, when Zorir rose. But no. Not now.

Laha was dead.

Taken from her by Cahan Du-Nahere. She found herself trembling, grief and anger mixing until they were indistinguishable.

"Shall I send the woman in, Skua-Rai?"

Her? For a moment she did not know what the monk was talking about. Send who in? Grief had washed away all sense. She took a breath. Sat straighter. Composed herself. What had the monk been saying to her? She could not show how shaken she was.

"It is rare the bearer of messages such as this," she held up the note, "would wish to see me."

"She came with the body, she is quite insistent, Skua-Rai. She has Laha's willwood rosette and it does not bleed her." The body? She had brought the body all this way? "She has also brought a prisoner." Saradis blinked away tears. If this woman had his rosette, and carried it without wound then she had Laha's confidence. And a prisoner? What could that mean?

"Take her to my rooms."

"Not here, Skua-Rai? Shall I send guards also?"

"No." Saradis did not know what Laha had told this woman. "Just send this Rai to me."

"She is not Rai."

"What?"

"She dresses like Rai. But the Rai say she is not one of them. They do not like her."

That at least was interesting.

"As I said, send her to my rooms." The monk nodded and backed out of the reception room. Saradis did not go straight there, let this woman wait while she walked off her grief. Instead she went to the Cowl-Rai, to look in on her and report on the gains in the south – if the Cowl-Rai was in any state to receive her words. She passed the silent guards, found herself in what had once been a throne room, now she thought of it as the cage room. It stank of animals and sweat. The Cowl-Rai lay on the floor, hair a corona around her head as she moaned softly.

Saradis's first thought was that Nahac was ill, her instinct to run into the cage and check on her, but she had fallen for that before. Seven guards had died caging Nahac again, and another ten she had been forced to kill as they had witnessed the Cowl-Rai's madness.

"Cowl-Rai," she said softly, and the figure in the cage rolled over groaning. She pushed herself up onto all fours like an animal. Her eyes were bloodshot and the blue lines beneath her skin looked brighter than usual. The stone on her head glowed.

"Take it out," each word a struggle, "please, take it out."

"I cannot, you know that. It will kill you."

"Please," the word barely perceptible, "the voice hurts so much."

"Voice?" said Saradis, and found herself focused on the Cowl-Rai in a way she rarely was. "What voice?"

"Please," her words growing stronger, louder and she clamped her hands to either side of her head. Her agonies shaking her body. "Take it away."

"The voice, what does it say?" asked Saradis again. Something cleared in the Cowl-Rai's eyes and she shuffled forwards, put her hands on the bars. Sweat ran down her face.

"If I tell you," she said, each word a gasp, punctuated by short sharp breaths, "will you take the stone out?"

"You will die."

"I do not care."

"Tell me then." She found herself whispering. "Tell me what you hear."

"Stronger," said Nahac, "it's getting stronger."

"Zorir?"

"The fire is coming!" The words a shriek of agony. Something soared within Saradis, Laha's death almost forgotten. Then Nahac spoke again, begging. "Take it out, you promised." Saradis took a step back, and another, and for every step the Cowl-Rai repeated, "Take it out," getting more and more desperate as Saradis backed away.

"Cowl-Rai," she said, "you are the conduit of a god now, I cannot take that from you because of a moment of weakness." With that she opened the door and slipped out; behind her the Cowl-Rai screamed and raged and the liquid darkness of her magic ripped apart the furniture in her cage.

When Saradis entered her rooms the woman waiting stood and gave her a small bow. There was something to it that made Saradis smile, not an unwillingness exactly, but it was not the way the Rai usually bowed to her. There was a resentment and an anger that radiated from this woman and she did not care who saw it. You want to see the world burn, thought Saradis, maybe we are more alike than you could ever know.

"You brought news of the death of Laha," said Saradis. She sat upon her most upright and uncomfortable chair, her stiff robes of many folds, and cage of twigs making her look suitably imperious. "He was dear to me, I have killed people for less." The woman did not appear frightened. She looked around the room, chose a well-padded chair then sat. "I am told you have brought his body with you too. I am curious as to why you think I would want a corpse."

"He requested it."

"Laha?" Did her surprise come through? She tried not to let it show. The woman looked up at her, something about her, not only resentful now but calculating.

"He said he was not dying, only becoming. I got the feeling he thought you would understand."

"Of course," said Saradis, "that makes sense." It did not, she did not understand at all.

"So you know why he does not corrupt?" said the woman. "A whole eightday dead, and he does not smell at all. Not even the wound that poisoned him stinks." Saradis had the strangest feeling the woman was somehow testing her. That a smile hid behind her face that could only be sensed, not seen.

"Tarl-an-Gig is powerful," said Saradis, "and Laha was one of the chosen."

"Of course," said the woman. You are mocking me, thought Saradis, and she studied the woman before her. Sharp eyes, white make-up cracked from travel. Once splendid armour now scuffed and used, a fighter. A survivor.

"Did Laha say anything else?"

"To put him on the stone." Saradis wondered about that. Then nodded as if it also made perfect sense.

"Tell me about the prisoner you brought."

"You don't want to know how your favourite died?"

"Did I ask?" The woman narrowed her eyes, then bowed her head in acknowledgement.

"My prisoner is Furin, Leoric of Harn."

"Then why is she alive? I do not suffer traitors to live."

"She is alive, Skua-Rai, because I believe you want Cahan Du-Nahere?"

"And?"

"She is dear to Du-Nahere." The woman smiled. "I have let him know she will be executed. I have told him where and when and that we will take him in exchange." Saradis would usually have taken exception at such plans being made before she was consulted. But she found herself – not liking this woman, she liked very few people, but admiring her, she was clever. Had seen an opportunity and taken it.

"You believe he will give himself up?"

"He is weak; even if he decides to fight for her, I will capture him for you."

"You will?" Saradis could not keep the surprise from her voice, or the disbelief. "Cahan Du-Nahere destroyed an entire army, but you will capture him?"

"He took my cowl." The woman stood, breathed through her nose as if to channel her anger. "Now I am one of your dullers, but walking," she said. "I am the weapon you need to capture him."

So this was Sorha, thought Saradis. She had tried and failed to take Cahan before. Though what she said was true of course, a warrior who could stop a Cowl-Rai using their powers was priceless to someone like Saradis and Laha would know that. If he was dying, maybe he saw her as a replacement?

But a warrior who failed, that she could not put up with. To forgive would make her look weak. Truly, her god guided her through a troubled landscape.

Yet Laha must have seen something in her.

"How was Laha killed?"

"He heard Forestals and Cahan Du-Nahere were attacking caravans," said Sorha. "He intercepted him, killed the two women who protected him. Almost finished Du-Nahere but the Forestals intervened."

"Why would Laha do that," she said, "if you had this woman who is dear to Du-Nahere?"

"He did not know I had the woman." Saradis nodded again.

"And you really think he will simply give himself up?" The woman before Saradis smiled. Nodded.

"He will, he has done before. He walked unarmed to me for a village full of people who despised him." She straightened up. "Imagine what he will do to save someone who really cares for him as he cares for them."

"So he comes here, to Tiltspire?" Sorha shook her head.

"No, if there is one thing Du-Nahere had shown it is that he is full of surprises. It seemed foolish to risk him coming here."

"Then where? How?"

"The execution grounds of the eastern Slowlands."

"The viewing stand there was damaged in the great

shaking of the last season, when a rift opened between the taffistone and the Slowlands."

"Surely it can be fixed?" said the woman. Saradis stared at her, insolent, sure of herself despite her failures.

"If I approve your plan," she replied.

"He is coming whether you approve it or not."

"You should have told them to bring the trion as well."

"With Cahan out the way," said Sorha, "there will be no one to stop you taking the trion." Saradis thought on that, the woman was right of course, but she did not want to say that, not now. Not here.

"You say he has aligned with the Forestals?" Sorha nodded. "Their bows are dangerous. A city hampers them, denies them range, forces them into close combat where they are weak."

"The Slowlands are empty, flat. We will see him coming from a long way off. He knows to come alone. If he does not we kill the woman and leave. We are no worse off."

"Well," Saradis stood, "it seems you have it all worked out." She walked forward. "But you cannot kill him." Fury passed across Sorha's face, a brief and intense flash before the woman gained control.

"He is too dangerous to keep alive."

"My god wants him alive so he will be taken alive. It is not a discussion." Saradis waited as the woman fought for control, and realised she had decided she would use her.

"Very well. Alive," said Sorha. Saradis tapped a finger against her knee.

"I will send people to rebuild the scaffolds. The rift will need a bridge as well, we do not know which direction he will come from. We will make a celebration of it. Maybe execute some others while we wait. It has been a long time since I have seen a Slowlands death. I miss it."

"But I will be the one who takes Cahan Du-Nahere?" said Sorha. Her hatred was impressive. Saradis wondered if was what kept her going, and what would keep her going once Du-Nahere was taken.

"Yes," said Saradis. "Give me Laha's rosette." The woman dug into the coat she wore over her armour and passed the rosette over to Saradis. A willwood star of Iftal, a circle with eight points growing from it.

"This is a symbol of my authority, you have to earn it," said Saradis. "Do so and I may give it back to you." Sorha stood back.

"What else should I do to earn your trust then, Skua-Rai?" Even now, beaten, she could not hide the mockery in her voice. You truly are dangerous, thought Saradis.

"Go to the Slowlands, ready it for the executions. I will follow with the prisoner when it is ready."

"Very well." She bowed her head.

When she was gone, Saradis called her monks. Had them take the body of Laha to the room where she communed with Zorir's stone. While they did she reapplied the white make-up to her face. The lines of her rank replaced, she found her centre, breathed and calmed herself.

When that was done she went to look upon the body of Laha. He looked peaceful, except where the arrow had struck him and the darkness around it. Poison put into his body by cowards with cowards' weapons. She touched his face. So serene, the fragments of stone in his forehead still glowed slightly.

"The stone," she said to herself. Closed her eyes, swallowed.

From her waist she took the ropes which cinched her robes tight and tied them around Laha's wrists. His body was slack, cold, and heavier than she thought his slight frame should be. With much struggling, grunting and fighting, she pulled him up until he was draped over the stone. His back against it, hands stretched over the top.

It exhausted her, took all her strength. She squatted before the stone as if about to commune with Zorir, but not this time, all she wanted was her breath back. To rest a little.

Behind the stone, the Light Above fell below the horizon, and in the darkness she saw the faint blue glow of the taffistone. It not only ran across the stone but over the body of Laha, and she wondered what gift her god would give her, give him.

She had a flash.

A momentary vision of the world below, the growing loom of Zorir's power, and at the centre of it a great, dark, eight-pointed star. Did she hear a scream from far below, where the Cowl-Rai was imprisoned?

She bowed her head.

"Zorir," the word a breath, "your power is growing, our time is near."

44

Dassit

Dassit Gan-Brinor had never been so confused in her life.

At first she was struggling to understand how she could be alive. Struggling to understand what had happened at Fin-Larger. A rock that opened and became a door into a different place. Pushed through it by the Forestal, her and Vir, and the monk and all that remained of her Fifty. She didn't remember much of the moment, only pain, though she knew from talking to Vir and the others it was not caused by the travel. She was hurt, sick, and the Forestals had treated her, along with the monk and Vir who had sat by her side through her days of pain and delirium.

She had hallucinations in that time, of walking along the Star Path, watched by the vast, glowing forms of every god she had ever heard spoken of, gods of every grove and stone that had been dedicated. She accompanied herself, spoke with herself but these versions of her were strangers. The gods watched and she felt unworthy. Like she had not fought hard enough, that she had run when she should have died.

In her dreams, she had been a moment away from falling

from the path to tumble down into the world of the punished, the Osere below. Only the words of herself, her other selves, stopped her.

Stay on the path.

Eventually, she had woken.

Then she had been brought here.

Down through the Forestals' tree town.

Walking through Woodhome, she had wondered if she really had died, had walked the Star Path and found herself in the promised land of the Cowl Star: the paradise of the worthy dead. She was sad, but not surprised that Vir was here with her, also dead.

If she was dead.

She thought she must be dead. The forces of the Blue had overwhelmed Fin-Larger, sad that Vir had paid with his life for his loyalty. He deserved more.

"Strange all this, innit?" he had said as they walked along a path suspended far above the ground. "The Rai never told us about all this. Not sure I like it. They don't have firstwives you know, or second or third, or the same for husbands. They just do what they want. With who they want." She didn't answer, not at first. Couldn't answer. "You all right, Trunk Commander? Or those mushrooms they gave you still got you spaced out?"

That was how she knew it was real. Vir's voice, his suspicion. It was exactly how he should act in a Forestal city. But not how he would act on the Star Path, she was sure.

There were groups of people everywhere, laughing, joyful children running. The guards in hoods and dark make-up smiled at her as she passed. Music, the singing of people and rootlings. She did not know rootlings could sing. There were gasmaw farms and the smells of good food on the air. More rootlings and garaur everywhere. Even crownheads. Herds of crownheads, in a tree.

"You are right, this is not how they told us the Forestals lived," she said.

"Not natural," said Vir. "Living like this, in a tree."

"How many got out of Fin-Larger?" she said.

"Not including us?" he shrugged. "Twelve."

"Twelve out of fifty," she said, and found she had no appetite for more conversation.

Now, she waited in a room inside the hugest fungus she had ever seen, a room that was pleasantly cool despite the heat of the air outside. With her were others. The death monk, the Forestal who had brought them here. A trion who was small and thin, shy, but gave her a smile before turning to stare out across the forest from a hole cut into the bracket fungus. Another man came to join them, very tall, and he carried with him a quiet authority. He went and stood with the trion. Dassit's side hurt, she put her hand against it.

Another man arrived soon after, he was huge, but looked as shocked as she felt. His clothes were bloodied, his make-up smeared with dirt and something about him made Dassit think he had come straight from battle. He held a forestbow, but did not seem like the other Forestals she had seen. There was a brief conversation. From it she learned the tall thin man was Tall Sera, leader of the Forestals, the trion was called Venn and the huge man was Ont, monk of a god called Ranya, one who Dassit had never heard of.

Tall Sera left soon after. Leaving the rest of them alone. It was not a comfortable silence. The trion continued to stare out of the window, the rest sat there. They were there for a long time, the night grew thicker, the sound of it increasing in volume. The air cooling until eventually, the death monk, Fandrai, spoke.

"It's very quiet," he said. "Maybe we should get to know each other."

"It is a waste of time anyone getting to know you," said the Forestal woman.

"Are you absolutely sure they are going to execute me, Tanhir?" said Fandrai.

"Yes."

"They are taking their time."

"They needed you to look after the Trunk Commander."

"I thought you were not meant to bring strangers here," said Fandrai. "On pain of your own death." That was news to Dassit.

"She gave me my life when she did not have to. I owed her."

"Why bring me as well?"

"Because I want to watch you die," said Tanhir, her voice dripping with venom. Then she added, grudgingly, "And I needed you to heal Dassit after the poison you gave her." The Forestal glanced across at her, gave her a smile and Dassit thought, for a second, maybe there was more there than just a debt owed.

"You are a healer?" said the trion, going over to the bound man.

"It is not my primary purpose," said Fandrai with a smile, "but I know my way around the human body."

"He is a murderer," said Tanhir. "That is why he is condemned. Have nothing to do with him, child." The trion looked shocked, stepped back and ran a hand through messy, thickly curled dark hair. Fandrai chuckled.

"I am not a murderer, I am a devotee of Hirsal, Lord of the Swarden."

"For whom you murdered."

"Devotion takes many forms, the forest will be fed and its armies must be replenished," said Fandrai, looking over at Tanhir. "Your own hands are hardly clean of blood. Or do you claim the Boughry to be gentle and sweet?"

"Have you just come from the same battle as Ont?" said the trion, stepping between the old man and the Forestal. Dassit did not immediately realise they were speaking to her, as they did not quite look at her.

"No," said Dassit eventually. "I think the man – Ont? –" she nodded at him, he nodded back "– has only just arrived.

I came here a few days ago." The trion studied her, there was something very attentive in the way they considered her.

"You were hurt in a battle?"

"I was hurt before the battle, stabbed. But the battle did not help."

"Could I try and help you?" said the trion.

"I am not about to undress in front of strangers," said Dassit. It was as if her words, spoken quickly and in embarrassment, were a weapon that wounded the trion. "But thank you."

"I . . ." They tripped over the word, blinked. "I need only lay my hands upon you. For a moment." They were plainly embarrassed. "If you will allow it?" Would she? It seemed foolish; if Fandrai with all his arts could do little then what could this child do with a touch? On the other hand, she had travelled through a stone to this place and the pain in her side, it was like something lived within her and was trying to eat its way out. What could it hurt to try?

"Very well," she said. The trion placed their hands on her shoulders. At first there was nothing. Then a gradual warmth that spread through her body and when it got to her side, where the pain was sharp and cold like shards of ice, it lingered there. The pain slowly ebbed. She wanted to speak but could not, the trion above her was lost in some other place, eyes closed, in communion. The oddest feeling came over her. Like wandering out of camp at night and sitting on the grass in the warmth, letting the silence soak into her as she watched the Cowl Star above. Like a moment of peace in the turmoil of her life.

"What are you doing?" The warmth fled. The trion stepped back, looked half ashamed.

In the entrance to the mushroom stood a man, big. Not as big as the monk, Ont, but far more threatening. He blocked the light, it made him into a silhouette. A dark figure, clad in close fitting, jagged armour that hugged the lines of his body. He turned his head, looking at those gathered. He wore no make-up and sported a beard, something rare in Crua. But none of these things were what really struck her.

What hit her hard was the aura the man brought with him, something powerful and frightening. She had seen spearmaws move through the woods, known on an instinctual level that they were inimical to her, that they would kill her without a thought. This man made her think the same thing. He was exactly what she had always thought Forestals were, something primal and dangerous, and yet he did not seem to be one of them. Tanhir did not look like she recognised him. In fact, she moved back a little in her seat when he came in. He smelled strange too, like forest loam when it was wet, like dark still pools among the trees that you knew were not safe to drink from.

Tall Sera came in behind him.

"This is Cahan Du-Nahere," said the Forestal leader, "some of you know him. Some of you do not." He looked at Dassit. Another Forestal came in behind him, a woman who looked like she would rather be somewhere else; she nodded at the monk, Ont, and sat by him. "I have two problems," said Tall Sera and he turned to her. "The first is you, Trunk Commander, and your troops, even though they are not many." Any trace of the warmth put into her by the trion fled. "And you, Tanhir, and your obsession with that man," he pointed at Fandrai. It had never occurred to Dassit that Tanhir may be acting without the permission of her people in pursuit of Fandrai. "You have brought people here who should not be here. Who," he turned and gave a small nod to Dassit and Vir, "and I apologise for saying this, we do not know well enough to trust." Dassit shrugged, what he said was fair. "The other problem is Furin, Leoric of New Harnwood, and Harn before it."

"What of Furin?" said Venn. "Is she all right?"

"They have taken her," said the man, Cahan, his voice more of a growl than speech, there was something cold and distant about him. "They intend a Slowlands execution for her. In the east." The trion visibly shrank. Dassit wished a Slowlands execution on no one. The thought of it made her blood run cold. "It will not happen," growled Cahan. He did not look at anyone, his hands were balled into fists. Did Dassit imagine it or were spikes growing from the wrist guards of his armour? "I will not let it."

"And there is my problem," said Tall Sera. "I will rob the Rai, we have always done it. They expect it. But I will not send an army of my people to stop a Slowlands execution. We are ambush fighters, not an army."

"They will come for you," said Cahan. "As soon as the south is dealt with you will be the last inconvenience."

"That may be true, but the later it is, the better for us." Dassit was not sure she agreed.

"Bad idea to let your enemy draw breath before you attack," she said. The lack of pain had made her bolder. Tall Sera cocked his head, looked at her.

"That may be true but I have made a decision. The Forestals will not assist in the return of Furin. However," he looked around the room, "Tanhir has told me you are quite the tactician, Dassit."

"Me?" She was not sure she liked the sound of that. Tall Sera nodded.

"Yes. You. This will be dangerous, some troops will be needed and you have thirteen soldiers with you, all of whom need to prove their loyalty to Woodhome."

"Or?" said Vir.

"A swift trip to the forest floor from the top of the city," said the Forestal who had come in last.

"Ania is brutal, but right in a way," said Tall Sera. "Those who have not proven their loyalty cannot be allowed to leave with memories of this place. Though we will not execute them, we have ways of removing their knowledge of us."

"Should throw 'em from a tree," said Ania. "Much simpler."

"You want us to save someone from a Slowlands execution?" said Vir. He shook his head. "There's nothing there, nowhere to hide, no way of escape. Dassit, me, twelve soldiers. They'll slaughter us. I choose forgetting."

"I will be there," said Cahan. It did not make Dassit feel much safer, though there was a real sense of power from the warrior. "And the Reborn walk once more. Where I go they follow. They are an army in themselves."

"And you will go, Tanhir," said Tall Sera, "you have disobeyed me and a price must be paid. You will take the monk of Hirsal with you."

"What?"

"You heard me," said Tall Sera, "you may need a healer."

"I can do that," the trion stepped forward but Cahan shook his head.

"We cannot risk they may take you, Venn. They want you. You are important to them." Under his breath, Dassit was sure he heard the man say, "and me." For a moment the trion tensed up, then Tall Sera was there.

"He is right, Venn. And there is much here for you to learn." That seemed to convince the trion, they stepped back.

"Very well," said Tanhir. "If a fight is the price of my transgression I will ready my bow."

"I will go too," said Ont. "I can use a bow, and Furin is my Leoric."

"I'll go." Tall Sera looked surprised as Ania stepped forward. "Someone needs to keep an eye on 'em ," she said, "and I like to kill Rai."

"Did no one hear me say I choose the forgetting?" said Vir. Dassit was looking around the room. Thinking. What Vir said was sensible, to leave here with no knowledge of the place and start again? Hard, but they would be alive at least. At the same time, she had the oddest feeling of familiarity, as if she knew the people around her from somewhere. Maybe some had been there when she was in her sick bed, hallucinating?

"I know we ask a lot," said the monk, Ont, and he was speaking directly to her, "we can fight, but we are not soldiers, your help would be of great value to us."

"You are not soldiers," said Vir, "and we're not suicidal. Anjiin's ruins, Dass, this is madness."

"I'll go," said Dassit and she was not even sure why. Just, looking at the monk, it felt right, like her own voice whispering in her ear, the same one she always listened to on the battlefield. Vir looked as though he was about to fall off his seat. "I can't speak for my troops, and will not force them to come, but I'll go." Beside her Vir sighed and shook his head.

"We should leave soon then," he said, "Osere-cursed long way to the eastern Slowlands." The Forestal, Ania, turned to him.

"Not necessarily," she grinned. "I believe there's a taffistone there?"

45
Udinny

As I walk, in darkness-not-darkness, with good Syerfu by my side and my needle spear in hand, I listen to the whispers of a thousand Udinnys behind me. They are hard to understand, their words are heard as if they are voices in a dream, loaded with meaning but that meaning so clouded it is impossible to understand. The words had a weight – though it sounds strange I cannot think of any other way to describe it – and that weight leaves me feeling that I have walked further along the path of Ranya than any other, that much is now expected of me.

Though, it could just be that I feel like I have walked an awfully long way.

It does not do for a monk to get above themselves.

The tunnel is tight, not much larger than I am, pulsing lights run along it, some bright, like Ranya, and others dark, like the tentacles I found everywhere in this realm. A shiver runs through me, a familiarity, a feeling that people I know and care for were close to me. Then it is gone. At the same time a flash of bright light passes down the tunnel. I try to follow it but cannot, though it vanishes not far ahead. I follow, thinking about how long I have been walking and how this place insists on remaining the same. It could be I am not even moving, or maybe that this tunnel only goes in circles; the walknut has ceased to be of assistance. It is foolish of me to expect this place to make sense, this is after all a realm of gods and there is no reason for it to obey the rules of the land of Crua I am used to.

I walk and muse until Syerfu stops, staring at the tunnel wall as if she finds something delightful in the matter of it.

"Come, Syerfu, we have things to be about for your mistress. We have no time to inspect the architecture."

Syerfu turns her heavy head towards me and bleats. Then turns back to stare at the wall.

"What are you doing you foolish creature?" She bleats again. "We cannot stop, we have a long way to go, we have to get to . . ." Well, I am not actually sure where we have to get to, but I am intent on getting there. "Now come on."

Syerfu bleats.

"What is this nonsense?" I walk back to the crownhead and she turns her head from me once more to stare at the wall and bleat plaintively. "It is only a wall, Syerfu." In the darkness her eyes glow a myriad of different colours. "Do you see something I cannot?" A shiver. A feeling of familiarity. A faintly glowing line of light along the wall that vanishes at the point where Syerfu stands. "I cannot walk through a wall, Syerfu."

Another bleat.

"Look!" I place my hand upon the wall, it is solid though warm, which surprises me. The volume of Udinnys past rises in my mind. Syerfu bleats more urgently and backs up. Then using her great and heavy head, she gently pushes me forward. "Syerfu! You will crush me against the wall." I raise both hands, placing them against the dark surface. The susurrus of voices grows. For the barest, briefest moment I am blind. It should bring on a terrible sense of panic, but it does not, it feels natural and normal and with it comes the sensation that I am visited by another me, a long-ago me.

And I see.

But I see in a different way, not with my eyes but with some other sense that I do not understand, but feels entirely right. It changes the world around me. I see more, I see beyond. Lines of strange light that run through and around and up and down the material of the place. Ranya's web is here, touching upon everything. Also, the dark web of the tentacles, not as widespread as Ranya's, not as pervasive but far more menacing. Its threads so thin in places as to be almost imperceptible. In other places it clusters, thick and pulsating with a sense of dread. Between these two webs is another, different and somehow more permanent and powerful. A sense of energy and movement flows through it, vast and strong. It pulses along the tunnel and, in front of me, where Syerfu pushed me, it turns a corner and goes through the wall. All around me the lines of energy bend and I see an entrance to another tunnel. My hand still feels as though there is a wall, but this new sense shows me there is not.

Syerfu bleats.

I push.

Syerfu bleats.

The wall before me dissolves and a new tunnel opens, leading off in the direction I have seen the light going. Syerfu's bleating stops as I enter the tunnel and she trots along beside me. The strange light is gone, and once more I am in a black tunnel, though larger than the last one. As I walk I feel for that strange sense I had used to find the tunnel, and like the skills of the needle spear I find it at my fingertips, ready. The tunnel lights up, energy pulsing along it, *travelling*, the world a framework of glowing power. Just as easily I send the vision away.

What other strange abilities would Udinny's past gift to me? What magics are hidden in the people I have been?

No answers come. No doubt when they are needed they ill step forward. For now I walk, as I have walked ever e I first heard Her voice, in trust, and my crownhead with me, my walknut in my hand, and my needle t my back.

nnel grows larger as we move down it, and then nother vast cave, like the one that had been h tentacles which I flew Syerfu through, though ar of the vile things. When I look with my ee energy pulsing round it, the gossamer s web and far above me a fracture, a place lines are broken, where their clean lines rooked, flowing hither and thither to d I wonder what this shows on the k, way above me is something else, een before. A huge, vast, shim- Was that the correct way to dead, the energy of death has where it is not polluted by urse.

As clearly as I know I

I do have toes, but

ive and living, it s from another d find a new A true and d my mind,

away; ottom shadows, han my ankles om Cahan and Venn.

Cowls. These were cowls, hidden within the frames of people I could not see. Who were these tiny people?

Or am I huge?

In this place, I have nothing to measure myself by. As I think on it I shrink and reform to be the same size as the ghostly cowls, and find myself within a maze, thick with energy, moving and changing and twisting, groups of cowls move through it.

And something else.

Within the strange space I inhabit is another intelliger and as I realise I hear the cry of all the other Udinnys

"Escape!"

Escape what? I do not understand. Around me shadow cowl-people stop their movement, turn and tate themselves in one direction. Then begin vanishi the crevices and alleys of the maze. With their va comes a feeling of oppression, like a cold rain Running feels like a good idea but it is too late. A it, whatever it is, I become very sure it has someh me.

"This, Syerfu," I told my friend, "does not bo good."

In the direction the cowl-people looked gr of blue and purple tentacles. Had it been t am not sure. If it has then it had been s enough to see. It is not small now. It is gro changing and feeding, the lines of blue en it are thickening. In the maze, the things t were walls are doing something, movin feeding the nest of tentacles. No, not all some.

"We should go, Syerfu." Syerfu ble be agreement.

I mount up, and as I do the nest writhes *and* I hear a voice but not not a sound. *Some*thing I have neve with it comes a deep and instinctual terror. This is a language long forgotten by me, by Crua, but known to my ancestors and passed down in the same way a raniri knows to run from a garaur without ever having seen one before. A voice that freezes my insides.

Something far back along the line of Udinnys screams. Screams a word I know and fear. That all fear.

"Osere!"

At the same time, the nest of tentacles bursts open and from it come shapes from my time in the forest with Cahan, long, streamlined and dangerous. They leap into the air, reaching out with vicious poisonous tentacles.

Spearmaws.

"Go, Syerfu! Go! Run and may Ranya guide our steps!"

Oh, how useful it would have been to be huge again in that moment. I could crush the spearmaws in my hand, but much as I may wish it different, I remain the size I am. Syerfu gallops through narrow spaces as the spearmaws launch into the air. My loyal mount fast as the circle winds, flashes down long corridors and past strange walls full of possibility. None are flat like normal walls, more like cave walls, rutted with hollows and outcroppings but at the same time strangely regular.

Syerfu screams, skids to a halt.

A spearmaw in front of us, hovering in the corridor, tentacles squirming and twisting.

Behind us another.

Above us two more.

"Syerfu," I say, taking my needle spear from my back, readying it in my hand, "you may already have come to the same conclusion as I have, but this does not look good for us."

46

Cahan

They were in the hollowed-out fungus, making final preparations to free Furin. Cahan felt like he was in a dream. The story of the mushroom people had bothered him more than he had words for, and there was no one he could tell. A whole town corrupted, and those that had not been affected had chosen death in order to protect the rest of their people. Would he have to make that choice? Because he knew the darkness within was growing, the bluevein spreading imperceptibly inside him, and if he used the power it granted then it would grow more quickly.

But it promised so much, power without stealing life from another. If he could find a way to control it then maybe he would be able to help others with it.

Though why help them?

He did not know these people gathered round a table making plans. He did not have any reason to trust them. The Forestal, Ania, she did not like him, maybe she never would, but after the battle at Harn he had believed he could trust her. A lie. She had kept secrets, all of the Forestals had kept secrets. If they had been more truthful Furin would never have been taken, and there would be no reason for them to risk their lives now. It was plain that he remained to them what he had been all his life. An outsider. Unwelcome, not to be trusted.

Only the people of Harn had been different, but even then maybe not. Ont was clearly close to Ania now, and Cahan did not like that. The others gathered here, the old man, a killer who worshipped the swarden? Cahan wanted nothing to do with him. The woman Tanhir was right. He should be executed if the litany of crimes he claimed was true, preying on travellers to feed the swarden's numbers.

As for the woman, the one who was sketching out the plan, and the man with her and their soldiers who waited in Woodhome? They were of the Red. They were the same tyrants who had held down the north, who had ruled with heartwood-hard fists, who had tilted the land to take the warmth and kept it for themselves. Lived in plenty while the north shivered. They were here only because of misfortune. They could not be trusted. No doubt the first chance they got they would run back to their own. The woman's second, Tir? Hir? Vir? He was constantly looking around himself when he thought no one was looking, it had taken Cahan a while to pin down the expression on his face.

Distaste.

He could not be trusted, and as such Cahan did not trust those who put their trust in the man.

Furin. She could be trusted. Even thinking her name was a stab of hurt. How much time had they wasted, had he wasted, pretending he had no feelings for her? Too much. What did they do to her now? Torture? Or did they save that for the Slowlands? Tradition said you only put whole prisoners into the Slowlands, but did tradition matter to a woman like Sorha? She was a ball of hate and rage. He felt a cold inside, the writhing of what he had taken into himself.

Purpose.

"Cahan, are you all right?" Ania was staring at him. "You look like your ancestors disowned you."

"I am fine," he said. But he was not. The darkness within had been growing and now it had spoken to him. It had never spoken before.

It was not like the voice of his cowl, that had been part of him. This was *apart,* without. It was dark, and it was cold and he wanted nothing of it. Though that word, *purpose,* felt like a promise. A promise of power. He considered those gathered. They were few, and from what he knew the woman, Dassit, had already lost a battle and that was why she was here.

If he was to bring Furin back he would need strength.

He took a deep breath. A decision for later; death was one of the few constants in Crua, it was everywhere though the bluevein was not. He may not even be able to draw power in the Slowlands.

He was still in control.

"The execution ground is here," said the woman, Dassit, tapping on a crude map drawn on crumbling bark. "They are repairing an old viewing stand, looks like it holds about a hundred people. We were lucky not to be noticed by the workers when Tanhir took us through the stone."

"Lucky the door in the stone faces away from the stand," said Tanhir.

"We got close enough to have a good look," said Dassit. "The stand faces the Slowlands, looking east. North of it is a crevasse that cuts it off from the taffistone, which is north of the crevasse. Looks relatively new and a rope bridge has been built over it. The stand is tall and has a covered box at the top." She pointed on the map.

"Looks like someone important will be coming to watch," said Vir. Cahan wondered who.

"Beneath the stand are cages," continued Dassit, "enough to hold five or ten people, maybe more if they crowd them."

"Now we have seen the place," said Vir, looking across at Cahan, "getting your friend out may not be as impossible as we thought."

"The crevasse," said Dassit, "here," she tapped the map. "Between the taffistone and the execution stand. The rope bridge over it is the key." She turned to Ania. "You say there is another taffistone, not too far away?"

"To the south. Near an abandoned village called Hurna, about a day's walk away." Dassit nodded.

"Well," she said, "I can think of a hundred clever plans and ways to do this. But for all of them I would need more people, and more time. So the only plan I have is simple." Dassit looked across at Cahan. She was frightened of him. He was not used to that, people disliking him, yes, distrusting him, that too. But fear like hers? That was new, he tried to push it out of his mind, not to think about it. "You, Cahan. They want you. So we send you to the stone at Hurna. You walk to the execution ground from the south as if to hand yourself in. Then we come through the stone to the North and disrupt the execution. In the confusion you save this person, Furin?"

"She is not just a person," said Cahan, his voice harder than it needed to be, he knew it and yet he could not stop it. "She is a Leoric." Dassit licked her lips, then nodded.

"My apologies, Cahan. You get the Leoric, we will run interference until you are both over the rope bridge. We cut it behind you and then we escape back through the taffistone and they will remain trapped on the other side."

"What about Rai?" said Cahan. "There will be Rai."

"You must deal with them, Cahan," said Ania. "Tanhir, Ont and I will help with our bows." He nodded.

"The real problem," said Dassit, "is timing. Knowing when Cahan is there, and when we should turn up."

"I can solve that," said Ania. "In fact I had already considered it." She walked to the back of the room and came back holding out a mixture of leaves and vines in her hand. Cahan stared at it, he recognised the vines, common enough around the forests of Crua, but not the leaves. When he looked closely he saw they were bonded in some way, vines and leaves melting into each other.

"What is it?" said Dassit.

"An entanglement," she said. "Don't ask me how it works, I do not know. All I know is that it does."

"What do you do with it?" said Cahan.

"I rip it apart, give you half, keep half. When you want to send a signal then you tear your half apart and mine will fall apart also. Forestals have used them for generations."

"More secrets," said Cahan.

"You should leave soon," said the Forestal. "Find Venn, tell them you are going. They will be hurt if you do not." He could not do that. He could not bear to face the trion. They knew something in him was wrong and their naked desire to help him was hard to look at. Maybe when he had Furin back, when she was safe then he would ask Venn for help. See what could be done. But for now he needed the power, or at least the possibility of it.

Somewhere, deep within, he was also frightened. Frightened that if they could not rescue Furin and if Venn could not remove the darkness in him then he would be left cold and empty of all but rage, like the woman, Sorha. Or worse, that he would somehow infect the trion with what was within him. That his darkness would spread to the one person he had come to think of as better than he or Crua deserved.

"I should leave now," said Cahan. "I have a long walk ahead of me."

47
Venn

Tall Sera had introduced Venn to a Forestal named Issar, one of their guides. At first they had thought Issar would take them through the forest, show them things but she did not. Instead Issar led them up the trees and onto one of the lifts. Venn paused before stepping on.

"It is quite safe, Trion." Venn looked up at the woven vines it hung from. "Even if the vines break there is bladderweed woven into the fabric of the cage," she shook the bars, "it will mean we drift slowly to the ground." Venn nodded and stepped on. Such a strange feeling, similar to when they had first harvested floatweed for Cahan and, despite that being a time of real terror, looking back it somehow seemed simpler, easier. They had been terrified then, but all that had happened since was they had become more and more terrified. Learned to put a face on it so it was not as obvious to others.

The cage began to rise through the air. "Tall Sera said cowls are rare among trion where you are from." Venn opened their mouth, didn't speak, not at first. Those few words held so many things that surprised them. That there were trion here, first of all. That from the way Issar spoke it was clearly not strange for trion to have cowls among the Forestals. Those things felt too big for Venn to touch upon now, they would wait. For now they only asked one question, the one that felt the most manageable.

"Where do you think I am from?"

"Somewhere outside Wyrdwood," said Issar. "It is all the same to me."

"You have never been outside Wyrdwood?" Issar chuckled, and Venn wondered how old she was, it was hard to tell through the make-up of white and green stripes. "I am a focus, a guide, but no traveller," she said, "that is for the intrepid and the outcast and I am neither." She sounded friendly.

Outcast? Venn hid that away as another thing to ask about later.

"Then what do you guide?"

"The cowls," she said, and put out a hand. "Give me your hand, it does not need to be your hand if that is too much. We just need to be touching." Venn stared at her and the cage continued to rise. Amazing how far up it went. They reached out and took her hand. She was warm, her skin slightly rough. "You are strong," she said.

"Cahan said so, said I should try to get stronger." The smile fell away, not from her face but from her eyes.

"That is a very outside way of thinking." The lift slowed at a branch, swayed slightly. "Strength is useful, finesse is better." She let go and stepped out of the cage onto the branch. "Power is all around us, the cloudtrees hold more power than it is possible to imagine."

"Do you use it?" She shook her head.

"We would only take from the trees in the direst emergency, and then whoever did it would be stripped of their cowl after." It made Venn go cold inside; Cahan had taken from the trees. Issar walked on.

"Why is their power taken?" She stopped. Turned to them.

"Someone who is thirsty will always go back to a well

once it is discovered." Venn thought of Cahan, the way he struggled with what he was. The way events always forced him to use the power within.

"Cahan's cowl talks to him." Issar shrugged.

"I have heard others say that, but my cowl has never spoken to me." They passed statues of the Boughry. Venn tried not to shudder. "You do not like them?" said Issar.

"They . . ." How to explain it, Venn had never met them, never seen them. But knew them. When they had been the conduit between Cahan and Udinny, the Boughry had been there. Venn had felt them, a huge and alien power. Cold and indifferent but also interested, invested, full of need. "They took my friend." Issar bowed her head a little.

"They have taken some of mine too. The Boughry are not kind."

"What are they?" Venn stared up at the statues, a mixture of all things. Shaped like the people of Crua but much taller, much thinner. Skulls like crownheads, horns like branches, but no tentacles, no bladders that allowed them to float.

"I do not know."

"But you worship them."

"No," said Issar, quickly, the word sharp and hard in the warm air. "We do not. We respect them and we recognise we must live with them. They are of the forest not the people, they are wild and dangerous."

"They felt like more than forest," said Venn, the words surprised them. They had not known that until the Forestal made them think about it, but here, in the womb of the forest, Venn felt more alive and in touch with something beyond than they ever had.

"Some say they are the remnants of Broken Iftal," said Issar, "that they are cruel because they are incomplete."

"We are all incomplete," said Venn softly.

"Aye," said Issar, "but we are not all gods." The forestal began to walk away. "Now, come, the House of the Trion waits."

"I thought no one had their own houses?"

"That is sort of true, yes. But trion are different to the rest of us."

"I have heard that all my life." Issar came back and took Venn's arm.

"They are not forced to gather together, and they do not live there, Venn." She walked closely, companionable. It was sort of like being around Furin. "Trion have different abilities to us. It is good they have a place for them."

"They heal." Venn felt safe saying that.

"We can all heal, to some degree," she saw how stung Venn was to hear that, "but the trion have more of an affinity."

"That is the difference?" Issar shook her head.

"I will let Brione explain it, they will do it better." Venn nodded and they approached the House of the Trion. A great longhouse, like Furin's had been in old Harn. They walked along the bough, past groups of adults gathered everywhere, all dressed in shades of green, light robes of wool so sheer it was almost see-through. There were children too, like flyers attracted to flowers they moved from group of adults to group of adults. Taking food when they wanted it, causing laughter. Sometimes adults teased them, sometimes they only smiled. "It is a good way to grow up," said Issar, "yes?"

"Yes," said Venn, "it looks to be." Venn did not want to talk about their upbringing.

"Well, here we are, Venn, go in. Brione will be happy to welcome you."

"Are you coming?"

"We do not enter the House of the Trion."

"You are not allowed?"

"I am sure we are, but we do not enter out of respect." With that Issar took a step back and Venn looked into the darkness of the longhouse, swallowed, and walked in.

The house was even darker within, the heat a wall of

moist air and to Venn it felt more like they swam than walked. As well as moisture the air was thick with strange smells: smoke, herbs with high, acidic notes and low earthy tones. Out of the darkness came another trion, tall, dressed in the same sheer wool as the rest of the Forestals, baring more skin than it covered and Venn did not know where to look, though the Forestals felt no shame at nudity. Their face was made up with the same pale green base and darker stripes as the rest of their people, and they wore a necklace of feathers and tiny gasmaw beaks.

"Venn," they said with a smile and nod of their shaved head. "Welcome to the House of the Trion. Where you will find the Lens."

"Lens?" they coughed, smoke working its way into their lungs and the darkness around them took on a new quality, as if it was alive, moving. In the rear of the longhouse there were more people, Venn could not see them but they could feel eyes on them, curious and unthreatening, but strange.

"We are the Lens of the Forestals." Brione looked down on them, they were very tall. "Has nothing been explained to you?"

"I know your power is to do with touch, I know you do not take from the trees. But nothing else." Brione nodded.

"A start," they turned, "now, come with me to the rear, meet the members of the Lens who are here." They took Venn into the back of the longhouse, Brione having to duck slightly between the beams. As their eyes got used to the gloom Venn saw the house was not constructed, but grown from the branches of the cloudtree. Four trion sat around a glowing rock that added to the heat, above it was a pot that gently bubbled, fragrant steam rose from it.

"My friends here are only part of the Lens, but others are with their current, or being parent."

"Current?" said Venn.

"Outside, in your world, you have first and second and third and fourth and more, fathers and mothers. Among the Forestals there is no such thing. If we are the kind to take lovers, we have a current, those we chose to be with for a time, until that time is over."

"It hurts when people leave," said Venn.

"It can," said one of those sat before the stone, their voice was rough, like unsanded wood. "But we are encouraged from childhood to celebrate what we had, not what we lost."

"Even death?" said Venn.

"Even death," said the trion. One of the others chuckled.

"Sendir thinks too much of death," they said, "that is what comes of being old as tree boughs and having one foot already on the Star Path." More of the trion chuckled and Sendir waved a branch over the steaming pot, spreading smoke through the room that made Venn's head spin. "Sit," said Brione, and they reached out a hand. As they did Venn noticed the other trion move, so they were all touching. "Take my hand." Venn did, Brione's hand was large, warm and slightly wet from the steam. It felt like it enveloped them.

The room was full of motes of light.

"Strong," said Brione.

"Dangerous," said Sendir. "They have touched something dark." They looked up, eyes sparkling. "Dark and powerful."

Cahan.

"Tainted," said another of the trion. Venn wanted to let go. Fear flowing through them. They could not.

"Young," said Brione, "teachable." There was a moment when Venn was sure they heard voices, a discussion that lasted a long time and took only a moment. Like when Least became Harsh and it seemed the leaves of the trees turned ever so slowly then, one morning, all the branches were bare, like the trees had decided the season had changed that night. So it was with the Lens of the Trion's discussion.

"If you wish to learn," said Brione, "we will teach you." Five sets of eyes bored into Venn.

"I know nothing of what you are," said Venn, "what you will teach."

"If you do not learn," said Sendir, voice harsh, "then what you are cannot be allowed. We will strip the cowl from you." Venn swallowed, they had not expected this. The Forestals' life seemed a paradise where all were free, but it was not.

"They deserve to know what they are," said Brione. "What is required."

"Or maybe they are only danger," said Sendir, "and we should strip them, now."

"The decision is made," said one of the other trion. Venn did not want them making decisions for them. They wanted out of here but when they tried to stand they could not. It was as if something as gentle as it was strong held their body still. Venn would have trembled but they could not.

"Let them go," said Brione. There was an edge to their words, a spike of command. Sendir shrugged and the hold vanished. Venn could have left then but did not. It did not feel safe to try and leave.

"Much was lost, Venn," said Brione and they sat before the glowing stone. "There is much we do not know about how the land once was." The other trion nodded. "What we do know, is that the Rai are an aberration; to take power from life is a fault, not a true way."

"And you know the true way?" said Venn. Wary of anyone who believed they were right, Cahan had been raised by people like that. Venn's mother had been like that and in both cases it had brought nothing but pain.

"We know a way that causes less harm," said Sendir, "one we think is the will of the Boughry. We do not interfere. We help one another."

"You share power?" said Venn. Brione nodded.

"Yes, we share. All the Forestal have cowls, to some degree, to be raised in Wyrdwood is to have a cowl. We have no blooming rooms, we do not force it on anyone. It is in the air." Venn did not understand, but nodded. "We do not have cowls of great power, the Rai do because they feed theirs in unnatural ways. And that makes them hunger for more. Do you understand?"

"I think so," said Venn.

"Among us," said Sendir, "some are stronger than others, they act as focus, and the rest lend their strength. That is how we work."

"I have seen Ania make shields," said Venn. "I would like to learn to—"

"That is not your place," hissed Sendir.

"Peace, Sendir," said Brione, "the child does not know anything."

"Then tell me, and I am not a child," said Venn. Brione smiled.

"Compared to these members of the Lens that sit before you, Venn, you are very much a child. That is not an insult. We are long-lived." Venn had no answer, or rather they may have but it was a very long way off and they could not reach through their thoughts to get it. The smoke made thinking hard.

"Put a trion between the givers of power and the focus who uses it, and we not only add our own strength, we concentrate what is passed to the focus further, make them stronger. Together, we can achieve miracles. This house?" Brione waved a slender delicate hand at the building. "We helped make it, the focus used the branches of the tree, and we magnified what power they needed." Venn was about to say something but then Brione continued to speak. "To be a trion is to be a conduit, We stand between male and female. We stand between the power and the wielder."

"But we do not wield," said Sendir in a low growl.

"That is true, mostly," said Brione with a smile. "We largely act only as conduits, Venn. So we heal, as that is just to be a conduit for life, and we also oversee the taffi-stone network."

"But I saw Ania . . ."

"The Forestals can use the network, but we have a deeper connection. With our help the people can travel further and more safely."

"Safely?"

"Taffistones do not always send people where they wish to go. Ania and Tanhir both managed to bring large groups a long way, that is unusual."

"Maybe Ranya guides their steps." There was silence for a moment.

"Maybe she does," said Sendir, and Venn could not help thinking they had only touched the surface of a pool of secrets, one that had depths they were yet to understand.

48

Sorha

It was a long time since she had been to the Slowlands. She had fond memories of them, laughter and feasting with the other Rai while executions were carried out. There were Rai here this time too, and they were laughing and feasting but she was not invited to join. She had been sent away, not even allowed to be among the soldiers who flanked the stand. She was below, by the cages with the prisoners. She told herself she was glad, it was shady here, cooler away from the Light Above, but when the Rai moved into the stands she knew she would have to move again so she did not affect them, make them uncomfortable. Saradis had brought duller pods, but they were placed each side of the stand, far away enough not to affect the Rai within. One pair at the north towards the bridge, the other opposite on the plains approach from the south so Cahan Du-Nahere would be caught whichever way he came.

She looked out, and wondered how she could ever have been amused by this place. The Slowlands were a nightmare made flesh. She had a vague memory of being horrified the first time she had been here, but familiarity over many years had made her forget. The horror of it slowly became mundane, the way things were. Normal. But now she saw it again and saw it in a different way.

She pushed the idea she had changed away, did not like it.

The Slowlands were the opposite of Wyrdwood; the great forests were at the north and south of Crua, the Slowlands were at the east and west. The grass of the plains died before it met the Slowlands, and the land here was flat and hot. The Light Above beat down, the air was full of dust carried down the edges of the Slowlands by circle winds. There was no shade here for relief from the heat.

Through the dust the Slowlands, the true Slowlands, were a shimmer in the air. If they had not been used as an execution ground then they would be easy to miss. But not now. The Slowlands were one of the strange miracles of Crua, a place where you could go no further east. It looked like you could, it looked like it went on forever, but as you moved further into the Slowlands you became slow. She did not understand it, could not explain it, but she had seen it. Seen the condemned run into the Slowlands in hope there may be some escape. The offer was always there, if you could make it to the unseen other side, you could go free.

But Sorha felt quite sure there was no other side.

She had watched runners try. Watched them slow, at first gradually, then it became more and more pronounced until it appeared they barely moved at all. As they slowed the spear throwers would move up at a leisurely walk. Then throw, and the spear was also slowed by whatever mysterious force affected the runners. It was thought the condemned would know, that they would see or feel the spear coming towards them and know there was nothing they could do to escape. That when it hit them, depending on how far in they were, their deaths could take whole seasons as the spear made its way through their body.

Sorha was not so sure it worked that way. She suspected

that those trapped in the Slowlands may not be aware of what was happening. That to them they moved at the same speed as anyone else. If they looked back it would be those left behind who appeared to move strangely. Though she did not know for sure, could never know unless she herself was cast into the Slowlands and the thought of that made her shudder.

It did not matter of course. What mattered was the fear the Slowlands instilled in people. Of all the many and painful ways to die that the Rai could come up with, the Slowlands was the most feared because it could be seen. Looking out into the Slowlands you saw generations of victims. Sorha stared at them, and wondered if she was wrong about time being the same for those cast into the Slowlands. Recent victims were there, frozen mid-stride, still moving imperceptibly no doubt, some pierced by spears, some about to be, some that had been.

Then there were the skeletons. Hundreds of them. Stood in the position they had been in when death came to them. And if time worked the same way in the Slowlands, to those trapped there, how could that be? The skeletons should be on the floor. But they did not fall. They stood, a thicker forest than even Wyrdwood, a thousand years of executions and in among them what looked like living people, those few who had somehow escaped the spear. They were a long way off, and those furthest off wore strange armour, like none Sorha had ever seen. Their clothing became gradually more recognisable, more normal, the nearer they were to the Slowlands border.

"They hate you, don't they?" Sorha turned. Furin, the Leoric of Harn, speaking to her. There were nine other prisoners in the cages. Most meant nothing, they had been picked because the Rai wanted something to amuse them while they waited for Cahan Du-Nahere. They were foolishly sure of themselves.

The Leoric looked tired, drawn. Thinner than she had

been as she had not been fed well. Her face was not made-up, prisoners were not allowed such privileges. No sign of her clan lineage and she had covered her face in dust, to hide the nakedness of it. She was no one here. Sorha began to turn away. "Why do you serve those that hate you so much?" said Furin.

"I serve the Cowl-Rai," said Sorha. Why did she answer the woman? Furin snorted, laughing to herself. "You find honour funny, Leoric? Find that I do what is right, what generations of Rai have done, amusing?" Sorha walked over to the cage, expecting the woman to back away but she did not and Sorha was now face to face with her.

"But Rai Sorha," the woman said, "surely you of all people know that the true Cowl-Rai of the north is Cahan Du-Nahere?"

"Do not speak of him," said Sorha softly, "or you will regret your words." Furin laughed again.

"What in the whole of Crua could you do," said Furin, her words definite and unwavering, fearless, "that would be worse than sending me into the Slowlands?" Sorha had no answer. "Well," said Furin, still smiling, "think quickly if you wish to threaten me. It sounds like they are taking their places above us." She was right; the sound of shoes on the wooden stand above like thunder. "They will want you gone. I saw how they treated you on the way here."

"While they treated you so well."

"I travelled in a cage, that is true," said Furin, "a lot easier than walking." Soldiers appeared, one pointed at a cage, the one next to Furin's.

"That one first." The other soldier nodded and undid the locks. The first soldier turned to Sorha. "You are to leave here, and take position one hundred paces away from the stand. By the bridge dullers to the south."

"What have you come to, Sorha," shouted Furin, "being ordered round by a common branch commander?"

"Quiet, prisoner!" said the soldier. Sorha walked away, not looking back but still she heard Furin's voice.

"They hate you, Sorha! We both know it!"

Sorha found the walk uncomfortable, she was stiff-legged, aware of being watched. She wanted to hurt that woman. She half hoped Cahan did not show up, she would enjoy watching the Leoric walk into the Slowlands, knowing she would die over the space of weeks or months as the spear slowly moved through her. She would make pilgrimages back to this place to watch her slow death. Sorha took her place near the bridge, under the hot sun, grit and dust swirling around her, getting under her armour and scraping her skin. She felt the Rai on the stand watching her. It annoyed her that the woman in the cage spoke the truth.

"You are right, I hate them," she found herself saying as she walked over to the dullers in hope of a little shade, "and they will know my hate."

She stood, watching the forest of the dead held in place by the Slowlands. From the corner of her eye she could see the Rai in the stands, ten or more of them. Below them mostly soldiers, favourites picked especially. That made her smile. Saradis had not met Cahan Du-Nahere, and just like those before her she underestimated him. Presumed he was a fool she could easily beat, because she thought Sorha was a fool, who had been beaten three times by him. Well, she was no fool. If Cahan planned something, and he undoubtably did, he would aim for the bridge over the crevasse, it was the only safe way out. Far too wide to jump, and like them all so deep the bottom could not be seen. Cut the bridge behind him so he could not be followed and use the huge taffistone for cover and he could conceivably escape. She had advised the leader of the Rai to put people on the other side of the crevasse, or to bring a marant to fly troops over, but they had ignored her. Sorha had looked to Saradis, expecting her to see the sense in it but she had shrugged.

"If he comes all this way for this woman, he is hardly likely to run." Sorha had bitten her tongue rather than speak. Let them be fools. She would be ready and then they would know her worth. She put a hand on the hilt of her sword. They may have power, here and now, but she had wits and sharp wood at her hip and that would serve her better, power could be lost or taken away. A good mind could not, and a blade was a dependable servant that would never betray you.

They sent the first prisoner into the Slowlands not long after she took position.

She could not hear them, the circle wind was too strong, whistling and howling across the flat landscape, but she knew he begged. Could tell from his posture. Weak. She had no time for weakness. Begging would not help and he should realise that. One of the guards walking him to the Slowlands boundary raised a fist and the man cowered before him. Stand up, she found herself thinking. Stand up and meet your end like you're better than them.

When had the Rai become "them" to her?

She did not know.

The other guard drew his blade and made to stab the prisoner. The man turned and ran. He tried to run along the edge of the Slowlands first, marked by fluttering flags on small poles, many tried this, she had seen it before. It made sense.

It never worked. The swordsman lunged at the prisoner pushing him slightly deeper into the Slowlands. He dodged around a flagpole and like a flyer in a nettile string he was caught. The Slowlands had him and he headed deeper in, a look of panic on his face, an inability to understand how, no matter what he tried he could not run out. He was being pulled in, his movements becoming more and more languid the deeper he went. They waited and watched. Laughter came from the stand, the Light Above moved through the sky, a sixteenth, an eighth. Then a cheer and one of the Rai walked up, the wood of their armour burnished to a deep bronzed red, a spear in one hand. They raised it over their head and elicited cheers from the stand. Saradis laid on a couch at the top of the stand in a white woollen gown, bright despite she was in the shade. She was paying little attention to the execution. The spear thrower lined themselves up, made a few practice run-ups, stopping two or three paces short of the flags. A couple more practice throws. Finally they took a true run; at the moment they let go of the spear they channelled their cowl, sending the spear into the Slowlands in a gout of flame. At first it moved too quickly to be seen, a fast and lethal dart, then it slowed and it slowed, the fire around it doing the same until it resembled brightly coloured smoke slowly vanishing into the air. All this to a roar of appreciation from the assembled crowd.

Then, of course, nothing happened. It became a race between a man and a spear, both of which appeared to be hardly moving. The man facing forwards, seeing only the dead and dying and knowing what awaited him, that one day he would be nothing more than a nameless skeleton among so many others. But first there would be pain and there would be terror. A thought entered her mind. A strange one. Almost alien, like it had come from another person rather than her.

What was it all for?

For the Rai. For the Cowl-Rai. For Tarl-an-Gig, the god in ascendance, for the glory of Broken Iftal.

Did she really believe that?

She watched them bring out more prisoners, going through the same ritual, each time with a different spear thrower, a different show of power: flame, and water and ice. Cheers and disinterest and fear. At one point she thought something moved in the corner of her eye, across the bridge from her, but she could not turn to check. She was meant to be watching the executions, so she sweated, her skin burned where it was rubbed by grit beneath her armour. The light baked her, the wind chafed her cheeks.

What was it all for?

She found tears running down her face. She did not understand it, and hated herself for it but could not move to rub them away. Told herself it was grit from the winds. More prisoners died. They were running out of them and Sorha began to wonder what would happen if Cahan did not turn up? Would they send Furin into the Slowlands anyway? What would be the point? Would she feel it? Did it hurt? Would the Leoric of Harn beg for her life?

If Cahan did not show up it would be her failure. Again. Would they send her into the Slowlands after Furin?

Probably.

Would she beg?

No. She would not.

If they tried to put her in the Slowlands she would kill as many of them as she could. She moved in front of the duller pod, back into the small shade that had crept away from her as time passed and began to plan a route of attack, how she could use the stand as a shield from the Rai's power until she was among them. Then what she was would rob them of their power and she would be the predator, without their power they were nothing. They were lazy, just like Cahan Du-Nahere.

Eventually the guards brought out the woman, Furin. Walked her to the flags at the edge of the Slowlands, but they did not send her in, not immediately. There was noise on the stand. Pointing. Something was happening. She squinted, trying to see in the distance, into the haze caused by heat.

A figure approaching, across the plain from the north, outline wavering, a darkness seen through the dust – and even though she could not know, she knew. It was him. He moved with very certain intent.

"He came," she said to herself. "You are a brave man, Cahan Du-Nahere." Odd she thought that, once she would simply have thought him a fool. The noise from the stand slowly died away as the soldiers and the Rai watched Cahan

Du-Nahere approach. He stopped, slightly more than a spear throw from the stand, just out of range of the dullers to the north. His armour looked different. Sharper, more serrated. More dangerous. He did not have his bow with him. Saradis stood.

"Come forward," she shouted, "and stand between the dullers, Cahan Du-Nahere."

"Send Furin south, over the bridge," he shouted back. 'And then cut the ropes so I know she is safe and you cannot follow."

"No!" The woman, Furin shouting back. "Do not do this, Cahan! You are too important!"

"Stand between the dullers," Saradis shouted back, "and then we will send the woman over the bridge," shouted Saradis.

"Do not—" Furin's shout was cut short by a blow from one of the guards, knocking her to her knees.

She is strong, thought Sorha.

"Very well," shouted Cahan. He bowed his head, beaten. Walked forward to take his place between the dullers, there he would become only one of the people, and the soldiers of the Rai could chain him. Something in Sorha seethed, she wanted to be the one to shackle him. He was hers. He had cursed her, she deserved her revenge. She put a hand on her sword. Took a deep breath. Cahan was not a stupid man. She did not believe he would simply give himself up. He would have a plan. he would make a move.

When he did, she would be ready.

Then everything went wrong.

49

Cahan

"Do not—" Furin's shout was cut short by a blow from one of the guards, knocking her to her knees. His hands went to his axes. Stopped. He was too far away to stop them pushing Furin into the Slowlands. He had to trust in others, wait for them to move.

"Very well," he shouted. Let go of the axes, bowed his head as if resigned. For a moment, he felt panic. What if they didn't come? No, he had to believe they would. The entanglement lay in pieces five hundred paces behind him. They knew, they would come. He advanced, each step became a struggle, his body fought him. It felt like walking through deep mud but the ground was hard. His legs were stiff, his muscles fought him until he entered the dullers' field. Strange, the loss of his power was not as complete as the last time he had felt it, when Sorha cut him off from his cowl; he was not as weak as he should have been. He was not strong, not by any means, but something was different.

He raised his head.

Saw Furin move.

She pushed away one guard, they were not expecting

her to attack, not ready for what she did. The second guard had no time to react as Furin came to her feet. There was no doubt in her movements, no slowing, no second thoughts. She was sure of herself, of what was needed. Of what she intended.

Furin, Leoric of Harn, threw herself past the flags and into the Slowlands.

And then he was moving, he was screaming.

"No!" The word filling his mouth, becoming everything. An entreaty. A terror. A hatred.

A statement of intent.

There was bluevein here, squirming through the soil.

Death everywhere.

He would bring more.

He ran. As he left the dullers field, was opposite the stand, figures appeared across the bridge around the taffistone to the south, in their hands something burned and they threw it, great clouds of smoke filled the air, so thick the circle winds could not whip it away. Whatever created it made more and more, building up and around the figures until they could no longer be seen.

In the stand the Rai stood. Flames licked round their arms as they gathered power to themselves.

He did not know which way to go. To his left the Rai were readying to launch fire and death at those who had come to help him. To his right Furin was running into the Slowlands. His allies could not stand against this many Rai alone.

But Furin.

Furin.

Her movements slowing as she pushed on. Dirty woollen robes moving around her in a slow, stately billow, like the sails of a skyraft as it moved to catch the wind. One of her guards drawing back an arm to throw a spear.

No one could be saved from the Slowlands. Everyone knew that.

"Furin!" A roar, a statement of intent. He would not give up. Not on her.

Axe in his hand. Throwing. The weapon tumbling through the air to bury itself into the back of the spear thrower's head and then Cahan was running hard for the edge of the Slowlands.

Furin.

He would save her. He would pull her from the Slowlands. He would find a way. The second soldier threw their spear as Cahan threw his second axe, but some trick of the land, some disturbance of this place. Some darkness within him made his arm twitch and the axe missed.

The spear flew true.

Furin!

Beneath the ground, the bluevein twitched and writhed.

Within he felt a heat.

It was not the fire of the cowl, not his own anger roiling within him. A different heat, a liquid heaviness that sat within his stomach, like one of the rocks the Forestals heated had been placed within him. It filled him, it made him nauseous. It burned. From it came molten branches, reaching into his veins, giving him strength. Beneath the ground he felt an answer to his strength. The bluevein reacting. He felt it and a deep desire to connect with him, there was strength there. A huge web, a vast presence and it touched the death around him. Found power in generations of death in the land beneath him. Thousands executed in the Slowlands.

A corruption.

An offer of strength.

Everything hung.

On his.

Acceptance.

Like the final breath of the condemned. One last moment of seeing. Of feeling. Of hyper-reality where even this beige and sandy windswept place of murder took on an almost hallucinogenic beauty. He saw the colours in all things. Felt he slowed just as Furin did. Felt all power flowing around him. The angry, sharp and misshapen power of the Rai in the stands. A moment of being aware of Ranya's web, soft and cooling. The blue throb of the death power, and beyond it, more, so much more. A great thudding heartbeat that echoed in his temples and promised so much it swamped even the power of death.

People became dots of heat and possibility.

The glow of the taffistone a white light in his mind.

The Slowlands. Vast and monolithic. Dwarfing everything. As much a part of Crua as the cloudtrees, channelling the power of the land into something Cahan knew he could never understand, it simply was. A power beyond any person. To broach it was to be taken by it. To be human was to be simply too small to affect it.

Despair. Touching him.

A promise from below.

Sound rushing towards him.

Dassit and her soldiers appearing from the smoke around the taffistone, launching spears towards the stands. The Reborn leading them. Rai burning weapons in the air and throwing back a deluge of fire and sharp ice. Screams. Those who survived running towards the stand. Arrows, too fast for the Rai to burn, and he felt two Rai fall. Then he was at the edge of the Slowlands. Furin almost within his reach. Passing over the flags marking one world from another. Like falling into water. Like diving into a still, cool, pool. Like breathing his last breath. Like being born. Like becoming the Light Above. Like the beginning of existence and the end all wrapped into one.

He was caught, prey in the tentacles of a spearmaw. Drawn inexorably into the Slowlands. A field of bodies, standing like stalks of grass waiting the scythe, dried and ripe. A spear hanging in the air before him, stretching out towards Furin. The woman he loved. Did he love her? Yes! Accept that. Too late.

The Slowlands, only now he really understood its strength.

This was the end.

He could not save her.

He could not save himself.

The Rai would kill all those who had come to help him.

What had he done.

Power below.

It wanted him.

It frightened him.

He had no other choice.

Once, and never again.

He closed his eyes.

Accepted.

Eruptions from below, breaking through the ground, bluevein spearing through his feet.

Corruption.

He took.

Agony.

Like nothing before. The heat within him, all consuming.

Burning Cahan Du-Nahere.

Burning all he was away.

50
Dassit

She felt better than she had done in years. It was a pity she was going to die today.

Though, being sure she was dying today seemed to have become a habit for her, but she still lived. How much longer could her luck hold out?

"Chyi, give me one more day," she said under her breath and looked around at those who had come through the stone with her. She hoped they had not heard her call on her god, though she did it more from force of habit than belief. The northerners had no love for Chyi, and no reason to love them. But no one had heard her from the looks of them, all preoccupied with their own worries as they hid within the shadow of the taffistone.

"Shall I light the smoke pots, Trunk?" She turned to Vir, behind him her remaining twelve soldiers. Behind them the two warriors they called the Reborn, swathed in yellow wrapping that covered elaborate and expensive armour. They set her teeth on edge.

"Not yet," she said and peered round the edge of the stone. One of the Rai was on the other side of the rope bridge, then she slipped behind one of the dullers. There were maybe thirty more of the enemy, a mixture of Rai and soldiers in the stand. A woman at the top dressed all in white.

"That's a lot of Rai," said Vir.

"Could be worse," said Dassit, though she was not sure how. Vir shrugged. At the edge of the Slowlands two more guards held a woman. Furin, thought Dassit. She must be pretty special for all this fuss.

Past the stand were two more dullers. The woman at the stand was gesturing at a figure who looked very far away, obscured by the heat haze. Dassit wiped sweat from her face, wished she could take her helmet off but if she did her soldiers would and they needed all the protection they could get. The woman was saying something, to the man, Dassit presumed it must be Cahan. She couldn't hear it even with the circle wind blowing towards her. She closed her eyes, tightly. Hoping when she opened them all this would have gone away and she would wake in her bed in Seerspire.

She didn't.

Instead everything was worse.

The prisoner, Furin, pushed away one of the guards and ran straight into the Slowlands. Cahan screamed her name, running forward. Then Dassit stopped watching. Not the time for it. Her job was to create a distraction when the time came, and it just had.

"Smoke!" she shouted. "Smoke!" Vir was there with a sparker, lighting the fuses and her soldiers were out, throwing the pots to the edge of the crevasse, sending up huge clouds of fragrant smoke.

"Can't see an Osere-cursed thing," came a voice from behind her. She turned, thought it was the Forestal Ania who spoke, she was with the big man, Ont, bows ready in their hands. The Reborn passed her at a run.

"Neither can they," said Dassit and she raised her voice. "This is it! Grab your spears and into them!" She ran, leading her troops through the smoke. The Forestal behind her shouting, "Put arrows in those dullers, we don't want them holding Cahan back!" A heartbeat of darkness, then into the light. Reborn already across the swaying rope bridge, the crevasse yawning beneath her as she followed, making her head spin. She put it aside and ran on. The Rai on the stand were drawing power, fire dancing round them.

"Throw when you're in range!" she shouted as the Reborn warriors launched spears at the stand. Four, five, six steps and she threw her own spear. Where was that Rai who had been guarding the bridge? Dead? Hiding? Behind them? No time to think.

Fire in the air, burning the spears to ash as they flew. She heard Vir shouting.

"Separation! Separation!" And she knew that behind her troops would be spreading out. Fire hit. An explosion behind her, a blast of heat that knocked her to the floor and sent her tumbling across the hard, dusty ground. The smell of burning hair and she slapped at her face in panic, but it wasn't hers. Someone was screaming. She shook her head. Forced herself up. Soldiers were coming from the stand. The Reborn had already engaged them, Chyi's blood but those women could fight. "Into them, into them." She could hear shouting, screaming. Didn't look back, daren't look back. How many were left? In the stand one of the Rai was raising a hand, fire dancing around it and something hissed past her head. The Rai fell back into the stand, an arrow in their chest. Other Rai were taking cover. Dassit could feel power in the air. She glanced back.

Don't count the bodies, she told herself. Don't look for Vir.

The archer, Ania at the edge of the smoke, drawing her bow. By her the big man, Ont. Bodies on the ground near the bridge. The old man, Fandrai, dragging one back. More fire arched over her. Arrows wouldn't be enough. Her people wouldn't be enough.

A scream cut the air.

So much pain in it.

Even the wind felt like it stopped for a moment.

The noise was like nothing Dassit had ever heard, and she'd been at many a cruel execution performed by the Rai. Seen and heard the slow bleeding-away of life for power. Watched people beg for death but still never heard anything like this.

The Reborn no longer fighting, as if life had fled from them and they stood there while enemy soldiers stabbed and slashed and cut at them until they fell.

It came again. The noise. A man's voice. Tested beyond anything Dassit could imagine. It came from him, from Cahan. He was in the Slowlands and it looked like every muscle in his body was tensed to the point his bones were about to snap. Hard, thin spikes were emerging from his armour, anchoring him to the ground. He screamed again. The air changed, like it was pressing down on her. She could smell rotten meat and ruptured bodies, felt like she stood in the centre of a week-old battlefield. Something unpleasant moved around Cahan. Something dark and liquid, purple-blue and black. A high-pitched whistling in Dassit's ears and she felt the ground beneath her shake, a tremor passing through the land and the bridge over the crevasse let out an alarming creak, as if the uprights were straining to support it.

Dassit had never felt fear like this. Pure and animal. It pushed everything from her mind. All thought of battle and Rai were gone. And it was not just her. None were moving. No spears flew, no arrows or fire or ice.

All looking at Cahan Du-Nahere.

The impossible happened. Cahan Du-Nahere, who was stood in the Slowlands, moved. Not a tiny amount, not like he was slowed. He reached out and plucked the spear heading for the woman Furin away, threw it back towards the stand. As it flew, it split, into ten, twenty, thirty shimmering purple-black spears that cut through the air between him and the stand. Crashed into it. Screams of agony from the Rai and the soldiers as the stand came apart beneath them. Spilling them to the ground. Cahan reached out again. Found Furin and he pulled her from the Slowlands. Threw her out of them and, plainly unaware of his own strength, she sailed through the air, crashing into the ground, rolling and twisting like a broken doll. Cahan screamed again. His armour ragged and serrated, the axes he had thrown somehow in his hands once more. The solid spears of material that had come from his armour now waved around him, four deeply unpleasant tentacles that dripped something noxious and vile and moved like they thought for themselves. His head moved but she could not see a face, the visor of his helmet covered him, no eyes, no features, just darkness. He took a heavy step towards Furin. Out of the Slowlands.

Dassit came to her senses. Fought away the fear.

She was here for a reason. Furin. And bringing that woman back meant life for what remained of Dassit's people. She glanced back toward the bridge. The three archers stood, bows at their sides, frozen by what was happening. The old man was with one of her people. Trying to help them up. She saw Vir, holding his side and struggling towards her. Some of her people were nothing but smoking corpses, the rest were as shocked and lost as the archers.

Cahan, huge, monstrous, took a step towards them. The ground shook.

"The woman!" shouted Dassit at Vir, pointing in Cahan's direction, at where Furin lay unmoving. "Help me get the woman!"

It took all she had to run towards Cahan Du-Nahere, if you had asked her what the Osere were like then she would have imagined something like him. Maybe not how he looked, but how he felt. She tried not to see him, to hear him roaring, concentrated on the woman. Made it to her. Checked for a pulse. Weak but there. Arm broken, bone sticking out through flesh.

"She's hurt," said Vir.

"I'm not blind," she snapped it, knew Vir didn't deserve it but she could feel Cahan, feel his attention on her. "Pick her up." Then Dassit was shouting: "To the bridge! Back to the bridge!" With the help of Vir, dragging Furin with them. Cahan following. His steps heavy, threatening. The land groaning and shaking as he moved. Fire burst against him from a brave Rai and he reached out a hand with a tormented scream. Something left his body, black and wet. The Rai took over the screaming. Dassit and Vir reached the bridge. The ropes stretched taut. It made noises she didn't like but there was nowhere else to go. The others were already across. Archers loosing at the stand. Moving as quickly as she could. Behind them Cahan spoke.

"Furin." It was like a thousand gasmaws burrowing through her head. She could feel him. She looked over her shoulder. He was leaving the Slowlands, monstrous, his steps shaking the land, making it hard to walk as she put her feet on the bridge. Running across. His form twisted, tentacles writhing around him. He was coming after her but he was slow, they had to hurry. He would bring the bridge down if he stepped on it, she was sure of it. She looked back again, struggling with the dead weight of the unconscious woman. Cahan was nearly at the bridge, then a figure stepped in front of him. The Rai, the one she had seen by the duller. Sword in her hand. Insanely brave. Something happened to Cahan as he approached her. The purple-blue liquid fire dying away. The writhing tentacles withdrawing into his armour, the black visor melting away.

"You and I," said the woman, "we're not finished."

"No," said Cahan, and he sounded more human, more real. His face looked haunted, scared, but Dassit didn't think he was scared of the woman.

"Dass," said Vir, "come on." Then they were going as fast as they could, making for the taffistone that hid the rest of their small force. Archers covered their retreat, Ania and the big man, Ont. Fandrai was dragging a moaning body towards the stone. They picked up the pace. As she passed over the threshold of the door in the taffistone she heard the roar of cowlfire landing behind her, wondered how she had managed to live through another day, and how much longer her luck could hold.

51
Udinny

Four Spearmaw hunt me through the black maze, the sharp, streamlined deadlier cousin to the gasmaw. Two circle above, one slips behind and one in front. I slide from Syerfu's back and she moves to protect my rear. I feel that strange tensing within my body of Udinnys past coming to me, a blessing from Ranya as I become a hunter. A hunter's knowledge floods my mind. A hunter's muscle memory flows into my body. I take my needle spear in my hand with a light grip for thrusting and slashing. Behind me I sense-more-than-feel Syerfu change – a brief look back and she is no longer a crownhead, now she is a vast garaur, lithe and thin and vicious.

I know so much.

I know the spearmaw, how dangerous it is. Fast and sleek, eight tentacles: four strong for grasping, suckers with barbed hooks that will rip the flesh rather than be loosed. Two longer, sharper, barbed tentacles that end in heartwood-hard spears. Two more long tentacles that end in paddles which drip a viscous poison to paralyse, though not kill. Within this nest of writhing dangerous weapons, a sharp beak that can slice through the hardest armour.

Its gasbag long and spear shaped. The beast is built to hunt.

But they are not invulnerable. Tentacles can be cut away, they are soft. The big eyes, with their lozenge-shaped pupils, are vulnerable, a pathway straight to the brain of the creature. The front of the gasbag is armoured with chitinous sheets that will deflect a spear thrust, but get behind them and the bag can be burst and then the creature is helpless.

I know all this. I know the acrobatic hunting moves. I know how to make my body sway and spin and twist in ways long lost to the people of Crua.

My hands itch for a bow and, almost, I do not feel fear.

Though hunter Udinny knows that not to be scared of such a creature is foolish.

And normal Udinny is quite happy to be at least a little bit scared.

Maybe more than a little.

The spearmaw came. So fast. A streak of blue light. Its stabbing tentacles extended in an attempt to run me through. I let myself fall to the right, turning the fall into a roll as its body slides by me. It smells of forest leaves, of canopies, of leaking sap and menthol. Reversing my spear in a single, fluid movement, the sharp end of it sticking out from behind me and digging into the gasmaw. The creature's speed carries it past, ripping open the gasbag and filling the air with a foul smell and a piteous squeal.

No time to feel pleased with myself for the first kill. A second gasmaw, hissing through the air, closely followed by another. They have learned from the mistake of the first. Keeping their distance, darting in and out. Hovering, using their syphons to push themselves around in a circle above me. Always facing my spear. Sharp tentacles thrusting. Clattering off my spear as I deflect their attacks. Past them Syerfu launches herself through the air, landing on a fourth spearmaw. The two creatures smash into the ground in a spinning, hissing, growling mass of tentacles and fur. I expect one of the attacking spearmaws to help their fellow, but they do not, they remain focused on me. Slashing and darting. Tentacles come at me from all directions.

I move like liquid. My spear a thing of light, sharp as broken glass. One of the spearmaw overreaches. I cut through a stabbing tentacle, rewarded with a hiss, whether of pain or fury I do not now know but in my attack I also overreach and am hit by the second maw. A spear tentacle crashing into my shoulder, held off by armour I do not even know I wear. I stagger and something brushes my leg. No more than the lightest touch.

Lit up in pain.

Waves of agony passing through me. Fighting both spearmaws and pain. Fighting a losing battle. Being backed up against the strange edges and roundels of the alley. Syerfu ripping into the spearmaw she fights, but blood runs down her lithe body.

I stumble, the wounded spearmaw comes in for the kill but it is only an animal and I am not. The stumble is a desperate ruse to bring it near. As it swoops in, tentacles spread wide to envelop me, I thrust with the spear, breaching the beast's eye and killing it instantly.

I twist to meet the last one, something wraps around my leg.

The first spearmaw. Grounded. Dying. But not dead. It pulls, hard enough to take my legs from under me. I roll. The final spearmaw diving. Tentacles wrapping around me. Beak snapping as I desperately tried to hold it off, hands struggling to find purchase on skin that is both dry and slippery at the same time. Hooks snag my flesh. Screaming pain as more of its poisonous tentacles find bare skin. Muscles slowly weaken, refusing my commands. The snapping beak coming nearer.

A pressure in the air.

The same awful presence as before, the one that sent the spearmaws. It intensifies, as if it suddenly grows in strength.

At the same time I feel its attention is moving away from me. Its servants began to lose interest. They hold me, but they no longer attack. The beaks no longer snap. The vast eyes no longer hold any life.

Something has distracted the presence. The great oppressive shadow of this down-below place, the thing that sits at the centre of the shadow web hanging parasitically off the golden weave of Ranya. It is drawn away by something more important than Udinny, warrior of Ranya.

Upwards.

Something up there has its whole attention and the spearmaws, a moment ago so dangerous and so lethal, simply fade away. Whatever the presence sees, or feels or needs, it is taking all its power. As the spearmaws' bodies vanish, becoming ash on the air, so does their venom. The effects flee. The pain is gone. I stand. Find Syerfu, once more a crownhead ready to carry me, and as I climb on to her back I know where we must go and hate myself for knowing it.

"That way, Syerfu." I pointed in the direction of the presence, whatever it is, that is the source of the danger. "I wish I had bow, and a shield." As I say it, the strange gullies and knobs and sharp edges of the maze I stand in light up with golden lines of light. I hear the soft voice of Ranya, as if from very far away.

"Some small gifts I can give." The walls of the alley move, pull more glowing lines to them, and on the wall before me appears a space for my spear and my walknut. I placed them within it and the golden light bathes them, they change. The walknut becomes a shield, the spear a bow. I take them. Hold them. These golden things.

"This place, it is magic."

A knowing, an Udinny past speaking through me. A vision of this place but different, a million people within it, magic flowing through and around it. A place made to keep Crua safe, I think, but now it sleeps. "What is this place, Syerfu?"

A whisper, an old-beyond-knowing Udinny says a name.

Anjiin.

Anjiin. The first spire city. Anjiin, the home of the gods. Fabled Anjiin, lost to time and war.

And I have found it.

52

Saradis

The Skua-Rai had, as she watched Cahan Du-Nahere, been considering how good it made her feel to be in control. To have her mistakes rectified. To be about to see this man bow before her once more, as was right and proper. As was his place.

Laha had warned Saradis once, long ago, that the clanless could never be trusted and she had ignored him. A mistake. She made another when she ran from the forces of Tarl-an-Gig, unaware then they were simply doing the work of Zorir, albeit unknowingly. That mistake she had corrected. Now was the time to correct the other. Cahan would be hers, and together with the dullers and the woman Sorha, he could be controlled.

He would be controlled.

She may even let the Leoric woman live, another lever for her to use against him. A carrot to dangle when the stick was worn out from beating him.

She let herself be pleased. Let herself enjoy the feeling that this was how things should be. Only this morning she had felt like events were running wildly out of control. Laha showed no signs of life, a skipper had come in bearing more bad news. Her forces which had been sent south were making too much progress. Going too quickly despite her instruction. Add that to the problems in the north at Treefall, the depredations of the Forestals, and the way the forest had turned on the mission, constant attacks from rootlings and wildlife. It had unsettled her. A visit to the Cowl-Rai in her cage had not helped, the woman was practically catatonic, a drooling imbecile begging for death.

But if she had the woman's brother, Cahan Du-Nahere, the sister would no longer matter. Zorir's will would be done. She would not need Nahac, the false Cowl-Rai, when she had the real one.

She let herself be calm. Fanned herself for a little relief from the terrible heat of the Slowlands. This was how it should be. Her god commanded, and she carried out their will. This would have been how it was in the old days, when Iftal walked, and ruled from ancient Anjiin. People like her, in charge.

Then everything went wrong.

Her pleasure, her sense of control, her surety were stolen from her by a woman she had barely even considered worth a thought: the Leoric of a small village in the northern Wyrdwood. The village had caused her trouble, but she had put that down to Du-Nahere. What were its people after all but villagers? Foolish, weak, there to serve. It had never occurred to her they could be anything but tools.

The woman sacrificed herself, rather than have Cahan taken prisoner; rather than be used she threw herself into the Slowlands, committed herself to a horrible death. Had she not been so shocked maybe Saradis would have admired the woman for it, but she did not have time for admiration. With a shout of "Furin!" Cahan attacked. She looked for Sorha, too late realising she had been sent away, the Rai would not allow her near, she interfered with their power. Before Saradis could command Cahan be stopped one of the Rai shouted.

"Look!" Pointing towards the ravine. Figures appeared around the taffistone. Then thick smoke surrounded them.

"We are attacked," said one of the Rai.

"Ignore them," shouted Saradis, "stop Cahan Du-Nahere."

"Archer!" another Rai shouted. Troops burst from the smoke and ran across the bridge. They threw spears, and the Rai exploded into their power around her. Flames from most, water from others which they turned into shards of ice and flung at the incoming soldiers.

Fire all around her. Saradis was used to the Rai using their power, but had never been within them when they fought, she had always been removed from it. It was different to be in it. Her heart raced and her breath caught in her throat. Everyone was shouting. No one was taking control and she wanted to, she wanted to more than anything but something had stolen her voice. There was a hollow within her that she did not recognise, she had not felt so helpless and lost since her monastery had fallen, so long ago. She had almost forgotten this feeling. Her soldiers were running towards their attackers. To be met by two warriors shrouded in yellow scarves who cut through them as if they were not there, then ran on towards the stand.

The horror of it.

To see her triumph turning to defeat before her eyes.

A scream. A sound of pure pain. Like it had been dragged here from her torture chambers beneath Tiltspire.

It came from Cahan. He stood within the Slowlands. The fool. By trying to reach the woman he had doomed himself.

Then she felt it.

Power.

Waves of it, coming off him.

Pleasure.

Running over her.

Hair on her skin standing on end, a breathlessness, a fluttering in her stomach. Her muscles threatened to give way. A name on her lips, breathed as much as spoken. "Zorir."

Cahan was communing with her god.

Violence and pain exploded around her. Arrows cut down Rai, and Rai cut down soldiers. The two warriors who had done so much damage, the ones in yellow, slowed in their fighting. Soldiers closed on them, stabbing and slashing and they did not defend themselves. Only fell to the floor. She barely saw any of this. She watched Cahan. Saw his agonies as his armour erupted. Felt the ground shaking as he screamed. Felt the power he drew and it drove her to her knees, her breath coming in gasps. Her body soaked in sweat.

"Cowl-Rai," she hissed. He was barely human. Four tentacles reached from his amour. Power, raw and liquid, flowing around him. Every scream he made was a promise and she knew it. She knew it. The time was coming. The fire was lit. Zorir was coming and she need not fear anything now. Need never fear again.

Cahan moved further into the Slowlands.

Impossible, but not for him. Not for the Cowl-Rai of Zorir. The spinning dark, liquid power around him allowed him to walk. The land shook with every footstep. He threw something. A split-second movement. A flash of noise. Cries of pain. Wood splintering and shattering. Creaking and breaking and Saradis was falling. The stand beneath her feet giving way, coming apart and she thought she would die. As she fell she saw a Rai, impaled on a broken spar. It felt unreal, like the Slowlands was reaching out beyond the barrier.

The stand came down and she was buried beneath wood, armoured bodies falling against her, some struggling, some inert. She could still hear fighting. She could hear shouts and screams. She felt the land beneath her vibrate and the broken spars of the stand shiver and creak. Parts of it falling, bringing up choking clouds of dust and she was reduced to nothing but an animal. Cared about nothing but escaping. She had heard of rootlings chewing off an arm or leg to be free of a trap and now she understood. A groan of sliding wood and she was pushed against the body of a Rai. One of his arms was trapped beneath a fallen beam, crushed by it, his head was held by the same beam, his eyes wide and she knew that look. Power hungry. He would take her life to preserve his own. His free hand reaching for her. He was covered in blood.

She could not allow him to take her, she mattered too much. In the dusty, choking confines of the fallen stand he could not quite reach her. A spear lay near and she grabbed at it but it was caught between broken bits of wood. The Rai reached for her again, so desperate. He was trying to move, to free himself. Sparks of fire danced round his hand and then her spear came free. She was bleeding. Her head ached. She slid the blade out, having to push her elbows in tight, holding the spear with hands covered in blood where the sharp end had cut her as she pulled at it. The Rai still reaching for her. She had to turn the blade in a complete circle in the tight space, cutting her fingers further on the razored edges of the dark wood. Then she thrust it into his groin where the big veins were. He screamed as he died. She had never killed with her own hand before.

But in that moment she did not care.

She only cared for freedom. About fighting past the warm corpse. A glint of light, a gap in the broken wood. Splinters digging into her flesh. Hands slick with blood. Choking on dust. The ground shaking. Mad with fear she pulled herself from the wreckage.

Some of her Rai had escaped the stand.

They were not fighting, they were watching.

"Help me." Too quiet, barely even words. "Help me!" Louder this time. One of the younger Rai turned. Hands, dragging her out. Helping her up, supporting her. She saw what they had been watching. Sorha and Cahan. She was blocking his escape. Behind her two soldiers were running across the bridge, supporting the Leoric. Cahan was slowly forcing her back until they were on the bridge. The rest of the enemy were running around the back of the taffistone. Archers covered their escape. An old man dragged a wounded soldier to the stone. A Rai launched fire at the soldiers and archers retreated. It landed and she heard screams but she did not care about them. She cared about Cahan, he could not be allowed to escape.

The world twisted, changed. Became dark, spattered with lights and thick with longing. For a moment she was no longer there. In the distance a strange and writhing star. A voice:

To me.

"Zorir!"

"Skua-Rai?" said the Rai who held her arm. For a moment she did not know what to do. Who this person was. Then it was clear. With the words had come a sense of her god. Of where they were. What they wanted. Zorir was in the below, maybe the Osere held her god prisoner, she did not know.

But Zorir wanted Cahan.

"The bridge," she said. The Rai looked confused, her make-up cracking as she furrowed her brow. "Cahan cannot be allowed to escape. Destroy the bridge."

"The abomination Sorha is on—"

"She does not matter."

The Rai grinned, turned, called fire to her hands and released it. A ball of glowing incandescence streaked through the air. It hit the upright of the bridge, splashing across the ropes and planks. She heard Sorha's voice, a single shout of "No!" But the fire did its work, with a crack the ropes of the bridge gave way and she was sent, with Cahan Du-Nahere, into the deep, into the earth, to the god he had been born to serve.

53
Cahan

Desperation.

Strength

Exultation.

Fear.

He walked in desperation along a path to save Furin. Knew there would be a price paid but he would not let her die. He gave himself to the power so that she may live.

In his desperation he gave completely, aware of the vast amount of power needed to fight the strength of the Slowlands. It was old and constant and part of this place, and compared to it he was young and transitory and small.

But what he tapped was also old, and constant, but not of this place in the same way the Slowlands was. At the same time, more of this place than he was. There was a communion between him and this power, it was not simply a web, it was alive. Something in it was alive.

It saw him.

It wanted him.

Strength

He could not think clearly because of the power flowing into him. A flood of it. More than he could bear, more than his body was made for, rending his flesh, racking his bones. This was not like taking life, or the slow seep of the land or even tapping the huge power of the trees. This was the gush of cut arteries, an unstoppable flow that he could not shut off. He screamed but he did not know he screamed. He knew nothing but the power. Nothing but overwhelming strength.

Such exultation. Surely he could control the world? Split and reform the parts that made it. Bend it to his will. He pushed on the Slowlands. Beneath his feet lay the essence of it, the creation of it. Further in, where it wanted him to go, where it would push him to go. Or suck him in; it was far stronger, harder. But here, on the edge, he could affect it. He found the essence of the place, found what made it real, its *heaviness*, and held it. He could describe it no other way. The strain upon him was immense. Every muscle and sinew stretched, every bone aching, every pore leaking sweat and the power flowing into him was flowing out as quickly as it came.

Little by little, he was forgetting who he was. There was only power.

Furin.

That mattered.

Something was screaming at him.

Furin.

His mind cleared.

A spear reaching for her. He flung it away and his consciousness followed its path. Saw the gathered Rai. Felt their power. They were little more than a stain on the canvas of Crua compared to him. But a threat to her. He willed the being of the spear to become more. Willed the air behind the spears to harden and push them on faster. Turned away as the stand became a mess of breakage; wood and bodies.

Fear.

This power was not a gift.

It was taking over, binding with him. Whatever was left

of his cowl atrophied – it did not die, it was still there, only stripped back to a framework on which a new thing was built and unlike his cowl this thing was not willing to share his body, it wanted him. There was a roaring, a hunger. A desire and a purpose and he was part of that purpose. Images flashed through his mind. A key. A door long ago closed. A huge and shining city flickering into darkness. Vast towers falling to the ground. The pure terror that was the Boughry. He did not know what this meant. What they meant. With every heartbeat he became less.

Furin.

His hand closed on her. She was real.

He pulled her out of the Slowlands. Too hard, far too hard. Had he killed her? The thought ripped him apart but at the same time he hardly cared. He was a whirlwind. He was crushed by something far beyond his understanding. It wanted him out of the Slowlands before it overwhelmed him.

Even this power had limits.

He moved, his body uncomfortable and unfamiliar. The tentacles of his armour dragging him along. He was the wrong shape, his mind twisted in ways it was not meant to. He should be bigger, more pliable. As he left the Slowlands his strength grew but Cahan shrank. Every step a battle. Someone had Furin. Two someones. They were taking her. He wanted to help them or to stop them, to save them or to kill them.

The taffistone.

Get to the taffistone.

Save Furin.

The taffistone.

A way in.

A way through.

Two sets of thoughts, no longer sure what was his and what was imposed on him. He was going after Furin. He was going after the taffistone.

Somewhere, deep within he was screaming but he could

no longer give voice to it. The stone, he feared it. Not the stone itself, but the consequences of reaching it. The smaller he became, the more control of his body was taken from him. His mind was being sorted through. Every memory examined and thrown away. Scattered around like so much rubbish and then one image held, examined in detail.

Venn.

The trion.

A surge of feeling. A surge of memories, from the day he first saw Venn in the forest to him leaving Woodhome without saying goodbye.

Venn.

Venn.

In the sounding of that name he knew the trion was doomed. The corruption within would seek Venn. It needed Venn the way it needed Cahan.

He felt nothing.

He was becoming nothing. His memories hidden away. The next image was one of Udinny

Ud—

Gone. Power ebbing, he stood before the bridge. Every part of him hurt but he did not care. He was flowing back into himself like water from a wetvine filling a trough. He was Cahan again. The thing, whatever it had been, was gone.

"I've been waiting for you."

Sorha stood before him. Blade in one hand, shield in the other. She had stopped the thing taking him over. She was a barrier. He was not weak, not like he had been when she blocked access to his cowl, but the thing was pushed away. Cut off.

She came at him. He was forced to defend. He was still strong, fast. She looked surprised but it did not stop her. She was fast too but he knew he could kill her. He could finish her. With what was in him he was stronger, faster, better.

Blocking her attacks. Pushing her back onto the bridge

while the Forestals and the soldiers ran to the taffistone, the last of the smoke dissipating. He watched Ania and Ont run for the stone, a great explosion of flame and a shout of agony followed them.

Cahan fought, but as he did he found himself in an impossible position. If he killed Sorha the barrier she made against the power would be gone. He would be lost once more and knew it, he had passed some threshold, what was within was no longer under his control. When he was lost, Venn would be next.

He made a decision. The only decision.

Let his axes fall to his side.

"Do it," he said.

She paused. Shocked. Surprised.

The world shook.

She raised her sword.

Fire, the heat of it on his back.

"No!" shouted Sorha.

And then he was falling, falling, falling.

54
Venn

It had been a long time since they had seen the Light Above and Venn realised they did not miss it. There was a harshness to the light of Crua that was absent in the forest, here the light was gentle, diffused by the canopy of the cloudtrees and the mists that gathered below them. You could look up and the light did not burn your eyes, it bathed them. The trees, when you really looked, had their own illumination, a soft glow. Everything here had a light and the more Venn worked through the exercises set for them by the Lens of the Trion, the more they saw it.

Sometimes it was obvious, the fungi that grew everywhere: in the newly established farms, on trees and houses, nearly all of it either glowed or could be crushed to release juices that did, the same ones that were used to paint the armour of the Rai. The Forestals did not paint their cloaks, or the little armour most of them wore beneath. They were like the creatures of the forest, they did not want to be seen. The Rai were more like the poisonous creatures that glowed brightly, warning others that they were dangerous.

Venn breathed in, letting their consciousness meld with the cowl, move from them into the air. Imagining each outward breath created a cloud, and every breath after increased that cloud. Venn recognised the feeling, similar to the way Cahan had taught them to see the world around them. The Lens had stopped Venn using his method, they did not allow them to touch the floor with their hands, saying it was a crutch and that they should be able to sense life without seeking it physically. Brione had softly and seriously told them that Venn's power was "in your mind, not in your body". Insisted that they must use their mind to reach out. This was the first discipline, because a Lens needed speed and a mind was faster than a body could ever be.

So Venn used their mind.

It was hard, at first. Twice they fell asleep during the days of their learning, only to be woken by one of the Lens. Venn expected punishment but none came, no physical punishment. If it was Brione they would be understanding. They would say it was hard at first, gently encourage. If it was some of the others, Sendir for instance, there would be disapproval, not voiced, but plain beneath the stripes of their make-up. "Do better," they would say. Oddly, it was the ones that did not like them that made them try harder. Venn wanted to prove them wrong.

So after a fourday Venn rarely fell asleep, they put everything into their mental focus; and in the last eightday, a breakthrough. They could do this, could find themselves outside their body. The great weaving of life was what the Lens called it. They seemed puzzled when Venn called it Ranya's web. They presumed Venn spoke of the same thing they did, but Venn was not so sure. The Lens understood all life was linked, they understood a corruption grew in the web of life, but they did not seem to know of the delicate web that touched upon all things. They did not see it the same way as Venn. They talked of roots and trees, of larger things where Venn saw delicacy.

They understood much but not everything.

Venn felt for life. Reaching for the people of Woodhome

first, they were bright and easy to find. Moving between the similar-but-different life of rootlings and garaur. The gasmaw farm next, like a beacon, the light of the maws very different in feel and warmth, colder, bluer. Then other creatures of the forest, a million tiny lights and all these had one thing in common, they were self-contained, not part of the great cycle of the forest, not yet. Their light would not be released until they died and were given to the forest floor.

Though Venn was not sure about that, not sure the way the Lens were. Venn had briefly touched what lived within Cahan, knew it as somehow connected to death, as something that should not be, and yet death was natural. What was in Cahan was not. It was more like a sickness. The Lens knew of the corruption of death, how their tree had lost a branch to it, but they thought that was all it was. A strange fungus and if they were careful, and only raised the right mushrooms, then it would not come to them again.

Venn did not believe that.

They took a deep breath.

They were part of the Lens, they must not be distracted. Brione had told them that to be distracted in the moment of passing power to the focus was to be death, not only to themselves but to all in the chain. To be trion was to be the conduit, this was how they said the world was made to work, this was the true way.

Venn reached out again, past life which was easy and fleeting, trying to reach beyond into what was constant. But the life of the forest was too much, blinding, it shocked Venn from their calm state and they lost the connection. They bunched their hands in frustration. Let go of it. *Breathe*. Brione's voice in their mind. This happened to them all. It just happened to Venn more than the others, but they would learn to overcome it.

Breathing.

Sinking.

The shock of brightness filling their mind.

Let it. It will pass.

The trick was to expand your mind past all the life. There was an intensity in this that was lacking in the way Cahan had shown them. A completeness that both felt right and scared Venn. Once you were in the beyond it was hard to look away.

But they would. Gradually, the brightness of life died away and a glow was left behind. The constant background of Crua, a great, huge, living thing, not many organisms but one. The plants, from the smallest lichen to the great cloudtrees, were a system and it was all linked by Ranya's web, delicate lines of fungus that touched upon everything; no more than a flicker in the edges of their mind. When you saw all of it Venn could understand why the Lens did not see Ranya's web – the power of Crua was immense, it made the web invisible, and if they ever saw the web then it was easy for them to imagine it as an after effect of the mind.

The cloudtree behind them vibrated with power, and Venn looked at it with a clarity they had been lacking before. The tree was a model of the way the Forestals worked. The tiny leaves gathered energy from above, not the Light Above, something beyond even that and Venn did not even begin to understand it. The leaves passed power to the twigs and where twig met branch it was focused into more power, then where small branches met larger branches focused again until it was passed to the trunk and from there it ran down to the roots of the great tree and deep, deep into Crua. The amount of energy was breathtaking; Venn knew why those who touched it must be denied the power afterwards, if you could harness the cloudtree's power you could lay waste to the entire world. Just to skim the energy of a cloudtree the way Cahan had with the trees of Woodedge would take huge amounts of control, one step and it would incinerate you, leave you nothing but ash on the air, or suck you dry and pull your own bright spark into the flow. Not from malice, or even to defend itself.

It was simply the way it was.

Its nature.

Again, that strange feeling that the power was going somewhere, or meant to go somewhere. For just a moment, the most fleeting touch, Venn felt another power to the north, huge and terrible but unfocused and incomplete. It frightened them in a way nothing else had done so far, and at the same time there was a familiarity that they could not place. Not straight away. They worried it was what had touched Cahan, but if so that power was insurmountable, a fight already lost.

Venn felt themselves shivering.

"You feel it?" They opened their eyes. Brione was looking at them. "The tree?" Brione added. Venn nodded.

"It leaves me feeling very small," said Venn. "But I understand the role of the Lens now. The people are the leaves, we are the meeting of the branches and we pass the power to the trunk. It is the way of things." Brione smiled at them and Venn stood, knees and ankles aching from many hours sat cross-legged.

"You have learned in an eightday what it takes most of us many years to see." Venn did not know what to say to that. Brione put a hand on Venn's shoulder. "The place of a trion is between, neither one nor the other. We do not become male or female, we do not take one side or another." Venn wondered why Brione was telling them what they already knew. "But remember, that is an ideal, there are disagreements and jealousies even among us." She looked around, breathed in the evening air. "Sendir was the strongest of us before you came."

"You are saying they may try to hurt me?" Venn hated that, they had thought this a safe place.

"No, they will not. But it may take them time to adjust, they have pride. You travelled with Cahan, the forester who herded crownheads?" Venn nodded. "Then you must have heard the herders saying 'the new garaur gets the most nips'?" Venn had not, but they nodded nonetheless. Brione smiled.

"What is to the north, Brione?" said Venn, they did not want to talk of jealousy or being nipped. The Forestal's body became still, like a tree when the circle winds let up. Like a raniri in the moment before it bolted.

"It is unwise to look too far north, Venn," they said softly.

"Have I offended you?" Brione shook their head and delicate porcelain rings in their ears chimed.

"Not at all. But in the far north is where the Boughry hold court, it is best not to attract their attention. I believe you have already lost a friend to the Woodhewn Nobles?" Venn had no answer to that, it was true and to think of Udinny still hurt. "Now come, if luck has been with them your friends will be returning soon."

"And they may need healing."

"Yes," said Brione but there was no commitment to the words. "Night will close soon, I think you are ready for the last truth."

"The last?" Brione laughed, a sound with the same chime as their earrings.

"Well, there are many truths, the last we would have you understand if you are to stay with us." Venn nodded and followed Brione to one of the lifts. Standing in the woven cage while it descended, seemingly through nothing as the cover of night fell. Venn felt like they could be lost in the sky, the myriad lights of the flying creatures existing in a way Venn could never understand. Though they did not miss the Light Above, Venn realised they missed seeing the Cowl Star, the comfort of the single light in the night sky, the final destination of those who found favour with the gods.

Vertigo. The world spinning. A revelation.

It wasn't true.

Couldn't be true.

They had seen the truth of Crua. It was a closed system,

all energy feeding back on itself. Power coming from without but none ever leaving.

"There is no Star Path," said Venn softly. Saying it was like a stab in their heart. No Star Path meant Udinny was gone for ever. Their mother gone as well, no chance of a reconciliation Venn had never realised they wanted. If all was passed back into Crua, then how could anyone ever walk the Star Path? Venn's hand tightened on the cage of the lift. They had the strangest feeling, that this was something they had always known, like a memory. Yet they had not.

"Ah," said Brione. "Not in the way most understand it, no. That can be a hard thing for an outsider to swallow. And it is not a thing we share."

"You lie to people?"

"The outsiders who have come, we let them have their hope and do not steal it from them."

"But it is—"

"Do you feel good for realising death is for ever?" Words sharp as a fire-hardened spear. Venn shook their head. Partly because they understood what Brione was saying, but also because a part of them felt that Brione was wrong, though they could not explain why. "Then do not throw the seeds of others' sadness into the wind, Venn." They continued the journey down in silence.

On the forest floor Brione led Venn away from Woodhome. They walked for a long time, both aware of the forest and its creatures around them. Shyun and rootlings accompanied them as if an honour guard, gasmaws, floated above and littercrawlers dug through the leaf mulch. Far away Venn felt the presence of a skinfetch, that was a place Venn would avoid, and the brittle existence of swarden somewhere to the east. Orit everywhere.

Venn knew the rest of the Lens of the Trion waited before they saw them, grouped in a rough circle around two small trees. Nervous, their body full of unwanted energy, feeling like a corn doll whose limbs had gone soft they approached.

Walking became difficult and then Venn was surrounded by the Lens, standing in the centre of a circle. The trion were all beautifully decorated with leaves, and jewellery of expensive wood and ceramics.

"This will be hard, Venn," said Brione softly, "do not speak or interrupt, only think on the lesson." Brione put a blindfold around their head. The light of the forest creatures vanished. Venn took a deep breath. "Step forward, Trion. And stand between the two trees." Venn did. They felt the world, it pulsed with life that was glorious and real and true.

"Venn," all of them speaking as one. It was confusing, as if they were inside the sound. Venn felt like they may fall over, unbalanced, they had no sense of place, everything became blocked off beyond the circle of trion. "Tell us of the tree to your right." A moment when Venn felt for it. Found it. "Describe it and how it lives in harmony."

"It is strong," Venn said. "Bracket fungus grows on it, and the fungus takes from the tree but it passes back to the tree also. One supports the other."

"Now, tell of the tree to the left." A moment, a shift of their attention. It felt like they stood on the outer surface of a spinning ball.

"It is sick, dying."

"Why?"

Venn reached further, exploring the plant the way they would a body.

"The fungus," they said. "It has a parasite, another plant drawing off what it needs to live. So the fungus takes more from the tree than it passes back."

"And if nothing is done?"

"The tree, the fungus and the parasite will all die."

"How do we save it?"

"Remove the parasite," said Venn. It was obvious, they felt no doubt. One of the trion approached. The blindfold was removed and Venn found themself looking into the face of Brione. The light of the night forest distorting her features

"The Rai are the parasite, Venn," they said. "They feed off the people, weaken them and the true ways are dying. Like that tree, if they are allowed to continue we all die." They said these words solemnly, serious, intoning them as if they were practised.

Behind Brione, Sendir stepped forward.

"For years we have known this, and among all of the Rai the ones they make into Cowl-Rai are the worst of them. All the Rai's power flows to them, they are the hammer used to beat down the people of Crua."

Brione stepped forward.

"We have always lacked the strength to do anything about this," they said. "But you, Venn, you have the strength. And the Rai are weaker than they have ever been. War is their sickness, and they have weakened not only Crua but themselves with it."

Sendir took over again.

"The Cowl-Rai of the south is dead, has been for many years. The Cowl-Rai of the north is a pretender, getting by on illusion and artifice. The Lord of Murder is weakened by a sickness in the land." Venn blinked, how could this be? How could no one know? "Only one remains now, and if that one is allowed to ascend the Rai will gain strength once more."

"You mean Cahan," said Venn.

"Yes," said Sendir.

"I will not kill," said Venn.

"We do not ask that," said the old trion. "But if our world is to live, you must take his power from him the way we would pluck the parasites from this tree to save it."

Venn wanted to argue, to tell them they were wrong about Cahan Du-Nahere, but Brione had said not to answer now, only to think of what was said. It was true also, that Venn could not deny they had felt the darkness in their friend. Witnessed how unwilling he was to let go of it.

Could they be right?

What if they were right?

55
Udinny

It was to be caught in a storm.

Ancient Anjiin comes to life around me and I am battered by streams of power. The walls and the floor and the air shake. Strange blocks and roundels pulse and move of their own accord. The disturbances are so great I am forced to bring Syerfu to a stop, to hunker down and hide behind her shaggy body as the great energies of the lost city of the gods rage around us. Streams of power cut through the air, pass through the strange walls and stutter along the maze-like streets of Ancient Anjiin. Energy rises in sparkling purple-blue streamers, punching through as if the air fights against it, rising and rising to feed some great appetite in the world above.

I do not think it can be anything good.

Udinnys past whispered in my ear. Lost knowledge filters into my consciousness. I know what I see is wrong.

This was not how Great Anjiin should be.

For the briefest moment, an image overlays the dark city, pulsing with purple lines and twitching lights.

So different.

A golden city. Humming and bright as if the Light Above

shines down upon it. Great towers and spires, vast halls and huge buildings; and all of it moves. Eight-spoked leaves spin around on great poles, towers rise and fall and rivers of energy flood into the place from north and south, huge golden streams that split and twist as they come into the city. The energy shared among eight hundred thousand temples, and the incoming magic flows to each and on each a different god sits upon a throne, by them one of the people. Acolytes listen to their songs and obey their instruction and parts of the flow of power are split off, for who knows what purpose, maybe those gods eat it. What remains of the power is sent on. Joining the flow from other temples and spinning into a vast and twisting rope that rises up through the central spire of Great Anjiin; from there it is spread into eight smaller, though still immense ropes that connect with eight smaller towers and shoot into the sky, two head east, and two head west, and two head north, and two head south. There is no sense of storm or danger in this place, only contentment. I cannot understand the voice of the ancient Udinny who shares this with me – their words are strange and twisted – but I know I look upon a vision of Anjiin as it had been, when it was not ancient and Great Iftal ruled Crua and all was peace and all was good and the Osere had not yet risen.

The sense of peace does not last long. The vision flickers and once more I am buffeted by dark currents surging through Anjiin. The same dark and noisome strength that I fought in the tentacles, that animated the spearmaw. It was not using Anjiin as it should be used, not working with the great city. Instead it bullied its way through thousands of tiny parasitic nodes, fed them power which was directed by something at the centre that burnt like a dark Light Above, the opposite of Ranya, the adversary of my god.

My enemy.

Our enemy, I feel it from the whole line of Udinnys past. I know it. This is a returning darkness, this is the Osere rising once more. The terrors of our past have set their sights upon the world above and that is why Ranya has put me upon this path, Golden Ranya, who steers my feet. I swear I will not fail.

Or I will do my best not to fail.

After all, I am only one, probably, dead monk set against the power of a god.

Syerfu bleats.

One dead woman and a magical crownhead, against a god.

The city of Anjiin screams its pain and outrage. A flash of light. I see something in the distance where the ropes of power had risen from, three great spires. That is wrong, there should be more. Eight.

The power stops flowing.

I wait, but nothing happens.

I mount Syerfu, and we walk through a ghostly dead city towards where I felt the focus of the power. Drawn there, I do not think I will find anything. I cannot explain this to one who is not dead, but I know that what has drawn the power, sent it up into the lands above, is no longer there. Whatever it has done has taken much from it and it has fled, for now at least. I was as sure of that as I was of dear Syerfu's loyalty and the sharpness of my needle spear or needle bow or whatever it was at the moment. What had been in Ancient Anjiin is now gone, though not for ever, maybe it would be truer to say it sleeps. Its energies spent on some great endeavour, and I do not know if it had been successful or not.

A great groan passes through ancient Anjiin, the noise of rocks sheering, of vast trees falling in forests bringing down their smaller counterparts, the sound of destruction.

Syerfu bleats.

"No, I do not think that sounded good either."

We head towards the noise, past a city that becomes clearer and more real to me with every step. Yet again I speak of things that are almost impossible for the living to understand of the dead. I am part of this place. Physically part of it, a stone that used to build the walls of it. I know it makes little sense but that is the way of it.

We pass vast ziggurats, the temples of gods long gone, the huge spinning leaves above now still. There are what looks like dry beds for water to run into, huge amounts of it, but I know they should be filled with glowing and pulsing golden energy.

We slow a little as we approach the place I felt the energy focused to, and here the city ceased to make sense. I see an approximation of two cities. Anjiin as was and Anjiin as is. In one, a huge temple is in this place, one of the largest buildings of the entire city, but now it is no longer there. What I had heard was the destruction of this building, the focus of power and sending of it has destroyed what was here, and I feel a pain deep within, a shock from Udinnys past. As if what had been done is somehow unthinkable, impossible. That Anjiin is sacred to all, both Osere and those who fought them. Never, since Iftal fell, had any desecrated one of the great Lens.

Lens.

A new word to me. I do not know what it meant, though I felt sure it was a place of great importance.

What its destruction meant is more clear. Whatever enemy we fight cares little for Crua. Little for what has been and little for the memory of glorious Iftal to whom the city is a memorial, a grave even. I wonder what could be so important that this place should be destroyed. Has the enemy done it out of hate, or because they have no use for it? Or maybe they are not from the past, not risen Osere at all and have no concept of what this place was.

Not that I know much apart from its importance.

What matters enough for this destruction?

As if in answer, I look up, and see movement. Two bright stars falling from above, hurtling down towards Ancient Anjiin.

"Well, Syerfu," I say. "It seems Ranya answers my question."

56

Cahan

Falling.

Strange, to fall was relaxing in its own way. To be free of the pressure of the land, the constant wearing of it on his muscles, the friction of traction and movement, the weight of thought and the constant fight just to be.

This was freedom.

This was an end.

He would fall and he would hit the ground and never have to think or worry again. How far was the ground? He did not know. Maybe they would fall forever.

Inside something roared, something fought and screamed and wanted. With it came a sure and certain belief; a knowing. He was wrong. There would be no freedom, there would be no crushing impact followed by death and silence and escape and a foot upon the Star Path. Not for him. In his desperation he had given himself over to something terrifying and dark and it had him. He belonged to it. His body was its puppet, who he was, his essence, would be pushed back into the corner of his mind while the rot within him raged.

If he broke his body it would fix it.

It wanted him. It needed him.

The only reason it did not have him was because of the woman, Sorha.

And the fall would most certainly kill her.

She was falling below him, bits of bridge spinning and twisting around her. Her arms flailing as she clawed at the air, trying desperately to slow her plummet. She deserved death. She was the catalyst of everything, an easy figure for him to blame. A woman who gloried in the pain of others, the essence of what it was to be Rai, hateful and concerned only with herself.

But if she died?

What happened to him if she died?

A roaring within. A fire waiting to be kindled.

Iftal's star, he could not let her die.

He brought his arms in close to his body, angled himself like a spearseed, copying the way they made a flat plain against the air that sped them through the air to bury themselves in the ground. Air rushing past him, bits of debris hitting him as he hurtled towards Sorha. Darkness closing in, light fleeing. Only one chance, if he missed her that was it. He would have too much speed and he could not fly, to go back upwards. Swaying back and forth. Altering his direction. Closer and closer and closer. Darker and darker. Soon he would be unable to see her. At the last moment, as he was about to hit her she saw him and spun in the air, twisting out of his way. He cried out.

"No!"

Shooting past, the air howling in his ears, wind whipping his hair about his face, blind from the moisture being forced out of his eyes. Blinded by the lack of light. Reaching. One last desperate action. His hand closed on material. He pulled. Felt her struggling against his grip, they began to spin. Dancing through a veil of windborne tears, she struggled, trying to slip out of the topcoat that he had grabbed. He pulled harder, getting another hand on her arm. The smooth sheen of her armour. Hard to grip but he would not let go. She was hitting him. Screaming at him. But there was no skill in her attack. She was overwhelmed by the terror of the fall. It had driven all sane thought from her mind and left her a scratching, biting, unthinking creature, wanting only to escape death and in her panic attacking the only thing that could waylay it. Him.

He pulled. Harder. Dragged her closer. Nails raking his face. Her breath loud enough he could hear it over the whistling wind. She began shrieking, screaming in fury and then he had her. Spinning her round so her back was against his front. Clasping her with his arms and legs, moving so his back was to the ground and his body would be a cushion against the impact that surely must come soon, and the last thing he heard before they hit, before the darkness took him, was her voice.

"I'll kill you! I'll kill you!"

"Wake up."

Everything hurt.

"Wake up!" Another hurt added to the rest. A pain on the side of his face. "Wake up!" His eyes opened. The night almost absolute, no luminescent animals pierced the darkness. He could just make out a face above his, a weight on his body adding to the agony of knitting bones and stitching muscle. He tried to focus. Failed. He could feel his body mending, faster than it ever had before and it distracted him. At the same time it did not feel quite like his body. As if what fixed him was not the substance of who he was, it was something other. He squinted, focused on the face above his. Sorha.

"Why?" She let out the word as a grunt of pain. "Why did you save me?" He couldn't reply. His mouth was wrong. Whatever was fixing him was concentrating on what mattered most. He could feel it as heat in the trunk of his body, ribs and organs knitting. His skull burning as it corrected fractures. For a moment he did not know who or where he was. The world blurred again. "Tell me or . . ." Her words fell away, overwhelmed by pain that came out of her mouth in a great rolling grunt. Blood running from her nose. Make-up smeared and dirt on her face. "Tell me or I will . . ." The words dying away, she was shaking, wavering. "I will . . . I will slit your throat." He couldn't tell her, his mouth would not open. His lungs were swimming in his own blood. "I will . . ." Then she fell forward, slumped against him and darkness took him again.

He woke. The pain had subsided and Sorha was gone. Relief, swiftly followed by panic. Expecting the thing within him to rise up and take him. It did not happen, instead it wallowed in his belly like a heavy meal, threatening sickness.

She had to be near.

Cahan forced himself to sit, every muscle making its presence known, his body alien and unfamiliar but it obeyed him and that was what mattered. It did what he wanted. Cahan rolled over until he was on all fours. Took a breath, the air down here was different, damper. It felt like the air in the forest after the circle winds had brought rain. But there was no rain here, no circle winds. The air was completely still.

Vague shapes in the darkness, buildings? They were huge, strange. Not like any buildings he had seen before. He tried to reach out the way he did with his cowl, but what stopped the rot within taking him over also stopped him being able to sense the world around him. Instead he peered into the black. Eventually seeing something against the base of one of the buildings, a faint glimmering, the reflection of something white. He crawled towards it, hoping it was her. Staying aware of what was in him in case it began to grow. His hand found something in the dirt of the cavern. If it was dirt, it felt strange, more like gravel. A knife, it must be hers. He must be going in the right direction. He pushed the knife inside his greaves.

It was her.

Still alive but only just. He wondered if something of her cowl remained, it must for her to survive such a fall. Without something to help her she would not have survived at all. One of her arms was twisted. The white he saw was the bone of her thigh where it had pierced the skin. He stared at her, taking her in. She would have lost a lot of blood but her leg must be fixed. He took off the belt around her middle and split it down the centre lengthwise with the knife. It took all his energy and he had to sit down afterwards. Rest, unsure for how long. No way of telling how much time had passed down here. When he felt like he had enough strength he straightened her leg, even weakened and unconscious she cried out. A sob in the dead quiet of this strange place. That done he took his axes and placed them either side of her thigh, lashing them in place with the belt to make a splint.

It took almost all he had. With the last of his strength he straightened her arm, and this elicited no more than a groan. Then he lay in the strange dirt of this strange place and slept once more.

She sat leaning against the wall when he woke next. Little more than a collection of gleaming lines in the darkness where the small amount of light touched the hard edges of her armour. When she spoke her voice was thick with pain.

"You bound my wounds." He saw her move, heard the creak of the crownhead leather beneath her armour. "Why?"

He pushed himself up, his muscles complaining and bones aching. It was very quiet, this underneath place. No sound of animals, no rush of wind or brush of leaf against leaf. Unnatural.

"If what we are told is true," he began, his words came haltingly, his voice sounded wrong. It was as if the vast silence of this place ate the sound up, as if hungry for noise. "Well, this is where the Osere reside. I would be fool to go on alone."

"And you would rather have an enemy who would stab you in the back than be alone?" She sounded disbelieving. "A wounded one too, one who will slow you down?"

"You will heal quickly," said Cahan, "that part of your power clearly still lives within you." He saw her nod, the way the highlights on her skin changed. Then she laughed.

"You make no sense," she said. "You are Cowl-Rai, I saw your strength up there. You do not need to carry a threat around with you, and especially not one who will slow you, make you weaker by her presence."

"Look around," he said quietly. "What is there to feed a cowl down here? What is there to feed anyone?"

Silence. A great and oppressive silence in a great and oppressive darkness.

Or was it lighter than it had been? Did the air have a faint glow to it? Was he becoming used to this place, adapting to it?

"Do you even need life any more, Cahan Du-Nahere?" He did not like what she said, what he knew would come next. "I saw you in the Slowlands, I saw what you became. Barely even one of the people, something monstrous. Is that the way of the Cowl-Rai?" He could feel her studying him, even though he could barely see her. "I feared you as you came at me. I thought I stood no chance, even when I took away your . . ." Her voice tailed off. Cahan thought he heard water dripping somewhere very far away. Laughter from her. No humour in it, a cold and unpleasant noise. "You do not fear the Osere," she said. "You fear yourself." He said nothing. Stood, turned his back on her. The laughter continued. "What have you done, Cahan Du-Nahere? What have you let yourself become that you loathe yourself even more now than you did when we first met? That you frighten yourself so much?" He had nothing to say to her. "You think I do not see it? How little you wish to be powerful, how foolish you were to think you could survive without power in Crua?" He turned, advancing on her without realising. Anger rising within.

"It is not me!" The words a roar. Dagger in his hand. "Something dwells within me and it is not me." As he approached he heard her move, the glint of a weapon in the darkness. In the two steps it took him to cross to her she had produced a second dagger. She held it to her throat.

"Stop!" she shouted. He did and she smiled, not that he could see, but he could hear it when she spoke. "You need me. You need me to keep whatever has you in its grasp at bay. Come any closer and you lose me." Her teeth glittered. There was definitely more light. "I will end myself."

"If you do," said Cahan, slowly, "everything will be destroyed."

"You are that powerful and that out of control?"

"I will no longer be me." The words dull, flat. "Something darker than even you can imagine has me." She stared at him, still smiling.

"But I will not care, Cahan Du-Nahere. I will be dead." He was about to rage, to scream at her but he did not. Instead he took a deep breath.

"No," he said, "you will not be. I saw the way you fought for life as you fell. You will not take your own life."

"That was the animal in me, the shock of it." Did she sound ashamed? He could not quite tell. "It is different to make the choice yourself. To realise revenge leads you along the Star Path." Her voice was drifting, he wondered if he was wrong. If her pain was outweighing the fierce need to live he had seen in her before.

"I do not think there is a Star Path, not now," he said. He crouched, had told no one what he thought before. Strange, that he should be unburdening himself here, to his sworn enemy.

"You would say anything," she spat.

"You saw how I did not want to take life." She was watching him, her eyes locked on his. "To fight you in Harn, the trees gave me power, but that was a one-time gift. When I needed it again it was not there. The land denied me. So I sought another way."

"You made a deal with the Osere." He shook his head.

"Crua is a cycle," said Cahan, and he no longer looked at her, he looked into his past, at a decision made he would do anything to take back. "All things are brought back, the trees take power from the Light Above, but they also take power from death, from what decays."

"That power is denied us, all know it. Only the Cowl-Rai who made the Reborn understood death and that knowledge is lost." She sounded fascinated, malice gone just for a moment. Cahan shook his head.

"If it was true it would be good, the Reborn should not exist. All that mattered to them is lost. Taste, love, pleasure, all gone." He wondered if the Reborn would come down here in search of him so he could fulfil his promise of death for them. "I sought to take power from death, and found I could not. The same way a person cannot eat gasmaw or littercrawler flesh, the power of death was denied to me."

"So what are you, then?"

"I thought I had found a way to use it, death," he said, "that I need not kill to protect those I love. The bluevein sickness was a way in, in my mind the worst that could happen was that it would make me ill."

"But you were not strong enough to control it," she said, almost a laugh, though it died on her lips.

"I controlled it until the Slowlands. But the power needed to save Furin overwhelmed me. Bluevein is not a sickness, it is a symptom of something deeper. And it is aware of us, of me. It wants me."

"Why?"

"It wants to destroy."

From his past a voice came back to him.

You are the fire.

No, it could not be. He would not be.

"If I help you," he said, "can you walk?" She shook her head.

"Not yet." Cahan nodded. Put aside his own weakness.

"Wait here." He walked away, careful not to go too far from Sorha. It was definitely getting lighter and that the light had a direction. Lighter to his left, darker to the right. He followed the light. A thin alley between two of the strange buildings, just enough light to see by. He could go no further than this, the corruption within was growing, roaring in his mind. The buildings that lined the alley had a strange skin over them, not wood, not stone or cloth. Cold to the touch, in places it was holed and flaking. He pulled at part of it and to his surprise found it came away from the building. Beneath he found a wall of strange smooth material as odd as the skin he had pulled off. He could make a travois with this stuff, and pull Sorha along. He picked up the material.

And saw the first body.

Mostly bone, but with a film of skin. It looked like it had died in agony, the limbs twisted in impossible ways. He looked more closely. Fire? It looked like fire had done it. As if something had burned them alive. As he stared he began to smell it, the scent of cooked flesh. This was recent. Cahan looked around, he did not want to be here if whatever had done this came back. He did not want to meet the people of this place either because he knew what lived below. Osere. Was this one of their servants, a punishment? Or were there Rai down here? Rai of the Osere who had fed from this body?

Cahan had no wish to find out.

He returned to Sorha, and now he had seen one body he found more. His eyes became used to finding shapes in the darkness that marked other burned corpses. How had they got down here? There were many, tens, maybe even hundreds.

Was it those sent here to be punished? Had he been sent here to be punished?

"I'll put you on this," he said to Sorha as he knelt by her.

She began to reply but he did not give her time. Made her cry out as he pulled her roughly on to the sheet of material. Then he took her outer tunic from her, cut the long coat into strips.

"Why are you in such a hurry?" she said. "There is nothing here."

"I do not think that is the case." As he said it he felt something, huge and powerful and hungry, though not hungry in a way he understood. Not hungry for food. Behind the hunger a purpose. Implacable purpose. He tied Sorha onto the travois, strung a handle and wished he had enough material to make something that went over his shoulder, but he did not. Instead he had to drag the travois behind him in a way that would be uncomfortable and tiring.

"Where are we going?" she said. Something of his urgency must have infected her as she was no longer mocking him.

"Away," he said. "Away from this place."

They moved off into the darkness.

57
Ont

There was darkness and there was pain.

The last thing he remembered was an arrow in among all the noise. His arrow. The soldiers had run across the bridge. The Rai were launching fire at them and he was loosing arrows. Watching them hit Rai, a killing blow with each arrow and the sense of pride that came with it. He had not realised how much he wanted this. How much they were not only a physical target but the target of his grief, and with each arrow he asked for Ranya's guidance and he said the name of one who had been lost.

"Ranya, guide this arrow for Darmant."

"Ranya, guide this arrow for Usest."

"Ranya, guide this arrow for Bryent."

He released each arrow with a sense of peace. A sense of rightness. He no longer hated the Rai for what had been done to his people. He thought of them more like a rogue gasmaw, or spearmaw, or orits when they came too near the village; they were simply doing what they did, it was their nature. That did not make them any less dangerous, or make the hunting of them any less necessary.

Then there was fire and pain. Voices and screaming. One

of those voices his. Clawing at his eyes, falling backwards. Pain like he had never known. A voice.

"Get the wounded back."

He tried to struggle, even through the pain, the darkness. He was there to fight. He had to fight. He was trying to tell them that but the noise coming out of his mouth was not words, only a harsh croak.

"I will get you to a healer."

All was pain.

"Have . . . to . . . fight."

"You have fought." It had been Ania, he was sure. "You have fought well, now you must fight to live." The strange sickening sensation of passing through the taffistone and the familiar scents and heat of the Forestals' home. Shouting. Voices but they did not matter to him. He was fading away.

He woke, feeling cool. A sheet covered him. It was dark and he was aware of pain the same way he was aware of rootlings in the forest back in New Harnwood. He heard them, knew they were there but they did not bother him.

The pain was far away.

"Ont? Are you awake?"

He did not reply, the voice was of no more concern to him than the echoes of pain.

"It is hard to tell if he is."

"Can he hear us?"

Something made a chattering noise, animalistic but not threatening.

"If he is awake maybe, but he has had so much sperrion syrup I doubt he cares what we say."

They were right, he did not care about anything. He was tired and moved through a dream. The noise of the world outside dissolving into a gentle, quieting hum. He felt like he had failed. Failed again but this was just another thing for him not to care about.

*

He woke and the pain was more insistent. The world less gentle. He could hear moaning, a low and constant sound. Someone breathing, rhythmic in the way of gentle sleep. Voices, talking among each other, keeping low as if they did not want to be heard. Ont thought he should open his eyes soon. See where he was. Somewhere in Woodhome, he was sure about that, but where in the great tree he did not know. For now he would just lie here and listen.

"We need to find Cahan." A soft voice. Venn, he thought.

"He is lost. You must forget him," said the other voice and Ont felt something slip away within him. Hope fading away. Cahan, lost?

"Sera," said Venn, "I know you do not trust him, but you are wrong. And I believe he—"

"He was seen to fall into the depths. The Osere have him now and considering what you tell me of him, that is for the best."

"Cahan is not like other people."

"Venn . . ."

"In the north, there is—"

"The Boughry; I know you think they would help him but my answer has not changed. They are too dangerous. So is he."

"But Cahan and Udinny went to—"

"And how did that work out for them, Trion? The Woodhewn Nobles have great power, and know many things, but there is always a great price for their knowledge."

"I would pay it." The dying hope within Ont grew a little at that. At the bravery of the trion, their lack of selfishness. Ranya had chosen well.

"Yes," said Tall Sera, "I know you would. But Brione has told me you are important to us, and I listen to their advice so do not ask again." Before the conversation could continue Ont heard the flap of the hut open.

"How is he?" A little brightness within at the familiar growl of Ania.

"Healing," said Venn.

"Thanks to you, Trion."

"And his own strength was great, and your presence should not be overlooked."

"I am not sure he even knows I am here." Strange, how sad she sounded.

"I believe he does. Will you sit with him today?"

"For an hour, then I must go; the forces of the north are making great advances in the south. They will send more troops to Treefall soon. We must do as much damage as we can, while we can."

"Walk Ranya's road, Ania, and stay safe."

"Thank you, Trion."

Footsteps, coming closer. A touch, someone taking his hand and they squeezed gently.

"Ah, Ont, I must be away for a few days. But I will come back." He squeezed back. "Ont?" He tried to nod and felt almost as if he had forgotten how to use his body. "Do not try to do too much," said Ania. "You have been hurt."

He turned his head towards her, slow and excruciating movements. He wanted to see her but could not, it was too dark in the hut.

"Light," he said, his tongue was very dry. The words were hard to make. "Bring some light."

"A drink," she said, he felt something against his lips and realised he was propped up in the bed, not lying down. The water was like nectar, and taken away far too soon. "Not too much," she said, "it will make you sick."

"Bring some light."

"Ont, how much do you remember?"

How much? He did not know. It would be so much easier if it was not so dark.

"I remember loosing arrows." Halting words, each one a struggle. "Then the Rai. I remember thinking you were in danger and . . . not much else." Another squeeze of his hand. He was tired again, just from those words. "For

Ranya's sake, bring a little light. I feel I have lain in the dark for ever."

"You killed three Rai," said Ania. "Saved lives."

"Stories later, please, a little light."

"Saved my life, Ont. The Rai loosed fire at us, and you stepped in front of me. Shielded me."

"I do not remember," he said. *A flash of fire, the brightest thing he had ever known. Pain like nothing before.* Something inside him growing, a suspicion he did not want to examine.

"They thought you dead. But I did not. I dragged you back here with the other wounded." Ont was seized by a desire for her to stop talking that was so strong, so powerful, that he could do nothing but give in to it.

"Please, no more, Ania." He did not want to know what had happened because there could be hope without knowing.

A silence.

He felt the need to fill it. "Did we get Furin out?"

"We did." Ont let out a breath. That was good. He needed good news. It was so dark. "She was sorely hurt, but gets better every day. Venn and the other trion here work miracles. The trunk commander woman, Dassit, and her second made it back also."

"The other Forestal woman? The murder priest?"

"The priest helped me get you back. Then returned to help others. Something happened, he hit his head and has not woken. His body lives but Venn says whatever was within it, the mind, they think it gone. Tanhir sits over him watching. I think she guards him from death, and cannot stand the fact he may escape her justice." A quiet, grim laugh from Ania. "He is near you, his breathing has kept us company for many nights. That and the occasional chatter of Furin's woodling boy, Issofur. He also sits with the priest, he will not leave his side though none know why and none will move one who belongs to the Boughry."

"How many nights?" Soft words, quiet words.

"Many."

"Oh." No answer. No more questions. Only one left and he was sure he knew the answer to it. The fear was still there, the desire not to know but the panic was gone, replaced with the knowledge he could not run from what was. "I am blind, Ania, am I not?"

"I am sorry." He felt trapped, like he needed to run but there was nowhere to run to.

"Surely Venn can fix me. I have seen them do such things and . . ."

"They can only work with what is there, Ont." She held his hand even tighter. "The fire took your eyes. It took so much." He did not speak again, not straight away. He had seen those few who had survived fire, and was not sure he would ever describe them as lucky. The fire of Rai was a strange thing, wounds would reopen years later, or never heal.

"How hurt am I?"

"It is remarkable you survived." He could barely hear her. She took his hand in both of hers, aware as she did that it did not feel right. Pain shooting through him as he moved. Blood in his mouth. His fingers, his fingers were not in the right place.

"What is left of me, Ania?"

Silence. Only the rhythmic breathing of the sleeping priest. The soft whine of what may have been a garaur or Issofur. It was not, in the end, Ania that answered though, it was the Forestal, Tanhir.

"You have lost most of your fingers to the second knuckle. Though the two first fingers on your right hand survive intact. Boots protected your feet, though the heat melted them into your skin and to get them off damage was done. But they think you will be able to walk again."

"My face?"

"Tanhir," said Ania, "there is no need for this now."

"Better to rip the bandage off," said Tanhir.

"My face?" he said again.

"Gone," she said. "They had to cut you a new mouth. Most thought you would never speak but Venn was confident that you would." He let that sink in, glad in that moment of his blindness and that he could not see the ruin of his body.

"I will need a mask," he said, the words little more than an exhalation of air. "Or people will think I am a skinfetch, with no features but those I can steal off others."

"You are more than your face, Ont," said Ania.

"I will never loose a bow again." That hurt, and mostly because he would no longer have time with Ania. It had been a long time since he had been anyone's first, second or third husband. He had all but given up on the idea of romantic attachment but he had cherished his time with her. "I had enjoyed our work with the bow."

"And you were good at it," said Ania.

"I think," he said softly, "I would like some time alone."

58

Sorha

Time had ceased to have any meaning to her.

To begin with, it was because there was nothing but pain. Every step Cahan took sending waves of it running through her as the broken bones in her body rubbed where they were knitting together. There was at least solace in that pain, because she knew it meant her strength was growing. She might hate Cahan Du-Nahere but he had done a good job of setting her leg and her arm. But there were other places he did not see, the bones in her foot and hand and her ribs were misaligned. Her body had already started healing them in these new positions. So while he slept one night she had re-broken the bones, swallowing her agony and pushing it into thoughts of vengeance.

And she would have vengeance.

Once she was fixed, once her body obeyed her.

He may need her, but she did not need him and when she was well she would kill him. He saved her life, but he did it purely for selfish reasons. He wanted her to save himself, that was all. Should that change no doubt he would be as quick to kill her as she intended to be in killing him.

She was able to walk now at least. Every step hurt but

better that than have to rely on him. He had tried to speak to her but she decided not to reply. Better to raise her defences now. To be a spire city, walled and protected from him, or better still a skyraft, floating above and unassailable.

So she walked and she hurt and she stewed in her own anger and hate. To keep her mind off him she studied the place they walked through. Dark, but not entirely dark, not any more. A glow had been growing as they passed through the city and the more they walked the more attention she paid to it. She began to think it was not a pervasive thing this glow, not everywhere. She had a horrible suspicion that it led them. That Cahan always headed towards the light, that it drew him onwards.

Foolish?

She was not sure. She did not trust it, but she preferred the light to the utter darkness.

So she walked and she hurt and she studied and she hated.

The more she studied, the more sure she became that they walked through a city, but not a city on a scale of the people of Crua. A city on the scale of something much larger. She almost spoke to him about it, shared her suspicions about the light and the city.

But she would not speak to him.

Instead she studied vast buildings with strange moving parts that made no sense and had no symmetry. Other buildings looked like they should move but had not in more generations than she could imagine. They walked down one huge thoroughfare and past what looked like a temple of some sort, the building massive and slab-sided, rising up and up and clearly for some purpose she did not understand. Around it stood what looked like taffistones, which made her think this was a place for sacrifice, for the taking of power. She wondered what sat upon the thrones within such temples. Maybe it had been one of her people, a Rai of huge importance and strength.

Because there were people in this strange city. Or at least the remains of them.

She was used to seeing burned bodies, from the fire she had made when she was Rai. Knew the contorted shapes of those dying in the flame well, and there was no doubt that the corpses they passed had died in fire. Or something akin to it.

She stopped to study another body, examining the way the flesh had been broken down into something hard that crumbled under the pressure of her grip. She felt the Forester's attention on her and tried to ignore it. She put her hand on the ground, ran the gritty substance of it through her fingers. She looked ahead, he had stopped walking, staying well within her influence. He looked tired, miserable.

Good.

A moment of pure anger. What had she become? A once powerful Rai and now her life was lived in pursuit of vengeance on him, some clanless loner from the far north where the people were barely civilised.

"I have seen hundreds of such bodies," he said. She turned away from him. "You will have to talk to me eventually, Sorha." She did not look at him, only at the floor. A feeling she was unfamiliar with growing within her. "If we are to leave this place we will need each other." He sounded pathetic, like he was beaten and she had, all her life, been taught to despise weakness. She turned back to the burned body; a little further along there was another, and another. "I think something took power from them," said Cahan. "Something like me, given how many bodies there are." She did not look at him, though she was aware of him in the gloom, watching her.

He was right, and it made her burn within. Did she care about returning to the world above? How often had she thought vengeance was all that mattered? She would have died content if she had died in the killing of him.

Would have.

Then why did she hesitate? Why had she not killed him while he slept already? Weakness, was her first thought. But it was not. Somehow, creeping up on her, had been change. She did not hate any less, but she was no longer blinded by it. She hated him because he had bested her, because he threatened her. She hated the Rai for the same reason. But without the power of the Rai, without being one of them she had slowly come to realise that she owed all the hate she felt to being brought up Rai. It was conditioned into her by them.

Above, before she had fallen, the Forester and his people had risked their lives to save one of their number when they knew the odds were stacked against them. Part of her thought that madness. Part of her wondered what it would be like to be so loved.

Who would fight for Sorha?

She pushed that thought away.

"Whatever, whoever did this," she said. "They have been doing it for a long time."

"What do you mean?" She heard him take a step closer. His boots crunching on the ground.

"That ground you walk on," she said, "it is not soil." She lifted a handful of the gritty material and let it run through her fingers. "It is the burned remains of thousands." He stopped walking. "You cannot hurt them by walking on them," she said, "they are long beyond your help."

"I think this is Ancient Anjiin," he said and she laughed.

"Anjiin is a myth."

"It feels like a place out of myth." She had no reply, it was hard to refute.

"Well, wherever it is, we are being led." She stood. He did not reply and she wondered if he suspected the same. "The light, subtle as it is, leads us."

"It glows wherever we are," he said, "the way the flyers glow when you walk through the forest and disturb them." Sorha shook her head. It hurt.

"No, I have been watching. It glows ahead of us and you take us towards it." She could tell her words angered him, he did not like being stuck with her any more than she liked being with him. He turned and looked in the direction of the light.

"Very well," he said, "we shall go a different way." He pointed towards the darkness and for a moment she wished she had not said anything. She did not want to leave the light but it was too late, he was walking away from it now. She followed into a darkness that felt absolute, solid. She had to follow the sound of his footsteps, slow, careful, steady. As her eyes adjusted, she began to make out dark shapes; they were disquieting and discomforting, their scale wrong, the lack of light played tricks with perspective.

They walked for a long time, and it was as if the light gave up on trying to lead them. It began to illuminate where they walked. She could see again. Cahan stopped. She stopped. Looked over her shoulder.

"The light is brighter behind us," she said.

"You were right." He did not look at her. "It was leading us." She did not reply, did not know what to say. Felt no triumph in noticing what he had not.

"Where do you think it was leading us?"

"I do not know," he said, looking around at the huge structures. It struck her how unsettling the silence here was. How total. "How long do you think we have been down here?"

"A fourday at least," she said. He nodded.

"Are you hungry?"

"No."

"Thirsty?"

"No."

"But we have not eaten or drunk. Were you told the stories as a child? 'In Ancient Anjiin no one wants.'" She did not reply, she did not want to be walking through a myth. That made her think she was caught up in some great event, and great events brought only great danger to those caught up in them. She laughed to herself. What had her life been since she came upon Cahan Du-Nahere in the forest? Nothing but great danger.

Maybe great events were coming. Maybe she was already caught up in them.

"Quiet!" he said and she was about to snap back at him. He was no trunk commander to order her about like a common soldier.

Then she heard it.

The irregular steps of something huge. A clanging and grinding as it moved, a sense of heaviness and slowness. A presence above them. Something passing over the tops of the buildings they stood between, meagre light shining off its oily underside, the light that followed them dimmed by its great bulk. A sense of oppression fell upon them and Sorha found she was holding her breath. Then it moved on. The oppression lifting.

"What was that?" said Cahan.

"I do not know. But I did not like it." They walked on, but more carefully, slower. Hiding each time the thing approached, which it did – again and again. She had the feeling it was searching for something. At one point it stopped a short way in front of them. Two tentacles, thick as the anchor ropes for skyraft, slowly unfurled from above them and reached down for the ground. Then they moved across the floor, exploring it. Running over the slick black skin of the thing were gently glowing blue lines. Sorha was about to say something but Cahan put his fingers to his lips.

They waited in silence as the huge tentacles moved, touching everything within reach, searching. Finally, they lifted back into the air and it was gone.

"I think it is searching for us," said Cahan.

"Us?"

"Me," he said more softly, a hint of bitterness. "I think

that is what fed me the power I used in the Slowlands. That or a servant to it."

"Why?" he shrugged.

"Glimpses seen in my mind, the smell of it," he looked away, "I cannot explain it. I only know it is true. We are linked."

"Surely if it is linked to you then . . ." She stopped speaking. Smiled. "It cannot find you because of me?" He nodded. "But it is still searching, by sound do you think? What is it? Do you know?"

"No, some huge gasmaw, maybe?" She had the distinct feeling he was keeping something from her, at the same time she was not entirely sure she wanted to know.

She looked away, staring into the darkness. "Well, whatever it is, I think it is better we stay away from it."

On they went, aware of the thing that hunted them, nervous of the darkness lest a huge tentacle appear and pluck them from the ground. Later, when they stopped for a rest they did not feel they needed, the silence was broken by sound again. Different sound, not their pursuer. It sounded like battle. Voices shouting and screaming in excitement and pain. The Forester stared at her.

"Towards it, or away?" she said.

"Toward," said Cahan. "Maybe there are more of our people trapped down here?"

She nodded and he led them towards the noise in the darkness and the light about them dimmed again, like it did not want them to go towards the fighting. It only made her more determined to, and Cahan too from the look of him. The way his body stiffened as he noticed the light ebbing away. He did not like being told what to do, being led.

They had that in common at least.

They honed in on the sounds of battle, and found they shared an instinct, knowing when they were near, going low to stay hidden. The final approach made at a slow crawl, though bending over was excruciating for her, her body had become a collection of a thousand small agonies as it healed.

They rounded a corner, and the battle was laid out before them in the dim light. Though Sorha did not, at first, recognise it as a battle. The shapes were wrong. Her view of it made little sense. She could hear people, running back and forth. Orders were occasionally shouted in a language that was both strange and familiar. How many voices? More than twenty, more than thirty? It sounded like they moved in small groups but the battle had an odd rhythm. Staccato. Forming and reforming. Bursts of movement followed by absolute stillness. The clatter of spears thrown and landing on the ground. What did they fight? She wondered if they were mad, minds broken by this strange, dark and silent place. Slowly, the dim light grew, and she saw more of what was before her. Her mind could not make sense of what she was seeing. The size of it, the strangeness of it.

"They fight what hunted us," said Cahan. Fear filled his voice, fear and awe. What they fought was vast. Half hidden and constantly moving. She only caught glimpses. A round body, covered with strange glowing protuberances and fruiting bodies. A gnawing beak within a circle of hundreds of small writhing tentacles. From the round body sprouted eight massive tentacles, ringed and veined with blue and if it had eyes she could not see them. In fact she could not see any features that made sense to her apart from the beak. It was like no creature of Crua. The only thing it resembled, and she circled herself at the blasphemy of it, was the Star of Iftal.

Before she could say anything, speak or ask Cahan what he thought, there was an explosion of fire, leaping from one of the groups of people and up towards the star-thing. A scream filled the air, as much fury as pain and the beast retreated at a furious speed, using four of its great tentacles and, half blinded as she was by the sudden brightness, she felt sure that the other four tentacles held people, small writhing figures.

"We should get away from here," said Cahan. She nodded.

They turned.

Found themselves confronted by a wall of spears.

59

Saradis

The journey back to Tiltspire was a hard one for Saradis, despite that she spent it in the plush staterooms of a skyraft, looked over by scowling, distrustful rafters. In the battle of the Slowlands she had lost all but three of her most loyal Rai. Saradis was already planning, deciding which of those in Tiltspire could be trusted, or who could be leveraged into a position where they relied on her. New alliances would be needed.

She was in pain, which made everything worse. Her left arm was broken, ribs cracked, and she could barely put any weight on her right ankle. The drugs that would numb her pain also dulled her thinking and she could not bear that, so she fought through the pain and planned the way ahead.

Despite all of this, she was also full of joy. Zorir had come. She had seen her God's power. She had seen what she had worked her entire life for come into being and known in that moment that she had been right to choose that clanless boy all those years ago. His weakness was not the flaw she thought it was. His weakness was the mechanism of Zorir's ascension, the spark that would light the fire. She had seen him lose himself, be overtaken by her god and Zorir had been pleased, he had spoken to her.

What power Zorir had! Power that rivalled even that of the Slowlands, she had never heard of such a thing. Even remembering how Du-Nahere changed, his body swelling, the four arms that grew from him, the way the Slowlands ebbed around him. It thrilled her in a way she could barely understand.

Looking back, she had only truly been scared once. It was not when the enemy soldiers attacked. It was not when the hated arrows flew and not even when the viewing stand collapsed around her and she had to fight for her life against one of her own Rai.

No, she would gladly give her life for Zorir.

The great fear was when Du-Nahere, lost, consumed by her god, followed the woman Furin. She knew at that moment that some small remnant of him remained. Even that had thrilled her, because she was sure in his confusion he would have wiped out their attackers, destroyed them all and maybe even the woman Furin, the power around him was so intense, so destructive. It had been more beautiful than she could possibly ever have imagined.

Then he was gone.

The woman her Rai called the abomination, the walking duller, Sorha. She put out the light of Zorir, the beautiful blue and purple fire, the liquid power that twisted around the chosen. Worse, she possessed the skill to kill him. In that moment there was the very real risk that everything she hoped for would be ended with one blow of Sorha's sword.

Then Zorir spoke to her. The god wanted the Cowl-Rai sent to them in the darkness of below and what release she had felt in that moment. The powerful thrill of contact with Zorir driving all pain and fear from her body, leaving only certainty. She knew what she must do with a crystal clarity. Watched as the Rai let loose with fire. As the ropes that held up the bridge ignited. Even then worry, how long would it take? Would she be in time?

Two figures on the rope bridge, fighting. Sword against axe.

She held her breath, until the moment the bridge disintegrated, rope and wood falling away, taking Cahan and the woman with it.

She was dead, of course. Sorha was no longer Rai. The fall would kill her, but it would not kill Du-Nahere. Zorir would not allow that. Even with his power dulled by the woman he would survive. She knew that the same way she knew the bones in her arm and shoulder were broken. It was part of her.

She spent long, excruciating hours writing down everything about the attack in the Slowlands. Everything that had happened and how they had been attacked. Sorha had set up the viewing stand, she had been in charge of the security around it. Easy for Saradis to imagine she set up some sort of betrayal. But that did not fit with what she knew of the woman. She cared about little but her revenge on Cahan Du-Nahere. To be in league with enemies, Forestals, it did not make sense.

Then Saradis wondered how the attack was possible. How they had managed to sneak up on the stand in the Slowlands without being seen when the land was so flat and so bare?

Fortunately, they had had the bodies of the reborn women. The deathless ones. When they woke she would find out. She would enjoy finding out, and what was more, she needed to find out. Knowing what had happened would help her when she faced the questions of the Rai of Tiltspire.

But not now. Not on the skyraft. She put down her pen, her account finished. There was little more she could do so she would take the drugs now and let them dull the pain and her mind. When she returned to Tiltspire she would be as healed as she could be. She would be strong and she would ready.

The time was coming.

Zorir's time was coming.

60

Dassit

She had somehow escaped without a wound.

Vir had not been so lucky, his arm had been burned by Rai fire and Dassit had been sure he would lose it and knew that amputation was always hard. Some survived amputation, but you could never tell who. Then the trion had come. The young one that was friends with the man who had become a monster, Cahan. They had performed miracles, Dassit had watched the burn heal before her eyes. She had never seen anything like it. She knew the trion had healed her but she had not been awake to see that; watching them work had amazed her. She knew the Rai healed themselves, but it had never occurred to her that their power could be used to heal others.

Vir complained constantly that his arm itched.

"At least you have an arm to itch. Nine of ours were not so lucky." He made a dismissive noise, he had always been able to shake off the death of his troops in a way she never had. Vir looked away, shook his head.

"There is that," he said. His eyes never stayed still. He was uncomfortable here, struggling to adapt to a new life among the trees.

They stood in one of the branch villages, high enough in the cloudtree canopy that there was a chill in the air. Uncomfortable – to be so high. Dassit had slowly become used to it. Come to trust that the edges of this kingdom high above the forest floor were marked, rails and ropes would stop her falling. She was not sure Vir felt the same. No, she was sure he did not. "Over there," he said.

"What?"

"One of them, those Osere-cursed animals." She looked along the branch, a height mist was coming in, drifting between the living roundhouses and longhouses. She did not see anything but knew what he would be talking about. Rootlings. The creatures were everywhere in Woodhome, ignored by the people who lived there. Sometimes they stole from the houses, though the Forestals did not see it as stealing. To them it was simply part of the price of living here. Sometimes the rootlings brought them gifts, fruits and mushrooms, histi and raniri. Forestal children played loud screeching games with them, running around the branches, up and down ropes over the great heights without any fear. Dassit found it endearing. Vir was distrustful, to him the rootlings were creatures of the forest which he thought unnatural.

"Just ignore them," she said.

"It's not right, they're diseased, vermin."

"That is how we thought when we were part of the Red, we are that no longer."

"They can make you into 'em, you know?" Vir scratched at his arm. "There was a hunter came with those villagers, became one, ran off into the forest."

"That sounds like a story for children, Vir."

"They do it to children too, you've seen that villager boy, ain't you? Boy's half animal." She had no answer to that – she had seen the child, Issofur, though she felt no threat from him. Vir shook his head, a small, almost unnoticeable movement. "We knew where we were in the army."

"Our army would have had us dead, Vir. They sent us to die. You lost Tryu because of them." He did not reply, only looked over at a group of Forestals.

"Can they not do that inside?" She glanced over, the Forestals were lounging against each other, men and women, kissing and touching. Hands running over bodies.

"Their ways are not ours, Vir."

"They don't even have firsts and seconds, they go with whoever they want." Disgust in his voice. He had always been more strait-laced than her. It was what made him a good second but she was surprised by the way he was acting.

"This is our life now, Vir. We must learn to live within it."

"It is not right," he said, turning away from the group of Forestals.

"Let's walk," she said.

"It is dangerous to walk here."

"Not if you watch your step. In that way it is no different to dealing with the Rai, and we have done that all our lives."

"That was different." No mistaking the resentment in his voice. "That was . . ." His words tailed off. "That was right. How life is meant to be. Tryu died fighting, like a soldier. Here . . ." She did not like this side of Vir, she thought he was better than this. Should be better than this. He turned away from the Forestal's entanglement. "Only five of our people survived the Slowlands, Dass, and that includes us."

"Far more of ours died in Fin-Larger, Vir."

"But that was orders, we obey orders. Here it was for what? So we can bring back some woman who is barely alive and mother to a child that's half rootling? And do that in service to . . ." He looked away, then went and leant on the railing of living wood, staring over the edge and down into the darkness.

Here they were, at the rub of it.

"In service to what, Vir?"

"You saw."

"What did I see?"

"The same thing I did. Osere."

"I saw a Rai, a powerful one."

"Is he even of the people?" Vir turned to her, his face dark, shadowed. "He was more gasmaw than man."

"I think that was his armour—"

"His armour is part of him!" He shouted it at her. Looked surprised by his actions. Thought about it then said it again, more quietly. "His armour is part of him." Vir's face changed again, every thought showing, every stress and every fear. "You must have felt what I did. It was in the air when he moved. The land shook, and I felt like I breathed the air of a battlefield full of corpses. You cannot tell me that is right."

"No," she said. "But he is Cowl-Rai, they are not like us. People like you and I, we are not meant to get close to people like that."

"It was wrong," said Vir.

"And when we burned villages, or executed those suspected of being traitors, that was not?"

"I told you that was different." Vir would not look at her, only fell back on repeating, "That was orders."

"There may well be something terrible about him, Vir," said Dassit. "But freeing that woman, it felt like the right thing to do." Vir shook his head, no longer looking at her. She wanted to change the subject. "Did you see those women, the Reborn? Anjiin's old walls, but they could fight, right?"

"Yeah," he said, non-committal. "Right up until he changed." He stared at her, a challenge in his expression, in the tension of his muscles. "Then it was like they forgot what they were there for, and the other side cut 'em to pieces."

"Well, yes," she said.

"I can't stay here."

"Then leave, Vir."

"But I can't, can I? Not knowing where their woodland paradise is." He shook his head. "They are degenerates, but not fools."

"They have said we can leave." He shook his head.

"With conditions."

"They make us forget, that seems fair."

"Let them grub around in my mind? Would you allow that?" She did not answer, because they both knew she would not. She did not know how removing a memory worked, but the thought made her deeply uncomfortable. "And how do I know they won't turn me into one of them?" He nodded at a rootling.

"I think I like it here. I think you could like it here." Happy sounds coming from the group of Forestals. "Find yourself a Forestal, Vir. They are a passionate people. Make a home here." He looked over his shoulder, the group of lovers could barely be seen as the darkness of Wyrdwood night fell.

"This place is not for me." He turned and began to walk away.

"Vir," she shouted and he turned. "Tell me you will not try and escape. I do not want to find you on the forest floor with an arrow in your back. We are soldiers, remember? We make the best of what we have." He stared at her, shrugged his shoulders.

"If that is what you order, Trunk Commander."

61
Cahan

It was difficult, in the moment, in the darkness, with the memory of the vast creature hunting them in his mind, with the wall of spears before them, for Cahan to keep his hands from his axes. Despite that he fought against his instinct. Violence was ingrained into his psyche by years of conditioning in the monastery of Zorir, by years afterwards of fighting to try and dull the flame within and only fanning it.

It was not being scared of the fight that stilled his hand. It was what was behind the row of spears and those holding them. Bows. Not like the bows he knew, not like his great forestbow back in Woodhome. They were shorter, more curved, they twisted back on the arch of the bow in a way that he had never seen before. Each was held at tension, short arrows ready to fly. The people holding them, if they were people – he was not sure as in the strange light of this place it was difficult to see them – it was as if the night had come alive, they wore make-up of all the many subtle hues of the night, greys and whites and deep, deep purples. They resembled the people of Crua and they did not, their heads were too long, with strange plumes and ridges. Their hips oddly sharp.

One of them spoke, shouting something out. The words twisted. Almost understandable but not. By him, Sorha shifted. He put out a hand, feeling more than seeing her tense up, ready herself to fight.

"No," he said. "They have bows." He felt her stand closer to him.

"What are they?"

Another of them spoke, in words almost within his understanding but not, like hearing the echoes of the language he knew.

"I don't know."

"What do they want?"

Again, the harsh vocalisation but in it the unmistakeable cadence of an order.

"I don't know," he carefully pulled the axes from his armour and lay them on the floor, "but I think they want us alive." As soon as his hands were away from his weapons they were on him, and on Sorha. Hands everywhere, running over him, voices, and clicks and whirrs, almost like forest creatures. An odd smell, harsh, unnatural. Arms pulled behind his back, ropes around his wrists, another round his neck and all the time the touching and the sounds in the darkness. He heard Sorha groan in pain but their captors did not care. They were like shadows, shadows come to life. Cahan did not think they hurt him or Sorha on purpose, but they were not gentle either. It was only at the end he really saw them. A face appeared in front of his. A collection of shadows, features distorted by make-up, and because of it he had not realised they had no eyes. Only a large smooth forehead, bulbous, strange, and it froze Cahan.

Who were they?

They pulled on the rope around his neck, making him follow. Sorha was leashed and attached to him, dragged forward with him.

"We were fools to allow this," she hissed. Before he could

reply, one of the creatures was in front of him. Hissing something he could almost understand. Or maybe it was just the aggression he picked up on, whichever, it left them both sure that they were not to speak.

So they travelled in silence apart from the clicking and the whirring of their captors, who despite their blindness managed to move unerringly easily through the dark streets around them. He tried to stay aware, keep a look out for the huge creature that had attacked them but he saw no sign of it. Not that he could see much, the small amount of light had fled and the darkness was total now. Occasionally he would see lights, gleams of it, running over the corners of the huge structures they walked through. He wanted to ask Sorha if she saw it too but he did not speak, only walked onwards following the line of those before. Behind them there were more of these creatures, he could not see them but he heard their feet.

They stopped only once.

Sat him and Sorha together and she leaned in close to whisper.

"Do you understand them?" He shook his head. Looked about in case they had heard but it was too dark to see. He thought he heard sounds coming towards them. He smelled something that could have been meat cooking and his stomach rumbled. "I feel like I almost do," she said.

"Almost?"

"When I was a child, some of the monks spoke a language for Chyi that . . ." She was silenced by a pull on the rope around her neck. A few words he could not understand were said and then they walked again, for how long he did not know. Time had no meaning in the darkness. There was only the monotony of his steps and when change came it was slow. Like being woken from sleep.

First, he was aware of a vague light ahead. Then a change in the rhythm of the column as they approached. It went from single file to fanning out. He knew all this by hearing not by sight, odd, he thought, how his senses changed to become more attuned to this place.

"Getting ready for a fight," whispered Sorha.

He nodded. But did not reply as hands were put on him. He felt the warmth of bodies close around him and he and Sorha were pushed, forced to run forward in the press. He heard the screech and the roar of the creature, the huge tentacled thing that had been searching for them before.

It was here. In front of them and from the way they were acting he was sure their captors had expected it. He heard the twang of bows releasing. No shouting, no commands given. Then he and Sorha were being pushed forward again. More bows. A glimpse of the creature, vast, lashing tentacles, a body was smashed through the air. All seen in the unreality of the faint glow which had reappeared.

They were running towards it.

"They're going to give us to it!" shouted Sorha. He started to fight them, but he was running and they were running and all trying to fight did was cause him to fall. Hands lifted him, dragged him onwards. They covered his mouth and he thought Sorha's too as he heard her struggling. The screeching of the creature and the smell of it and of the blind warriors filled the air. He could feel the thing was near, movement of the air as it passed over. The sounds it made felt like his bones were shaking in his flesh. The hand was no longer silencing him. He opened his mouth, wanting to shout but not knowing why.

Nausea.

A sense of dislocation.

Of falling.

Then somewhere else.

The noise gone. The sense of oppression gone. The flicker of a fire. The weight of bodies on top of him, struggling to get free. His hands had come loose. Trying to find something recognisable: a shoulder, an arm, wanting to follow it to a spear. He could hear Sorha, fighting, grunting.

Somewhere in the back of his mind a thought that made no sense. *I have just been through a taffistone.* The thought lost, blown away in the fight. His greater strength beginning to show.

"Stop! Stop or they will kill you!"

Shocked at hearing a voice speak his language. The moment he stopped fighting the creatures that held him began beating him. More words, the same voice but speaking in the creature's language. Calling something out at them. The beating stopped. The creatures withdrew, leaving him and Sorha lying on the floor, breathing heavily.

"Stay still and they will not hurt you. It may not feel like it but they have saved your lives."

Cahan rolled his head towards the sound. Saw a man like him. Though he had the same bulky hips as the creatures. In the firelight Cahan could see it was clothing, and what he had thought was a strangely shaped skull was a helmet with feathery plumes of some material he had never seen before. The speaker's skin was dirty, though not painted with the colours of this shadow world the creatures wore. In one hand he held a long staff. He was looking straight at Cahan. A half smile on his face.

"You have eyes," said Sorha. "You are not one of them."

"Oh, I am now," he said. "It is the only way to survive outside of Anjiin. They know how to get food, water, clothing." He touched the material on his hip. "But once I was of the above, like you. My name is Ulan Mat-Garhai." He looked around, said something else in the alien language of the creatures and the warriors around them backed away. "Please, sit up," he said. "It is safe now. You are safe here."

"Where is here? Who are these creatures?"

"They are easier questions to answer than you think. Firstly the where, you are in a village, somewhere under the Wyrdwood of the north. The people of this land call it Osereud."

"Impossible," said Sorha. "You talk nonsense, we were near the Slowlands in the centre of Crua and . . ."

"It is not impossible," said Cahan. "The taffistones of Crua, they are a path, like a shortcut between places. The Forestals know how to walk them. That is how you and the Rai were surprised by them in the Slowlands. It seems our captors also understand their use."

"That is correct," said Ulan, he smiled at Sorha. "I suspect my face looked much like yours when I first found out about the taffistones." He leaned on his staff and Cahan realised this man was old, very old. "Now, as to who these people are, I ask you to listen to what I have to say, and not to jump to conclusions." He looked from Sorha to Cahan. "These people are as ancient as the people of Crua. They were people of Crua."

"But not now?" said Cahan.

"They have changed, it has been many years since they were above ground. But they keep their people's name." He looked away, took a deep breath.

"And what is that?" said Sorha, looking around.

"Do not be frightened when I say this," said the old man, "but you know them as the Osere."

62
Ont

Without the tinctures and the teas and the fragrant smoke the Forestals used in their healing, Ont discovered the truth of his world. It was one of darkness and pain. He would no longer take the drugs, he did not think he deserved them and they dulled a world where he was already denied so much. The healers told him he was a fool and he chased them away with fury and blindly flailing arms.

He could walk, in a fashion, though he needed a stick and the stick was difficult for him to hold. In the end Ania made him a special one, carving it for his misshapen hands, running cords through it so he could tie it to his arms and ensure he did not drop it.

He was grateful, beyond grateful, for her small kindness. Yet when she had given it to him, explained its use, he had been surly and shouted at her, demanding she leave. He did not understand why, and when she had gone he found himself sobbing, though he could no longer cry, not really, as the fire had stolen his eyes. He felt ashamed to weep, all his life he had tried to be strong but in the darkness his strength had fled, sapped by pain and hopelessness.

He never travelled far from the hut the Forestals had given him, they allowed him to live off their charity and treated him as they treated their own. Sharing and asking nothing for it. Bringing food. He ate, though all food tasted of dirt, his mouth had been burned inside and out and even the small joy of food was denied him.

He raged at those who tried to help. Snapped at those who offered to guide him when he walked. Swore at those who warned him he neared an edge, and yet these people did not fight back, they did not begrudge him. They yielded, absorbed his blows, and his anger found no target. If anything they treated him like someone special, honoured him for his sacrifice. As time passed his fury became misery, his misery became grief and through it all, Ania still visited him. She spoke to him, told him stories of her life. How she had not always been a Forestal. How she had come to hate the Rai and how she had come to be here, in this place after losing everything and everyone she had ever loved. How Tall Sera gave her a bow and showed her how to use it. How, for her, grief demanded solitude and the bow gave her that excuse. Her skill was born of obsession, a place to run to when she felt she had nowhere to go.

When he broke, she held him. She did not lie, she did not tell him it would be all right. She did not tell him the pain would lessen. When he asked what he was now, where he would go, the only answer she had was, "I do not know."

In her truthfulness, her unwillingness to soften his situation, he found a strange comfort. This was the beginning of his healing, he thought. This was the place where he changed forever.

He had fought but he had not been a fighter, he had believed he must fight but that was duty, not a calling. He had been called to serve Ranya, to try and fill the shoes of Udinny and he had been put onto a path where he had put the weapon before the word. He did not believe he had been punished for that, it was not Ranya's way. Udinny had always said, "We do not pick the path, we only walk it."

But could it really be coincidence that the only thing he could still do, the thing that hurt the least, was walk? Oh, he had to be careful, and it was not easy, but what in Crua was easy?

Without sight, knowing the path became more important to him than ever. The path from his hut to the water. The path to the food. The path to the heat. He learned all these, step by step in his dark world. He used his stick to sweep the ground before him as there was always something dropping from the trees, always some new obstacle. He no longer shouted at the children when they ran into him. Instead he tried to laugh, despite the pain.

Sometimes Furin's boy, Issofur, came and sang to him in a language he did not understand.

And as if in reward for his patience, and his forbearance and his pain, his vision returned.

Not in a way that allowed him to see the world as he had, but in a way that let him see another world, one he did not understand. He saw flashes of colour, explosions of brightness. It was like waking in the forest at night, half asleep, glimpsing its wonders before being plunged back into unconsciousness. Sometimes he heard whispered voices, but could not be sure if it was in his mind or from the people of Woodhome. The strangest thing, the voices often sounded like his own.

In time he began to experiment with the drugs the healers offered him to combat the pain, the mixtures of plant powders and mushrooms. First to take the edge off the pain, seeing how much he could take before he began to feel stupid and slow. Then trying different mixes, spending long hours talking with the healers and Venn. The trion had avoided him at first, worried by his anger, but as the anger ebbed Venn had returned. The trion could do little more for his pain and Ont felt the trion's guilt whenever they spoke. He had worked with Venn, fixing what they could in his body and together learning about the properties of Wyrdwood, its plants and fungi.

Sometimes, the mixtures would expand what he saw, the lights would go on longer and it was then that Ont became sure he heard the whispering in his mind. It was not always the voices he thought may be his own, and it was definitely not how he imagined Ranya would sound. He thought his god more delicate than this voice. This speaking-but-not-speaking voice sounded like it delivered some imperative, some demand but one he was not quite ready to hear.

One night, when he sat by the stones, barely flinching from the heat, he spoke with Venn. The trion had, in their own way, been slowly withdrawing from everyone. Whatever they had learned from the trion of Woodhome weighed heavy upon them.

"Do you still follow Ranya, Venn?" No answer at first, only the rhythmic growl of Segur, the garaur, always accompanied Ont. A long gap before Venn spoke.

"Yes." It amused Ont, he imagined the trion had probably nodded, then eventually remembered Ont could not see the movement and spoke instead. "The Forestals, they revere the Boughry, but there is no comfort there." Ont did not answer, not straight away as he had found little comfort in Ranya lately.

"Does she speak to you?" he said. A gap, a space where he heard only the forest.

"No, she spoke only to Udinny." A thought in the air. Ont had become good at hearing the unsaid.

"And?"

"Maybe Cahan, once, at the end in Harn." At the mention of Harn, Ont had a flash, a vision as real as if he was stood in the place. It lasted only a moment, the smallest amount of time but there was comfort in what he saw. The bower of Ranya in New Harnwood. With it came such a strong feeling of longing that it almost doubled him over.

"Ont?"

"It is nothing," he said. But it was not. It was something. It was golden like the Light Above on his face and with it came a need, a desperate yearning to be in that place. To be where he had first devoted himself to Ranya.

That evening, when Ania visited him he told her of it. Of this wish that had come upon him and how he could think of nothing else now.

"Take me through the taffistone," he said. "Back to New Harnwood."

"It is gone," she said. "There is nothing of it left."

"I need to go there," he told her.

"Need?" He could hear her amusement. "You need to learn to live and to—"

"Please," he said. Only one word and that was answered by silence. The sound of her movement, the smell of damp material as she came closer to him.

"It is a true need?"

"Yes."

"Tall Sera does not want anyone leaving Woodhome, not unless he sends them out. He thinks the attack in the Slowlands has endangered us. It was too direct."

"I must go to the bower, my grove," he said. "I do not know why but I must." He heard her draw air in through her teeth.

"The Rai could still be there," she whispered, urgency hiding within the spaces of her words. "Even after this long. They will want to know how we escaped. Taffistones are our greatest secret, so if any are there to see us arrive they cannot be allowed to live."

"You talk as if you intend to go with me," said Ont softly. "You do not need to."

"Ont." The pressure of her hand on his arm, he tried not to hiss in pain. "A blind man stumbling about stands little chance of going unseen." *Stumbling*, the word hurt him somewhere deep inside. "You cannot go alone."

"So you will risk Tall Sera's wrath to help me stumble about?"

A laugh from her, bitter as ever but truthfully he liked her sense of humour. Liked how dark she could be.

"Aye, I will do that for you." Inside his pain was a warmth, and melancholy at what may have been but never could be now. "But it will take more than just me, and few Forestals will go against Tall Sera." Her hand moved off his arm.

"Then it cannot be done," he said, some light within flickering and fading, a promise the despair he thought he had left behind would return.

"I did not say that," she told him.

63

Sorha

Osere. The word echoing in her mind.

She was led through a strange village by an even stranger man. With her walked Cahan Du-Nahere and around them the blind soldiers of the Osere, bristling with weapons and barely hidden aggression. She thought about that name, Osere, one she had heard so many times but had never really believed. Cowls, Rai, even the Cowl-Rai who could wipe whole armies from the field, they were real but the rest? The Star Path? Broken Iftal? The Osere?

She had never considered them real, them or the gods. Just a way of control. Her secondfather may have been happy to give his life and burn for Chyi, but she had not been and there had been no punishment for it. Her life had been long and it had been one of luxury and pleasure. Though that pleasure was mostly found in other's pain.

Strange, how her desire for that had ebbed as she had come to understand pain more. She had felt pain as Rai of course, everyone felt pain. But she had believed there was higher purpose in the pain of others, it was worth it to make her strong, and her strength was important for Crua. For herself.

But now she truly knew pain, and knew it was without purpose, something to be suffered. Something to be avoided.

She was changing in more ways than losing her cowl, becoming something and someone else. She had seen Anjiin, city of myth. She had been saved from death by the man she hated most in the world. She had witnessed something, vast and inimical, something that radiated hate, that she knew instinctively she should fear.

So it was not hard for her to believe these strange eyeless creatures, skin painted with shadows, were the Osere.

Their village was made of small round shelters gathered round flickering fires. In the distance she could see what looked like a larger building, a tall shrine before it. She wondered what dark rituals the Osere did here, and what could be important enough about her or Cahan that they would have gone up against the creature in Anjiin to retrieve them?

There was no wood or forests down here, or there had been no sign of them in Ancient Anjiin. Maybe it was different in this place but clearly there was something the Osere could build with. She wondered what secrets were hidden here, in the vast cave of the . . . the what? The beneath? The otherworld? Was she dead? Sound was strange here. She had told herself it was the warm still air and the huge empty space above that ate up all sound, but maybe it was more. Maybe it was the quiet of death.

The man walking before them, the one who was from above, had said there were people here they must meet, and now they walked through this strange place. She wondered what they ate, what animals lived down here, what grew down here? All these things must happen somewhere, hidden in the darkness, or the people could not live. In Anjiin she had not hungered, but when they had left the city she had begun to feel a gnawing in her belly and she was desperate for water, which she had been able to smell on the air ever since she had thought about thirst.

She saw children, dressed like the adults even down to the strange plumes growing from their headdresses. It was like any village in Crua, except the people here were cursed, and if legend was true then both her and the Forester were being escorted by them to unending suffering.

No, she refused to believe it. They were not dead, and the legends said the Osere only took the dead. The Osere had made no overtly violent moves towards them since the fight in their village, they had been threatening, but only wished to subdue. They could have wounded them, or killed them, or left them for the beast in Anjiin, and they had not. The translator began to fall back so he walked between them. There was something of the monk to him she thought, the gentleness of his voice, the quiet chiming of the porcelain threaded through his clothes.

"We go to meet the leaders," he glanced across at Sorha, "you would call them a Leoric." She saw Cahan nod, though he did not look at the man, only kept grimly walking over ground which crunched beneath his feet. "I tell you now," the man said, "speak only the truth to them."

"Why, Ulan?" said Sorha, and even to her ears the sarcasm bit deep and was unneeded. "Can they hear lies?"

"Yes." He said it so simply she believed him, or at least she was sure he believed it. "I do not know if it is because they cannot see, but they can hear a lie. And they punish liars harshly." He held up his left hand, showing two fingers were missing from it. "I did not learn that lesson quickly enough."

"How long have you been here?" said Cahan. Ulan shrugged.

"I do not know, you cannot measure time down here. There are no seasons, the crops grow without sun. The animals breed when they will." He looked away, some sadness crossing his face in the flickering firelight of his torch. "I have been here longer than I lived above, I think." Cahan nodded then looked up. His brow furrowed in confusion.

"What is that light?" he said. "The glowing lines. What are they?" He pointed into the sky, or what passed for sky here. When she looked she saw it too, faint flashes as if light fell from above.

"That," said Ulan, "is cloudtree roots, they do that and more sometimes. I think, but cannot be sure, it means the end of day above. Or the beginning." He smiled, to himself, not them. "It is no forest lightshow, but it is what we have. There are other wonders here but—" He stopped speaking as the Osere warriors split into two groups. "Ready yourself," said Ulan.

Two Osere sat on thrones in front of a larger hut than any Sorha had yet seen, and although she had thought there was no wood down here, now she was not as sure. The struts that held up the hut looked like wood, though different to what she was used to. Maybe they used the roots of the cloudtrees.

The thrones were of some material she had never seen before, shiny and hard. Sat on them were two Osere, one male one female. Behind them more figures, she could barely make them out in the firelight, but as her eyes got a little more used to the poor light she realised what they were, felt fear. Four people of Crua, dead, impaled on spikes behind the thrones. The sharp points of spears emerging as the final screams of eternally opened mouths.

"Should we bow?" said Cahan.

"The Osere bow to no one, and they would not see it anyway," said Ulan. "Let me introduce you both." He stepped forward. Spoke in the Osere language and it was again a strange thing to Sorha, like he almost spoke words she knew. She heard her name spoken, heard Cahan's name spoken and felt like she could almost touch the meaning around them. The two Osere talked among themselves, pointing at Cahan, Sorha, Ulan, then above. Eventually the one on the right turned and spoke directly to Ulan. Then Ulan spoke for them.

"The leaders of Elmfarhad bid you welcome to their village. They have questions for the outsiders about the land above. If you lie you will suffer the fate of all liars." One of the Osere said something sharp and their warriors brought forward the impaled bodies from behind the screen. They were very old, the bodies long ago dried out to remain in death as an eternal lesson.

"You said only our fingers were at risk," growled Cahan.

"The Osere were not always as gentle as they are now." The woman on the left throne said something, cutting across Ulan's words and he stopped speaking. Turned back to her. There was another brief discussion among the Osere and then the woman spoke again. A long stream of almost understood language.

"They want to know," said Ulan, "if you were involved in the freeing of the god."

"What?" said Cahan, gruff as ever. She did not need the ears of the blind to hear his confusion – she shared it. "What god?"

"The creature that hunted you, it is a god freed from its prison of ages. The Osere," he motioned at the gathered people with a hand, "once chose the wrong side in a war. They brought about the death of Iftal, and the fall of Anjiin. For that, they lost their eyes and were banished down here, to keep the gods imprisoned and stop them rising again."

"Surely, if they were once their servants, they would be the ones most likely to free them?" said Sorha. Ulan bowed his head.

"Sometimes, it is only when the shackles are removed that you realise how heavy they were. The Osere will never bow to the old gods again." She looked across at Cahan, he looked confused, lost.

"You are saying the gods are our enemies," said Cahan.

"Many of them. Or that is what the Osere believe," said Ulan, and once more, the woman on the throne cut across him, angry words. The warriors around them lowered spears. "Please, answer their question, they do not like us talking among ourselves." Cahan turned to the two Osere.

"No," he said. "We have freed no gods."

She wondered if that was true; the monk, Udinny, had spoken of Ranya. Was that not a god? And one she had never heard of before. Should she speak up? Before she could, Ulan translated Cahan's words and the two Osere once more discussed among themselves what had been said. The woman nodded, said something to the man. Pointed at them.

"They believe you," said Ulan. Cahan grunted. The Osere talked more among themselves before once more the woman spoke to Ulan and he translated: "They wish to know what is happening above. If not you, who has freed the god from its prison? Will they free more?"

"The thing?" said Cahan. "That we ran from?" Ulan nodded. "I have never seen such a thing before. How was it imprisoned? Where? How can a god be—" One of the Osere barked something out.

"Please," said Ulan, "give only answers to what is asked. Your questions may be addressed later." You are leaving much out, Cahan, thought Sorha.

"Above, the old god – we called them Chyi – has been overthrown," said Sorha, her throat hurting and her bones aching. "A new god rises, they are called Tarl-an-Gig and their Cowl-Rai has taken nearly all of Crua." She stared at the Osere's rulers as Ulan translated. More talk between the Osere, bouncing back and forth among them until eventually some consensus was reached.

"No," said Ulan. "This is not what they mean. The above has warred over gods for almost as long as your people have ruled there. They say you waste what you have in war."

"Are you trying to tell me these people are not warriors?" said Cahan.

"They are now," said Ulan. "Part of the reason they kept me alive was I fought once. They had almost forgotten how." Cahan made a dismissive noise, as if such a thing were impossible and Sorha shared his thoughts. Ulan smiled at them. "Down here where less power was gifted, where life is far harder than above, war was not an option for the Osere. They have always worked together to live."

"But now they war," said Sorha. Ulan nodded. "When did it start?" One of the Osere barked something from their throne. Ulan turned to them and a conversation was had, plainly about Sorha and Cahan. Eventually the Osere shrugged and turned away.

"They want answers, but I have told them the answers will be more useful if I can explain a little to you."

"Explain then," said Cahan, and Sorha thought it odd that although this place was almost entirely silent, his voice did not carry at all, it was as if the air sucked it up, devoured it.

"The Osere believe themselves the jailers of the gods, not servants." He looked from Cahan to Sorha. "There have always been those who believed otherwise. That they should free the gods, take power back from those above. Small cults. Occasionally one such as me would come from above and tell tales of the light and plenty. The cults would grow afterwards, believing the gods would take them back above but they were peaceful. They had their own villages in the rootwood, and few followed them for long. Most would get bored or hungry and come back. Even those that did not would still trade with the villages." He scratched at the side of his head. "Then things changed. The god talkers turned against the people."

"God talkers?"

"Powerful Osere. Like Rai, I think, but I never met one and they do not like to talk of them so I cannot be sure," said Ulan. "After the god talkers turned, raids began. Warriors appeared. They were Osere but not. Strong and fast, but wrong and twisted. The Osere call these warriors the Betrayers, as they have left the path. They found they had no choice but to learn to fight."

"How long ago did this happen?" said Cahan. Ulan shrugged.

"Time is hard to tell down here, and I do not know why but I am sure I have lived far longer than I should. All this started maybe twenty or thirty lifetimes ago, as the people of Crua measure a life. I think, anyway; as I said, time is difficult here."

"These Osere Betrayers . . . what do they mean when they say they are 'wrong'?" said Sorha.

"The phrase the Osere use is that they 'walk close to death'."

"Hetton?" said Cahan, looking at Sorha.

"You know these creatures?" said Ulan.

"Do they look dead? Skin desiccated eyes white and . . ." His voice tailed off. "I do not know how they would look here, as these people have no eyes."

"They taste of the dead," said Sorha. "When you are around them, you can taste the dead."

As she finished speaking the Osere began to talk among themselves and she realised they must understand more of what was said than she thought. The woman leaned forward, the man put a hand on her shoulder but she shrugged it off.

"When?" she said. "When these appear above?" Her eyeless face focused on Cahan.

"At most, sixteen years ago, maybe less. I first saw them twelve or thirteen years ago, as we measure it." He looked over at Sorha but she had nothing to add. "They are a tool of the new Cowl-Rai." The Osere turned and said something to the man on the throne opposite. He nodded and vanished into the hut behind them.

"What is this about?" said Sorha. Cahan shrugged and Ulan only stared at the empty throne. He looked worried. Then the Osere returned, leaned in close to the woman and they whispered, occasionally pointing towards Cahan, Sorha and Ulan. Eventually they sat back and the trion once more spoke to Ulan. He turned to them.

"What can you tell us about these Hetton, and this Cowl-Rai?"

"Not much," said Cahan. "The Cowl-Rai rose in the north, the Hetton were rare at first. There are more now." Ulan translated for Cahan as he spoke. "The Hetton were not there when the Cowl-Rai first rose, I do not think so anyway. I did not see them. Then I fought for money, it was years before I saw one. Well, not one. They move in groups. I was told that two guarded the Cowl-Rai from the start and . . ."

"Tell of Cowl-Rai," said the woman on the throne. That she ignored what appeared to be the protocol of the meeting clearly annoyed the other Osere.

"Sorha would know more," said Cahan, and he motioned towards her with a hand. She swallowed.

"I have never met the Cowl-Rai," she said. "They rarely used their magic from what I have heard. Relying on overwhelming force or guile, attacking where it was not expected. I never heard of the Hetton until they had taken nearly all of the north." Ulan translated for her.

"But you have met with her."

"No," said Sorha. "but I have met Saradis." A look crossed Cahan's face when she said that name, one of such horror as she had never seen. The blood drained from him, and she thought he would collapse, but he did not. He managed to hold on. To keep his composure.

"Saradis?" he said, the word barely even there. "The Skua-Rai of Tarl-an-Gig is Saradis?" Sorha watched him, he looked as if his entire world had imploded and she wondered why, wondered what Saradis was to him. Something terrible, from the look of it.

"Why do you ask that?" said Sorha.

"I knew her, she was not always Skua-Rai of Tarl-an-Gig." His voice was hoarse and pain had tracked deep lines into his face, he looked like he had aged years in moments. "She made me, she raised me. Picked me out, took my sister and I from our home. Tortured me. Her devotion to her god was complete and it was utter. I cannot believe she worships another."

"Who was her god?" said Sorha. How could she have known that such a simple question would change her world so profoundly?

"Zorir," said Cahan, and all around them, the Osere either cried out in anger and fear, or brought their spears to bear.

64
Dassit

Vir was drunk.

Her branch commander had found a place where the Forestals brewed a foul-tasting alcohol from leaves and proceeded to drink himself insensible. Dassit supposed if that was how he coped then that was how he coped. She had decided to leave him to it and find her own ways of existing. There was no denying that she felt just as out of place here as he did, though less uncomfortable. She had seen more of the world than Vir, visited Woodedge villages who still followed the ways of ancient gods that most had forgotten. Experienced wild nights and festivals where most monks in the more "civilised" largers or spire cities would have been appalled at what went on. She had travelled the skyrafts and been among the families who followed their own ways and had no interest in the gods of the ground.

So she was not as upset as Vir by the Forestals, not upset at all and as she watched them, laughing and talking – and more – in their fluid groups she thought she could enjoy this place. She could end her days here and be happy, hidden away in the branches of the cloudtrees.

If she could get used to the heights.

And the rootlings.

It was still a struggle to see them everywhere; all her life she had been taught to believe they were vermin, dirty. Yet here they were treated as people. Or almost as people. Somewhere between people and pets. The Forestals were clearly fond of them but would also chase them off if they became too bold. Though, it was all done with good humour. Dassit looked over the railing she stood at, had the same awful feeling she had every time. As if the ground, so very, very far below was beckoning her, calling out in a voice so strong it was hard to resist.

"Dassit?" She turned from the railing and the call of the abyss vanished. "That is your name, Dassit?" It was the woman they had saved. Furin? Yes, that was her name. She looked very small, diminished somehow.

"I wanted to thank you. For coming for me." She did not look at Dassit, her hands were wrapped around her middle and her make-up looked like it had been left on for days. Her eyes were red and raw with old tears.

"It was Cahan, mostly," said Dassit. Furin nodded, but did not raise her eyes to meet Dassit's. "I am sorry he was lost. You were close? He seemed to care very much for you."

"Lovers, briefly," she said quietly.

"A clanless and a Leoric," said Dassit.

"Leoric of nothing," said Furin, even more quietly than before.

"Still," said Dassit, "power leaves a mark, it must have been a strong attraction." She had an odd desire to touch the woman, just a brief communion, an acknowledgement that she knew what loss was. Furin nodded, wiped at her eyes in that careful way the people of Crua did, not wanting to disturb face or eye paint.

"A high price was paid, many of yours lost. The priest that was with you still lies unconscious."

"I do not think the priest will ever wake," said Dassit, though she was not sure that was the most terrible outcome.

"Your village's monk was grievously hurt as well." Furin nodded and stood a little closer. Looked around and Dassit knew, from years of being close to command, that she was about to hear something likely to make her life more difficult.

"That is part of the reason I have come to find you."

"No," said Dassit. "Whatever it is I am sorry, but the answer is no."

"It is only to be a guard."

"The fact you need a guard is enough by itself." She turned away.

"Ont, our monk," said Furin softly, "he is not even a monk. He was a butcher. A proud and vain man once but he gave up everything. In the battle, well, you have seen him. He has little left now." Dassit turned to look at the woman, but she was not looking at her. She was leaning over the railing. Staring down into the nothing. "He wants to go home, to the grove he built. If I am truthful I think he intends to die there, though he is careful not to say it."

"And you need me to watch him die?" Furin shook her head. Dropped something over the railing and watched it fall.

"Ania says there are likely to be Rai forces there. That if we appear through the taffistone they will report back on it. That the Forestals will not allow us to go because the risk of being discovered is too great." Dassit looked around. At the tree village, the twinkling lights that marked out the hundreds of small houses in the gloom of Wyrdwood.

"You are telling me," said Dassit, "that Tall Sera has said you may not leave?"

"Yes. Leaving is not allowed without his agreement."

"But you are here. Talking to me."

"The taffistone here is guarded," said Furin. "But Ania believes that she can get Ont, her, and a few more out."

"We would never be allowed back," said Dassit. "They may even hunt us. They have forbidden us leaving without having our minds altered to forget this place."

"Did you intend to live here?" said Furin. Dassit stepped forward, nearer to the edge of the platform than she liked, and stopped. That dizzying feeling, the call of the abyss making her head swim.

"It is gentle here," said Dassit. "I had thought maybe to find myself an entanglement and join it. It looks like fun."

"And then?" said Furin. "Farm mushrooms on a branch? Set up a water garden?"

"Better than being cast out and having nothing." It was clear Furin had no answer to that, not immediately. She let out a sigh. Stared down into the gathering darkness of twilight. From all around them came the sounds of merriment and Dassit felt very alone. She was not of these people, she was not one of Furin's people either. Her own people had sent her to die. She had nowhere.

"Ania," said Furin softly, "is a favourite of Tall Sera's. She believes that he will forgive her and any who go with her. She will claim it was all her idea."

"I am sick of war."

"He is a good man." The Leoric of Harn was studying her as she spoke, no doubt wondering what sort of woman Dassit was. In turn Dassit wondered what type of woman Furin was. She closed her eyes. "He saved Ania you know, the monk. Wrapped his body around her to keep her from the Rai's fire. He would have done that for any of us, I think. Even you, though he barely knew you." Dassit took in a deep breath of the warm forest air, tried to ignore the Leoric's words. "He just wants to die in a place he loved."

Dassit let out the long breath. There was a calm here among the branches of the cloudtrees she had always longed for. But sacrifice for another, she understood that and it called to her. The need to let a warrior pass in peace was a powerful thing to her – even if the man was a monk. What he had done was selfless, it should be rewarded.

"How big is this grove?"

"No bigger than most of the houses here. And there is

one way in and out. Though the walls can be easily scaled." Dassit thought about it.

"These stones, when we move through them, is there light? Some signal?"

"Only what shines through from the other side." Dassit nodded again.

"I will speak to Vir. With Ania's bow and our spears, it may be enough. If we are quick and quiet." Dassit looked across at her. "Are you coming?" Furin shook her head.

"I want to," she said. "But Ania says I should meet with Tall Sera, distract him. That is the best way to ensure he is not watching the taffistone. Ania thinks she can bluff her way through if he is not there." Dassit nodded, more to herself than to Furin. Across from her, on a wide branch a group of Forestals were laying wreaths of flowers, food and small saplamps before an image of the Boughry.

"We sacrifice to our gods, so they bless the Rai who are meant to protect us," said Dassit. "What do you think the Boughry offer the Forestals?"

"I think they hope the Forest Nobles will take the gifts and leave them alone," said Furin.

"Well," Dassit nodded to herself, "I suppose that's a sensible enough thing to wish for."

65
Cahan

He did not understand.

His mind suffered the same turmoil from Sorha's words that his stomach suffered from the poison he had taken within for power. Saradis? Alive? Skua-Rai to Tarl-an-Gig? But how could that be? How could that ever be?

When he had seen the woman in the Slowlands, the Skua-Rai, she had reminded him of Saradis, but he had never considered she could *be* her. The idea she would turn traitor to her god was unthinkable. He felt like a child again, like nothing. Like the land of Crua was some vast and cruel joke played on him. He could barely think. His muscles refused to answer to his mind. He had shadow memories of the Slowlands, of the stand collapsing. Was she dead? Or did she live?

Was he still a puppet to her, playing out his part in some plan too complex for him to see?

She could not be a traitor to her beliefs he was sure of it. Zorir, the god, was her all.

And these people, they clearly knew that name.

How? That word flooding his mind, driving out all else. He did not react when the Osere pushed him to the floor.

He barely heard Sorha fighting them as they did the same to her, shrieking and cursing as she was forced down. He barely saw the spears above him. Felt no fear as they were thrust at him, only stopping short of skewering him to the ground at a shout from one of the Osere on the thrones.

Then silence.

Stillness and darkness, until it was split by the voice of Ulan.

"The leaders of the Osere have more questions of you," he said. "Be careful in your answers, for you walk dangerous ground."

"Why?" shouted Sorha.

"Say nothing!" shouted Ulan. Cahan heard the fear in the interpreter's voice but he did not care. He was numb. "You have put us all in danger with your foolish talk."

"What foolish talk?" shouted Sorha. "What is happening?" One of the Osere shouted something and Cahan heard wood on flesh. The grunt of Sorha as the air left her lungs.

"Answer their questions," said Ulan slowly. "Do nothing else." The female Osere spoke again. Not many words, but they were said slowly and with an intensity Cahan recognised as import, what they asked meant much to them. On his answer he knew the spears of the warriors crowding around him would fall or be stayed but he did not really care either way.

"They want to know," said Ulan, "why you have not told them of Zorir before." Cahan could not answer, he did not understand himself. "Say something," said Ulan, "the leaders of the Osere are not patient."

"Zorir does not rule," said Sorha. "Tarl-an-Gig, that is the god who rules above. Zorir-Who-Walks-In-Fire was a minor god, I thought their cult wiped out."

One of the leaders spoke again, staccato, urgent noises.

"How do you know Zorir?" said Ulan. "That is what they want to know, it is what matters." Cahan did not speak, not at first. The tension in the air was too great, the pain within too deep. It choked him. He coughed, tried to sit up a little but a spear stopped him.

"Let Sorha live," he said, but he did not know why. "She has nothing to do with Zorir. It is me you want."

"Why?" A harsh bark from one of the Osere on the thrones. "Why you?"

"I was raised," he said softly, "in the monastery of Zorir, by Saradis, to be Cowl-Rai of Zorir." Silence. Cahan expected an order, expected the spears to come down. Nothing. "Do they know what Cowl-Rai is?" he said to Ulan.

"They know," said Ulan. The Osere leaders spoke again. "She wants to know if they sent you down here, to be with your god."

"No." Cahan turned his head towards where the thrones were, he could only see feet. "The monastery was destroyed a long time ago, as Sorha said. The monks all killed by the forces of Tarl-an-Gig. Or so I always believed." How had he not realised when he saw Laha, not even considered Saradis could also live? "I never became what they wished. They thought me weak." Then, as silence once more entombed him he spoke again. "Why would our gods be down here?" Laughter in response to that. More words from those on the throne, then a softer voice said something to the warriors threatening him.

"Above world, do not know?" From the thrones, they sounded both confused and amused by this. Then they barked out orders in their own language. Cahan was lifted.

"They wish to show you something," said Ulan. "The woman stays here, run and she will be killed."

"No!" he shouted, and now he fought them as they dragged him forward, more hands grabbing him. "No! you do not understand! She must come! For all your safety." The Osere paid no attention, pulled him on. At the same time another group were pulling her away and no matter how he fought and shouted they did not listen. He felt the grip of Sorha's power loosening. Felt the pain coursing through him. His armour changing. A scream from his mouth as he threw off the warriors holding him, shaking them from him the way a garaur shook off water. A spear thrown and it took all his control not to throw it back, instead he caught it and thrust it into the ground. Forced himself to his knees. Lifted his arms to show he was not about to fight, though his armour was changing, serrating. His back screaming as tentacles of black wood began to grow from it.

"Sorha," he spat her name, almost begged it.

Then the pain ebbing. Control returning. Sorha near again. The Osere around him picking themselves up. One approached. Only one, the rest holding back. The Osere woman who was one of their leaders stopped in front of him. Her head orientated to his face. Then turned towards the darkness. Away from him. Turned back. Touched where a faint blue glow ran over his armour.

"She stops this?" He nodded. "You walk in sickness?" He shook his head.

"Not when Sorha is near."

"How?"

"I touched a power I should not have."

"Why?"

"To save another." The Osere stood above him, spear poised in her hand. "I thought I could control it. I was wrong."

"You a weapon for it?" He nodded. The Osere looked him up and down. Stepped back.

"You should kill me." It was all that made sense, the only reality he had. As long as he had been in Sorha's shadow he had been able to pretend it was otherwise. But without her, if he was taken from her, or she died, he belonged to what these people said was Zorir. He was the fire waiting to happen. "Finish me, it is what you should do." So difficult for him to read the woman before him, he had never realised how much he read from another's eyes. She hefted the spear, as if to throw it.

She did not.

"You worship Zorir?" She cocked her head as if to hear his answer better.

"Never."

"Then live for now," she said.

"Why?" he stood.

"A weapon," she said, "is that to who hold it. We hold you. Now come. Learn."

She walked away and he followed, out of the village, past the huts and through what he thought of as a wood, or a forest. The trunks of trees gradually becoming thicker and stronger, the pain within subsiding as Sorha caught up with him. No one spoke to him, not even Ulan, until Sorha broke her silence.

"Do you know where we are going?" she whispered. The trees around them occasionally lit up, not too brightly, but enough to give him a view of Sorha. In the light she was monochrome, her face thin as though she was starved. From the corner of his eyes he kept thinking he saw bright colours. "I did not think a forest could grow underground."

"I think it is the roots of a cloudtree," he said. "I think they get thicker the nearer we are to the trunk."

"Do you think that's where we are going?"

"I do not know, if the roots are as wide as the branches it could be a long walk." She nodded, glanced at him.

"You did not know about Saradis?"

He shook his head, hearing her name made his mouth dry. "I thought her dead."

"She was at the Slowlands," said Sorha. Cahan let out a laugh, a low and bitter thing.

"I saw her. Even thought how much the woman on the stands reminded me of Saradis. It never occurred to me she would betray Zorir."

"Well—"

"I do not want to talk of it."

They stopped later, drinking sweet tasting water out of

gourds like none he had ever seen before. The Osere served them a kind of bread with a strange texture, no crust, but no grit either.

"It is made from dried and ground mushrooms," said Ulan. Then added wistfully, "Almost everything down here is mushrooms. What I would give for a histi."

"How far is it to our destination?" asked Sorha, staring at the mushroom bread.

"A long way."

"How long, a day? Two days?" Ulan shrugged.

"Time is rarely measured down here," he said. "The Osere stop when they stop. Sleep when they sleep." He looked up. "I miss the Light Above, the sense of rhythm to my life."

"How many times will we sleep?" said Sorha.

"Once, at least. And eat maybe twice more."

In the end they slept twice and ate three times. That aside there was only the walking. To walk here was nothing like in the forests above, there were no bushes, no animals. Occasional stands of mushrooms loomed out of the darkness like pale sentinels, and Cahan presumed these must act as signs to the Osere. No doubt they would feel as lost in the great forests as he felt down here, in this featureless, unending, darkness.

Thoughts of Saradis filled his mind. Of what she had promised he was, how he had run from it and still it had captured him. A fear rising within that all of this was her plan, that he had never walked any path but hers.

The roots became thicker, though the light from them never changed, always dim and flickering at best. He began to notice that as the Osere passed close, colour shimmered across them but he did not know if it was an illusion or not, something conjured up by a mind starved of things to see.

"I think we are stopping again," said Sorha. All around the Osere were putting down packs, gathering into small groups to eat bread and drink water. Cahan had become used to this, and it was only as he began to sit that he noticed a difference this time. Ulan was not sitting, and neither was the woman, the Osere leader who had accompanied them. She stood, together with two of her soldiers. Rather than sitting, Cahan straightened up. "What is happening?" said Sorha.

"I know no more than you." He glanced around, noticing in the gloom what appeared to be a taffistone but no one was approaching it. Ulan came over.

"From here, we go forward in a smaller group. Me, the guards, Frina of the Osere, she is their leader, and both of you."

"Through the taffistone?" said Cahan. Ulan shook his head.

"Not yet. Leave anything here that may catch or entangle you, imagine you intend to go through a thornbush in Harnwood." Cahan nodded, though there was nothing he could remove, his armour was part of him. Sorha took off her helmet and left it on the ground together with her belts and scabbards. She looked at him.

"You could take your belts off too." He blinked, nodded. He had worn these clothes so long he had come to think of them all as part of him, and the belt he wore to hang a gourd from he had long since stopped thinking about. He placed it on the floor. For a moment wondered what had happened to his bow, if someone back in the Forestal tree city used it now, Ont maybe. He hoped they did, he did not want it to go to waste. It was a good bow.

"Come," said Ulan. "We have a way to go yet." He watched Sorha, she was staring at the taffistone.

"It will not lead you back," said Ulan. "The paths between stones here do not lead above." Sorha nodded and turned from it.

They walked on, over the grit of the landscape and around huge roots. Always heading towards some destination that he could not see. Slowly, a glow appeared before him, growing in intensity as they neared. At first it frightened him, it was similar to the glow he had seen around the Boughry; were they what waited? As he neared he became sure it was not them. This glow was criss-crossed with lines that, when he was very close, revealed themselves to be a cage of thick rootlets.

He turned to ask Ulan and the Osere what this was and saw something spectacular. The Osere, whatever they painted on their skin and armour was reacting to the light. He had not been going mad when he saw colours before, though what he had seen was weak compared to this. Frina and her guards shone in the brightest colours he had ever seen, streaks of green and pink and purple. Handprints in bright, bright pink adorned their bodies. Lines of white drawn across where he would expect to see eyes. They were beautiful, and he thought it sad they would never know.

The Osere were walking round the cage, in the darkness their bodies left behind after-images in his vision. Streamers of bright colour until they vanished behind the light and mass of tangled roots. They were gone for long enough that Cahan began to think they had been abandoned.

They had not been, the Osere reappeared, spilling colour where they walked. They said something to Ulan in their odd language. The interpreter turned.

"Follow," he told them.

They went around the cage of roots until the Osere stopped, she pointed to the cage and then put her hands between two of the roots, pushing hard and with a creak, the roots moved so she could force her way in. Cahan followed, Sorha close behind him and they made slow and painful progress. The cage was so thick with roots they could not go in a straight line. Instead they had to slide between, and over thicker roots. Moving aside thinner ones, a constant feeling of claustrophobia as they pushed through. Their skin scratched and bleeding before they had got far, but when they finally broke through Cahan did not feel the scratches. He did not feel anything.

He did not know what or how to think. He did not understand what was there, what he was being shown.

He felt a pulse, like a heartbeat felt through the ground – though it was very slow. He had felt it when he was pushing through the root wall, but it was weak and he had ignored it.

Now he was through it was no longer something he could ignore. And he found himself looking at something he could not understand. From above came a massive, thick root. Thicker than any other he had seen, nearly as thick as the trunks above, and it pierced the ground below them. Where it met the ground he found the light source that made the Osere a riot of colour. As Cahan watched a pulse of light ran down the root and into a strange, bulbous blister on the bottom of the wood that was the source of the light. It was many times taller and wider than him. Its outside semi-opaque, like glass. Unlike glass it looked soft, malleable. The Osere leader led him closer, saying something softly in her language. As she spoke he saw that there was something inside the blister.

The thing within was huge and black, slowly moving in time with the gentle pulse of the light. It was like watching something made of cogs or wheels, spinning, stopping, spinning. He could not understand it, not at first. Then he managed to decipher some of what he saw. It was like a gasmaw, but on the scale of cloudtrees. Tentacles as thick as he was, suckers edged in blades. The flash of a beak that could easily cut him in half. The overwhelming feeling of a presence, of a power.

His first instinct was to run. This was another creature like the one that had hunted him in Ancient Anjiin, but those around him did not appear frightened of it. Or worried it may attack them.

"Behold," said Ulan, "before you a god in its prison."

"Anjiin's ruins," said Sorha from behind him. "Is there one of these on every cloudtree?"

"I believe so, and the same in the south."

"They are part of the tree?" said Sorha.

"No, I think they live off it." The Osere Leader, Frina, said something to Ulan and he nodded. "When a cloudtree falls, the prisoner dies."

"Parasites," said Cahan. "Like fungus." Frina spoke again. Saying something long and complex, using her hands, which glowed a warm blue, to emphasise some words.

"No," said Ulan, "she says the fungal web lives with life, it is part of it. These creatures, they live off the tree but give nothing back." Cahan looked across at the Osere, her head locked on the blister in the wood. He wondered how she perceived it, if it was purely by sound, or if the lack of eyes meant the Osere had some other senses. Her talk of webs had made him curious.

"Do these people know the name Ranya?" All attention on him.

"Ranya?" said Frina; she stepped closer, talking all the while in her own language, and Ulan, shocked at first, eventually managed to speak.

"She wants to know where you have heard of the Visiongiver."

"Visiongiver?"

"The Osere believe Ranya to be the herald of Iftal, that through her they will have their eyes returned to them, if they stay loyal to their cause. But she is a god of the underground. The Lady of the Web." The Osere leader spoke again. "She is not a god of the overground, her web lives below."

"I met a man when I was a youth who told me of Ranya," said Cahan, and he addressed Frina, not Ulan. "Then later I met a monk, called Udinny, who said she heard the voice of Ranya. She called the god 'Our Lady of the Lost'. I found a kindness in her followers that was lacking anywhere else." He heard Sorha laugh.

"I don't think a soft god has any place in Crua." She shook her head. The Osere leader spoke again, her voice gentle.

"She says Ranya is kindness. The ones you call gods are mostly cruel. Or they were. Iftal was once aloof, but Ranya grew within them and looked down on the people and felt pity. When her web is complete, Iftal will rise again. Anjiin will be full of light and the Osere will be given eyes to see it." The Osere nodded. She pushed her way back through the cage of roots. Cahan looked at Ulan.

"Follow," he said.

They left the cage and the sleeping god, returned to the camp and spent the night. The next morning they stood before the taffistone and Ulan told them to put a hand on the person in front of them. Then they passed through the stone, the now-familiar feeling of nausea, of being upside-down and the right way up at the same time. Then they were on the other side in complete darkness. No lights in the sky here. No brightly glowing Osere. He heard Ulan speak, something coming back that sounded affirmative. Then a scratching sound, sparks, bright in the pitch black. A moment later a torch guttered into being.

"There is no light here," said Ulan. "It took a long time for me to get the Osere to understand light when I first came." He lit two more torches, passed one to Cahan and one to Sorha. "Follow," he said, pointing to the Osere who were walking away.

Again, they walked with little sense of time and more of a sense of unreality, everything here was black. The flickering of the torches painting bodies and faces with odd shadows, making the Osere look even stranger than Cahan already thought them.

They passed through another root forest, but this was different. Cahan tripped at one point, a hand going out to steady himself on a thick root. It crumbled beneath his hand and he fell into the dirt. The Osere stopped. Waited until he was standing and he reached out, touched another root. That one also cracked at his touch, it was dry, like paper.

He saw none of the mushroom clumps, nothing that helped him understand how the Osere navigated down here, and he felt a moment of terror. If they abandoned him he would be lost for ever in the darkness.

Eventually he began to see a light; at first he thought his eyes played tricks on him but as they got closer he saw it was a blue glow, so soft as to be barely there. It came from within another of those balls of roots, the prisons. But this one was not thick like the first, it looked like it had been exploded outwards and as they approached Cahan became more and more sure of what he would see within.

The Osere stopped at the hole in the root ball and he walked up to it. Looked inside. The thick root was there, and along it blue, faintly glowing lines. At the bottom was another blister, but this one was shattered, broken, the liquid it had contained splashed over the ground and the root, where it had solidified like ice. The occupant gone, and Cahan did not need the Osere to speak, to tell him it was the creature he had seen in Ancient Anjiin. In the end the Osere said only one word. She pointed at the empty blister.

"Zorir," she said.

"The name of the god that was here?" said Cahan.

"No," said Ulan. "They do not know the names of the gods. In their language 'Zorir' means 'escape'."

66

Udinny

There is at once so much for me to understand and so little time for me to understand it.

One of my many Udinnys, an ancient and most disagreeable one, has shown me how to communicate with the city of Anjiin, in a way. Through them I found Cahan, fallen from above, and chased by the same creature who had set spearmaws on me. With light, I tried to lead him to safety, and Cahan, ever stubborn and foolish, chose to walk towards darkness and danger.

But now Cahan is gone. Vanished into thin air. And the beast is still here. Roaring and waving its tentacles.

As it moves I feel it has a presence that is both in the world of life and in the world of death. I expect an immediate attack, for the ghostly spearmaws to leap from the creature and towards me, but they do not come. Instead the creature moves with a strange, spinning striding gait across a clearing within ancient Anjiin. As it moves I feel something else, a ghost of power from the centre of the clearing, and as part of me watches the creature, another part examines this echo. It is a slow ebbing away of something that makes the walknut in my pocket tremble, an image in my mind of a door and a moment of confusion until another Udinny past whispers to me of taffistones.

A blinding glare.

An image overlaid.

A world of golden people, flowing streams and fountains. Soaring buildings and linking it all a network of light and power that transfers people and goods across the land of Crua to where it is needed. The voice of an Udinny long dead says something I did not quite understand but it sounds to me like "Taffis web".

We could travel anywhere at will?

Yes.

So much lost.

Yes.

And all this happens in an eyeblink, a heartbeat. An understanding of what has been and what has happened. Somehow Cahan found a way into this network and used it to move north. So far north. Too far north for me.

The creature reaches the far side of the clearing and one of the huge blocky walls I have begun to think of as buildings – they are all buildings, of course they are. Anjiin is a city. The beast, the creature, the thing of tentacles and darkness attaches itself to the building. I have the distinct impression of wet and slick tentacles, sliding into the building, joining with it in some strange union, and as it does I feel a pulse, a draw, a syphoning-off of power. It is as if the city fights it, as if Anjiin does not wish to give of itself and something in this battle reminds me of the forest. The trees. Cahan once told me he thought the forests were alive and aware but in a way beyond our understanding. Where the beast draws power is a wound, no, an infection, growing slowly but still growing. It gives me time to streak across the clearing on Syerfu, to approach the place where the door had been and put my hands upon it.

A taffistone.

Inside it a hundred thousand lines of energy. Streaming

across and under and through and around Crua. Some feed energy to it, some transport it away, and all going in a vast circle. Thick lines of glowing power that begin and end in the cloudtree forests. It feels like some giant puzzle I am yet to unlock, or should unlock? Or can not unlock? Or should not unlock?

I do not know.

What I do know is the beast is drawing strength, replacing what it has expended before Cahan fell from the sky. I place my hands upon the taffistone, feel the energy moving through it, the last trails of power from when Cahan fled through it.

No. Not just Cahan. Him and others, many others. Udinnys past whispering to me again, telling me I should be able to read how many, who they were, where they had gone. There are hints, whispers, guesses within the stone, as if it tries to speak to me, but whatever is there has been disturbed, as if something alien to it has also passed through it.

Corrupted it.

I am lost in lines of energy, a web. Ranya's web? It is both alive and unalive, always altering itself, changing, trying to find some way to—

My thoughts interrupted by wild bleating from Syerfu and I wrench myself away from the stone. At the same time I leave some part of me there. A ghost, an Udinny past that detaches itself from me, a voice lost from the host, gone to decipher the taffistone, to unlock it and open the door.

Before it can, I feel another presence, a stranger, darker one. The creature senses me. Spearmaws leap from its body, four of them, shimmering into existence between the creature and the stone. Why always four, I thought as they hover there. Twisting in the air. Tentacles waving as if they sniff it.

"Bow," I say and my needle spear is in my hand, reading what I want and changing to be a bow. It looks exactly like the one I trained with under Cahan, except the string is a glowing line of gold, the arrow the same. The spearmaws are splinters of malice darting towards me; behind them the creature, huge, malevolent and purposeful. The spearmaws are much simpler, they have only one thought, to end me, to remove me from this place. But the creature is different, intelligent, calculating, aware. I have the distinct feeling it could have brought far more against me if the city had not been fighting it too.

Its hatred is a taste on the air.

The spearmaws find me, turning in the air to streak towards me and I draw the bow. Feel the strain in my muscles. Then comes the narrowing of the world into only what I see along the arrow. I let fly.

It does not fly like a real arrow, no arc, no great curve up and then down. This is a streak, a line of golden light across the ether. It hit the first spearmaw which explodes into golden light and is gone, the air filled with an anguished shriek from the beast. At the same time I feel something click into place behind me as past Udinny works.

Another arrow. Another explosion and shriek of fury. Another click of something slotting into place. About to draw again but time has run from me. Syerfu changes form, flickering and wavering until she becomes a huge garaur once again. As the final two spearmaws careen towards us we meet them. Her with claw and teeth and me with my bow, now returned to a spear. Tentacles reach for me, but I am a creature of light, a thing without substance or fear, not subject to the whims of the living's laws. I dance around the spearmaw's grasping reach. Stood on one leg I place a single thrust between the glowing eyes of the spearmaw and it is dead. At the same time Syerfu tears something from the other and it phases out of existence.

A scream of frustration and fury from the beast.

The feeling of power being drawn. Of the creature using its fury to widen the infected wound in Anjiin, to take more power. Spearmaws flickering into existence around it again, one, two three, four. A moment when it rests, then starts again. Four more, and more, and I know it will keep creating them until we are overwhelmed.

A voice from behind me. I look, a filmy figure, a ghost of golden motes. "Go!" it says, and I feel this Udinny of old, this ancient one let go, feed itself into the stone. Whatever power has kept it alive through a time beyond understanding is released. A gateway opens.

To where I do not know. But I know I must go.

"Syerfu!" The garaur turning and pushing its nose between my legs, somersaulting me onto its back. "The stone!" With that she throws us forward, into the gateway and we become one with the stream of golden energy, though where we go?

Well, that I do not know.

67

Saradis

Saradis visited the Cowl-Rai; safely caged, she sat at her desk, staring at a piece of bark. The room full of the familiar smells of gall-ink and histi.

"Your pain is gone?" said Saradis. Wishing her own was, Fighting not to show it.

"It went some time after you went to the Slowlands. Have you brought the trion?" she asked this calmly and softly as Saradis came to stand before the cage. Saradis shook her head, wondering what this could mean, this change in the woman before her.

"No," she said. "They are being hidden by the Forestals."

"Then we must destroy them."

"Yes," said Saradis and she moved closer to the cage. "But many have tried, they move through the trees like the Osere themselves."

"We will find a way," said the Cowl-Rai. "My brother, did he come? Is he dead? Or is he here?" Saradis took a breath, stole herself for the inevitable explosion of anger.

"No, not dead, but not here either." Saradis waited, watching the Cowl-Rai for the signs of her fury: the liquid darkness, the dark shimmering of her rage.

Nothing.

"I knew," she said. "I knew he lived, I can feel him."

"Zorir commanded me send Cahan into the depths." Inside the cage Nahac nodded, then began to sort through the barks and parchments on her desk.

"I felt it happen." She neither sounded annoyed at not having him, or pleased with his death. Nahac picked up a parchment. "My armies," she said, "they move too quickly. We will rule all of Crua soon and we do not have the trion. How will I tilt the world? How will I bring back the warmth without a trion?" Was there misery there, was there loss?

"I will have the troops in the north widen their search for the Forestal's base. And slow the armies in the south by sending more troops to assist in the north." Nahac nodded at this, putting her papers down. "We had one of their warriors but she died on the way here, we also took the Reborn who served your brother." At this Nahac looked up, interested. "But they are inert, insensible and dead as far as any can tell. I will have to capture some Forestals, I think." These words were said only to placate the woman before her. Zorir was coming. The war no longer mattered. Saradis wondered if the Cowl-Rai knew it. Something had clearly changed in the sending of Cahan into the depths. Nahac stood, turned to Saradis and walked to the bars.

"The pain is gone but I am losing myself," she said. "These lucid moments, they are more fleeting. The time I spend in the darkness is longer. I walk as if in sleep, I see a great glowing web of life and yet I cannot touch it."

"It is all part of Zorir's plan," said Saradis. "He sent me to you, and your battle is nearly won." Nahac turned, looked at the desk full of charts and plans.

"When it is won," she said, "what use will you have for me if the god has Cahan?" For a moment Saradis had no reply, so she fell back on platitudes.

"We cannot know the minds of gods, Nahac, you will have your place."

"I should have protected him," she said. "It was what I was meant to do. I was his sister, stronger, faster. I should have protected him and I did not."

"Because you realised you were more than him," said Saradis.

"Do not patronise me, monk, it was you that turned me against him. Do not think I don't know. Your honeyed words, your insistence I was meant for better things than servant."

Saradis shrugged, smiled to herself. "Well, you believed that then. Maybe you only care now because it has turned out he has power?"

Then the fury came. The violent magic raging and beating against the bars. Trying to reach her, to rend and tear her but unable to pass the twisted wood. Saradis backed away, left the room and the Cowl-Rai to her rage. She enjoyed it, she had put up with much from Nahac at the beginning, been forced to beg for her life. To kneel and agree to serve. It was hard for Saradis not to enjoy how total her victory was now. She needed that joy, and she knew part of her cruelty was because of what Nahac had said.

"What use will you have for me if the god has Cahan?"

She worried it may also apply to her.

Usually she would never have considered such a thought, but Saradis had been before the stone where Laha remained spreadeagled across it. She had stripped and waited and worshipped for hours and hours and heard nothing. There was only silence. She was used to that from Zorir. Silence was normal but, and maybe it was her own worries, but it felt as though this silence had a different property. The silence was usually like being in a room with someone who listened but felt no need to reply. This silence, it was as though the listener had turned away, she felt they were still there, but no longer paying her any attention.

Was it because of Cahan? She had seen his transformation, known that he was fulfilling his purpose, becoming Zorir's creature.

Until the woman, Sorha, intervened. The Rai called her abomination and now Saradis had taken up that name for her. She was glad that the abomination was dead, fallen into the depths to be smashed upon the floor where the Osere walk, though it was little consolation.

Saradis believed in vengeance, and she liked to take it herself. Liked those who had slighted her to know she was avenged upon them in their last moments, but now there was no one to avenge herself on but the Cowl-Rai, and Nahac's madness made it curiously unsatisfying to bait her.

So she returned to her room and sat before the stone, the body of Laha bent across it, arms spread, filling the room with the scent of sickness. The wound where the arrow had pierced his shoulder was black with rot, and threaded through with blue. His skin was cold to the touch but he did not corrupt like a corpse should. In places, where his flesh touched the stone it was fused with it by a strange blue substance she had never seen before. There was something of the Hetton about him she thought, but also he was most assuredly not of them. He was different; they were alive and she did not think Laha was.

Not any more.

Though she also felt that he was there. Existing, but in a way she did not understand. Was this it? Were events spiralling out of her control? Was she losing Zorir, the one thing that had ever really mattered to her? She had delivered Cahan du-Nahere and now was she to be thrown away?

She felt a tear track down her face.

No. It could not be. It would not be.

She would not allow it or believe it. Zorir had chosen her, and despite everything, despite all the setbacks she had succeeded. She was the power in Crua now. She ruled.

But ruling was hollow without a purpose. She was

nothing without her god and if Zorir had forsaken her she felt she would crumble away to dust and be carried into the ether by the circle winds.

She heard a creak, a sound like leather armour rubbing as soldiers walked. The scent of sickness in the room increased and she looked up. Laha moved, not much, only turning his head a fraction towards her. Opened his eyes, they were blue, deep, deep blue.

"Prepare," he said, in a voice that sounded as though it had travelled across all of the time that Crua had existed. "The fire is coming, beloved of your god."

68
Sorha

She did not understand.

Her world had been tumbling out of control ever since she first came across Cahan Du-Nahere: the loss of her cowl, her troops being beaten by villagers, betrayal by Saradis, falling into a dark world that existed below and finding out the Osere were little more than villagers, living in their equivalent of mud roundhouses.

Then to find out that the gods were real. They existed and they were monstrous.

Everything she had ever thought had been a lie.

They had camped back at the original taffistone and she had pretended to sleep. In the complete darkness of this place sleep was hard to come by, or maybe she did not need it as much. More than once she had found herself walking, sure more time had passed than she could account for. Part of her thought it was simply a trick of this darkness, but she was beginning to believe that she also slept while she walked.

When she closed her eyes she saw the way the Osere had lit up in bright colours before the prison of the god, blots and patches of colour floating in her mind that stayed when she opened them again, becoming slowly fading phantoms in the night.

Were they even gods, these creatures that slept within the roots of cloudtrees? To her they looked less like gods and more like some kind of gasmaw. Though the one back in Anjiin had been like no gasmaw she knew, it was no animal working off instinct. It had possessed purpose and intelligence, it had searched for them. She could not get out of her mind how, when Cahan Du-Nahere had been filled with power, when he had been this great throbbing creature in the land above, destroying what he wished at a thought, that he had resembled that beast. That he had, tasted the same? Yes, taste was the right word. Strange as it was, his nearness to her was something she felt in all her senses. She had never noticed it in the world above. Too many draws on her attention, too much going on. But down here it was dark and quiet. Down here she had time. The Osere were in no hurry to get anywhere now Cahan and her had been shown their gods. She had heard Cahan ask the translator what they were going to do next and the man had shrugged.

"We will head back to the village, the Osere think you should be given time to think."

She was not as sure that was the case. When they had passed through the taffistone, before returning to the camp, the Osere leader Frina had spent a long time talking with the other Osere. Laying hands on the stone and chattering back and forth. Ulan had looked worried but when she asked about it he said nothing.

They rested often on the way back.

It was not entirely dark down here, it had taken her a long time to see it though. The light of the cloudtree roots was obvious, but once they were away from them she began to see other lights. There were mushrooms everywhere that glowed with their own internal light, but it was so weak it was hard to even know if it was real. She had started marking off in her mind where she thought they were and then nodding to herself when she found actual fruiting bodies, pale and wormlike with no sign of light up close. But the light was there, it must be there or maybe some other sense hidden within her was working.

When they camped there was a lot of talk between the Osere, pointing back the way they had come, and Sorha sat closer to Cahan.

"Something bothers them," she said softly. He nodded. "Something about the taffistone we passed through to come back. Something that was not there when we left."

"It could be," said Cahan. "But it could be something else, we know nothing about this place, or about them." It was plain he did not want to talk, and not just to her. He was equally short with Ulan. Maybe he was also thinking, using the quiet and the dark to assess where he had been, how he had got here, who he was and what the truth of their gods meant. If it meant anything. Did it change the nature of their gods if they slept in the trees? If they sucked like bizarre littercrawlers on the cloudtrees while they dreamed?

She did not know.

But she thought a lot. She used the silence of their walks, of the rest time, to try and understand the world she had found herself in. To think about escape. How could she escape? She looked across at where she knew Cahan was. Where she could feel him. How odd it was. She could feel them all if they were within her influence. Though the Osere were different they were people, she was sure of that, but not the same as her. She did not think they had cowls the way she understood it, because they did not shrink from her. Though they could use the taffistone. Maybe something of their flesh was different. She was seized with a sudden desire to walk over and touch one of them, place her hand against their bare skin, see if they felt different to the people of Crua. Were they warm or were they cold to the touch?

She took a deep breath and turned over on the gritty earth.

Did any of it matter? She could see no way out of this place.

They set off again later and walked for a time indeterminate. Then the Osere leader held up her hand. Stopped them. Spoke a few words that part of her recognised in tone and action as worry. Something bothered the leader and Sorha was, again, sure it was related to the taffistone. A small group of Osere took up spears and left the camp. Cahan turned to the translator.

"What is happening?"

"Scouts are going ahead." Sorha watched. Cahan was twitchy with obvious irritation.

"Unlike your friends I am not blind." He looked over at the Osere, Frina, and Sorha had the distinct impression they were paying attention to him. Why? She wondered if it was because he did not keep his voice down. The translator did not answer Cahan, instead he looked to Frina.

"The taffistone," said Sorha, standing. "They think something came through the taffistone don't they?"

Silence. She knew she was right. Cahan must know she was right too, the way he reacted. The interpreter was staring at the leader of the Osere. She said something, no more than a click but Sorha had picked up enough around them to know that was assent of some kind, an affirmation. Ulan sighed.

"When the Osere betray themselves and leave the path, they lose the ability to use the taffistone." Ulan looked over at Sorha. "What makes them Osere is killed by what binds them to the god."

"But she," Sorha looked over at Frina, "thinks they have used the taffistone?"

The Osere leader spoke, a long stream of unintelligible words and clicks.

"Something has," said Ulan. "They are not sure what, or even if it was the Betrayers."

"Was it not their own people?" said Cahan. Ulan shook his head.

"They would know if it was their own. It was not them."

"Did I do this?" said Cahan. "I carry the beast's corruption within me and . . ." The Osere interrupted, talking to Cahan in their own language, then Ulan started to translate.

"She says the creature escaped from a prison that should have held it for ever, corrupted a cloudtree. It was only a matter of time until they worked out a way to get into the stones. You may have helped, you may not have. What matters is it is done." Cahan said nothing, not at first. Then when he spoke his voice was cracked like old stone.

"How can you forgive me when I have put you in danger?" No one spoke, not straight away. To Sorha, it seemed the best way forward, the way these people should have taken from the start, was to open Cahan's throat. She should have done it. Then the Osere spoke again. This time she did not use Ulan.

"Long ago," her voice was harsh, like cracking leaves. The words halting. "We choose wrong but forgiven. How can not also forgive?"

"No," said Sorha, surprised by what rose up within her, an anger. "You were not forgiven, you were punished." Frina, turned to her, angled her head up, then when she could not immediately find the words in Sorha's language she spoke to Ulan in her own.

"She says," Ulan cleared his throat, "that they were happy and at peace for generations once they accepted their new life. That to be changed is not to be dead, to be ended." Something burned in Sorha, an anger, and these words fanned it in such a way she could not even bring herself to reply. It was like they spoke of her, talked of what had happened to her. Like they thought they were better for accepting what had been done to them. "And since the Betrayers came, and one of the gods has escaped, they know how blessed they were in their peace."

"If they think I—" hissed Sorha but Ulan cut her off.

"There were over ten thousand Osere when I first came

down here, now there are less than five hundred." He stepped closer. "Those who are taken now, who become the Betrayers, they do not choose it like it is believed the first ones did. They have it forced upon them and most die." Frina gently pushed Ulan out the way, opened her mouth as if to say something then stopped, sensing something Sorha could not. Her entire body froze.

"You fight?" she said. Sorha felt her face screw up, confusion, annoyance.

"I can fight." Only now she noticed the Osere had a spear in her hand. Frina held it out. Sorha closed her hand around it. She did not know what had suddenly bothered the Osere, but she would never turn down a weapon.

Shouting carried through the air. Desperate, shouting. The Osere around her getting into battle array, spears ready, shields on their arms. Some held bows.

"Help fight," said the Osere, and Sorha readied herself.

She wanted to fight.

Needed it.

69

Dassit

Furin was in with Tall Sera and Dassit stood with Vir, watching Ania speak to the guards around the taffistone. Occasionally Ania would point back at them, making her case. She turned to Vir but her branch commander was not ready to speak, he was fighting off a powerful hangover gifted to him by the Forestals' strong alcohol. Behind him stood Ont, the huge man who had been burned in the Slowlands. He wore a coat of rags with a hood, and beneath the hood a mask of rough wood covered his burned face. Behind him stood the final three of her soldiers, Mestan, Bahin and Gruit; they had volunteered to come with her. Stood by them was the Forestal Tanhir, and Dassit was glad to see her. As Ania spoke Dassit walked over to Tanhir.

"I am surprised to see you here," she said to the Forestal.

"The forest paths twine and come together," said Tanhir. "Ours have done so, and so I will continue to walk with you." Dassit nodded.

"And your quest to kill the priest of murder means you are unpopular here." Tanhir laughed.

"Yes, there is that. It may be best if I am away while Tall Sera still feels slighted by my actions."

"Will this not make it worse?" said Dassit. "Not that I wish to dissuade you from coming. Those bows are worth ten soldiers in the field." Tanhir grinned at her.

"Either we will return having done a good thing, which he cannot gainsay, for to give a good death is honoured among us . . ."

"Or?" said Dassit; she found herself comfortable in the companionship of Tanhir.

"Or he will remain angry with me."

"Do you not fear what punishment Tall Sera will bring upon you?" Amusement on Tanhir's face.

"It will not be too terrible, he and I have been lovers for half my life, and he cannot give me the silent treatment any more than he already is. He will forgive in time."

"Are you not lonely, without your . . ." Her voice tailed off.

"That is not our way, Dassit, I am never lonely. You, however . . ." There was no mistaking the intention in her words. Dassit felt herself blush. She was no stranger to taking lovers but the ways of the Forestals and their freedoms remained odd to her. Uncomfortable in her mind, to have no rules and no commitments.

"Come, Tanhir," said Ania. "I will need you to help me open the stone."

"I will help," came a voice from behind them; they turned to find Venn stood there. "I want to help Ont."

"You are meant to be learning, with the Lens." Venn nodded but they did not move away.

"They have given me some time to think." They looked around at the small group. "And I think best in familiar places." Dassit looked the trion up and down, even though she did not really know them it was quite plain they lied.

"Still not ready to take up a spear though?" said Ania. Venn held up the staff in their hands.

"Cahan showed me how to use a staff," they said. Ania

bit her lip, shook her head and moved closer to Venn. Dassit was just near enough to hear her whisper.

"I will welcome your assistance in opening the stone, it will leave me more strength than I had expected should we meet resistance." She leaned in closer. "But I cannot take you, Venn; I do not understand your importance, but I know Tall Sera will never forgive me if I put you in danger. I already tax his patience with this." Venn's face fell, then they bowed their head.

"Very well," they said. "I will not cause you a problem." Ania clapped them on the shoulder.

"Come then," said Ania to the rest, "the guards will not stop this expedition as it is Tall Sera's will." She gave a lopsided smile and walked over to put her hands on the taffistone. Venn put their hands on her back and Tanhir placed her hands on Venn. A moment when it felt like everyone held their breath and then the stone opened, a path straight through to Ont's grove. Dassit put her hand on Ont's arm.

"Come," she said. "Your grove awaits."

They walked forward. Vir and their troops following her and Ont. One moment they were in the heat of Woodhome, the air moist and clinging. Then they were in the grove, the air clear, dry and icy. There was a fire. Around it a group of soldiers. One looked in their direction, hearing a noise. Dassit saw the woman's face change in the firelight, confusion as to where these people had come from. One minute the grove was empty, the next warriors were there, and worse, behind them. Dassit found herself running, reactions ingrained into her. There was nowhere to hide, nothing to be gained by stealth, so she ran, bringing her spear up. The first soldier began to stand, opening their mouth to call out and an arrow cut them down. Then Dassit was among them. A thrust of her spear, dodging to avoid a counterthrust from another soldier. Vir ran them through. Behind him came her remaining three soldiers, spears working, she thrust again and another enemy soldier fell and then she was through them. Turning. All resistance gone. All that was left was five corpses and not one of hers lost.

"Quickly," she said, and once more she was a leader. "Vir, get those corpses moved into the shadows and then everyone who isn't a Forestal sit around that fire. Ania, keep your archers in the shadows and if anyone looks in and gets overly curious, kill them." Ania and Tanhir took up station beneath the twisted tree that enclosed the taffistone. All that was left now was for Ont to find a place and welcome the embrace of death in the place he had come to love.

With the butcher stood Venn.

"No," said Dassit, and she ran forward, as Ania turned and did the same. She heard the Forestal hiss out words.

"I told you not to come."

"I had to."

"Why? To see a man who never liked you die?"

"He has changed," said Venn as Dassit approached. Ania turned, and if she had not heard the anger in the Forestal's voice then she would have stepped back at the look on her face.

"I told you, Trion, that some things Tall Sera will not forgive, and putting you in danger is one of them. We will open the stone, you will return now." Venn shook their head, and Dassit thought Ania about to grab them and bodily force them back to the stone. No doubt Ania would have if Dassit had not put herself between the Forestal and the trion.

"Why?" said Dassit. "What is so important that you risk Ania's wrath?"

"Ont has not come here to die," said Venn.

"Then why have we taken such a risk?" spat Ania.

"Because this is the nearest he has ever felt to Ranya, he has come to commune. To find answers." For a moment Dassit thought the Forestal would hit the trion. She shook her head instead.

"The world is complicated enough without bringing gods into it. We go back," she said. "If Ont had told me this I would never have . . ."

"That is why I did not," said the butcher, "please, it hurts within that I have misled my closest friend." He reached out, blindly grasping for the Forestal and though she did not move towards him, she did not move away. Eventually he found her. "I have prayed and begged Ranya to speak to me in Woodhome, and felt nothing of her. If I am to have some purpose, and I need purpose, then I will find it here."

"And if not?" asked Ania, anger still there, simmering beneath her words.

"Then I will lay down here and let the wood have my body. And you will not have been lied to." For a moment Ania did nothing. Then she stepped back.

"Very well," she said. "How long will this take?"

"Not long," said Ont.

"I am not sure," said Venn. Ania took a deep breath then blew out her frustration.

"Dassit," she said, "go look outside, see if more soldiers are about and make sure we are not going to be disturbed. Have your troops bring those corpses up here, we'll take them back to Woodhome so there is no sign we were ever here. Tanhir, you are strong. I want you ready to open the stone." Dassit nodded and left them. At the entrance to the grove she bent low, moved forward as slowly as she could until she could see out into Wyrdwood.

Before was what had once been New Harnwood. But was no longer.

Instead there were fires. Hundreds of them. She estimated two, maybe three trunks of troops were camped around the grove. She looked back and motioned for Vir to come up.

"Watch," she said, "whistle if anyone comes." He nodded but did not speak. She was not surprised, he had not had much to say recently and the hangover did not help. She made her way back to where Ania waited with Ont and Venn.

The trion was on their knees, one hand on the floor of the forest. Behind them Ont stood, and they held the trion's other hand. As she approached her steps slowed, the ground became spongy beneath her and she felt herself breathing, felt the forest move into her lungs and through her body, touching every part of her. A shiver passed through her. A voice tolled in her mind. Not her voice, not her own interiority that spoke as it saw and watched and questioned. This was something from outside. Something not of her.

North.

Then the feeling passed. She was just a woman standing in a wood. Venn stood, letting go of Ont's hand as she approached.

"I am sorry," said the trion, "but there is nothing—"

"North," said Ont.

"Yes," said Ania.

"What do you mean?" said Tanhir from her place by the stone.

"Did you not hear the voice?" said Dassit. "It said north, clear as clear."

"I heard nothing," said Venn.

"Nor me," said Tanhir.

"I wish I had not," said Ania.

"What of Vir?" said Dassit, and she turned to ask her branch commander and soldiers if they had also heard the voice.

But Vir and the three soldiers they had brought with them were gone.

"Ruins of Anjiin, no," she said, running over to the entrance of the grove. "I trusted you, Vir." The words were pain to her. So many years, so many fights. They had stood together when all seemed hopeless, he had never questioned, never doubted and in turn she had done the same. She had thought them closer than lovers, closer than siblings.

And he had taken the first chance he got to run, he had betrayed her.

70
Ont

For Ont, it was a night of terror unlike any other.

The battles around Harn had shown him fear. His life had been in danger, soldiers had come at him with weapons and he had fought. Grunting, screaming out in rage. Killing and smashing, not thinking about the lives of those before him, who they may be, who they may love, only that they were the enemy and they wanted to hurt him and those he cared for. The battles had started with terror, but it had been washed away by fury and the strange singing joy of battle.

And he had been able to see his enemy.

Here, in the cold and the dark of Wyrdwood, he could see nothing.

North.

That voice, it was not what he had expected. He had thought Ranya a gentle presence, a softness in a harsh world. A gentle push in the right direction and instead he got something else. An imperative, a word that took hold of him, left him shaking and weak. He felt in that moment as if he may collapse and his tortured body would give way beneath him.

"I am sorry," said the trion, and Ont could hear the misery in their voice, "but there is nothing—"

"North," he said, and the word was like ashes in his mouth. He had heard the Forestals talk of the north, they believed nothing but death waited there.

"Yes," said Ania.

"What do you mean?" That was the other Forestal, Tanhir.

"Did you not hear the voice?" The warrior of Chyi, Dassit. "It said north, clear as clear."

"I heard nothing," said Venn, and that shocked Ont. For the trion was his link to the numinous, to the outer worlds he could neither see nor sense any more than he could sense this one now.

"Nor me," said Tanhir.

"I wish I had not," said Ania. Did she sound, angry? Bitter? It was hard to tell.

"What of Vir?" said Dassit. Then there was a pause. As if everyone took an intake of breath. "Ruins of Anjiin, No," said Dassit. "I trusted you, Vir."

"What?" said Ont. "What is happening?"

"The Chyi soldiers," said Tanhir, "they have run. We must bring them back, they know of the stones and Woodhome."

"Vir will run straight to the enemy if it is escape he wants." Dassit's voice. She sounded cold, hard as she spoke and Ont recognised the voice of one fighting to keep their emotions in check. "He knows the worth of information and he will bring them here. If we follow we are likely to run right into them."

"Then we must escape," said Tanhir. "Back to Woodhome, help me open the stone." A pause, too long. "Ania, help me open the stone."

"No," said Ania. "Ont and I must go north."

"And I," said Dassit. It was strange to hear those words as they were clearly not spoken out of choice. Ont knew he could not deny the call, and it sounded like they could not either.

"Then we go back to Woodhome," said Venn, "and from

there you choose another taffistone in the north, away from here. One without soldiers."

"The trion speaks sense," said Tanhir.

"No," said Ania, "Tall Sera will never let me leave if I return, not now. Those soldiers of Chyi will bargain knowledge of the taffistones and Woodhome for their lives. He will say I betrayed him."

"We will not tell Tall Sera until you are gone once more," said Venn.

"He will already know we are gone, and besides, to open the stone here, and then once more when we get back? It will take all I have. The journey north is hard. I will need my strength."

"I will help," said Venn.

"You will, but not how you think," said Ania, and all the time Ont wanted to speak, but what use his opinion? As much use as he was. "You and Tanhir must go back. Tell Tall Sera what has happened." Venn started to speak but Ania cut them off. "No time to argue and Tall Sera must be told, quickly, about the soldiers who have run. You tell them I forced you to come with me."

"What of you?" said Venn.

"I am going North, with Ont."

"And I," said Dassit. No one asked Ont what he wanted.

"But the soldiers . . ." said Tanhir. Another of those pauses, and he could imagine Ania's face, calculating, thinking, planning.

"Venn, can you hold the gate open once Tanhir has opened it?"

"Yes," said the trion, no doubt at all in their voice. "I can do that."

"Very well – Ont, Dassit and I will leave, head north. Tanhir, open the gate, then come to the grove entrance with us. When they come, and they will come, distract them for as long as you can while Venn holds the stone open. Then return to Woodhome. Take no chances."

"You don't have to do this, Ania," said Ont. "None of you have to do this." He felt a hand on his arm, an unfamiliar touch.

"I heard the voice," said Dassit, "I know you must go, and that I must go too, you cannot make it alone. What spoke to us, it will not be denied."

"She's right," said Ania, "believe me, the last thing I want is to get mixed up in the business of gods. But you cannot move a tree when it's grown." He felt her hand on his arm. "Now come, Ont, we will guide you."

Gods. He had come to find Ranya but that voice, it was not her. It frightened him.

That was when the true terror began. The escape from the grove. He did not know where he was. How near they came to being caught. There was only the staccato stop-start of their movement through the wood. The pressure of a hand on his arm, or if they had to move particularly quickly a hand on each arm. He heard shouts, screams. The sounds of people running. Voices echoing around them. Ania's bow loosing. Ont wondered how they managed to hide. The images in his head of Wyrdwood outside the forest grove were of long open spaces beneath the trees, though he knew he had seen little of it.

"Stop." Dassit's voice and he was forced into a crouch. The hiss of arrows. One, two three.

"Only ten left," said Ania.

"Arrows or soldiers," said Dassit, and even though their position was tense, Ont heard humour behind her words. Ania did not answer her, she was not given to humour.

"That way," said Ania and he wondered which way she meant. Cursed for the thousandth time his misfortune.

"We cannot keep this pace," said Dassit.

"Are you getting tired?" said Ania.

"No," said the soldier, "but he is."

"I can run," said Ont. He heard Ania make a clicking sound, something she only did when thinking dark thoughts.

"We go north-east then," she said. "There is something there that will help us. But it is dangerous."

"Worse than the soldiers?" said Dassit. "The ones I've killed didn't seem that friendly." He heard a noise, like a cough and knew it for a laugh from Ania. A rarely heard thing.

"Come on," said Ania.

They were moving again, Ania speaking in a low voice to Dassit.

"It is important you do exactly as I say. Keep yourself and Ont on exactly the same path as me." They moved again, forward, but more slowly.

"Why are we going around this clearing?" said Dassit.

"Just do as I say," said Ania, pulling him on with a firm grip. They stopped again. "Now make some noise," said Ania.

"What?"

"Do it."

While the two women spoke, Ont had the strangest feeling of something near. Something huge and hungry. Not malevolent, not dark, but at the same time it was not friendly, or even uninterested in the way the trees were. It was waiting. He tried to make the feeling go away. Over the past few days such feelings had been coming and going. These imaginings that he could sense the world around him without his eyes. Wishful thinking and he hated himself for it, for his desperate desire to be useful.

"Dassit," hissed Ania, "scream if you want to live."

"Then we run?"

"No," said Ania, "we stay very still."

"This makes no sense, you will bring them on us and—"

Ont screamed, made the sort of noise that had been living in the back of his head, that he must have made when the flames engulfed him. All the frustration, of becoming useless, of not knowing whether he could trust his broken body from moment to moment, welling up and out into the most horrendous noise he had ever made.

"See," hissed Ania, "*he* can follow instructions."

Ont started to laugh, and then Dassit as well and finally Ania, all trying to smother, near hysterical laughter bubbling up out of them. Having to fight it down as the hours of stress, of running through the forest while pursued by the enemy overwhelmed them. Then the laughter vanished.

"They're coming," said Dassit. "I can hear them."

"Wait," said Ania. "Wait. And don't move. No matter what happens stay still."

Could he really feel something? Some great presence? Something in the ground?

"There!" A man's shout, a voice he did not know. The sound of people, he did not know how many. Ten or twenty, nearer twenty. Why did he think that?

Then the explosion. Something huge pushing itself up from below. The presence. He had not imagined it. Screams. He heard Dassit swear under her breath.

"Osere's blood, what is that?"

A hissing roaring, a sense of air being displaced as if by massive vines falling from trees. Shouts of panic.

"Littercrawler nest," said Ania, "now, we move slowly away. Very slowly, it feels you move. But hopefully it is distracted by those soldiers."

They moved, step by painful step, away from the beast as it roared and screamed and killed. Heading north. Always north and Ont could feel something in that direction. Something waiting. Something far more terrifying than the littercrawler.

It was waiting.

It was waiting for him.

71
Udinny

I was lost. Spinning through the lines of power, falling between moments in a place I could not understand. Beneath me Syerfu twists and turns, squeals and bleats as she changes form, trying to regain control of herself. Behind me I feel the stone I passed through. I feel it fighting against another presence. I can sense movement between places. Feel the footsteps of others. Cahan has used this. The darkness within him as he travelled through this un-place has left a trail of breadcrumbs that the creature behind me is desperate to follow and I can feel something else, some other effect I do not understand, just as I do not understand how to travel here. We twist and spin and we spin and twist and Syerfu cries out and I cry out.

Only one of us is a fool who has forgotten the walknut in their pocket.

Once the walknut is in my hand the spin steadies and stops. I find myself on a strand of golden silk in a night as black as black can be. Deeper than the black of Wyrdwood in the moments before the plants and animals explode into light. Through the darkness strands of light spread a million golden paths, all of varying thicknesses and strengths, like the paths through a forest, some wide and often walked, some thin and barely there. An infinitely complex weave of light, but the light of the paths does not spill over from them. From each path, or maybe to each one, are more lines, invisible but there, so thin as to be unseen, while carrying power that I cannot help but feel. Yet, it is incomplete. I sense this with the same sense that sees the lines. This web is makeshift, it is chaotic but should not be, there is a sense of order denied it.

Scar tissue.

Where that came from in my mind I have no idea, but it feels right. The way flesh grows differently when it is broken, so something here has been broken, and is trying desperately to fix itself. This must be what I was knitting with my needle, and maybe its breakdown is what I have been fighting. But I never stood a chance, the chaos is everywhere, and I can see great dark areas where there should not have been. Looking upon it I have the feeling of walking into a house that has been left to ruin, not through carelessness, but because its occupant was overrun. And I have no doubt, none at all, that we, the people of Crua, are somehow responsible for this. A sadness falls upon me as I think of the land I had travelled through as a monk. It contained such great beauty, the vast and verdant forests, the waving plains of grasses and the multitudes of animals. We had been given a great jewel and ground it in the mud. Ranya wants me to arrest this desolation of our world, and yet here, in the pathway between death and life, in a place I barely understand, I am overwhelmed.

Then Syerfu bites me.

The bite brings me back to my senses and she spins around on the spot, showing me the way we have come, far off a bright white spot of light.

"No, Syerfu," I pull on the steering rope, "that is where we have come from." Syerfu bleats in such a way that it convinces me she thinks I am a little stupid. Maybe more than a little. "We must find Cahan." I pull harder but Syerfu ignores me and I feel her body melting, taking up the form of the garaur which she uses for battle. "Syerfu, no!" I said "We must find Cahan!" I can feel where he has gone, his route through the web.

Ranya's web.

This is it.

Of course.

How could I be so foolish. This is what moves throughout Crua, what touches all, what is broken and must be fixed.

Too much.

It is all too much.

Syerfu bleats again.

"What is it?"

And I see what upsets her.

From the spot of light comes a darkness, a sickly blue glow leaking into the gold. In the centre of it a purple and blue tentacle, questing, tasting. It has the same sense about it as the path Cahan has left and his travelling through the web has, if not let this thing in, then at least kept the door ajar for it.

"You are right, Syerfu," I say, "it must be stopped." And with a shout of "Hai Syerfu!" we streak through a golden tunnel, moving at a speed beyond sound or seeing. Once more to raise my needle spear, once more to fire my golden arrows. Twice I have fought this creature's foul spearmaws, now I will fight it rather than its servants. Spear to tentacle, I will strike a blow for Ranya because whatever is wrong here, this beast is a large part of it. So I will fight this battle, and it may be against great odds but I will not shirk or run. I will use my Lady's name as my battle cry.

"For Ranya!" I shout. "For Ranya!"

And only at the last, as Syerfu and I close upon the creature, do I realise how very, very big it is. How it drips a strange and poisonous power. How a fearsome strength and noisome, differentness emanate from it that chokes me as I approach.

But we do not cower. We do not back down. I leap from Syerfu's back, my spear becoming a bow. My arrows fly straight and true, impacting against the creature, driving it back in a horrific cloud of screams and squalls. But more tentacles push through, seeking out what hurt it. Syerfu, screeches and launches herself at the beast. Sharp teeth cutting through ropes of purple flesh. Another scream from the creature. It retreats, and if we can only push it a little further back I am sure I can close the door. Use my needle spear to sew it up and deny passage. In I go. Bow becoming spear. A thrust, I parry, I jab, I cut. The air fills with a purple haze of blood energy that stinks like a battlefield sickroom. The creature's screams a physical force and yet I, Udinny Pathfinder, servant of Ranya prevail. My spear is fluid as water, bright as the Light Above. Bringing the vengeance of Ranya down on her enemy.

I am unstoppable.

Until the moment I am not.

A shock.

A stopping.

Looking down, a glistening tentacle pierces my chest. Through it I feel the creature's triumph, and its hatred. It grasps Syerfu in two tentacles and with a huge wrench it tears my companion apart. Then the tentacle withdraws from my chest, leaving a hole of sparkling gold and I can not move, can not do anything. The creature pushes through the door and past me in search of whatever such things search for.

Then, for the second time, I, Udinny Mac-Hereward, the pathfinder of Ranya, crumble into ash.

72
Cahan

Their attackers were coming from the south, from the direction of the settlement. In the distance he could see them, flickering blue like ghosts in the darkness and they screamed, made strange ululating noises the like of which he had never heard.

"Form a line! Form a line on me!" Screaming the words. Not knowing if the Osere would understand. Ulan joined him, standing by him spear in hand. On his other side stood Sorha with her spear ready. "My axes, I need my axes." Ulan echoed him in the language of the Osere. He felt a touch on his back. Turned, an Osere, holding out his axes, and he took them. Felt more complete with them in his hands. But the line was not forming, instead the Osere were spreading out.

"Ulan," he said, and he heard his desperation, his fear and worry about fighting here in the darkness against an enemy that knew this place better than he ever could, "we must form a line. We must meet the charge." He looked back to the attackers, the charge was coming, closer and closer, rushing forward and Cahan saw them clearly now, even in the darkness. Faint blue lights on their bodies, as if smeared over them. Not the same on any one of them, no uniformity, patches of dimly glowing blue on arms or faces or chests. They ran and howled and leapt and screamed. He stood where the centre of the line should be. He knew, even with a line, that if they had been facing Rai, or the troops of the Rai they would be doomed. They were too few and he doubted the Osere knew the discipline of battle, had shown it by spreading out. They were unsure of themselves and he could feel it. See it in the way the Osere nearest to him reached out to touch one another for reassurance. "Ulan, they must form—" And he was silenced. The hand of an Osere over his mouth, the same happening to Sorha.

His first instinct to strike out, hers too but they did not. Only because Ulan hissed a word.

"No."

They were moved. Dragged from where they had been stood. Not too far apart, keeping him and Sorha reasonably near. The Osere let go and quickly moved away from where they stood.

The air filled with the sound of their attackers. He looked to left and right where there should be a line, hoping that at the last the Osere would see some sense, but there was only Sorha. He waited for the moment the enemy Osere, the Betrayers, ran into them. The smash of bodies, the thrust of weapons and his skill, his familiarity with fighting would not save him, he knew it. They were many, and one man alone could not stand.

The charge stopped.

The noise stopped.

All was still and utterly silent. He saw the pale form of Sorha's face to his right, the glow of the Betrayers, vaguely people-shaped smudges in the darkness. He could have been adrift in sleep, alone and dreaming. The shapes of the Betrayers now advancing, very slowly. Using their spears to sweep the air before them.

Cahan did not understand.

What was happening here?

Where were the Osere?

Had they left him?

A noise to his left. A slight movement. The blue glow of one of the Betrayers, its spear had bounced off something.

It let out a cry. Clutched at its stomach and fell. More Betrayers converged on the spot, stabbing wildly. It took a moment for Cahan's mind to piece together what was happening. One of the Osere had been crouched in the dark, the Betrayer's spear had bounced off their head, or a shield, and then the Osere had thrust forward and up. Killing their enemy before moving swiftly away so they were not caught.

And then he understood.

The battle line of Crua was entirely wrong for this place. Combat here was different. The Osere could not see. How foolish he had been to try and put them all together, it only made them easy to find.

Instead the fight here was one of stealth and silence. He imagined Osere around him, still as statues, waiting for the Betrayers to approach. Relying on speed, that when contact came they would have the quickest reaction time. Listening for the sound of footfalls. Feeling for a disturbance in the air and hoping that your enemy did not find you first. Did not hear you breathing before you heard them.

Cahan could not imagine the tension they must feel. Like the moments before battle but magnified a thousandfold. How long did such a battle last? How did you know who won and who lost?

A sound from one of the Betrayers. A word he did not understand and those strange fuzzy blue spots in the air that told him where they were had stopped moving. Become still. More figures came forward, brighter, more of the blue on them and it looked to Cahan like they were on all fours, people moving like crownheads. He watched as one approached, accompanied by an upright betrayer. He tasted sickness on the air, like the Hetton but not as extreme. The four-legged Betrayer stopped. In the darkness he was sure he made out the brighter creature extending a malformed arm. In the dim glow he could see its handler. They were running a hand along the outstretched arm. Then they let go and launched a spear in the direction it pointed, and were rewarded by a cry of pain and the sound of a body hitting the floor.

For a moment, some trick of the dim light showed him both creature and handler. The handler was a Betrayer, like the others. But the creature was twisted, strange. Veins of blue running over it, and as it turned its blind head towards him he saw something that surprised him. The thing had eyes. No, not eyes, a facsimile of them, traced in bluevein on the bulge of its forehead. They did not sit right, not equal on the head, not opposite each other. At first he thought they were drawn on, then they locked on to him and the creature began to raise its arm again.

He could not move. He was transfixed because the creature had once, at some point, clearly been one of the Betrayers. Now it was something else.

A spear broke the spell, thrown accurately and expertly through the creature's head. He turned to see Sorha. Now weaponless, a look of horror on her face. The handler shouted something, warning its friends, and was immediately cut down by one of the Osere, a spear thrusting through their chest from behind as they reacted to the sound.

Silence again. But more of the sighted creatures were coming forward with handlers. An overwhelming advantage in this place of blindness. Carefully, he moved back until he was at the body of the first Betrayer to die. With their smaller numbers and the enemy's sighted creatures this was a battle the Osere could not win. But he, Sorha and Ulan could even the fight up. He reached the body, knelt, each moment taking an age. Watching the twisted, four-legged Betrayers coming forward. His hand going to the corpse, feeling along hard ridges that grew out of its skin for what he was sure he had seen.

There. One of the Osere short bows. Further down a quiver of arrows. He picked them up, put the bow over his shoulder, arrows on his belt. Continued to search, found a pack of short throwing spears. Moving slowly forward, watching as the Betrayers around him did the same. Feeling the air for movement, he made his way to Sorha. Held out the spears. They shared a look. Strange, they had once hated so strongly, and here, now, they were warriors, sharing the fight. Bound together.

He pointed to his eyes, then at the betrayers and Sorha nodded, readied a spear as he backed away, making sure his footsteps were loud enough to draw the nearest Betrayers to him. Four. Coming slowly and stealthily. Used to fighting this way and not knowing that he was not like them. They came on. He had watched them kill, and be killed in turn. He knew how they fought, in single, quick attacks that they expected to kill outright. They did not defend, or worry that their enemy may come back with a riposte.

One of the four coming fell, tripped and killed by a hidden Osere. One of the remaining three turned to strike them down and Cahan used the bow, shot them in the neck. Then he began to loose arrows. Trying to move every time he did. The noise of the bow began pulling them to him.

He put the bow over his shoulder and ran. Taking up his axes, passing between two Betrayers. One thrust at him and he dodged it. Cut back with his axe taking the Betrayer in the throat. The other thrust at the noise and Cahan danced around the spear, grabbed it with one hand, pulling the Betrayer forward and they fell. He buried his second axe in their head.

Then froze.

The noise was bringing even more Betrayers. Spears began

to cut through the air. Felling the approaching figures. Sorha taking out the sighted. Precision throws. Her skill was impressive. He gathered up fallen spears, and quivers from the dead, and began to loose from his bow again, backing away. A death for each shot. When he reached Sorha he passed her more spears.

The Betrayers had no defence against them, because their defence was to be still and that only made it easier for Cahan and Sorha. They were something the Betrayers did not understand. They were unknown, of the outside. Warriors the like of which they had never met, and in his killing Cahan was relentless and pitiless. A cry went up, a garbled shout and the enemy were running. The glow of their bodies receding. He expected some congratulation, some noise from the Osere or Ulan, but instead he was grabbed by the interpreter.

"We must run," he said.

"But we have beaten them."

"No, that is not why they left," he pulled on Cahan's arm, "the Betrayers do not fear death, they do not stop."

"They have not come across us before," said Sorha.

"No," Ulan hissed it, desperation in his voice. "They did not leave from fear."

"Then why did they go?"

"Because it is coming. The god, Cahan, it is coming."

"How?" said Sorha. "You said we are far from Anjiin, that it could not use the taffistone." Ulan shrugged.

"How does not matter. It is coming," said Ulan. "We run."

They ran into the darkness. Cahan heard the Osere around him, they let out clicks and squawks, harsh noises that told others where they were and it did not take long until they were in the root forest once more. Or maybe it did, Cahan could not tell. He had no sense of time, and his blood was singing from battle, from winning. Ulan brought them to a stop. When he turned Sorha was by him, flushed.

"I enjoyed the fight," said Sorha, leaning on a thick root, breathing heavily, bathed in its faint glow. "The run less so. Do you think we have escaped it?"

"Quiet," said Ulan. The Osere leader whispered something to her people, so softly it was hard to tell they were words.

"What did she say?" Sorha's words just as quiet.

"That what comes is of the darkness, and you cannot use the darkness to hide from it."

"Joyful," said Sorha with a snort. "Hard to believe anything can find anyone down here." Then she turned to Cahan, maybe hoping to share the humour but he was not looking at her. He was staring at the ground. One hand on it.

"Can you feel it?" he said.

"What?" She looked around, only noticing now there was something different about the Osere, some strange posture that spoke of worry and fear to her. She turned her head, looking at the root she clung on to. At where her hand grabbed it. "The root. It shakes."

Cahan nodded, the ground shook too. It had a rhythm to it. Not the rhythm of people but the rhythm of something else. Something massive, with too many legs and too much weight.

"It's coming," said Cahan.

A crack in the air. An Osere was cut in two. A wetness on his face. Voices crying out around him. Bows raised and shot but the thing attacking them did not care about arrows. It descended from above, black and writhing through the roots. Eight massive tentacles in constant, oily motion. Four it used to cling onto roots, propelling itself through the darkness; a vast and dripping shade within the shade. Its other four tentacles it used as weapons, cutting and killing in the darkness. Like the roots and the mushrooms and the Betrayers, it had its own light. Lines of blue that crossed its flesh and allowed him to follow it. Though its shape was some relation to the gasmaw and spearmaw of the forests, it was also twisted, unnatural in a way they were not. The blue that ran over its flesh in ridges and rills cracked as it moved, spilling a glowing liquid. The scent of it was sickness, vomit and rot. It was everything that was a warning to keep away. He was paralysed by it. His body unable to move and he did not know why. It took time for him to recognise it, as he stared up into the snapping, glowing beak of a god. This was fear, but not fear of death. Fear of being lost again, of being consumed by this terrible thing and he had no doubt this was it. This was the creature that had escaped the prison of the cloudtree. This was what had fed him power in the Slowlands. This was what Sorha's presence saved him from. This was what *wanted* him.

This was Zorir.

A tentacle, writhing and curling down towards him. Something hit him. Sorha. Shouting his name. "Move, Cahan!" With a flick the tentacle caught her a glancing blow, sending her flying through the air to collide with a root and fall, slack as a wet corn doll. His senses returned. He pulled himself up, no use fighting, he knew it, the Osere knew it. No choice but to run. The world spinning, the beast overwhelming his senses, the stink of it on the air. Where was Sorha? Did she live? No, he knew she lived, or he would no longer be himself. The Osere were leaving, streaming away. He found her, a crumpled ball. Keeping low he ran towards her, stopped.

Not by choice.

Something cloudtree-strong around his centre. He grabbed it with one hand. Tried to hack at it with an axe and was rewarded with a sound, a great basso thrumming that shook the air. He was thrown. Hitting a root. The world losing focus, his weapons gone. Grabbed once more around his centre. Pulled into the air.

Then he was moving.

Away.

Away from her.

Away from himself.

Within him something terrible rose up, the fire that he had spent his life running from consuming him, a sickly power spreading from the noisome rope gripping his waist, taking over his body and burning through his mind.

Cahan Du-Nahere was lost.

73
Dassit

She hated Wyrdwood.

Up until the creature, the littercrawler, that huge and awful force of nature had destroyed an entire branch of troops it had been the simple fear of the place that she had known her whole life. An understandable, knowable fear that was as much part of her as breathing.

War was spear against spear. Tactic against tactic and though luck played some part in it, you could tell yourself that your skill and knowledge contributed to it, were even the biggest part of it and so you could go into every action believing you made your own luck.

Not in Wyrdwood.

In Wyrdwood monsters lurked beneath the floor. In Wyrdwood the ground grabbed at your feet. In Wyrdwood the trees towered over you and forced you to take detours just to go around their trunks. There was something monstrous about this place. She liked it best when they hit the stands of short trees with thick green leaves because then she could pretend she was in a real wood, Woodedge, or Jinnwood, where the dangers were known. Not Wyrdwood, where she felt like the darkness watched their every step.

North.

The only consolation was their pursuers clearly felt the same, they might still follow but it was hours since they had heard any sign of them. At one point, Dassit was sure soldiers were lurking in the bushes, waiting for them. She had hissed for quiet and gone forward, softly and stealthily, her spear at the ready until Ania almost bowled her over, grabbing the end of her spear and pushing it into the dirt.

"No."

"We are watched." Dassit wanted to fight her. The tension in her muscles manifesting in anger. "They are here."

"It is shyun," said Ania, "the forest children." She pointed at a little pyramid of sticks. "That is one of their shrines, they always watch. But will not hurt us if we do not hurt them." They did not move, not immediately. Dassit found she was breathing hard, air hissing in and out through her teeth and she wanted to strike out, at Ania, at these shyun whatever they were. Most of all she wanted to go back.

North.

She could not go back.

"What is happening?" That from Ont, stood ten paces away from them, walking carefully forward using the staff that had once been his bow to guide his steps. "What is happening?"

Dassit closed her eyes, let the tension flow out of her muscles. "I want to go home," she said softly.

"Nothing is stopping you," said Ania. There was no bitterness in her voice. In fact Dassit thought there was an understanding there, as if she too once had everything she knew turned upside down.

"I am not convinced that is true," said Dassit. She met Ania's gaze, saw what she had suspected for a while as they walked through the forest.

North.

Not only a word, but an imperative, an order, and even

to think about disobeying made her head ache and her legs go weak.

"Aye," said Ania, softly, "you're probably right." She let go of the spear. "Trust me, Dassit Gan-Brinor, and I will do everything I can to get you safely through Wyrdwood."

"Everything you can?"

"You must feel it," Ania looked around, "what all of us Forestals know. This place feels strange, I know, but it does not care about us. It does not hate us. Listen to what I say, obey, and we will get through this."

"What is happening?" said Ont again.

"Nothing," said Ania, standing, "Dassit was scaring away some orits, that is all."

They went on but Dassit found herself unable to relax, unable to let down her guard despite that Ania had said to trust her. She was more aware than ever of being watched, of the hidden eyes of these "shyun" fixing on her through the gloom. She imagined them in every bush, behind every mushroom that rose in monumental grandeur to tower over them, slender grey stalks that exploded into feathery caps of a thousand different colours.

Worse, she was starting to doubt herself. The one thing she had been sure of, her whole career, was she was a good judge of people. She knew her troops. She knew how they thought. But Vir betraying her? She had not seen that coming. Nor the attempt on her life in Fin-Larger. That she could excuse, she hadn't known her would-be assassin well, but Vir? She had thought she knew him as well as she knew herself.

It hurt, and as she thought on it, she began to wonder if she had simply been blind to him. The things they had done out of duty, the executions, the burnings, maybe he had actually enjoyed them? Should she have stopped that? Found him other work before he became so hardened? Helped him somehow?

Or maybe he was not who she had thought he was at

all. Maybe he never had been. Maybe she was not who she thought either?

She wanted to be wrong.

As they travelled Dassit began to see rootlings everywhere, weaving in and out of the bushes, burrowing into the undergrowth, lying flat on the needle-strewn ground. More and more she found herself lost in this place: its size, the strange noises. She was not only lost here but lost in herself. She recognised nothing, had no sense of direction, no way of comparing to things she understood. More than anything she wanted a little comfort, to feel just a little better and not like someone who had failed so drastically.

Then she saw Vir.

At first she told herself it could not be. He had run, taken her soldiers and run to the enemy, abandoned her. Betrayed her.

She looked again and he was there, in the shadows between two of the huge bushes. Smiling at her, beckoning her to him. Was she wrong? She must be wrong. Maybe he left the grove for some other reason? Probably trying to protect her as he always had done.

The man she saw was not the Vir she had known over the last years, the hard, unforgiving man. This was a younger Vir, quick to laugh like he had been when they were lovers. Somewhere, in the back of her mind, she knew this could not be, but that voice was very quiet. Becoming quieter with every moment she looked at Vir, because he was back. Vir was back. He had not betrayed her.

"Dassit!" A voice from behind. Ania. She did not want to answer the Forestal. "Dassit, what have you seen?" The answer was in her mouth but she did not want to let the words loose, something in her said she would chase Vir away. Because it was the Forestal's fault he had gone in the first place. They had been too much, too different. She missed Vir so much, this version of him.

North.

The hateful call, but quieter. Vir beckoned her again. He had been a good man, and if she looked away she knew he would be gone, eaten up by the forest. Dead, and all because of her. "Dassit!" Her name harsher this time, she did not turn but managed to speak.

"Vir," she said. "He did not betray us." She took a step towards him. Behind her she heard footsteps. Two sets. Then a hand on her shoulder.

"Dassit, look at me."

"It is Vir," she said.

"Do you remember a light?"

"No." Vir was still waving but he was moving away now. "He is going." She tried to go after him but Ania's hand on her shoulder tightened.

"Stay still, Dassit. Because we are all going to die if you move." Despite the complete conviction in Ania's voice Dassit would have followed Vir, but at the moment she was about to shrug off Ania a stronger, more commanding voice echoed through her mind.

North.

Louder. More urgent. The tolling bell of a voice and it forced her to turn from Vir.

"What do you mean?" she said. To her surprise, Ania had her eyes shut and she was holding on to Ont's hand tightly.

"I thought it may be a golwyrd that has you, but it is too late in the season for them." She sounded frightened, breath coming in short sharp stabs. "Around us are hareft trees. We have walked into the territory of a skinfetch." That name, like icy water poured over Ania even though she knew little of them, only that they came at night and took unwary travellers from forest paths. That they were one of the nightmares fathers and mothers used to terrify children. "Close your eyes, Dassit, and hold on to Ont," said Ania.

"Why?" said Dassit, and still something lingered, a desire to turn and find Vir. To find forgiveness.

"Because we are lucky," said Ania. "I happened to be

looking at you when you saw the creature, so I know you are you. And I was stood by Ont, so I know he is real too."

"I do not understand."

"It calls one of a group away with visions. The weak skinfetches, they show something general, someone in need of help. The old ones, the really strong ones? They reach into your mind and show you what you want the most. It wants to draw you away so it can come back in your skin, to wear your face and prey on the rest of us. I have known them take ten or more, each time changing who is taken. Returning in the guise of friends." Her words came quick and urgent.

"Surely, now we know about it . . ." Dassit's voice died away, because knowing had not changed her desire. She still wanted to turn, to look out and to see Vir again. To go to him.

"If it's strong enough, Dassit, knowing will not help. We all have things we desire more than our lives." Dassit swallowed, put a hand on Ont's arm. "Ont, put your hand on my shoulder." He did and Dassit wondered if she would have read the same horror on his ruined face that she felt. Ania ripped lengths of cloth from her clothes. Used one to bind her eyes, then passed the other to Dassit. "Quick, we must all be blind now." Dassit bound herself up, found herself near to sobbing. What was this place? It offered such a gift to her as Vir of times past, but only as a cloak for something monstrous to wear. "Ont, you told me you could feel north?"

"Yes."

"Then you must lead us. Walk two thousand steps at least."

"But I cannot see."

"And are more used to it than either of us." Each word polluted by fear and Dassit found it infectious, that the skinfetch made even Ania, who had seemed cold and hard as stone, frightened. What other horrors did Wyrdwood hide? "Walk, Ont and neither of us are to let go of you for any reason."

"What if it takes advantage of our blindness?" said Dassit. "What if it attacks us or . . ."

"No," said Ania, "that is not how it works, it has no body of its own. It is . . ." Her voice tailed off as she searched for some way to describe something indescribable. "It is like a thought, a malignant idea. When it is close it comes in through the eyes, and then you are it. And you do its bidding. But as long as we stay touching, we know none has wandered off and been taken."

So they moved.

Stepping on, passing through darkness in their own darkness, in a world that already terrified Dassit. Every nerve in her body jangling.

"How can such a thing as this be?"

"I do not know," said Ania, "the forgotten weapon of some past Cowl-Rai maybe. But it is a horror, and we must pass out of its territory if we wish to live." Step after step. Dassit felt herself trip, managed to right herself at the last moment. "Do not let go!" Ania's voice on the edge of panic and Dassit did not know how much longer she could take it. Each step wound her tighter and tighter, she ached for the vision of Vir. The ghost of a man she had loved. Maybe it would be worth it, to become lost just to see him once more. "Dassit!" Ania's voice, commanding. "You are slowing. Do not slow. Keep hold of Ont and keep walking." She did, and wept silently for all she had lost, all that she once knew and all she had once cared about, knowing it was all gone.

But none knew she wept, the blindfold soaked up her tears as she stumbled on. Occasionally, she thought she heard the laughter of a child and Ont would change direction to go toward it. They walked on in blindness, it felt like hours passed until eventually, Ania called a halt.

"Can we remove our blindfolds?" said Dassit.

"Yes, I think we are safe—" The words stopped. Dassit pulled off her blindfold. Immediately froze.

Skeletons surrounded them. Some had spears and some had swords. They held their weapons pointed at the small group, and their bones were wrapped tight with grass. In the distance was a light, a strange, flashing light that filled Dassit with a familiar fear, the same one she had felt when that word first reverberated around her head.

North.

"What is happening?" said Ont.

"Swarden," said Ania. "Hundreds of swarden."

"That is not good," said the butcher. Dassit did not know what to do. Then the grass-wrapped skeletons moved, creaking and swaying, making a pathway that led out of the bright, yellow grassed meadow they had found themselves in and north, deeper in to Wyrdwood. Down it came a lone rootling, limping with every step. Its sharp, furry head looking from side to side as it walked. It stopped in front of Ont. Lifted its head so it looked up at him. The butcher tilted his masked face down as if he saw the creature.

"What?" he said, as if in reply to the rootling. Dassit was confused. She heard nothing. "But I am so tired," said Ont, and it was as if all the despair in the world was in him. "I want only to lie down."

"What is it, Ont?" said Ania.

"I do not really understand," he said. "It says the web is failing and the fire is rising, that the Boughry are waiting to make us weavers and builders, but we have a way to travel yet." Dassit looked from Ont to Ania, to the rootling.

"What does that mean?" she said.

"I do not know," said Ont, and then the rootling put out a small, fragile hand and the butcher took it in his burned fingers, let it lead him onwards. "Maybe the Boughry will tell us more when we meet them."

The ground shook, the bones of the gathered swarden rattled around them, but Ont walked on, as if the earth below his feet did not shiver and shake.

"Starting to wish I'd walked into that littercrawler pit," said Ania. Then her and Dassit followed him across the shifting land and deeper into Wyrdwood, deeper into the unknown.

74
Venn

Venn and Tanhir stood in the treehouse, the warmth of the air uncomfortable after the familiar cold of the north. The humidity made Venn feel as though they were drowning, or maybe it was the fear entwining itself around them, like the vines holding the building together. Luminescent mushrooms grew around the outskirts of the room, providing a gentle green light and suffusing the air with an earthy smell. Effigies of the Boughry, all long bone and branching horn, threw frightening shadows. Tall Sera stood at one end of the house before a set of seats, and with him was the leader of the Lens, Brione. They were whispering and occasionally looking across at Venn and Tanhir.

"We could be in trouble," said Tanhir, which made Venn feel no more comfortable. Instead they watched as Tall Sera and Brione continued their hushed conversation, throwing occasional glances their way.

"We did the right thing," said Venn.

"That will be little comfort when we can no longer remember as much as how to feed ourselves." Venn's breath caught in their throat. They had not really thought as far ahead as punishment, and how the Forestals administered it to their own. There were no whippings or giving over the condemned to the Rai as sacrifice, the way they did in the rest of Crua. The Forestals considered themselves different, gentler. Venn was not as sure; what they did here felt just as cruel, only in a different way. To take from someone's mind, to wipe away who they had been to, as the Forestals put it, "allow straight growth away from what was twisted". Venn had seen the punished being collected by relatives, or past lovers. Seen the faces of them when they were not recognised and thought it punished loved ones as much as the one who was to be punished.

Though for Venn it did not matter, they had no real friends here and definitely no lovers. Their only friends were gone. Udinny and Cahan dead, Ont fled deep into the forest, called by a voice Venn had not been able to hear.

The door to the house opened and a figure came in, slight, face aglow with white make-up and Venn felt a deep sense of guilt. They had been so busy feeling sorry for themselves that they had forgotten about Furin, who had at least as much to lose as they did. She had risked herself for Ont. And there was the rest of the villagers of Harn, who were scattered throughout Woodhome now, and always had a smile or a word for their trion.

Maybe everyone was better off without them, Venn thought.

"I think we are in trouble," said Furin as she stood by the trion. She tried to smile but it was a fragile thing, it may have been because of the situation, but she had been friable and sad ever since she returned from the Slowlands and Cahan had not. Her sadness only made worse as her child, Issofur, became more and more of the forest and less and less of the people. Venn put a hand on her arm.

"It was worth it," they said, and it was almost a surprise that they found they believed that. Venn had carried a sense of disappointment when Ont heard a voice and they did not, but that was foolish, selfish and childish. Venn had not travelled to the grove so they could commune with Ranya. They had done it for Ont, to give him at worst a good death and at best a reason to live, something he had found. Venn's actions had given a man who had almost lost everything a reason to go on. Tall Sera glanced over, gave Brione a nudge and then the leaders of Woodhome approached.

"Do you know what you have done?" said Tall Sera, there was a bubbling rage beneath his voice. "For generations Woodhome has been a secret, hidden from all, so far above none could find us from the forest floor." Behind him Brione nodded. "And even more of a secret has been the taffistone network. Now you throw it all away for a dying man."

"He was burned in a fight for you," said Tanhir.

"Quiet!" Tall Sera roared it. "Not a fight for me, a fight for these incomers who I let into our world." He shook with the effort to suppress his anger. "I liked Cahan when I met him, thought him brave. Thought maybe we were wrong to look upon the people of Crua as different to us. But I was mistaken, they are raniri and we are spearmaw. It was always the way. The hunter and the hunted. My mistake has brought us misfortune, just as many said it would." He turned away, walked four steps and Venn could feel how he did it to walk off his anger. He stopped, walked back. Fists opening and closing with every step. He looked to Tanhir, then to Furin. "I cannot undo what has been done. But there must be payment." He turned to Venn. "You, Brione tells me you are powerful, she is not sure the forgetting can be done to you." Then he turned to Tanhir. "Your punishment will be not to forget, but every Forestal will know what you have done. And if the Rai come to Woodhome they will know whose name to curse. You will be an outcast among us." Venn heard a cough, a sob, Tanhir bowed her head. "Do not feel sorry for yourself, you brought those who ran here, these soldiers of Chyi who betrayed us." Tanhir nodded and Venn could feel the depth of her misery radiating out from her. Tall Sera turned to Furin. "But you, someone must pay and you came here, into the place I call home to distract me so Ania could get past my guards at the stone. Without you this would not have happened."

"It was all my plan," said Furin. "Ont came to me, asked my help. I felt it my duty." She raised her head and looked him straight in the eye. "I feel no guilt for loyalty, you would have done the same for one of yours. Do what you must." He stared at her, for only a single beat of the heart, then nodded, as if what she said proved him right but also won his approval.

"Brione," he said, "take everything from her." The trion stepped forward, no words, only a hand, stretching out towards Furin's head. Venn wanted this to stop, found they were waiting for someone to walk in, to end this.

Tanhir stood with her head bowed.

Tall Sera only watched.

Furin waited, resigned to her fate.

For a moment, Venn hoped Ania would appear, that she would burst in through the doors in her brash, aggressive way to end this, but she did not.

There was no one here to stop Brione.

Then someone did.

A hand reached out, grabbed Brione's wrist.

A voice said, "No." Brione turned, looked at Venn. Tall Sera looked at them and Venn was almost as surprised at what they were doing as the Forestal leader.

"Let go of Brione, Venn," said Tall Sera.

"No," said Venn.

"Please, Venn," said Furin, "do not do this." They saw then through the mask of caked make-up, how it covered her grief. "To forget would be a gift."

"What of your son, Furin, what of Issofur?" She shook her head and, if anything, the sadness upon her only deepened.

"He is as much rootling as boy now, I love him still, but his true parent has become the forest."

"No," said Venn again, "Issofur is not gone, and Cahan would not want us to give up."

"This is not your choice," said Tall Sera. "Let go of our Trion." Venn found they were shaking, afraid, but from somewhere within flowed a well of strength they had never truly acknowledged. For so long they had been moved around by others, put into place by them, told what they would be.

"It was my idea, not Furin's." Venn looked around. "We took Ont for Ranya, who tells us we all walk a path and must choose to follow it or not."

"Forestals do not care about the soft gods of—"

"Listen to me!" said Venn. Tall Sera's face hardened, as if he moved from Least to Harsh. "The ground quakes and opens all over Crua. A god rises who pushes away all others and brooks no disagreement. Ranya's web, which is as real as you or I, is touched upon by some sickness no one understands but it is something so strange and dark that your own tree, that has harboured you and held your people for generations, lost an entire branch and all those who lived upon it. You walk the path even if you do not know it." They were not sure where these words came from, but they knew them as real and heartfelt and right. "You look, but you do not see the signs around you. It is like you track raniri and ignore spearmaw gathering to hunt you." Venn wondered, looking at Tall Sera and Brione, who was more shocked at the words that had come from their mouth. They let a cloak of silence fall around them before speaking again. "Take Furin's memories if you must, but you will lose me."

"We will take your mind if you try and leave," said Brione and they felt something touch them, as if a mind wandered over Venn's skin looking for a way in. With a thought Venn pushed them off. Brione let out a hiss of pain.

"Do you think you can?" The words coming out a sob, guilt flooding them for hurting another, even though they had not meant it. "You need me, Cahan may be gone but there is another Cowl-Rai out there. If I am as strong as you believe, and they are coming here then you need me." Brione stared, but they did not gainsay Venn, they did not disagree because they could not. "I say it again, clear as I can. Hurt any of those that came with me, and you lose me." Venn looked around. "I do not know why I am what I am. I have never wanted it. But it is the path, and I must walk it."

"I rule here, Venn," said Tall Sera, and they took a step forward, one hand on the knife at their hip. "And in Wyrdwood the word of the Boughry is the one that matters, not your soft god." He slipped the knife from its sheath. "And I am not frightened to make hard decisions. Let go of Brione, let her do what she must." Venn stared at Tall Sera and his words echoed in their mind. An understanding came upon them. They let go of Brione and stepped in front of Furin who was, in urgent whispers, telling them not to do this. Venn did not listen. Because they knew now that Brione and Tall Sera would not touch Furin, or Tanhir. Or Ania, if she ever came back.

"We went in search of Ranya," said Venn, standing straighter than they ever had, more sure of themselves than they had ever been. "But we did not find them. I heard nothing from my god. But Ont heard something. Ania heard something. Dassit heard something."

"What of it?" Tall Sera coming forward, knife in hand. "As I said, we care nothing for your gods."

"They heard one word, Tall Sera," said Venn. "They heard 'North'. Clear as day. They were called North." Tall Sera blinked. "Now tell me, leader of the Wyrdwood Forestals, what lives in the north? What scares you, and all your people so much that you bless each other by wishing they look away?" Tall Sera blinked. Brione stepped back. "I thought so," said Venn, looking at the two Forestals before them. "The Boughry, the Woodhewn Nobles of Wyrdwood, called Ont, and they called Ania and they called Dassit. Furin and Tanhir, they did the bidding of the Boughry. Will you punish them for that?"

Silence, for a moment.

"The Boughry do not . . ." began Tall Sera.

"I have told you," said Venn, "walk the path. Read the signs. Change is coming. The old gods call. I saw what happened to Cahan, something took him over. Something terrible, all that were at the Slowlands, saw it and they felt it. Take a side, Tall Sera, and do it now. I think the Boughry feel your people have stood in the shadows for too long. Ranya shows you the path. Walk it, or move out of the way of those that will."

"I . . ." began Tall Sera, then the air shivered, and the hard and sturdy wood that they stood upon shook. A tremor passed through all of Crua, shaking the Cloudtree the tree and it was as if something terrible and powerful moved far beneath the land.

"Take a side," said Venn again.

75
Sorha

She walked in a daze.

There was always this moment of confusion when combat finished, win or lose. Sometimes there was only a second of quiet while you realised you had won, that the enemy was fleeing. Sometimes long hours of reflection on how you had lost and what it would cost you.

Sorha was still not used to losing and in the moments after the creature – the god? – left she was stunned. Locked in a darkness within herself deeper than the darkness of this place. She could not stop seeing it, the thing – though she had never actually *seen* it. There had only been glimpses, a huge body, a screeching beak clacking open and closed, ridges, spikes and rills of glowing blue, dripping strange liquids.

The curling, shivering, writhing of tentacles.

And that last moment when it had taken him, the noise Cahan had made. A strangled scream, part fear, part fury, that twisted, increasing in volume, becoming something else.

He had become something else. His armour changing, blue fire flashing around him, his voice turning as harsh and cracked as the voice of the creature. Agony cutting through the darkness as long tentacles grew from his back. He too became a thing of spikes and rills and darkness; he resembled the creature in the final moment she saw him, two arms, two legs, four tentacles: in constant motion as he was pulled into the air through the forest of roots.

Then he was gone.

And she was alone.

Breathing hard. Feeling lost in a way she never had before. Not understanding why. He had helped her, yes, but only for his own purposes. Only because she kept in check what was within him, not because she mattered to him. But despite that, she had begun to feel a camaraderie with him. She had never had that with anyone, she had always been alone. Down here, they only had each other. And he had not hated her the way others had. Did he like her? No, he did not like her. She did not like him. But she felt that they were tied together in some way, and, Osere curse it, she owed him her life.

But there was more than that. As she had watched him taken, as she had seen him change, as she had fought that great beast, she had known it was wrong. Past the horror of the creature, she felt some ancestral memory deep within her, some loathing that rose up, overriding the gut-wrenching fear the beast made her feel.

She looked around. Found Ulan, he was lying on the floor with two of the Osere stood over him. She walked over, feeling the mask she had worn since Cahan took her power away slot into place, the hardness of it. She pushed Osere out of the way, sending them sprawling and grabbed Ulan, pulling him up and making him shriek. Not thinking it may be dangerous, that she may take a spear in the back, only knowing, deep within, that something must be done. The creature wanted Cahan so badly it could be for nothing good.

"Where has it taken him?" she spat at him. "Where?" Shaking Ulan and he cried out in pain. She could not see a wound, but in the darkness that did not matter. If she had seen a wound it would not matter, she was gripped with a certainty. She must get Cahan back and with every moment that certainty grew. "Where?" she shouted again. Ulan did nothing but whimper.

"Anjiin." The word came from behind her and she turned. It was the Osere leader, Frina. She had a spear, pointed at Sorha's throat and other Osere were gathering. "Put down," said Frina, nodding her head at Ulan.

"We have to stop it," said Sorha. The words were raw in her throat, she felt near to tears and knew it for battle fatigue, the wearing on her body and mind of so long in the darkness, to have come so far and through so much and then to lose.

"Yes, stop it," said the Osere leader. "We need his words." She pointed at Ulan and Sorha nodded, let go. Once more the Osere were around Ulan, treating his wounds. Then they pulled him away, groaning and moaning to sit against a root and Frina took Sorha's arm, pulled her over to him. The Osere spoke to Ulan, a long stream of words. Now she had time to look at him she knew what ailed him was deep hurt. He was struggling to concentrate, his eyelids fluttering.

"She says, it will have taken him to Anjiin, to one of the great temples where the gods once ruled from."

"Why?" she asked. Ulan looked to Frina who spoke again. Then she turned to one of her soldiers, spat words out into the darkness and the soldier walked away, quickly swallowed up by the darkness.

"The gods were banished from the land," said Ulan, "their connection severed."

"I know the myths."

"Not myths," said Ulan, the words coming out as gasps. "Truths. How it escaped, we do not know. But those who attacked us, they are us." Behind her she heard the sound of dragging as a body was brought forward.

"Betrayers, it is in the name." Ulan nodded, a weak gesture, his energy fleeing.

"Not as simple as it sounds. The blue glow, they force it on those taken. They become part of it. It uses them to talk to the land. To try to break through. But they have never given enough for it to be so brazen as to attack us. It always hid, always ran. We hunted it. It feared the power inside the Osere. The cowls." She stared at the Osere, so these people did have cowls, or some form of it. Cahan had explained how you needed one to use the taffistone network. "It wants power to escape, they all want to escape."

"But it has escaped," said Sorha, confused. "We saw the broken tree, the bubble within."

"Not escape the tree," said Ulan. "Escape the here."

"And escape from here is in Anjiin?"

"Yes," said Ulan, air hissing painfully through his teeth. "The stories tell that the gods rose through Anjiin. The taffistones, they do not reach above. Anjiin can if the beast can channel enough power. That is why it wants Cahan."

"Then we are going to Anjiin," said Sorha. "I can stop this. I need to get near it though." Ulan looked up, smiled.

"I hope you can, the gods bring nothing but ruin. The fire of their escape will destroy everything." He coughed. "But I am afraid my journey, it is over now."

"No." She tried to grab him but was held back by the Osere. Found herself fighting them but they were many and they held her tight, pulling her away from Ulan.

"I am sorry," he said, and with a flicker she saw the life leave him.

"Anjiin," said Frina, and Sorha turned her head to look at the woman. "You go to Anjiin?"

"Yes," said Sorha.

"We go to Anjiin." The Osere leader touched her chest, then motioned toward her people. Sorha nodded, wondering how they could do anything when they barely understood one another. Frina barked words and Sorha was let go. She said more words – names, thought Sorha, as each bark of her growling clicking language brought Osere to her.

Standing around her, touching constantly in the way of them. Then the leader's hand was on Sorha's arm, pulling her on. Frina touched Sorha's chest.

"So'ha," she said. Then touched her own chest. "Frina."

"Frina," said Sorha, and the Osere woman nodded, then pointed, and together with the Osere all speaking soft words to one another now, she began her journey through the darkness.

"Itafston," said Frina pointing ahead. As they moved she thought she counted twenty Osere with her, all had bows and spears and they ran almost entirely soundlessly. She had not noticed that before, never really thought about it, or them. When she found herself tiring they pressed food on her that filled her muscles with energy and allowed her to run with them. They never slowed, never stopped. As they ran they guided her with a touch here and a touch there, subtly altering her course so she did not trip or fall. Sometimes Frina would point at a thing and say its name and Sorha would try and copy her, then say it in her own language. Inside she worried about what they would face, what fate awaited Cahan and the world above, but she also felt strangely comfortable. Accepted. When they reached a taffistone they barely paused. Just long enough for Frina to point at and say "Itafston." Then she felt a disturbance as the stone opened and she was guided through.

A moment of dislocation. A feeling of nausea.

Through.

Then knocked aside by the impact of a body and she felt something pass close to the side of her head. One of the Osere that ran with her fell. Frina threw a spear, a cry answered and the rest of the Osere spread out. Froze. Sorha did the same.

Trying to not make a noise.

Trying not to breathe.

Letting her eyes adjust to this new place. It smelled different, in the north the air was drier and smelled of the earthy mushrooms that grew everywhere and leaked their weak light. Here, in Anjiin, the air was dry and smelled of deserts. It made her think of the great grasslands in the heat of Plenty when she had been young, before her cowl, when the world was full of old gods whose statues stood in every field, whose straw-built effigies were found on every corner.

The tell-tale blue glow of the Betrayers around them. First it was so faint it was like something floating in her, but as she became accustomed to it she could make out individuals. None of the four-legged "seeing" ones, thankfully. Slowly she took a bow off her back, she had no memory of retrieving it and she was not confident with it the way Cahan had been. She would rather have a handful of spears but the bow was small and, more importantly, quiet to draw where her spears would clatter as she took one out of the quiver. She began to pull the string taut.

To her right a noise. A sudden shift of feet and a groan of pain. A body falling. Spears cutting through the air and she threw herself down. The noise drew Betrayers to her. A glow of a movement as a spear was raised. A shadow in the darkness cutting it down. Sorha had the impression, from nothing more than faint shuffling, the occasional groan, that all around her a vicious, silent and slow battle was happening. One fiercer than they had fought before. This must be a rear guard, left by the creature to stop any who followed. Sorha had no idea who was winning. She stood with her bow slack in her hand. She could not use it, she did not know if Osere stood between her and the glowing patches of the Betrayers.

The ground shook.

She was used to quakes, Crua had been shaking all her life in some form or another. The regular, calendared quakes that were known and the increasingly frequent tremors that ran through the country creating new cracks and crevasses like the one she and Cahan had fallen into.

This one was different, deeper, stronger. It tossed the Osere and her and their opponents from their feet. It shook the great buildings of Anjiin, dirt rained down and she worried that the roof, the land above, may come crashing down on her. The noise of it, a deep, basso roar took over Sorha's body, stole all control from her. It made her muscles limp as if the life was cut from them.

Then it stopped.

Light flickered into being, running along the buildings. Sickly blue lights everywhere. Control of her body came back and she pushed herself up. In the light she had the advantage. Dropping the bow she began striking out with her spear, cutting down Betrayers left and right. Frina was being pressed by three of the enemy and Sorha attacked, a spear through the back of the nearest. One turned on her, raising their weapon to strike back and Sorha dodged, let them strike at thin air and thrust her weapon into their side. The last of the three Frina dealt with in a single strike.

The earth shook again.

Not as powerful this time, and Sorha managed to keep her footing. Staggering over to lean on a wall, waiting for the tremor to subside. It did not, and in the sound of it was something grinding, like great stones being forced together, and above it a great wail, as if some vast and foul creature were being tortured and felt a pain beyond bearing.

More lights. Blinding her and she had to shade her eyes with a hand. The lights threw both the Osere and the Betrayers into confusion. Though they may not have been able to see it they could sense it in some way Sorha did not understand. They stood in small groups facing towards the light and Sorha lowered the hand shading her eyes.

One of the temples was rising into the air. A black, slab-sided pyramid surrounded by eight short spires. The whole of the construction was wreathed in curling, twisting, lines of blue. Like the roots of some great plant had grown over it and it was from these the light was coming. On the centre of the pyramid, at its apex was the god, tentacles raised, writhing upward towards Crua as the plinth and pyramid slowly rose. It left the spires behind, ripped itself loose from the pulsing blue roots as it rose.

Below where the creature, the god, writhed she could just make out the tiny figure of Cahan – he had been stuck to the pyramid, plugged into it by a spike through his chest. Blue fire danced around him. The screaming, the tortured noise she heard, it came from him and she was as sure of that as she was of the ground she walked on. He was being used as a power source so that this creature from the past could emerge once more into the world above.

"Over. It is over. Osere failed." She turned. Frina dropped her spear. The rest of her people were falling to their knees. The Betrayers had lost all volition, one by one they began to collapse into the dirt and it was as if, now the god had got what it wanted, they were no longer of any use to it. They were discarded like the husks of seed grasses.

"No." Sorha picked up Frina's spear and took her hand, placed the spear in it. "We will not give up. If I have to climb that thing," she looked back. The temple was mounted on a smooth-sided pillar growing beneath it, pushing it up. As it did, it bathed Anjiin in a sickly blue light, "then I will climb it." Frina cocked her head, pointed her spear towards the grinding sound made by the rising temple.

"Up?" she said.

"Yes," said Sorha, and she stared towards the noise and the light and the terrifying, waving figure of the god above it. "If it can go up," she said, "so can we." She grasped the hand of the Osere leader. "Will you come, Frina?"

There was a pause, the Osere leader cocked her head as if studying Sorha with eyes she did not have. Then she squeezed her hand.

"We will come."

76

Saradis

Today felt like a good day.

So much of the time since she had lost Cahan in the Slowlands had felt bad. The Rai had been moving around her, jostling to unseat her. She could not prove it, could not find anything that said they were about to move against her but she felt it in the air of Tiltspire.

Sideways looks, whispers that stopped when she entered a briefing, questions that challenged her when she proposed a strategy. Mounting losses around Treefall in the north had set them off, the annoying ability of the Forestals to melt in and out of the trees. The way the outlaws always targeted Rai, always took the most valuable goods from the cloudtree rafts.

That and the feeling Wyrdwood itself was working against them.

Few Rai were true believers and she had always known that. For generations the gods had only been a way for them to get what they wanted, the Cowl-Rai was less a leader and more a way of keeping them under control.

Setbacks, and the fact the Cowl-Rai had not been seen for so long, meant the Rai were beginning to whisper, to plot. It would only be a matter of time until they decided someone more malleable would be better in her place.

The Cowl-Rai had been at once worse and better since Cahan had fallen. Her lucid times were longer, but spaced further apart and when she was not lucid she flickered between fury, self pity and believing she should not have betrayed her brother, raging or begging to die. Saradis had been waiting for the latest episode to pass in the hope she could somehow be convinced to help her.

Now she stood before Nahac's cage, watching the woman as she thought about what she had been told by the man, Vir, newly arrived, who had betrayed the Forestals that had taken him in.

"They move through the taffistones?" said Nahac again. She studied the map before her.

"Yes," said Saradis. "It explains everything, why they can never be found, how they appear to have such great numbers that they can be everywhere." Nahac nodded. Touching the locations of the stones on the map.

"And they have a whole city up in the trees of the Southern Wyrdwood?"

"Yes."

"And you are sure this is true?"

"I had the common soldiers that came with him questioned, they never wavered in their story, right up to death." Nahac stood from her desk and walked over to the bars, the stones in her skin glowing.

"And the branch leader, what about him?"

"There is an anger in him I thought may be useful. He considers himself betrayed by the trunk commander he followed all his life, she is now with the Forestals."

"He is not annoyed that you tortured his soldiers to death?" A half smile on Nahac's face, as if an amusing thought had landed in her mind. "He may decide to avenge them." Saradis shook her head, the sticks of her formal dress hissing against the material. She liked this Nahac, the cold one, the planner.

"He is a pragmatist, he gave them to me as proof of what he said. He knew what would happen. In his words, 'soldiers die'." She smiled; the man Vir was bitter, it made him easy to manipulate. "He thinks the Forestals are savages." She straightened up, letting out a hiss of pain as something in her back pulled, some wound left over from the wreck of the platform in the Slowlands. "A man who wishes for vengeance is a useful tool." Nahac nodded. "I will find a use for him."

"And how will you find this city in the trees? Will you use our skyraft?"

"That did not work out," said Saradis. "It turns out, they are hard to pilot and it crashed." Nahac nodded again. "Without rafters to pilot the thing we cannot use a skyraft, and they are too precious with their great rafts to take them into Wyrdwood."

"Then send me," she said, standing and walking over. Putting her hands on the bars. "Send me after the Forestals. Let me go after them." Saradis heard the desperation the woman was trying to control, to keep in check. "I have learned to hold the power in. I have had nothing else to do in this cage. You must have noticed how much longer my lucid periods are." Such misery, and Saradis almost felt a stab of pity. Nahac and her had been through so much, done so much. She was clever. This woman had convinced the Rai she was Cowl-Rai, even though what power she had then was nothing but illusion. She had made herself powerful. She had done it by using her mind, her strength. Raised an army. It was sad that Nahac had ended up in a cage, that Zorir's power was too much for her. She had been useful but she could never be trusted.

"No," said Saradis. "Not yet."

"You," spat Nahac, "are no better than those Wyrdwood savages. You are a betrayer. You betrayed me, you betrayed my brother. You care only for you." With her words came the anger, and the outpouring of power, liquid, black and poisonous. The screams of pain and agony and Saradis was glad of it. She could leave now. She had important things to be about and she was glad she no longer had to look into Nahac's eyes.

From the cage room she walked through the great hall, past Rai guards who watched her in a way she found little comfort in. Under waving flags of the counties of Crua, past wicker statues of the Balancing Man. She walked through corridors where more Rai watched, stopping what they were doing to silently study her as she passed. She did not look at them. She never as much acknowledged their existence.

But they watched her, and she did not like it.

The pressure in Tiltspire was growing, she felt violence lurked around every corner and it would be violence aimed at her. She went up, to her shrine room; one of the Rai stood before the door. Dashan Ir-Vota, a Rai who had stood by her many times on the battlefield. He did not say anything, only waited. Did not move as she approached.

"I must offer sacrifice to my god," she said. Dashan stared down at her, the skin of his face had that odd texture that only the really old Rai had.

"There have been more losses in the north. Sacrifice is definitely needed," he said. "Maybe we could visit your shrine together."

Well, she thought. Here it is. The time has come. She let herself smile, more because she wondered what he would think of the room – the blue-veined stone, the body of Laha stretched across it – than because she had any plan, any way out.

Maybe, in the moment of confusion when he saw the stone she would be able to strike. To kill the Rai. If she killed one of them it would buy her time, though she knew it was unlikely she would succeed. Saradis wore a knife at her belt but it was purely ceremonial and always had been.

And the ground shook.

The shards of stone on the floor rattled against each other. Her body betrayed her, a sudden weakness came with the relief of still being alive. She fell among the shivering stones. They cut her skin, each cut a shock, as if they touched something deep within her. The Rai fell at the same time as her, muscles jerking and spasming. Blood seeping out around the stone in his neck. Where it was embedded in their skin blue lines grew from it. Laha looked at her.

"It is coming," said Laha again, and the world shook. Laha raised a hand and pointed towards the great square, where the taffistones were, and the huge plaza with the market.

She pushed herself up, stumbling over to the huge window. Was this it? What she had lived for? Planned for? Sacrificed for? Shards of stone rolled beneath her feet. It was not enough to watch from above. She had to be there. Turning, running through the strangely shaped corridors, down through the great hall and out the huge doors. Fighting to stay upright, her path swerving crazily as the ground shook beneath her. Part of her fearing the whole spire would come down. A particularly strong tremor and she fell, right at the edge of the great plaza. Beneath her the market was set out. Colourful stalls everywhere, people kneeling, sheltering in fear beneath their stalls for all the good it would do if the spire fell.

The shaking stopped.

In the stillness she heard screams from the city beyond the spires. Smelled fire, there were always fires after the big quakes. She could see thick smoke, flickering flames where the city was alight.

But there was something else, something in the air. An expectance. A difference. It was not simply that Laha promised Zorir was coming. She could feel it.

Another rumble. This one familiar. The way the land moaned before the geysers went up, but it was not the right time for the geysers. She looked at the Light Above, to make sure.

No. Not time for the geysers. Not the day for the geysers.

With a roar they went up. She could see the nearest. A vast plume of water that shot up so high the water was taken by the circle winds to fall as rain in the north and south. There were seven, the others she could not see, too far away, or on the wrong side of the city but she knew they were spouting too. She knew it. Saradis counted, waiting until she reached fifty when the geysers would stop. Then spout again.

But they did not stop.

How?

They always stopped. There was a pattern to them. First spout, never for long. Then another and another, each longer than the last until they had done it eight times and then they stopped, but this was different. A huge, continuous stream of water arcing above the city. Falling as rain.

The land was celebrating Zorir's coming.

A new noise. A vast sigh. Like an outpouring of breath, like the last gasp of a corpse. The air filled with a foetid smell, mixing with the petrichor of rain and the woodsmoke from the city burning. She heard cries of disgust. Fools. They did not understand. The earth shaking again. Not as fiercely this time, more constant.

The centre of the market plaza cracked, not a crevasse or a rupture. It cracked along clean tracks, outlining eight curved leaves. With a slow grinding sound they began to pull back. People ran, falling over each other, getting in each other's way trying to escape the opening crevasse beneath them. Stalls fell into the widening, gaping hole, people followed them screaming and crying as they vanished into the darkness. The maze of wooden huts and stalls trapped people as it was forced against the edge of the plaza, crushing any who were caught between the stalls before they fell into the darkness below.

"They sacrifice to you!" shouted Saradis, pushing herself up despite the continuous shaking of the earth. "The god is coming!" She was screaming it, her voice lost amid all the noise. "The True God is coming!"

From the hole, rising up from the darkness below came Zorir, huge, thick tentacles writhing in the air. It sat, perched atop an eight-sided pyramid that was wrapped with glowing blue roots. On the side facing her, the side facing the spire, was him. Cahan Du-Nahere, physically plugged in to the rock by his armour and a spike through his chest, blue fire spitting and twisting around him, and she felt nothing but triumph. Nothing but a desperate desire to rejoice as the black pyramid locked in place with a sound like a vast tomb door closing.

Silence fell. The god on the throne at the apex of the pyramid cried out in triumph. In their triumph. In her triumph.

"Zorir is come!" she said. "The fire is kindled!" She watched those few who had escaped the opening of the market floor and smiled as they ran into the city in panic. "There is no escape from the fire." She screamed it after them, though no one heard her. She felt someone behind her, turned. Laha, and by him stood Dashan, eyes blank, the blue lines radiating from the stone in his neck had twisted around it, like a collar.

"It is come," said Laha and Dashan together. She looked at Dashan, how he stood and waited to be commanded before the god, at the stone buried in his neck, and smiled.

The breaking of the stone made sense now. A collar to control her Rai with, to control Zorir's Rai. They would have an army, an army that would never question or plot. One of utter loyalty. Saradis smiled.

She had won.

Despite all the setbacks, all the mistakes, she had won. She would stand at the front of Zorir's army, and she would burn the world.

She walked forward to meet her god.

Epilogue

I was not pleased, about being dead again. It had most definitely not been my plan. I did not imagine it was Ranya's either, though when her golden light washes across me it is gentle, and forgiving. I sense no disappointment, no desire to chastise me.

I want to sob.

"I have failed you."

"You have done more than any Udinny before."

"But I have still failed. That thing, it killed me. It killed poor Syerfu."

"Plans and schemes for more years than any can imagine, Udinny Pathfinder. A slow corruption, first below, then above. Too weak to fight. Too distracted trying to keep the world together."

A flash, an image. Tiltspire but not Tiltspire. A huge stone ziggurat, and around it lines of blue. Atop it, the creature, waving tentacles in triumph. Before it, hanging from a spike a figure that sends a physical pain through a body I do not have.

But it still hurts.

"Cahan."

"It has reached the lock, found the power but it lacks the key."

Another image. Familiar, friendly.

"Venn."

"Hope is not lost."

Images.

Three figures of light, silhouetted by the terrifying presence of the Boughry. Anjiin, and ten, twenty people, at their head another light. Making its way up a steep staircase that goes on for ever, curling around a huge pillar that rises right to the roof, dwarfing them, turning them into tiny creatures crawling on the trunk of a cloudtree. Woodhome, its people sleeping, playing, loving and with no idea of what was to come. A light within it.

"What use showing me this? I am dead."

"Udinny Pathfinder, your time here is done. They are impatient. They will sacrifice all for the Star Path. The web must be rewoven. Iftal Reborn." I saw Anjiin again, I saw eight pillars, three standing tall and the others fallen.

"What do you mean?"

"Wake, Udinny Pathfinder."

Darkness.

A headache.

The smell of herbs and woodsmoke. My body aching like I had been beaten for a week and then drunk every drop of cheap alcohol in Harnspire. A groan. A voice, someone young. The strange, foresty smell of rootlings.

"He is waking, Trion!" The sound of a door opening, footsteps.

"I have told you, Issofur, no matter how much you wish it, he will never wake. The priest's mind has long since fled along the Star Path, all we can do is let him leave this life peacefully." Footsteps, coming closer. "Will someone get this crownhead out of here," said another voice. I tried to push myself up, and was rewarded only with more pain. "Anjiin's ruins! He really is waking." The trion raised their voice. "Quick, get me water, and food. He will be starving."

So, I was back in Crua.

And it seemed I was also a man now.

Ranya, truly you lead your servant down the strangest paths.

The story continues in . . .

Book THREE of
The Forsaken Trilogy

extras

meet the author

RJ BARKER lives in Leeds with his wife, son and "a collection of questionable taxidermy." He grew up reading whatever he could get his hands on, and having played in a rock band before deciding he was a rubbish musician, RJ returned to his first love, fiction, to find he is rather better at that. As well as his debut epic fantasy series, the Wounded Kingdom trilogy (*Age of Assassins*, *Blood of Assassins* and *King of Assassins*), RJ has written short stories and historical scripts which have been performed across the country. He has the sort of flowing locks any cavalier would be proud of. RJ's novel *The Bone Ships* was the winner of the British Fantasy Society's Best Fantasy Novel, aka the Robert Holdstock Award.

Find out more about RJ Barker and other Orbit authors by registering for the free monthly newsletter at orbitbooks.net.

if you enjoyed
WARLORDS OF WYRDWOOD

look out for

THE BONE SHIPS
The Tide Child Trilogy: Book One

by

RJ Barker

Two nations at war. One prize beyond compare.

For generations, the fleets of the Hundred Isles have built their ships from the bones of ancient dragons to fight an endless war.

The dragons disappeared, but the battles for supremacy persisted.

Now the first dragon in centuries has been spotted in far-off waters, and both sides see a chance to shift the balance of power in their favor. Because whoever catches it will win not only glory, but the war.

1

THE CASTAWAY

"Give me your hat."

They are not the sort of words that you expect to start a legend, but they were the first words he ever heard her say.

She said them to him, of course.

It was early. The scent of fish filled his nose and worked its way into his stomach, awakening the burgeoning nausea. His head ached and his hands trembled in a way that would only be stilled by the first cup of shipwine. Then the pain in his mind would fade as the thick liquid slithered down his gullet, warming his throat and guts. After the first cup would come the second, and with that would come the numbness that told him he was on the way to deadening his mind the way his body was dead, or waiting to be. Then there would be a third cup and then a fourth and then a fifth, and the day would be over and he would slip into darkness.

But the black ship in the quiet harbour would still sit at its rope. Its bones would creak as they pulled against the tide. The crew would moan and creak as they drank on its decks, and he would fall into unconsciousness in this old flenser's hut. Here he was, shipwife in name only. Commander in word only. Failure.

Voices from outside, because even here, in the long-abandoned and ghost-haunted flensing yards there was no real escape from others. Not even the memory of Keyshan's Rot, the disease of the boneyards, could keep people from cutting through.

"The *Shattered Stone* came in this morran, said they saw an archeyex over Sleightholme. Said their windtalker fell mad and it nearly wrecked 'em. Had to kill the creature to stop it bringing a wind to throw 'em across a lee shore."

"Aren't been an archeyex seen for nigh on my lifetime. It brings nothing good – paint that on a rock for the Sea Hag." And the voices faded, lost in the hiss of the waves on the beach, eaten up by the sea as everything was destined to be, while he thought on what they said – "brings nothing good". May as well as say that Skearith's Eye will rise on the morran, for this is the Hundred Isles – when did good things ever happen here?

The next voice he heard was the challenge. Delivered while he kept his eyes closed against the tides of nausea ebbing and flowing in hot, acidic waves from his stomach.

"Give me your hat." A voice thick with the sea, a bird-shriek croak of command. The sort of voice you ran to obey, had you scurrying up the rigging to spread the wings of your ship. Maybe, just maybe, on any other day or after a single cup of shipwine, maybe he would have done what she said and handed over his two-tailed shipwife's hat, which, along with the bright dye in his hair, marked him out as a commander – though an undeserving one.

But in the restless night his sleep had been troubled by thoughts of his father and thoughts of another life, not a better one, not an easier one, but a sober one, one without shame. One in which he did not feel the pull of the Sea Hag's slimy hands trying to drag him down to his end. One of long days at the wing of a flukeboat, singing of the sea and pulling on the ropes as his father glowed with pride at how well his little fisher boy worked the winds. Of long days before his father's strong and powerful body was broken as easily as a thin varisk vine, ground to meat between the side of his boat and the pitiless hull of a boneship. His hand reaching up from black water, a bearded face, mouth open as if to call to his boy in his final agonising second. Such strength, and it had meant nothing.

So maybe he had, for once, woken with the idea of how wonderful it would be to have a little pride. And if there had been a day for him to give up the two-tailed hat of shipwife, then it was not this day.

"No," he said. He had to scrape the words out of his mind, and that was exactly how it felt, like he drew the curve of a curnow blade down the inside of his skull; words falling from his mouth slack as midtide. "I am shipwife of the *Tide Child* and this is my symbol of command." He touched the rim of the black two-tailed cap. "I am shipwife, and you will have to take this hat from me."

How strange it felt to say those words, those fleet words that he knew more from his father's stories of service than from any real experience. They were good words though, strong words with a history, and they felt right in his mouth. If he were to die then they were not bad final words for his father to hear from his place, deep below the sea, standing warm and welcome at the Hag's eternal bonefire.

He squinted at the figure before him. Thoughts fought in his aching head: which one of them had come for him? Since he'd become shipwife he knew a challenge must come. He commanded angry women and men, bad women and men, cruel women and men – and it had only ever been a matter of time before one of his crew wanted the hat and the colours. Was it Barlay who stood in the door hole of the bothy? She was a hard one, violent. But no, too small for her and the silhouette of this figure wore its hair long, not cut to the skull. Kanvey then? He was a man jealous of everything and everyone, and quick with his knife. But no, the silhouette appeared female, undoubtably so. No straight lines to her under the tight fishskin and feather. Cwell then? She would make a move, and she could swim so would have been able to get off the ship.

He levered himself up, feeling the still unfamiliar tug of the curnow at his hip.

"We fight then," said the figure and she turned, walking out into the sun. Her hair worn long, grey and streaked in the colours of command: bright reds and blues. The sun scattered off the fishskin of her clothing, tightly wound about her muscled body and held in place with straps. Hanging from the straps were knives, small crossbows and a twisting shining jingling assortment of good-luck trinkets that spoke of a lifetime of service and violence. Around her shoulders hung a precious feathered cloak, and where the fishskin scattered the sunlight the feather cloak hoarded it, twinkling and sparkling, passing motes of light from plume to plume so each and every colour shone and shouted out its hue.

I am going to die, he thought.

She idled away from the slanted bothy he had slept in, away from the small and stinking abandoned dock, and he followed. No one was around. He had chosen this place for its relative solitude, amazed at how easily that could be found; even on an isle as busy as Shipshulme people tended to flock together, to find each other, and of course they shunned such Hag-haunted places as this, where the keyshan's curse still slept.

Along the shingle beach they walked: her striding, looking for a place, and him following like a lost kuwai, one of the flightless birds they bred for meat, looking for a flock to join. Though of course there was no flock for a man like him, only the surety of the death he walked towards.

orbit